THE
HIMALAYAN
CODEX

The Himalayan Codex

An R. J. MacCready Novel

BILL SCHUTT & J. R. FINCH

wm

WILLIAM MORROW
An Imprint of HarperCollins*Publishers*

THE HIMALAYAN CODEX. Copyright © 2017 by Bakk Bone, LLC. All rights reserved. Printed in the United States of America. No part of this book may be used or reproduced in any manner whatsoever without written permission except in the case of brief quotations embodied in critical articles and reviews. For information, address HarperCollins Publishers, 195 Broadway, New York, NY 10007.

HarperCollins books may be purchased for educational, business, or sales promotional use. For information, please e-mail the Special Markets Department at SPsales@harpercollins.com.

FIRST EDITION

Photograph of Tibet by HelloRF Zcool/Shutterstock, Inc.

Library of Congress Cataloging-in-Publication Data has been applied for.

ISBN 978-0-06-241255-3

17 18 19 20 21 LSC 10 9 8 7 6 5 4 3 2 1

For our mentors.

To every man is given the key to heaven. The same key opens the gates to hell.

—A BUDDHIST PROVERB, APPROXIMATELY A.D. 700

In these matters the only certainty is that nothing is certain.

—PLINY THE ELDER

THE HIMALAYAN CODEX

On the Shelf

1,500 feet above the East Himalayan Labyrinth
July 9, 1946

I hate fog," the helicopter pilot announced over his headset.

"I thought it was flies you hated?" answered a woman seated behind him.

"Yeah, I hate flies, too. But—"

The Sikorsky R-5 gave a sudden lurch in the wind and the pilot concentrated on steadying the cyclic stick in his right hand. He could feel the 450-horsepower Pratt & Whitney struggling to generate lift. "—but thin air is quickly movin' up my shit list. You see anything like flat ground?"

"No dice," said Yanni Thorne. "Still lookin'."

Behind a pair of polarized aviator glasses, the passenger on the woman's right side remained silent. He was also scanning the uncharted, mist-covered valley below.

"Jerry?"

"Bupkes, Mac."

"Swell," the pilot replied. "I *did* mention the potential for a high-pucker-factor landing, didn't I?"

The passengers quickly exchanged glances and head shakes.

"Not in the last two minutes there, Redunzle." Yanni continued to scan the mountainous terrain for a landing site free of fog or driving snow.

She was intense and insightful, two of Mac's favorite qualities. She was also an indigenous Brazilian with an incongruous Brooklyn accent that she'd picked up from her late husband, Bob. Much had happened to them in and around the plateau of Hell's Gate, most of which their passenger knew nothing about; yet the bottom line was that a lot of people died back in Brazil— including Bob.

But Mac and Yanni did not die, and after two years it was an outcome that still haunted them both.

The chopper's second passenger was Lieutenant Jerry Delarosa, a polymath, currently serving in the U.S. Army Special Forces. He and MacCready had last worked together three years earlier, during a South Pacific "suicide mission" to retrieve a kid with powerful East Coast connections whose torpedo boat was missing in action. The fearlessness and drive he had shown on that mission convinced Mac he would be a real asset to this team.

Presently, Yanni was pointing to something out the port-side window of the chopper's cramped cabin. "Mac, I think I see a place to land but it ain't on the valley floor. Three o'clock and down about five hundred feet." During the space of only a few seconds, sheets of wind-driven snow had begun dissipating, in the direction Yanni was pointing.

Mac increased the pressure on the right tail-rotor pedal and a moment later the chopper responded by swinging its nose to that side. There *was* something—a shelf carved into a lower section of a cliff face twice the height of the Washington Monument. He feathered the cyclic control stick forward with his right hand, adjusting the pitch angle of the rotor blades. In response the R-5 struggled forward through the high-altitude air.

Mac swung into a satisfyingly incident-free flyby over the patch of flat, snow-covered ground. *So far, so good.*

The site they had chosen for landing was not quite three hundred feet long and extended into the mountain almost half as far.

"That's a pinnacle approach in a confined landing zone," Mac announced.

"English, please," Yanni said.

"A double bitch of a landing in these crosswinds."

Yanni nodded. "Check."

"Plus that shelf's not completely smooth," Mac continued, pointing to a pattern of elongated ridges where the snow seemed to be piled up higher. "Problem's going to be snow blowing up from the rotors and screwing up my visibility."

"What do you suggest?" Jerry asked.

"Switch seats with Yanni. You're gonna have to put on a monkey belt and hang out that door a little bit."

"Hang out that what?" came the headset-distorted cry.

"Right before we land, I won't be able to see squat, so I'll need you to tell me when the wheels get close to the ground."

"You mean sit there with the door open?"

"Well, actually more like leaning. But—"

"I'm not switching seats with anybody," Yanni announced, cutting into the conversation. "Where's this so-called monkey belt?"

"Yanni—"

"Save it, Mac," she said.

MacCready knew that there was no time to argue, and that he'd never win this argument anyway. "It's tucked in behind your seat—pretty self-explanatory. The other end attaches to that hard point."

Yanni shot him a look. *"English."*

"To that metal *hook* to the left of your seat."

Less than two minutes later, Yanni was strapped into the canvas harness. From the moment she slid the side door open, the safety cable and clamp would become her only firm connection to the helicopter. Jerry double-checked the monkey belt and gave her a thumbs-up. Yanni nodded.

"It almost looks . . . man-made," Mac said as they flew in closer to the newly designated landing site. "Like it was carved right out of the mountainside."

"That's a lot of carvin'," Yanni added, adjusting her headset. "This could be quite the find."

"All right then," Mac called back, "Yanni, open that door slowly and *don't* let it go. It'll be a cold ride home if that slider comes off its track."

Yanni followed Mac's instructions and slid the lightweight door toward the rear of the fuselage, taking care to guide it into a fully open position before releasing it. The effect was instantaneous—it was as if someone had opened a car door at sixty miles per hour—in the Antarctic.

While Yanni maneuvered herself into position, MacCready slowly swung the R-5 around, bringing its nose just over the ledge at a height of only twenty feet. He nudged the craft forward and down, churning up swirls of rotor generated "whiteout."

Half-standing, half-crouching, Yanni braced herself on either side of the open door frame. "Fifteen feet, Mac," she called to the pilot, though the wind and increased engine noise made it even more difficult to hear. "Tail's nearly clear of the edge."

MacCready had decided to take the chopper in facing the mountain and hopefully into a headwind.

Unfortunately, the mountain had other ideas, summoning a

massive gust that swept up the side of the ledge and slammed into the chopper's tail rotor. The force tipped the R-5's nose down and threw Yanni forward into the door frame. As she struggled to steady herself, vortices of snow buffeted the helicopter from below, sending a turbulence-driven blizzard into the cabin. With the rotors now spinning in their own downwash, the aircraft continued to jerk nose-downward and slip sideways. Lift all but disappeared. Mac, desperate to abort the landing, pulled hard on the collective lever with his left hand while simultaneously fighting to move the wildly bucking cyclic stick to the right. It was clearly too little and too late.

"We're going in. Hold on!" Mac called over the headset.

Amid screaming engine parts, cracking rotors, and blasts of snow, and at the start of a violent clockwise roll, R. J. MacCready shot a glance back into the cabin.

He had but one thought. *Where's Yanni?*

After what seemed like five minutes, but was in actuality all of five seconds, the R-5 rolled to a sudden stop on its right side. Mac, uninjured, quickly undid his seat belt and scrambled aft into the cabin. Jerry seemed dazed but otherwise okay, and even now he was unbuckling himself from the overturned seat.

Turning to the open passenger door, which was now facing skyward, Mac could see the tether from the monkey belt extending out of the chopper. Giving it a tug, he felt a sickening lurch in the pit of his stomach as the safety line streamed through the door and into the cabin. There was no one attached to it.

"YANNI!"

MacCready quickly hoisted himself through the open passenger door frame, barely noticing that the craft had pitched up against a nub of rock only a few paces from the edge of a thousand-foot drop. He gave a quick glance over the precipice, then felt his guts tighten another notch.

"YANNI!" Mac called again. He clambered over the metal and Plexiglas framework of the cabin before staggering past the remnants of what had been a forty-eight-foot main rotor blade. He heard a grunt from behind, but it was only Jerry, who was making his own exit from the broken craft.

Mac frantically searched the snow- and debris-covered ground. Almost immediately, and to his great relief, he saw a figure lying prone in a snowbank between the R-5 and the mountain. He struggled to run through the hip-deep drifts, pumping his arms as he went, then fell to his knees and began brushing the snow and long black hair away from Yanni's face.

"Yanni," he cried, his voice cracking. "Yanni?"

Amazingly, her violet-colored eyes popped open and blinked. "Nice landin' there, Ace," she said.

At this moment, Yanni mocking him again was the sweetest sound MacCready had ever heard.

S oon enough, Yanni Thorne was not only up and about, she was examining the perimeter of the oddly placed landing zone. It was, of course, surrounded by precipitous cliffs and bordered by what her late husband would have described as "a doozy of a first step."

Yanni, though, was far more concerned with the low line of rocks that had stopped the tumbling helicopter from rolling into the abyss. A similar bracework of block-shaped stones had shielded her body from flying debris after what they could now appreciate as an admittedly spectacular exit from the spinning chopper, this one involving a roll-generated whip snap that somehow flung her into a well-protected snowbank instead of against the rock wall that loomed just beyond it.

"It's a building foundation of some kind," Yanni told Mac, who was taking a break from helping Jerry recover supplies and the cold-weather gear they were now wearing. "And if you want my two cents, it ain't very recent and it could even be ancient."

Mac nodded toward the squat-looking wall adjacent to the former flying machine. "However old it is, I'd definitely call it fortuitously placed."

Yanni did not hear him. Instead she straightened her back as if just touched by a live wire.

Mac heard it, too, a strange whistling sound. "What the—"

"Shhhh," Yanni said, cocking her head to determine direction, but by then the haunting warble of notes had ceased abruptly. What they *could* hear was the crunch of snow underfoot, coming from behind them, and they both turned quickly, relieved to see that it was only Jerry.

"Hey, did you guys hear—"

Yanni held up a hand and the Special Forces officer quickly took the hint. After a half minute, and when the sound did not return, Jerry continued.

"Maybe it was just the wind, blowin' through the rocks or something."

Mac and Yanni did not respond, their eyes methodically scanning the rock wall.

As if on cue, the high-pitched whistling resumed again—alternating this time from several different points along the soaring cliff face.

"Call and response," Mac muttered.

"What?" Jerry asked.

"We ain't alone," Yanni said.

R. J. MacCready's eyes ticked back and forth, scrutinizing nooks and crannies in the cliffs of rock and ice. As Yanni confirmed what Mac already feared, the scientist part of his brain responded as it generally did in such situations—with a question of its own.

How in the hell did we get here?

CHAPTER 1

Mission Improbable

Prepare for the unknown by studying how others in the past have coped with the unforeseeable and unpredictable.
—GENERAL GEORGE S. PATTON

Metropolitan Museum of Natural History
New York City
June 18, 1946 (Three weeks earlier)

L ike most disasters, the chain of cause and effect could be traced backward through time to an event that, to any outside observer, might seem as dry and inconsequential as an old bone, or as mundane as an elevator door sliding open. As he stepped onto the museum's fifth floor, the tall, red-haired man had no inkling that he'd just initiated a wrong turn surpassing that of the Donner Party some hundred years earlier. He carried a four-foot-long, oilcloth-bound package in both arms, bride-across-the-threshold style. A guard downstairs had offered him the use of a cart, but even though the package was awkwardly shaped and weighed upwards of thirty pounds, he had politely declined, uneasy about anyone getting too close to the objects he was hauling around.

Hurrying along a wide, cabinet-lined hallway, the man took a sharp right at a sign that read VERTEBRATE ZOOLOGY. He ignored a series of specimen-filled display cases, some housing mounted skeletons from animals he had no interest in identifying, and stopped finally outside a closed door. From inside he could hear a radio playing quietly—"The Gypsy," by the Ink Spots. He tapped out an arrival announcement with the side of his foot.

"Come in," called a familiar voice.

The red-haired man looked up and down the hall and, seeing no one, he gave the door a final hard rap with his shoe. "Open up, Mac," he called, impatiently.

From within, Captain R. J. MacCready followed the first of what would become an annoyingly lengthy list of orders issued by his longtime superior officer and friend, Major Patrick Hendry.

From a separate wing on the fifth floor, a second figure was also converging on MacCready's office. Charles Robert Knight was, without argument, the world's foremost natural history artist. Over a storied, five-decade career, the bespectacled seventy-one-year-old was renowned for the murals of prehistoric life he had created for museums across the country. Secretly, the Brooklynite was most proud of the fact that, while he had never been on the staff of any particular institution, his artwork had nearly single-handedly sparked a public fascination with long-extinct creatures—dinosaurs in particular. Just as fulfilling was the fact that the public's sense of wonder seemed to be growing stronger and more widespread with each passing year.

Knight had begun the day looking forward to wandering the halls of the great museum with his six-year-old granddaughter. But those plans were scuttled after an in-house phone call from one of the research fellows.

The old artist loved associating with the museum's array of taxidermists, exhibition builders, and curators, but R. J. Mac-Cready was a different kettle of fish—a war hero, but one who never spoke a word about his military accomplishments. Mac was also a top-notch field zoologist, though Knight had admired the man's biting sense of humor most of all. He also appreciated, if only vicariously, MacCready's refusal to suffer fools. Yet like so many young men these days, the friend who had come home from the war was not the same one who had gone off to fight nearly five years ago. Mac's unbridled enthusiasm had been tempered, and his wit—when he chose to display it—was darker now. Knight suspected that Mac had endured some unspeakable tragedy.

The goddamned war, Knight thought. *The goddamned war.*

The artist knocked and entered MacCready's small office without waiting. He always appreciated the unique view from just above the tree line and the cool breeze blowing in from Central Park. The office itself was nondescript, although a book lover might spend hours poring over the shelves here, which held everything from first editions of Darwin and Wallace to more recent works by "upstarts" like their museum colleague Ernst Mayr.

Today, Knight found that two others were already present. One was a military type he'd seen on several occasions previously. The artist remembered some recent museum scuttlebutt about a carrot-topped Army officer and so he needed no field guide to identify this particular specimen. The other was a strikingly beautiful young woman with dark, waist-length hair. Knight had seen her around as well, which he considered a far more pleasant experience.

"Afternoon, Charles," MacCready said, gesturing toward his visitors. "You've already met Yanni Thorne. And that's Major Pat Hendry, a friend."

Knight, an ever-present cigarette dangling from his mouth, acknowledged them with a nod, then noticed the room's other new addition: a tray holding an assortment of bones. The oilcloth and packing material, which had been carefully unfolded, told him that one of Mac's guests had likely brought the bones. Varying in size and shape, they were being illuminated by a pair of gooseneck desk lamps.

"Well hello," Knight said, stepping toward the lab bench as both of Mac's visitors moved aside, providing him with some elbow room. Never one to make assumptions, Knight turned back to MacCready. "May I?"

"Go right ahead, Charles. Those are the specimens I called you about."

There was a partial skull, alongside approximately a dozen bones, the smallest of which spanned the length of Knight's pinky. Knight noticed that Mac had conveniently placed a magnifying glass beside the tray, a respectful nod to the fact that the artist possessed only one good eye—the other had been damaged at the age of six by a pebble-tossing playmate. These days an ongoing battle with cataracts raised fears that his bad eye might one day become his good eye, but he had vowed to do as much as he could, until he couldn't. With a degree of caution that he'd developed during decades of handing delicate (and indeed, priceless) fossils, Knight picked up the largest of the specimens—a nearly complete lower jaw that was a shade less than two feet in length.

"I must say, this is a wonderfully preserv—" Knight stopped suddenly, then, snatching up the hand lens, he began to examine the bone more closely. "This can't be," he said, shooting MacCready an incredulous look.

Mac returned him a wry smile. "Yeah, that's what I thought, too."

"But Mac, this . . . this isn't a fossil."

"I figured you might find that an interesting feature."

Major Hendry cleared his throat, loudly. "How old *is* it, Mr. Knight?"

Knight responded by using the magnifying glass to carefully examine the complexly surfaced molars embedded in the thickened, rear portion of the jaw. "I can't be certain of course, but it's . . . it looks recent!" He turned to MacCready. "But this is impossible."

"Why's that?" Hendry asked. "It's an elephant, isn't it?"

"Well, no, not exactly," Knight replied, then paused for a moment. "It appears to be a type of mammoth."

Knight expected a chorus of skepticism, but instead, Mac's female friend stepped forward. "A baby mammoth?"

"What? Yes . . . I mean no," Knight replied, somewhat unnerved by their apparent acceptance of his outrageous pronouncement.

"Go on, Charles," Mac said, encouragingly. "Show us."

Knight held the upper portion of the jaw toward his small audience and pointed to the occlusal, or crushing, surface of a large flat molar. "Do you see this cusp pattern? It's quite different from that of a modern elephant. So yes, it's definitely a mammoth." Then he aimed the front end of the jaw at the trio. "But look at this mandibular symphysis."

"English, please," injected Major Hendry.

"The fusion of these dentary bones," Knight replied, turning toward the military man, who shook his head. "The right and left lower jawbones, for Christ's sake!"

Hendry nodded, flashing a smile that the artist found instantly irritating.

Knight continued, too excited to remain annoyed. "The way they're fused to each other at the . . . *chin* . . . tells me this specimen was an adult! Some unknown, dwarf species or a hell of a bizarre mutation."

"How bizarre?" the major asked, clearly trying to mask his concern.

Still holding the jawbones, the artist gestured to a pair of large openings in the front of the skull. "See those holes?"

His audience nodded.

"They're nasal cavities," Knight continued. "There's supposed to be one, with a septum running down the middle—like we have."

"And?"

"And this fella had *two*."

Hendry shrugged his shoulders. "A pair of nasal cavities. So?"

"So," Knight said, turning to the major, "I think this individual had *two* trunks. Is that bizarre enough for you?"

"But Charles—" MacCready began.

"Wait a minute, Mac," Knight interrupted. "It's my turn. Where on earth did you find this thing?"

MacCready nodded toward the redheaded officer, who was leaning against a rolltop desk. "Pat?"

The major crossed his arms. "That's classified information."

Knight, whose dislike for Hendry was growing by the second, began to throw his arms up, mock surrender-style, then, mindful of the specimen he was still holding, he gently returned the jawbone to the white-enameled tray.

"Classified, he says," Knight mumbled, using the Sherlock Holmes–style magnifier to scan across the spread of smaller bones. "Well, these *all* look recent," he said, mostly to himself but unable to hide the excitement in his voice. "Now how the hell can that—"

Knight held a long, narrow bone—approximately eighteen

inches long and bent somewhat like an archery bow. "Remark-able," he said, examining one end of the object ever more closely. "*Unbelievable!*"

"What is, Charles?" Mac asked.

"This rib."

"What about it?"

"It's also from your mammoth. But you see these?" Knight asked, pointing to a section of the narrow shaft. "They're cut marks—made by tools."

"What kinds of tools?" Hendry asked, his interest ratcheting up a notch.

"Sharp ones," the older man answered, shooting the major a wry smile before shifting his gaze to MacCready. "We can exam-ine these slashes for microscopic fragments and that'll tell us what made 'em. But at first glance I'd say this was a metal blade."

Deftly shifting the bone in his hand, Knight used a magnifier to examine one knobby end. "And there's something else going on. The epiphysis here's been gnawed on."

"Gnawed on—like, by a rat?" Major Hendry asked.

"No," Knight responded, squinting at a telltale set of spatulate grooves that had been chiseled onto the bone. "More like a hu-man—a big, hungry one."

Yanni stepped forward, watching as the artist ran an index finger along the tooth marks. "So, Mr. Knight, you're saying somebody butchered a miniature mammoth *recently* and then chewed on one of its bones?"

"As close as I can tell. But whoever did this is nobody you'd want to meet on the subway."

Yanni smiled. "Kinda like something out of your Neanderthal paintings?"

"Kind of, Yanni," Knight responded. "But different—much

larger, with massive incisors and premolars. More humanoid than human." He turned to Mac. "Look, I've got some friends over in Paleontology who would literally trade five years of their lives to have a peek at these. Now if you'd just—"

Major Hendry shook his head. "I'm sorry but that won't be possible."

"What?" Knight said, exasperated. "For crying out loud!"

"Like I said, 'classified information.'"

Knight turned to Mac, who shrugged his shoulders, before turning his attention back to the officer. *This is definitely the same knucklehead the other curators had been jawing about,* Knight thought. "So classified that you let me handle them but I can't know where they came from?"

"For the time being, that's correct," the major answered, impassively. Then he prompted MacCready with a nod.

"Um, Charles, we're asking you to please keep a lid on this—a tight lid."

"Tell no one," Hendry added.

"For the time being," Mac emphasized, trying to end things on a hopeful note.

Knight, who had a lifetime of experience dealing with decisions that made little or no sense, knew there was nothing to be gained from arguing—at least not now. Without acknowledging MacCready or the major, he placed the rib back on the tray, bowed slightly to Yanni, and exited.

Yanni turned impatiently, aiming the stylus of a fountain pen at the officer. "So, Major, now that we've got that settled, where *did* these bones come from?"

"You mean, where are you going?" Hendry said. He stood beside a wall map, got his bearings, then moved a finger from left to right, crossing the Mediterranean and the Middle East. Slowing down as he reached India, he traced a path northeast but then stopped abruptly. "Those mammoth bones," he said, "came from here. A clan of Sherpas had them."

"Looks cold," Yanni said.

"Colder than the major's heart," Mac chimed in. He had abandoned his examination of the specimen and was looking over Yanni's shoulder. "Southern Tibet, huh?"

Hendry ignored Mac's dig. "It's a region the locals call the Labyrinth. Definitely on the chilly side climate-wise, Yanni."

"But quite the hotbed of political fuckery," Mac added, thoughtfully.

Yanni continued to examine the map. "So who's running the show in there?"

"If you ask the locals, *they* are," Hendry continued, "the Dalai Lama and his Buddhist pals. They're on number fourteen I think."

Yanni shot the major a puzzled look. "Fourteen what?"

"Dalai Lamas, spiritual leaders, head monks. Whatever you want to call them."

"Although this one's no more than a kid, right?" Mac asked.

"So I hear," Hendry said. "But whether he's eight or eighty, officially speaking, our government doesn't talk about Tibetan independence."

"And why's that?"

"Chiang Kai-shek wouldn't like it. He considers Tibet to be part of China."

Mac rolled his eyes. "I hear Chiang's got bigger problems brewing than Tibetan Buddhists."

"You got that right. Some of his Stalinist pals are chomping at the bit to take over, and pretty soon they might be chomping on Chiang's ass. It's the *real* reason we want you in there *yesterday*."

MacCready shook his head. "I was wondering why the Army had suddenly gotten all lathered up about miniature wooly mammoths."

Hendry let out a laugh, then gestured toward the tray holding the bones. "Just consider Dumbo there to be a perfect cover story. If anyone catches wind of this—then it's all just a museum-sponsored collecting trip. The famous zoologist and his Brazilian associate, well versed as she is in elephant talk—"

"—hot on the track of a living fossil," Mac added.

"Now you're talkin'," Hendry said, with a smile.

"But why send us now?" Yanni asked, ignoring his reference to her recent and highly publicized work on animal communication at the Central Park Menagerie.

"Like I said, we want you both in and out of there before the hammer falls on that whole region. Our intel is pointing towards a communist takeover—imminent, maybe."

"Nothing like cutting these things close, huh, Pat?" Mac said. "But you still haven't told us why we need to go in there in the first place."

Hendry held up his hand. "Before we get to that, I've got one question for you. This guy Knight, can we trust him?"

"A hundred percent," Mac replied, without hesitation. His impatience was now in full view. "Now are you gonna answer *our* question or what?"

"Yeah, spill it already," Yanni added, allowing her own annoyance to tick up a notch.

"I guess you'll want to take a gander at this," the major said, withdrawing a folded manila envelope from inside his jacket and spreading out several eight-by-ten photographs.

MacCready picked one up, Yanni took another, and they squinted at what appeared to be sections from an ancient text. Some of the writing was accompanied by carefully labeled drawings of plants and animals.

"Well, this is definitely Latin," Mac said, squinting at the diminutive symbols. "What is this, Pat? It looks Roman."

Hendry smiled, clearly enjoying the proceedings. "It is. Somewhere between 70 and 80 A.D."

Mac thought for a moment, then used a hand lens to get a better look. "Well . . . the author's clearly a naturalist. Pliny the Elder?"

Hendry smiled. "Not bad, Mac."

"But where are these specimens supposed to be from?" MacCready continued leafing through the prints. "There's gotta be at *least* three different primate species here. And these plants? I'm no botanist but I sure as hell haven't seen any like the ones in these drawings."

"Me, either," Yanni emphasized. "Maybe this Pliny made 'em up."

"Or it could be a forgery," Mac said, picking up another of the photos. "I've read Pliny's *Naturalis Historia* but I'm not familiar with these writings."

"That's because we've only recently rediscovered them. The 'Omega Codex,' our boys are calling it."

"Codex?" Yanni asked, unfamiliar with the term.

"An ancient book," Hendry replied. "Usually made of papyrus."

"Or paper," Mac added. "The format allowed people to look stuff up randomly instead of having to unroll an entire scroll." Then he turned to the major. "Okay, so why's the Army all fired up about an ancient Roman text?"

"Well, for one, because Pliny evidently took a little side trip and then never talked about it."

Mac gestured to the map. "Lemme guess . . . Tibet?"

"You got it."

"And?" Mac and Yanni replied, simultaneously.

"*And* it's what he found there, and what the Chinese may have already found, that's got us worried."

"Which was what?"

"According to Pliny, the key to shaping life itself."

As the major expected, his audience of two paused to consider the statement before Mac slid into zoology mode. "Look, Pat, we've got departments full of researchers all over the country delving into the secrets of life: developmental biology, genetics, evolution. What could there be in a two-thousand-year-old codex that these folks don't already know about? And this 'shaping life' reference? I mean, ya gotta admit that's pretty damned vague."

The major waited until MacCready stopped for a breath. "Funny you should mention evolution, Mac. I've been reading up on your boy Darwin's theory about natural selection. What's your take? You buying it?"

"It's the engine that drives evolution," Mac recited, transitioning easily into science-speak. "Changing environmental conditions select the best-adapted individuals—the ones with fortuitous variations. They're faster or taller or better camouflaged than the norm."

Yanni chimed in. "Which also makes 'em less likely to starve or get eaten and more likely to survive long enough to mate—"

"—and pass those adaptations on to the next generation," MacCready said, completing the thought.

"Hey, you two should work together one of these days," the major said, taking a moment to relish the twin frowns they flashed at him. "So this natural selection's a pretty perfect process, huh?"

MacCready shook his head. "It's far from perfect, Pat. Plenty of mistakes. Plenty of fits and starts along the way. Then there's the fact that most of the variations produced by mutations don't do shit. Others are harmful and some end up killing the individual. In fact it's so imperfect that a lot of species go extinct *before* they can adapt to an environmental change—a blight or a new predator or whatever."

"Well, thanks for the biology lesson, Mac. But what if there was a way to avoid the mistakes, a way to create a superior organism *quickly* and without all the trial and error?"

"You're talking about a perfectly adapted species?" MacCready shook his head. "They don't exist in nature."

"And how would you do that anyway?" Yanni asked. "Create this so-called perfectly adapted species?"

"There's selective breeding I suppose," Mac suggested. "Farmers and livestock breeders have been doing that sort of thing forever—bigger ears of corn, more breast meat on a chicken. But still—it's never perfect, and more importantly, it takes generations. How would you deal with *that* little problem?"

"We don't know, exactly. But the brain trust down in D.C. suspect old Pliny may have stumbled onto something during his visit to Tibet—and it might be just the ticket."

"Something that speeds up the evolutionary process?"

"Speeds up. Smooths out. That's what I'm hearing. Unfortunately this codex of his is in shambles—sections missing, other parts completely confusing or impossible to translate."

Mac shuffled through the photos again. "But you *have* uncovered something that's important enough to send us into the middle of Frozen Nowhere?"

"Yeah, word coming out of China is that their scientists have started cranking up the bioweapons labs the Japs left behind. Now the Chinese army is swarming over the Tibetan plateau like ants—which has got the bigwigs in D.C. plenty scared."

Mac shot the major a hopeful look. "Did ya ever think that maybe this Omega Codex is just what Yanni suggested: a work of fiction—no more real than Plato's Atlantis?"

"In which case you and Yanni get to look for Dumbo's weird, pint-sized cousin, get him to pose for some pictures, then head home to shitloads of egghead acclaim."

"There *is* another possibility," Yanni added, and the two men turned to her. "Since this codex is supposed to be two thousand years old, maybe what *was* there isn't anymore."

Hendry glanced at the photos, and then nodded. "Then I'd welcome that great news. But right now we just can't take any chances. I mean, how many soldiers they got in the Chinese army? A hundred million?"

"No . . . but far more than we've got," Mac replied, "or anyone else for that matter."

"Damn right. Now imagine jazzing up even a fraction of that army's next generation with something that makes 'em stronger or faster, or better adapted to operating at night."

"Didn't Hitler try that one already?" Mac shot back. "His super race?"

"Yeah, but the Paper Hanger and his psycho pals didn't have access to something that could speed up evolution, right?"

MacCready said nothing, knowing full well that this particular argument was over, and that the only things to be determined were the specifics of the mission.

"Mac, we can't take the chance that this shit *doesn't* exist. Like I said, the commies could overrun that entire region at any moment."

"And if it does exist?"

"If it *does* exist, then find it and bring it out of there."

"Bring it . . . out?"

"You heard me," Hendry said. "Shouldn't be too hard to put it on ice."

"And then what?"

"What you can't bring out—destroy."

"Destroy it?" Yanni asked.

"Right. We can't have it falling into the wrong hands—if it hasn't already."

"Whatever *it* is," Yanni said, quietly.

"Exactly," Hendry continued. "Whatever *it* is."

Mac held up a hand. "Look, Pat, I've only got a coupla thousand questions. But let me start with just one. Who did all the gnawing on that rib? From what I've seen so far, whatever it was isn't in Pliny's figures."

Hendry hesitated. "We don't know, Mac. Like I said, some of that codex is in shit shape or missing." Then he gestured toward the bone. "But from the look of those bite marks I'd say the current inhabitants of that region might be a lot more interesting than a herd of little elephants."

And a whole lot more dangerous, Mac thought.

Hendry turned to Yanni. He knew that her rather unique skills related to animal communication had landed her a job at the Central Park Menagerie, working with their elephants. He believed that those same skills might be perfectly matched to the mission he was planning. "And no offense about those pachyderms, Yanni."

The woman gave him the briefest of nods. "I've got a question for you, too, Major."

"Shoot," he replied.

Yanni pointed to the stack of photos. "What's Omega mean?"

The major flashed Yanni something Mac had been calling Hendry's "mortician smile" for years. "It's, um, one of the symbols they've been finding over and over again in this codex." Then the officer appeared to give the revelation a dismissive wave. "This Pliny guy seemed obsessed with it."

"It's the last letter in the Greek alphabet, Yanni," Mac said. "It often means, 'the End.'"

Yanni shot both men a quizzical look. "As in—?"

"As in the end of the world," Mac said.

He and Yanni turned toward the major.

"Yeah, that, too," Hendry replied, sheepishly.

CHAPTER 2

Cerae

Some mischievous people always there.
Last several thousand years, always there.
In future, also . . . always there.
　　　—THE DALAI LAMA (#14)

Terra incognita: three weeks sailing, and more than 13,000
stadia* from Taprobane†
April, A.D. 67

An early thaw.
Or so he believed.
That is how it began for Gaius Plinius Secundus. "A cataclysmic melting," he hypothesized, though it was strange to consider that without it, Pliny could not have hoped to complete his mission. During the past four weeks, he and his centuria of eighty soldiers had traveled uphill, using the channeled scablands as a well-placed trail, carved by nature. Nevertheless, it was a disquieting path, knowing as he did that

---

* According to the ancient Greek historian Herodotus, 1 stadium = 607 feet in length.
† Modern-day Sri Lanka.

the same water-blasted wounds over which they walked had been far from well placed for those living below.

The path of destruction descended from the mountains into what had previously been a fair-sized city, named after the family lineage of the late Prince Pandaya, the most recent and final governor. From what Pliny could determine, a new and terrible river, glutted with sediment and debris, had come roaring and frothing through the city, sparing none and leaving behind only traces of buildings torn from their foundations.

All of this, he concluded, had occurred within the past year.

But Pliny also knew that the surge of mud, trees, and other natural battering rams had been more effective than a thousand trailblazers and road builders. Had the doomed city not met its fate when it did, there would have been no way up through an obstacle course of local politics, forest, ice crevasses, and sheer cliffs—no matter how early in the season they tried, and no matter how many times Emperor Nero would have commanded them to *keep trying*.

For a time, Pliny was grateful. But now he realized just how easy it had been to mistake bad omens for good fortune.

Now listen, Proculus, because I record these words for your eyes, and for my conscience, and for the dust of the earth. So began Pliny the Elder's account of a lost expedition. *Remind me, old friend, that these strange and terrifying things really occurred. Remind me Proculus, that you recall them as I do.*

Sailing forty days from Sinai past the horn of India we made landfall and trekked far inland. After a journey of great length but little intrigue or danger we arrived finally upon scenes of desolation and destruction. These evoked a new and immediate respect for a natural world that holds us so frighteningly at

the mercy of its moods. Boulders, greater in size than Phidias'
statue of Zeus at Olympia, were dislodged and carried downhill
by the flood, with a single stone obliterating what had once been
the royal palace. A city of frescoes and marble concourses, of
sapphires and silk, built over generations, must have vanished
in only a few heartbeats.

Climbing for twenty days along the path cleared for us by
the catastrophe, we detected no blade of grass, no sign of life. I
wonder if it will be possible for me, ever again, to be complacent
about this world upon which we live. I cannot escape the feeling
that Nature watches us all with the barely repressed fury of
Poseidon and Talos, waiting to lash out.

Above an altitude of ten stadia and nearly reaching the snow
line, the mudflow over which Pliny and his men walked had
solidified into plains of semihardened earth. Already these had
been cut through by new glacial streams and it was here, at last,
that they began to encounter evidence of the local inhabitants—
footprints and handprints along the water's edge. Most of the
markings seemed to have been made by people of small stature
but even so, Pliny could see that they appeared so deformed in
their extremities that they might only vaguely be called people.
He shared an unspoken question with each of the men who saw
the prints: *Are these the Cerae?*

Pliny's mind formulated another question, though this one
he knew he could answer himself. During a decade in which he
had survived African fevers, a shipwreck, pirates, and nearly every
other disaster the gods could inflict upon him, the Roman asked
himself:

How did I get here?

As a young man, Pliny had entered the army as a junior officer, demonstrating both heroism and keen intelligence in conflicts spanning all of Germania to the African provinces. Between a string of promotions, Pliny began to write extensively—of his travels, of military conquests and natural history.

Beginning with Nero's paranoid stepfather, Claudius, Pliny's ability to write about anything more controversial than grammar and cooking had become a dangerous endeavor. Then, just when it seemed that life in Rome could not get any worse, the gods made certain that it did. With the death of Claudius (poisoned, it was rumored, by his own wife), the seventeen-year old Nero ascended to the throne. Standing before the Senate, he took the name Nero Claudius Caesar Augustus Germanicus—which became wildly popular with his sycophants and ghouls. Others, though, who spoke in hushed tones, came up with a more appropriate title—one that forced Pliny to realize that even writing a cookbook was now a risk. For neither Pliny nor any other reasonably sane person in all of Rome would knowingly attract special attention from the Cannibal Emperor. It was a name spoken only in whispers, and one Nero had earned from his penchant for dressing up in the skins and claws of a wild animal before attacking his terrified victims and consuming their genitalia.

Pliny was grateful, therefore, when Nero became obsessed with a mythical race of half-human grotesqueries said to inhabit an unknown land beyond the Emodian Mountains.* The obsession led the emperor to assign Pliny three ships, along with eighty battle-hardened soldiers and their officers. Nero's orders had been clear: "Find the Cerae, learn their many secrets, then return to

---

* Latin term for the Himalayan Mountains

Rome and teach them to me." As an afterthought, the emperor had added, "And bring me a Ceran head, pickled in spirits."

Pliny hoped that his immediate enthusiasm for what might seem to some a suicide mission hadn't betrayed a strong secondary motive—to embark on a trip of such duration that it might outlast Nero's rule.

But did the Cerae even exist? he wondered. *And if so, were they people, minor gods, or perhaps even monsters?* Pliny had tried to compare the strange markings in a patch of streamside mud with everything he knew about the Cerae. It wasn't much. They were said to have thrived in the time before the Ogygian flood described by Plato—a primeval deluge that brought with it calamity on a worldwide scale. Then, while the ice and water receded into the Emodian Mountains, so too did the Cerae recede from the rest of humanity. As legend told it, they lived at the gateway to Hades, a region home to all manner of fantastic animals, plants, and trees, some with fur or leaves of stark white—the color of death.

Beasts, they may be, Pliny wrote. *But beasts with skilled hands. What we discovered twenty days' march beyond the prints and scratches in the ground should have removed most every doubt of this. The scablands over which we had walked, and the destruction of Pandaya were not created by a cataclysmic thaw of alpine ice and mud. Colossal and clearly hand-hewn blocks of stone had been formed into a dam, and then levered intentionally to either side.*

This alone should have been warning enough to turn back; but curiosity, and my own fatal pride, led us into thinning air and deepening snow, even as the mountain pass narrowed and the tall massifs on either side grew more imposing. Even after a level and easily traveled plain of ice collapsed beneath our feet, revealing itself to be a cleverly constructed trap bridging a bottomless ravine, I callously measured the lost (nearly half of our men) and the injured against those still able to continue the expedition. I sent the Medicus, Chiron and nineteen deemed unfit to trek higher, back down to the ruins of Pandaya, and pushed the twenty who remained with me to higher ground.

One of our finest young engineers, the centurion from Libya known as Severus, held contrary views to everything I believed we had seen. To him, the ground that collapsed beneath our feet could have been a natural formation. In his mind's eye, the prints in the mud were made by ordinary animals—at least three different types. The great dam could have been built by the Pandayans themselves, to control the flow of water through their city—with the destruction that followed a result of flawed design rather than intent.

Then listen, Severus—for I can tell you now that conjuring what could have been, inevitably attracts its dark twin, what is.

CHAPTER 3

Morlocks

I want to go ahead of Father Time with a scythe of my own.
—H. G. WELLS

We are not retreating—we are advancing in another direction.
—GENERAL DOUGLAS MacARTHUR

On the Labyrinth's shelf, South Tibet
July 9, 1946

We ain't alone."

No sooner had Yanni confirmed Mac's suspicion than the strange whistling ceased as abruptly as it had begun. He found this to be even more unnerving than the sounds themselves.

Yanni's stare was fixed on one of the car-sized boulders arrayed at the base of the nearest cliff face.

Mac nudged her with an elbow. "You see something?"

"I think so," she replied, quietly. "In the space between those two boulders."

Mac squinted. "I don't see anything. Just some—"

What he saw then was movement. A snow-packed section of

the wall visible between the stones seemed to have shifted. Now, though, it was still.

"Some, *what*?" came a voice from behind, and Mac gave a start. It was Jerry.

"—rocks, ice, and snow," Mac said, completing the thought. "But they don't ripple in the breeze, do they?"

"Nope," Yanni responded. "But fur does."

Jerry sniffed at the air, which had picked up a thick, musky odor. "Jeez, you smell that?"

They did.

Yanni ignored the comment. "I'm gonna try something," she said, turning to Mac for approval.

He nodded without hesitation.

Yanni turned toward the space between the boulders again and began to whistle, pausing, to mimic as best she could the high-pitched sounds they had heard earlier.

There was no response, and the section of rock wall where they had seen movement was apparently unimpressed as well. Yanni resumed her whistling.

"I found the crate with the weapons, Mac," Jerry said, keeping his voice low. "And pretty much everything survived intact." By way of demonstration he opened his parka to reveal the Colt .45 he had holstered to his belt.

As he did this, an ear-piercing shriek rang out—then several more, coming from different directions. Mac caught a flash of movement from the rock wall and then another movement, farther away along the cliff face. Then another.

It appeared to R. J. MacCready as if eight-foot-tall, vaguely humanoid sections of snow and rock had stepped out of the very face of the mountain itself.

Metropolitan Museum of Natural History
Fifth Floor

C harles Knight was clearly unimpressed with the typewritten communiqué Major Hendry had shown him several minutes earlier. In stodgy, official Army jargon, it gave the officer permission to appoint anyone he chose to an advisory role in "Project Kelvinator"—the mission title, a less-than-subtle nod to the ubiquitous household refrigerator company.

"So let me get this straight," Knight said, holding up a codex photograph. "You think these weird-looking simians Pliny drew might have been what chewed on that elephant rib?"

"With no other suspects, that's the current theory," Hendry replied.

"Well, it's not a theory. It's a hypothesis," Knight countered, sounding a bit too much like MacCready for Hendry's liking. "And it's wrong."

The major frowned.

"Anybody paying attention can see that the primates in your codex were man-sized or smaller. And whatever gnawed that bone was big—a lot bigger than a human."

Now the old guy was *really* beginning to remind him of MacCready. So instead of replying, Hendry eyed the sketches, paintings, and sculptures that seemed to cover every square inch of wall and every flat surface of the artist's office. "You did all these?"

Knight ignored the question. "And now you've lost contact with them as well."

"That's correct."

"But you're not too concerned about that?"

The officer answered with another question of his own. "You *do* know MacCready, right?"

Knight thought about it for a moment. "Okay, you've made your point. So what can I do for you, Major Discomfort?"

"I don't know, *Chuck*," Hendry said, pausing to relish the sour expression he'd hoped to generate. "But Mac seems to think you're a whiz and he trusts you. So . . . what *can* you do for me?"

"Let me think," Knight responded, still wearing an annoyed expression. "Well, for one, I can probably translate this god-damned codex faster than the clowns you've been working with."

"All right, you're in!" Hendry said, slamming his fist down on Knight's desk, the blow causing a sixteen-inch-high statue of *T. rex* to shift precariously. Then, just as suddenly, he turned to leave. "I'll have a photo set of all the originals here by tomorrow."

"Hold it," Knight said, adjusting the King of the Dinosaurs to its former position. "You'll have all the *originals* here by tomorrow," he responded calmly. "And I'll be working with an assistant."

The major hesitated. "An assistant? Wait a minute. Who?"

Knight waved the major away from the closed office door and the puzzled officer took a step to the side. "Patricia," he called.

Almost immediately, the door popped open and a bespectacled head appeared. "Well hello!" came a cheerful greeting.

Now it was Hendry who winced, before turning back toward the elderly artist. "You had this all planned out, didn't you? Right from the start!"

Knight flashed his best "who me?" look, then smiled. "Now if you'll excuse us Major, Miss Wynters and I have quite a bit of work to do."

Hendry dropped a handful of new photographs onto Knight's desk. "Here, start with these."

The artist picked up the first photo in the pile and used his hand lens to examine it. A passage by Pliny immediately drew him in and he roughed out the translation in his head.

"Unbelievable."

A moment later Knight's arm shot out and he passed half of the prints to his newly arrived colleague before returning to his examination of the photo.

"Well . . . I'll leave you to it then," Hendry said, but neither of the museum workers acknowledged him. The major considered emphasizing something about the top-secret nature of the project but instead he exited the office, making certain to close the door very quietly.

South Tibet

May, A.D. *67*

D uring what Pliny eventually came to call his "last night of the old world," the notorious insomniac had joined Severus and the rest of the night guard, adding his watchful eyes to theirs. The hours passed slowly and in silence. On this night, the air was so thin that only by chewing a third of the way through his remaining ration of coffee beans was it possible for Pliny to maintain his breathing without growing faint. Observing the moon as it passed behind a fleet of rapidly advancing clouds told him that the uncanny stillness of the narrow mountain pass— through which not even breezes stirred—would not last much beyond dawn.

"A storm is coming," Severus said.

The commander nodded, weakly. Though they had reached a point at which the path could not possibly ascend more than a day's walk higher, to Pliny the absence of sounds was more oppressive than the thin air. He listened with increasing intensity, for noises that never came. As dawn approached, he discovered that, with the high-altitude absence of trees and life's usual background noise, the human brain created its own forests of the night. Something moaned threateningly among the nearer of the cliffs, and something howled back from the opposite cliff face. Pliny glanced at Severus with startled surprise, but he and the rest of the night guard had heard nothing.

"The sounds were born of my own imagination," Pliny explained.

"The mind is a skilled deceiver," Severus replied.

"Good line," said the historian.

"I'll be honored to have you steal it from me one day," the centurion joked, but Pliny did not respond. Instead of imaginary sounds, his oxygen-deprived mind had now begun generating imaginary figures—misty and white and vague, gliding within and between the rocky nooks and crannies overhead. The longer he peered into the distant shadows, the less distinct the shapes became, and thus he was able to cast them aside. *This is no different from reading animal shapes into cloud formations,* he convinced himself.

The ghosts on the massifs were gone and did not manifest again; after sunrise Pliny quickly forgot about them.

According to scraps of legend Pliny had been able to collect before their voyage, the Cerae, despite their secretive nature, had somehow arrived at an understanding with Prince Pandaya and his predecessors. Apparently this had come after his family's successful defense of the lowlands and their mountain passes from an attack by the Scythians—a tribe of horse-mounted nomads with an appetite for human flesh. But if the prince ever actually met with the Cerae, he had never recorded the encounter. Even the means of trade between the two groups was an enigma, since it did not appear to involve any actual exchange of goods. And while the white-leaved trees from the Ceran homeland yielded medicinal oils and something akin to silk, the Cerae apparently asked for nothing in return for their resources. Instead they deposited their treasures in secret, outside the city. Despite his centurion's belief that the Cerae might not even exist, Pliny suspected that what the prince had interpreted as a naïve generosity was really a message, a command: *Take these gifts but stay away.*

Far above the Pandayan ruins, during the last day in which Pliny's world still made sense, the storm Severus had predicted seemed determined to freeze them all to death. As their leather armor and shields became wet with snow, the remains of Pliny's regiment ascended to what he believed to be the uppermost reaches of the "trail" and it became possible to hope that soon they would be moving down into more breathable air. Presently, even without the burdens of deep snow and wet, ice-swollen gear, each step seemed to require three times as many breaths.

Though his men were far too exhausted to care about such things, Pliny wondered how high the tallest of the Emodian Mountains stood. At a guess, based upon what he had already seen, the mountain range rose so high that it rendered the earth an *imperfect* sphere. It was a scientific revelation he would have shared with like minds in Rome over wine and good food, but here and now, philosophy counted for nothing. Nature's flaws mattered only in the present reality of slippery rock walls and wind-driven snow.

Against his better judgment, Pliny unbuckled the scabbard holding his short sword, then passed both to his personal attendant. *Anything to lighten the load,* he thought. *Anything to help me draw another breath.*

"Remain at my side, Antoninus," he said, between gasps.

"Of course, sir," replied the dark-haired teen. A storyteller and poet who had been in his service for the past six years, Antoninus somehow managed a smile and a dutiful bow. Pliny, though, could read the plea written in the boy's eyes. *Can we turn around, sir? Can we go home now?*

But they did not turn back. Instead, Pliny led them to yet another rocky outcropping, from which sudden, snowy gusts threatened to launch them screaming into the underworld. Pliny decided that they should rest for an hour in the shelter of an icy overhang, consuming light rations of dried meat, taking turns warming their feet against a portable brazier, and melting snow into drinking water. After providing his own body with what he had calculated to be reasonable time to recover, Pliny began to scout the route ahead. Intermittent breaks in the obscuring veils of snow suggested that they had indeed passed the highest and most physically demanding point along the path. Pliny looked back at his men, their wind-chapped faces covered in turbans so that only their eyes were visible. Tugged and battered by the gusts, they had their backs pressed tightly against the cliff face that ran alongside the trail. Pliny shifted his grip on the rock wall as he descended, his own movements labored by exhaustion and the thick hides he wore. Through the worst of it, he allowed himself a moment of optimism. *By tonight, breathing will be easier,* he reasoned.

The moment passed, as he knew it would. Not very many paces from where he stood, a pair of opposing rock walls converged to form a narrow, V-shaped passage—as if a doorway had been thrown open.

"The lair of your Cerae, I suppose?" Severus grumbled, doing his best to restrain any actual expressions of anger or sarcasm.

"Perhaps," Pliny responded.

But with nowhere else to go, Pliny and the centurion led their party downhill and through the jagged entranceway.

Although they were still being buffeted by windblown snow, now and again the white veil parted for a moment, allowing tantalizing views of what lay ahead. Collectively, each glimpse built upon the previous one in Pliny's imagination, helping him to form a picture that could not be real. There appeared to be towers, sharp-edged and cleanly cut.

His men moved with an accelerated pace through the narrows, driven by a combination of foreboding and excitement. They could all see the structures now.

Descending into a mountain valley, Pliny watched the entire curtain of snow draw back for several long seconds, granting them far more than a glimpse this time. His next thought was a revelation, for Pliny knew at once that even after coming to appreciate the strategic significance of the Pandaya-obliterating dam and the trap that had been sprung against his own group, he had vastly underestimated the Cerae. Sunlight striking the towers and domes was too bright and the wrong color to be illuminating mere works of stone. The turrets were composed of gleaming crystal or glass, or perhaps even ice—supported by foundations and ribs of granite.

Oddly, Pliny's next emotion was jealousy over an undeniable realization: *Rome's greatest architects could never have—*

A movement along the nearest rock wall drew his attention. Ghostlike, and so exquisitely camouflaged that the Ceran must surely have been standing only a few arm-lengths in front of his face all along, it—*they* moved as if they had been part of the snow and ice itself, summoned suddenly alive. Pliny instinctively reached for his sword then felt a flutter in the pit of his stomach as he realized he had given it to his young aide. He turned to Antoninus, who was still carrying the weapon, but in the next moment his view of the boy was obscured by a warm mist accompanied by the metallic scent of blood in the air.

In the space of five heartbeats, and in a silent whirlwind of arterial spray, the Cerae burst upon the Romans.

Metropolitan Museum of Natural History
Fifth Floor

An hour after Major Hendry's departure, Knight looked up from his work, stretched and yawned, realizing only now that the officer had gone. "Not the best writer, this Pliny guy," he said, removing his glasses to rub his eyes. "Not by a long shot," Knight emphasized. "Now his nephew, *he* could write."

There was no response from Patricia.

Squinting, Knight replaced his spectacles and turned around. He could see that Patricia had cleared a new space on a nearby lab bench and was using a desktop magnifier to examine the codex photos.

"He was confiding to Socrates in this section," she said, holding up a photo and without a hint of mockery. She wrote something down on a yellow legal pad.

"That's nice," Knight said. They both knew that by Pliny's time, the old Greek had himself been dead for nearly five centuries.

There was no further comment from the pair, and unaccustomed as the researchers were to small talk, they went silent and they went back to work.

I don't know what's more disturbing," Knight said at last, "this little dilly about what can happen to anyone bearing weapons, or this new stuff about worms?"

"I vote for the worms," Patricia replied, morosely.

"Well, either way, I'm starting to see why they sent Mac in there. I mean, if there's even the possibility that this world we're unraveling was real and that some of it could *still* exist—"

"Agreed," the black-clad woman replied, not bothering to look up from her own sample of codex photographs. "And Charles, about those worms—I think we need to bring in an expert on invertebrates."

Knight gave a mirthless laugh. "Yeah, that's gonna go over *real* well with Major Disaster. Let's just invite everyone we know."

"Speaking of invitations," Patricia said, "don't forget the concert Friday night and the tour afterwards with that movie guy."

Knight glanced over at the strange, cabinet-like instrument that had arrived two days before—a gift from its inventor. "Right, right," he said. "Remind me again. What's that movie guy's name?"

"Hitchcock," Patricia said.

Knight gave a brief nod. "That's it," he said. Then the pair returned their full attention to the codex.

> *I may truly say Socrates, that no one is meant to*
> *understand what I have seen. When you gaze upon the*
> *kingdom of which I speak, even wisps of snow gaze back*
> *at you, and into you. My soul has become a strange*
> *and dark companion. In the course of our journey, I*
> *seem to record my discourses more for the ancients than*
> *in memory of those among whom I travel. I suppose,*
> *in essence, I have my dialogues with the dust. Then*

listen, dust. Listen to a tale which, though difficult to comprehend and more difficult to relate, is a fact and not a fiction. And we know, we who have seen. We know, we for whom the tale began in a white blur, and gushes of scarlet, and the whole of existence ceasing.
—PLINY THE ELDER (AS TRANSLATED BY PATRICIA WYNTERS, MMNH)

South Tibet
May, A.D. 67

Pliny remembered struggling to regain consciousness in air that was too agonizingly rarefied and cold. Until the awareness of pain set in, he wondered if in fact he had perished during the attack—wondered if he had become part of the whirlwinds of red mist. The sudden confusing slaughter occupied the same instant of realization of *The Cerae have us,* and *This is the end of me.* Then, stillness and nonexistence, without ice or sky, darkness or light.

In the next moment, a breath was drawn in pain, fear, and anguish—for he had caught a glimpse of the short but exceedingly muscular creature dragging him by one foot. Having nearly believed himself dead, Pliny had a new realization: *I have not been that lucky.*

Dropped at the base of a wind-sculpted snow dune, Pliny feigned death on ground that seemed unnaturally warm. A loud thud and a sickening crack forced him to give up the pretense. Opening one crusted eye, he found most of the view blocked by several pairs of legs, vaguely human yet covered with thick white fur. Here and there burlap-like strands of fabric had been braided into the fleece, camouflaging them against darker splotches of rock amid snow and ice. He also saw that Severus had been correct on one detail: there were at least three kinds of them among the dozen creatures present.

Grotesqueries. The Cerae are monsters.

With his senses beginning to clear, Pliny had a pair of simultaneous revelations: First, he had been discarded in a pool of coagulating blood—*the blood of my own men.* Second, the Cerae were building two orderly piles: the bodies of men whose heads appeared to be missing, and the weapons that had been taken from them.

A moan drew his attention elsewhere and Pliny realized that he was not the sole human survivor. A soldier whose name he could not presently recall was crawling toward a half-buried sword and, though already missing an arm, he was still determined to fight. In a flash of movement, one of the nearly man-sized monsters grabbed the Roman by a foot and swung him headfirst into a pillar of ice, crushing the crown of his skull down to the level of his eyes.

"No!" Pliny cried out.

The murderous Ceran ignored him, focusing instead on the precise arrangement of the soldier's body on the pile of similarly "headless" men.

"Save your voice," came a weak call. It was Severus. "And your life."

South Tibet
July 9, 1946

Sensing that Jerry was about to withdraw his pistol, and in what seemed to Mac to be a single continuous move, Yanni blocked the man's right arm, grabbed the weapon, and flung it as far away as she could into the snow.

"What the *hell* are you doing?" Jerry cried, having acted just fast enough to stop a reflex to strike the person who had suddenly disarmed him. "Are you nuts?"

Yanni remained calm, exhibiting what Mac thought to be an equally extreme degree of self-control, considering there were four towering humanoids standing before them—their bodies covered from head to toe in long, translucent hair.

"Did you hear those shrieks when they saw that heater?" she replied quietly.

As MacCready watched the creatures closing in, he saw that any argument between Yanni and Jerry had ended as quickly as it began. He could tell that Jerry's anger had already been circumvented by the fight-or-flight portion of his autonomic nervous system.

"What on earth are they?" Jerry muttered.

"Morlocks," Mac said, under his breath, reminded of H. G. Wells's fictional subterraneans.

"Pliny forgot to mention these big ones, huh?"

Mac did not respond. Instead he watched as the two figures to his far left and right shifted position—moving to encircle them. *Incredibly graceful,* he thought, noting that despite their size (which he estimated to be somewhere north of five hundred pounds), there was no wasted motion. They seemed to glide across the ground, and within seconds a pair of giants stood between the trio and their shattered helicopter—effectively cutting off any possibility of retreat. *Smart, too,* Mac thought. *Shit.*

R. J. MacCready slowly raised his hands, watching out of the corner of an eye as Yanni and Jerry followed suit. "*Bom dia!*" Mac said cheerfully in Portuguese, missing the brief incredulous look he'd gotten from his Brazilian friend.

The "Morlocks," whose faces and palms were apparently the

only body parts *not* covered in thick, whitish fur, ignored him. Instead one of the creatures approached Jerry, who responded with a reflexive step backward.

"Do . . . *not* . . . move," Yanni said, through teeth clenched in what Mac thought was a rather scary-looking grin.

The man froze and closed his eyes. He never saw the blur of movement as the giant brushed past him. Reaching into a snow-drift, it gingerly picked up the .45 and, without hesitation, flipped it off the side of the cliff. Then it gave a short whistle. Each of his hirsute colleagues responded by taking up positions behind one of the three humans. Then, simultaneously, the newly cap-tive humans each felt what Bob Thorne would have considered a "somewhat less-than-gentle" poke in the back. All three obeyed the finger prods in exactly the same way.

They shuffled forward.

CHAPTER 4

First Impressions

Somewhere, something incredible is waiting to be known.
—CARL SAGAN

The greater our knowledge increases, the greater our ignorance unfolds.
—JOHN F. KENNEDY

Metropolitan Museum of Natural History
Fifth Floor
July 9, 1946

Well this isn't very cheery," Patricia Wynters said, having just translated another section of the Pliny codex.

Charles Knight never looked away from the desktop magnifier. He was using a pair of rubber-tipped forceps to examine a tattered one-inch square of papyrus. "I never said we were going to be reading the funny papers."

"I'm terribly worried about Mac and Yanni," she said. "Aren't you?"

"Of course I'm worried," he replied. "I read about that attack on Pliny, too. But we've got a job to do here and the quicker we can—goddammit!" Knight's progress translating a fragment from a later section of the codex had been stymied by the fact that the second half of what looked like an important page was in tatters and mostly missing.

"For the first two paragraphs he goes on and on about worms again. Then there's a big hole in the next section. All that's left is something about 'molding life as if it were—' Then there's *another* hole."

"Oh, dear," Patricia said, quietly.

"I'm sure Hendry caused some of this damage himself," Knight muttered, before glancing over at his friend. "The codex spends two thousand years intact and in another week the Army would have turned it into powder."

Patricia kept quiet, knowing better than to interrupt Knight when he was on a roll. Not for the first time, though, she wondered if it would have been better for all of them if Pliny's work *had* been completely destroyed, long ago.

South Tibet

You got a German cousin named Sergeant Schrödinger?" MacCready asked his towering Morlock shadow. There was no response (aside from another annoying finger prod) and no alternative, except to continue along the rocky trail that led them farther and farther away from the downed helicopter and, more disquietingly—farther away from their supplies.

Mac took the opportunity to retreat into zoology mode, mentally tweaking the standard mammalian field measurements for primates: They were all adult males ("Penis—pendulous; scrotum—primate-like," he would have written had he been filling out a field notebook). Arguably, their second most obvious trait was the long, dense hair that covered their bodies. This "pelage" ranged in color from pure white to a sort of cream, but remarkably, the creatures seemed to darken and lighten depending on their background. Mac noted that they looked almost slate gray when standing beside a rocky wall but within seconds of stepping onto the snow, the Morlocks blurred and changed before his eyes.

Textbook example of cryptic coloration, Mac thought, although he reasoned that the first trait he'd noticed might not make it into high school zoology texts.

As for *total* body size, in spite of the low oxygen levels, these guys had managed to pack on a great deal of high-metabolism beef. With muscular bodies of between seven and a half and eight feet in length, they made boxer Primo Carnera look like a toddler. Having had time to look them over, Mac *now* estimated that they'd weigh in at around six hundred pounds—or twice the weight of the six-foot-six-inch former heavyweight champion known to fans and foes alike as the Ambling Alp.

Of far more immediate concern were the creatures' oversize canine teeth, which reminded him more of a baboon's dentition than anything that might be considered human. MacCready also noticed that the tops of their heads came to a low front-to-back ridge. "Sagittal crest," he mumbled, knowing that the increase in bony surface area meant more room to attach a set of massive temporalis muscles—all of which translated into some *serious* jaw strength.

Although the mystery about what, exactly, had gnawed on the mammoth rib had been solved, Mac hoped to leave unresolved any questions about just how painful their bite could be.

After marching approximately three hours from the crash site, and to the point of exhaustion, MacCready realized that they were approaching what appeared to be a natural wall. It completely dead-ended what had, up till now, been a rugged path. Of course there were no handholds or, for that matter, anything that might give purchase to anyone insane enough to attempt climbing it. Mac guessed that any traveler taking this route would have determined the trail to have become impassable and, unless they possessed either a Buck Rogers rocket pack or sophisticated mountain climbing gear, been forced to turn back.

The Morlocks, though, continued herding the humans forward, until they came within several arm lengths of the roughly ten-story-tall barrier of rock.

"Now where, pally?" Mac said under his breath. He looked over at Yanni, who shrugged her shoulders but remained silent.

"Looks like somebody forgot the map," Jerry said.

Mac suddenly felt himself being grabbed around the waist while almost simultaneously being swept off his feet. With an ease that circumvented all thoughts of escape, he found himself literally tucked under a hairy armpit, his body held roughly parallel to the ground. From this strange though not entirely uncomfortable vantage point, Mac glanced around as the giant effortlessly scaled the rock wall, paying no heed to the 180-pound load it was now carrying.

The creatures carrying Yanni and Jerry in an identical manner followed up the rock face in rapid order until they had deposited their cargo atop the wall, where the path resumed, in a new direction. Glancing back over the edge, Mac could see the fourth climber literally running up the side of the sheer edifice.

"You see the dogs on these things?" Mac asked Yanni. He'd noted earlier that the Morlocks were equipped with huge, broad-soled feet and strange toes with rounded tips, the largest of which faced inward ("great toe offset from digits II-V and directed medially!").

"Like a house gecko," Yanni said, sounding excited at the sight of the creature, though clearly struggling for air.

"You got it, Yanni," Mac added. "I wonder if they've got the same type of friction pads on their fingers and toes?"

"I'll bet," she countered. "More gecko mimicry."

"And can you imagine the lung capacity—"

Jerry cleared his throat. "Um, excuse me folks," he wheezed, pausing until they both turned to him. He caught his breath. "If you could possibly take a break from all this swell science talk, I've got about a million fucking questions—most of them dealing with us not getting killed."

Mac gave him the calm-down sign. "If they wanted us dead, Jerry, don't you think we'd *be* dead by now?"

Jerry thought about it for about a half second. "Yeah, and some cats will play with a mouse for hours before they finally decide to kill it."

"Well, they're definitely not feline, Jerry, but I do think they're as curious about us as we are about them."

Jerry frowned. "I suppose."

"Unless they plan on eating us," Yanni chimed in, a bit too cheerily.

Mac shot her a disapproving look. *Not quite the support I was looking for, kiddo.*

"Or . . . there's that," Mac offered, sheepishly.

"This is just great," Jerry responded, shaking his head and looking even more dejected—if that were possible.

Mac took the opportunity to shoot Yanni a quick *give the guy a break* expression, and she returned it with a shrug of her shoulders. He knew she had initially voiced the opinion that Jerry was too young for this mission, but in that regard she wasn't alone. Back home, Mac had explained that although Jerry always looked a bit wet behind the ears, he had in fact mastered six languages by age twelve and graduated from Columbia at nineteen. But it wasn't all academics, and baby face or not, Jerry had saved Mac's life in the Pacific, and could therefore be counted on whenever the chips were down.

"Look," Mac said to his young friend, trying to sound confident, "we just play this by ear, right? There's no other option. I think *they* built this wall and now we're going to find out what's on this side of it." He looked Jerry in the eye. "You good?"

Jerry nodded.

"Well all right. Just don't look too threatening, huh?" Mac said, nudging his friend with a gentle elbow to the ribs.

Jerry managed to flash his trademark you-can-depend-on-me smile. "Got it."

"They eat the threatening ones," Yanni added, just before they each received another prod from behind.

South Tibet
May, A.D. 67

All told, Pliny counted just one other, besides himself and Severus, who had survived the massacre—*for only a liar would have described it as anything else.* The entire encounter could not have lasted more than the count of ten. Early in that count, a young Nubian cavalryman named Proculus had stumbled backward upon his own sword. In retrospect, the accident and an uncharacteristic fault in craftsmanship had saved his life—the sword tip breaking off as it struck his femur, and the blade itself cracking in two. The Cerae evidently considered the weapon to be useless, thus sparing Proculus a speedy trip to Hades.

"I'll be a Poseidon-cursed Cretan!" cried the wounded Roman. He was always one of the more profane members of the expedition but now he was lisping through a space where three front teeth were missing. Back home, before he became an adventure seeker, Proculus had been a much-sought-after architect, as stoic in striking deals with government officials as he was at hiding the pain of sucking in cold air over freshly broken teeth.

The three survivors and their captors were on the move now, setting out on a forced march toward whatever short and sorry future might await them. Trudging single file down a rocky path away from the carnage, each was shadowed by his own grotesque escort.

Pliny also noted that Proculus made a perfectly admirable display of hiding his limp, though muscle and even bone must have been pierced. The great blood vessels had remained unsevered, since the man had entirely stanched the blood flow by applying pressure to a well-placed rag.

"Why have they spared us, sir?" the wounded man asked.

"I think . . . because we lost our weapons," Pliny answered, between gasps of thin air.

"Perhaps," Severus said. "But I think you should *both* save your energy by not speaking."

A sharp prod to the centurion's back not only ended the conversation but reminded the Romans that there was no way to tell whether the vanquished were being marched toward their own executions.

Pliny concluded that any questions their captors might have about Roman fighting capabilities had already been settled. Now, it seemed, only pain thresholds were being explored with each successive prod—the latest, a thwack across his centurion's shoulder blades, had come from the flat side of a confiscated sword. Ahead, cradled in his well-muscled arms, a short-legged but disconcertingly stocky Ceran carried the remainder of the Roman weapons, and Pliny marveled that the creature exerted little if any extra effort.

"Who are these animals?" Pliny asked breathlessly. His companions, though, remained silent, as fresh waves of snow streamed in and broke upon them in stinging, blinding gusts.

After an especially strong blast of wind, Proculus began to stumble, teetering perilously close to the edge of a bone-shattering drop-off. A flash of movement followed but instead of falling, the soldier was dangling by an arm over the precipice, held aloft by his Ceran escort who, seemingly without effort, placed Proculus back on his feet and along the path.

During the episode, which had taken all of five seconds, the wounded Roman gasped but did not cry out, even though Pliny thought the "rescue" must have nearly disarticulated the man's arm at the shoulder. Instead Proculus brushed himself off in an exaggerated manner and threw the creature a nod. The only response from the Ceran was a gesture that could be interpreted as nothing other than *Keep moving*.

Proculus straightened his spine, obeyed the gesture, and gave an audacious nod that boasted, to his Roman onlookers, *Notice the restraint I have shown in not hurling this monkey over the edge*. "As you know," Proculus called back to his commanders, "for all warriors there are but two kinds of prisoners: assets and liabilities."

Severus shook his head. Despite the worsening conditions and their recent and unimaginable losses, he seemed truly amused by the man's audacity. "And which one are you?"

But the soldier's answer, if there was one, went unheard as the wind continued to roar and gale-animated blasts of snow whipped around them like maddened wasps.

July 9, 1946

The first thing R. J. MacCready noticed about the plants that ringed the walls and ceiling of the cave entrance was that they were stark white. The second was that they possessed teeth.

The Morlocks had deposited the trio of humans outside the fifteen-foot-wide opening and were currently huddled up nearby, deeply involved in what appeared to be a whistle-driven, hairy-arm-waving conversation.

"They almost look like snakes," Jerry said, pointing to the top of the opening.

"Yeah, but I think they're vines," Mac responded, squinting up at the impossibly weird life-forms.

"I don't know, Mac," the younger man went on, clearly unconvinced. "You ever been inside a bat cave?"

Mac and Yanni exchanged looks.

"I think I've got that one covered," the zoologist replied.

"Well, I was outside this cave in Puerto Rico once, and at dusk the boa constrictors would come out and hang down from the cave opening." He gestured upward. "Kinda like that—to snatch at the bats that flew out."

"Do they have bats in Tibet?" Yanni asked.

"Yeah, but nothing like the diversity you had in Brazil," Mac said.

"No vampire bats, though. Right?" Yanni asked.

"That we know of," Mac answered.

At that point the conversation died and the trio stood silently, peering into the cavern—which seemed to drop off a few feet just inside the entrance.

Moments later the finger prodders were back, and, having assumed their positions, they directed their captives in single file into the mountain itself.

Mac, who was the first one in line, paused for just a moment to get a closer look at the snake-headed vines—and as he did, something white and sparrow-sized streaked out of the cave, causing one of the plants hanging from the peak of the opening to snap closed.

"I think the breeze from that bird or whatever it was triggered those jaws," Mac commented.

Yanni squinted up at the vines as she passed beneath them. "Like the modified leaves of a Venus flytrap."

"Yeah, only this one seems to be lined with silica teeth."

"Interesting," Yanni responded. "Now, what was that you were telling Hendry about there being no perfectly adapted species in nature?"

Mac pondered the question silently as he entered the cave. "If it was a *perfect* adaptation, it would have caught that bird, right?"

"Well anyway," Yanni added, "do *not* buy one of those for my apartment."

Although a part of Mac's mind was still considering Yanni's comments about adaptation, another part concluded that the idea of having a few of these plants delivered to some of the bachelors living near her apartment made for some interesting visuals. Before his daydream could get *too* interesting, though, Mac received another finger poke in the back.

Had he and Yanni been allowed to stick around for another thirty seconds, they would have been even more puzzled by some very un-flytrap-like behavior, as the snake vine's "mouth" snapped back open. Elsewhere in the world, the Venus flytrap reset was a far more gradual process that could take up to two days.

Once inside the cave, the walls converged rather abruptly and the trio was soon being herded through a narrow passageway, roughly twenty feet high and less than half as wide. The straight sections led to a series of hairpin turns—and so the effect was one of continuous and gradual descent. *They really are subterraneans,* Mac told himself. Suddenly his funny nickname for them—Morlocks—seemed more apt than he had guessed, and his arms broke out in a chill of gooseflesh. Surprisingly, and to Mac's relief, instead of a nightmare march through a pitch-black maze, they soon discovered that there would be no need for torches or head-lamps. The cave walls themselves were lit by what seemed to be a great multitude of bioluminescent microorganisms.

Bacteria and algae mostly, Mac guessed, *each giving off its own spectrum of light.* Remarkably, some of the colonies appeared to be blinking at different frequencies, while others were simply "on." He made a mental note that while blues and greens were predominant, there was definitely some red light as well. Mac knew that many nocturnal and cave species, including a certain population of vampire bats formerly thought to be extinct, had been blind to the red light emitted by specially designed lanterns. *But here at least some of the subterraneans seem to have evolved beyond that red insensitivity.* Mac waited for Yanni's comment on the phenomenon but for now, at least, she was silent.

A stone arch under which they passed drove home the message that the world into which they were descending could be as strangely beautiful as it was dangerous. Along the arch's horizontal underside, hundreds of thumb-sized "glowworms" had draped an array of sticky silk feeding lines—each one baited with luminous beads that glistened like wet pearls on a string. The pearls were actually a gluey secretion and one of the lines was already being reeled in, having ensnared a chillingly vocal species of cave moth.

Another new species, Mac thought. Triphosa thorni—*Bob would appreciate that one.*

As if to emphasize the diversity of the cave environment, almost directly underfoot another previously unknown animal let out a squeak. MacCready, who reacted with a start, knew that this species was decidedly mammalian. About the size of a large white rat, it had nearly run across his boots before disappearing into the shadows. As their downward trek continued, Mac saw more vague shapes, scurrying in and out of the bioluminescence—but these, too, vanished into hiding places just before he could attempt to identify them.

I'd pay a million bucks to be able to stick around and study this ecology, Mac thought, before flashing back to his last caving experience—an outing that included voluntarily burying himself in a three-foot layer of living bat guano.

Well, maybe half a million.

But while R. J. MacCready focused on what was clearly a remarkable and unique troglodytic ecosystem, Yanni, as expected, was far more fascinated by the complex pattern of whistles and grunts that the Morlocks were exchanging with each other. More than once Mac looked back in response to a strange warble of notes only to find that it was Yanni who had made it.

None of the giants seemed to pay much attention to her linguistic exercises but at a brief rest stop beside a pool of what turned out to be deliciously cold water, one of the creatures did something remarkable.

After allowing the three captives to drink their fill, the alpha Morlock (a designation stemming from the fact that it did more whistling and no pulling of guard duty) ambled over and squatted down at the water's edge. Mac noted that its fur looked very different than when they were outside the cave—having darkened now to match the stony background. He currently suspected that, like polar bears, their hairs weren't really white. Instead they were likely pigment-free—transparent and probably hollow, thus providing them with the ability to scatter and reflect visible light. It would also explain, to one degree or another, how the Morlocks had taken camouflage to new levels of complexity and effectiveness.

This particular individual, who like the others gave off a strong musky body odor, was not looking for a drink. Instead it dipped its hand into the shallow water and appeared to fish around for a few seconds, as if gathering something. Once the lead Morlock withdrew his arm, Mac could see that its forefinger was now covered in a dense mat of cottony material.

Was it algae? MacCready wondered. *Probably, but it certainly isn't getting its energy from sunlight.*

Unconcerned about such questions, "Alpha" glanced over at Yanni before slurping the mess off its finger. Then it directed a short series of whistled notes at her.

Yanni hesitated for a moment, apparently not wanting to interrupt the big guy's meal. Then she shook her head and emitted a single, whistled note of her own. The creature responded with something that was *clearly* an expression of exasperation—which Mac thought was actually a distinct improvement over the aggressive, bared-canines look they'd generally been sporting up till now. The giant followed up by thrusting its hand back into the water and withdrawing a baseball-sized handful of the white glop. This time, though, instead of eating it, the big guy flipped the material through the air, the flight path ending with a splatter against Jerry's chest. The man's fear of the creatures had abated not at all since their initial encounter, but now he forced a phony-looking smile. The others, Morlock and non-Morlock, watched as the sticky mass plopped down onto his lap.

The algae flipper's three colleagues responded with what sounded very much like a hissing laugh, and though their expressions were anything but comforting (a return of the flashing fangs made that a certainty), the absurdity of what had just taken place caused Yanni and Mac to laugh as well.

Jerry responded by popping a chunk of the strange slime into his mouth. "Thi tuff ess great," he managed.

Less than a minute later, they were all eating the white stuff and all agreeing that despite its mucus-like consistency, it was indeed quite palatable.

Another new species, Mac noted, though he knew he'd never be mistaken for an algae expert.

After quickly eating his fill, Mac stood up, eyeing a semicircular alcove just up ahead.

"Gotta see a man about a horse," he said.

Jerry nodded, knowingly, while Yanni threw him a puzzled look.

Alerted by the movement, Mac's personal bodyguard broke away from his own group and followed, uttering an angry grunt as he did. MacCready turned and held up his hands, in what he hoped was *still* the universal sign for peaceful guy. Then, making sure that Yanni wasn't looking, he used a somewhat ruder gesture to explain why he had wandered off. The creature made no response except to move into its familiar position behind him.

"Hey, spread out, huh? Ya know how hard it is to pee when someone's st—"

MacCready's wisecrack was halted by the sight of a neat pile of unfamiliar bones in the alcove, sitting beside a small circular pool. As he moved in closer, the water was clear enough for him to see that a similar geometrically arranged mound sat submerged about two feet below the surface.

Mac wondered why anyone would create such an arrangement, but before he could get a better look, his hirsute shadow was back and a less-than-gentle shove (instead of a prod) followed. Adding to Mac's annoyance was the fact that he had been forced to leave the alcove without carrying out his original mission.

Yanni was studying the cluster of Morlocks rather intently, so Mac took a seat next to Jerry. "There's something over there on the ground that I really want you to see."

Jerry responded by scrunching up his face in an odd way. "I'll pass," he said.

Mac threw him a puzzled look that ended with a head shake. *What the hell's wrong with him?* he thought, before turning to see what had drawn Yanni's attention.

Off to one side, the now-reunited Morlock quartet continued to converse in their vaguely birdlike language, and Mac noticed yet again that the giant who'd dodged guard duty was doing most of the whistling.

He's definitely *the* jefé, Mac thought, wondering if his personal bodyguard was now taking flack from the boss for allowing one of the humans to poke his nose where it probably didn't belong.

Yanni acknowledged MacCready's return and gestured toward the Morlocks. "If you think about it, Mac, whistling's the perfect means of communication over long distances and mountainous terrain. I wouldn't be surprised if they were using low frequency as well."

"Like your elephants?" Mac said.

"And those musky secretions are probably some kind of scent marker," she added.

"Sounds about right," Mac replied with a nod. "Hey, I saw an interesting arrangement of animal bones in that alcove."

"An arrangement?"

"Yeah, one stack on the ground, another one submerged in a smaller pool."

Yanni paused for a moment. "*In* the water?"

"Sittin' there in a neat little pile."

"Maybe they're feedin' their algae friends."

Now it was Mac who hesitated. "Calcium, phosphorus, and protein. Could be," he said. Then he gestured toward the lead Morlock, who seemed to be in monologue mode. "Can you make out what he's saying?"

"Not yet," Yanni replied, "but I'm workin' on it."

CHAPTER 5

The Shape of Things to Come

To be a naturalist is better than to be a king.
—WILLIAM BEEBE

The happier the moment, the shorter.
—PLINY THE ELDER

Metropolitan Museum of Natural History
Fifth Floor
July 10, 1946

Major Patrick Hendry was peering over Charles Knight's shoulder—which provided no little annoyance to one half of the Army's new Codex Translation Team.

"Can you make out what he's saying?" Hendry asked.

Knight turned and shooed the officer back a few steps, having just worked on a particularly ratty-looking section of ancient papyrus. "Well, it's not just strange primates they'll need to be concerned with. As you've suspected, the bad news comes in a smaller package."

"And that is?"

"It's in the valley Pliny keeps talking about. That seems to be where the real trouble is."

"Was," Patricia chimed in. "Two thousand years is a long time. Who knows what's going on there now?"

"Okay, 'was,'" Knight said, relenting.

Patricia cleared her throat and, after a pause that went on a beat too long, Knight got the message. "So, Major," he continued, "what about sending some additional men in there? In case half the stuff Pliny described turns out to be true."

Patricia nodded in agreement, though it was obvious whose idea it had been.

Hendry simply folded his arms, assuming what had quickly become Knight's least favorite example of body language. "This mission doesn't exist, folks."

"Yes, I know," the artist said, struggling not to lose his temper. "But how do you expect our people to handle something that can reshape flora and fauna the way we shape modeling clay?"

"Especially when they have no road map to the source of that kind of power—no clue what they're searching for?"

"I understand, Miss Wynters," Hendry replied. "Even looking at the sketches of these weird apes, I can see as well as you, that . . . that . . ." The major did not know what to say next. The words did not exist yet, to articulate how, nearly two thousand years ago, someone had discovered and used an advanced genetic engineering system.

Hendry continued—slowly this time, as if measuring each word. "From what I can gather," he said, "some as-of-yet-unknown people in ancient Tibet learned how to fiddle around with their plants and animals—like those monkeys and apes that Pliny drew. And they used this . . . whatever it is . . . to make 'em smarter and nastier."

Now Knight stood, turning to face the much larger man. "First of all, Major, you *don't* understand—any better than any of us can really understand, yet. But more importantly, those are our friends and colleagues you sent in there."

"Mac's my friend, too, Knight," Hendry shot back. "And he knew *exactly* what he was getting into. So did his two pals."

"Did you not just hear me?" The artist held up a yellow legal pad filled with their recent translations. "They *knew,* you say? Well, according to this, they didn't."

Knight handed the note pad to the major, who began reading immediately.

"I hate worms," the officer muttered. "Shit."

"Yeah, shit," the Codex Translation Team replied in unison. It was the first time that Charles Knight had ever heard his old friend utter a curse.

In the Valley of the Cerae
May, A.D. *67*

W hen Pliny turned his open mouth into the gale, the just-past-his-prime and slightly asthmatic Roman discovered that the wind brought a certain amount of relief, for it squeezed higher-pressure air into his lungs. But he also felt the cold air biting deep within and knew that if the Cerae did not allow him shelter by nightfall, he would be a frozen corpse—with Proculus to follow, despite his outward defiance.

Too many deaths, Pliny thought. *Forty in the Ceran trap. Almost twenty more today. I'm the leader of a ghost expedition.*

Gasping and now mute, Pliny tried to peer over the heads of his shadowy captors and through the whiteout conditions. There was little to see. His other senses told him only that their trek had veered gradually and more sharply to one side of the mountain pass before turning downhill. Trying to drive thoughts of a death march out of his head, Pliny stiffened his spine, coughed, and, with renewed determination, picked up his pace. *I've visited dangerous new lands all my life and I've always survived. And somehow I always will.*

Pliny tried to search through the storm—hoping to see some additional hint of Ceran architecture, and the possibility of shelter. But though the wind stalled from time to time, the light remained dull and gray, the air itself still angry and driving a billion tiny needles of ice.

"*Maggot!*" Proculus cried out against another prod. Though his call was muffled and distant, it served to bring Pliny back to a new concern: even in the soldier's wounded condition, he and his escort were now a full hundred strides or more ahead of his own slog.

Pliny exerted all his strength to keep moving forward, quickening his pace trying to catch up. His short and lanky guard kept up as well. A sharpened spear point, formerly one of their own, remained within jabbing distance of Pliny's spine, following his motions with remarkable precision.

"What in Hades?" It was Proculus, again—nearer, this time, though his shout conveyed surprise, not anger. "Stop, you mother of whores!"

Now *he is angry,* Pliny thought, wondering what the man had seen.

"Poseidon's teeth!" Severus called, also from somewhere ahead.

Though his lungs ached and he felt his own heartbeat throbbing against his temples, Pliny threw each leg more quickly before the other until he was closing the distance at a trot. The gale, as he advanced through it, shuddered, stalled, rose strong again. His vision reeled, coming and going with the on-again, off-again blasts of blinding snow, until finally he stumbled and rolled forward into clear air, as if tumbled out through a ghostly white lens.

Immediately, Pliny glanced backward. The wind and snow were abandoning him, racing back up the hills and along the mountain pass through which the three survivors had marched.

Pliny's Ceran captor allowed him to approach his men, who were on their knees in the snowfield, both of them staring in the same direction. Pliny put a hand upon Severus's shoulder and gripped. The centurion's breathing was hard and fast, not so much from exertion as from astonishment.

"Do my eyes deceive me?" Severus asked.

Pliny ignored the question, for the sight that lay before them had replaced all other words and all other thoughts.

Spanning the entirety of a wide valley floor, what appeared to be a frozen lake was in fact a form of frozen mist. Though the mist lake was strange and beautiful to the point of being spellbinding, it was the enormous spire extending upward through its center that had stolen Pliny's voice. Seemingly constructed out of crystal and stone, the glittering tower stood far higher than anything he had expected to see in this part of the world—a cyclopean spire assembled from stacked terraces, narrowing at each successive tier. Adding another facet to the power of this landscape came the revelation that the crystalline tower was clearly inhabited, for Pliny could detect movement—figures within the structure itself as well as on the outside of it, the latter clambering acrobatically between the terraces on a meshwork of branchlike supports.

Although the tower alone could easily have held Pliny rooted to the spot, his attention was drawn back across the mist to a wider view of the valley, where scores of less lofty though no less impressive structures were clustered—elongated domes, each taller than the Imperial Palace in Rome.

There was plant life as well. Most of it was ghostly white, but the pattern was occasionally broken by more familiar-appearing cables of thick greenish vine, climbing into the hills surrounding the valley. Pliny noted that the latter very much resembled the outer architectural elements of the tower, which the Cerans used to move with ease from level to level.

"What is this place and who are these . . . people?" It was Proculus, and once again, Pliny could not and did not respond.

Despite the difficulty of breathing the thin air, Pliny was able to concentrate on the details of the level overlook onto which they had been led. He began to suspect that the Cerae had reshaped the entire valley. Out there, in the center of the fog lake, the tower's lower terraces were awash in gently rising and falling swells of white. He wondered how much deeper below the mist the actual foundation must stand. The portion that stood above the strange vapor was taller than the lighthouse at Alexandria, and yet the abrupt cessation of the blizzard revealed even nearer wonders.

Here, along the "shore" of what he would come to call "the Opal Sea," one of the domes appeared to be undergoing the final phase of construction. Once their captors decided that their rest period was over and marched them forward toward shelter, the astonishments continued to add up. Overhead, dozens of Cerae were moving busily to and fro along handholds and footholds set into branches and ribs that served as buttresses. Pliny noted that these were members of a leaner and more graceful race than their captors.

They seem as different from those brutes as we are different from the people of Asia or Nubia. Perhaps even more different.

Within the mountains of southern Tibet
July 10, 1946

I think I see daylight," Mac said, noting that several hundred feet ahead the passageway became suddenly brighter. This seemed impossible. By everything he knew, nightfall had certainly overtaken the world above. So he was surprised but not completely shocked to discover that the impression of daylight was illusory—nothing more (*or less*) than an intensely bioluminescent, cathedral-like chamber. All around, crystalline arches and carefully hewn rock walls bore the marks of being shaped in the recent geologic past. Whoever the Morlocks were, they had obviously chosen to hide at least a portion of their civilization deep beneath snow and rock.

As they moved toward the center of the immense space, they passed below rows of thick glassy pillars that were strangely organic. Each of them soared a hundred feet upward before splitting into branches that reinforced an arched ceiling, which was itself shaped from sections that resembled leaves.

"Feel familiar?" Mac said to Yanni.

"I feel like I'm in a forest," she replied.

"No forests up here though, right?" Jerry asked.

Yanni continued to stare upward. "Not anymore."

Jerry rapped gently on a column base. The Morlocks did not stop him.

"It's mostly ice," he said, "mixed in with some sort of plant matter. Cute trick. I've heard of experiments with this sort of stuff in the Aleutians, during the war."

Yanni gave him a quizzical look. "Where?"

"Off the coast of Alaska," Jerry replied, and she shot him a nod. "So anyway, you mix ice with the right material—even cotton balls or sawdust—and you can make it as flexible as steel beams and strong enough to take a direct hit from a cannon."

"Or from an earthquake," Yanni suggested.

"Definitely a high likelihood of quakes round here," Jerry said, without looking away from the architecture.

"Well, whoever built this was thinking long-term," Mac said. "Perfectly functional yet—"

"—constructed with an eye for beauty, too," Yanni finished, for him.

Jerry nodded toward their escorts. "Do you think *they* built these?"

Mac shrugged. "I don't know. But I'm bettin' their origin story turns out to be a real doozie."

"Mac, your breath," Yanni said.

"What?"

"Your *breath*," she repeated, more forcefully this time, before turning to Jerry. "Yours, too."

"Jeez, I'm sorry," Jerry snapped back, clearly annoyed now. "This has all been a bit too stressful for me to worry about brushing my—"

"No, you ninnies," Yanni said, shaking her head. "Your breath—you've gotten it back."

Jerry stopped in mid-rant. "Hey, she's right," he said. "No more wheezing."

"Now that *is* odd," Mac followed. "Especially since we haven't been up here long enough to crank out the extra red blood cells that mountain types have in their bloodstreams."

"You mean Sherpas and the like," Jerry chimed in.

"You got it. More erythrocytes equals more hemoglobin."

"Then what coulda—"

"Wait a minute!" Mac interrupted. "When Pliny mentioned

the reshaping of life itself, we were all thinking about speeding up evolution by skipping over a few steps. Maybe cutting down on the number of generations required to develop new adaptations."

"So?"

"What if this works a lot faster than generations?"

"You mean evolutionary change within an individual?" Yanni asked.

"Hold on," Jerry interjected. "Didn't a guy named Lamarck get hung out to dry for that one?"

"You lost me," Yanni said, with a shrug. "La-who?"

"Early-nineteenth-century Frenchie," Mac said, picking up the story. "Lamarck believed in evolution but thought it worked when individuals needed or desired specific adaptations. He even incorporated environmental change."

Jerry jumped in. "When the ground foliage died, short-necked giraffes stretched their necks to feed from higher branches. Then they passed those longer necks on to their progeny."

"Exactly," Mac followed. "Only evolution doesn't work like that."

"So then why would it work in this case?" Yanni asked.

"Okay, I'm only hypothesizing here," Mac said, "but what if there's something in the water or in that glop they fed us—a bacterium—something that initiates a positive feedback system? In other words, once inside our bodies, it somehow calculates what needs fixing, then fixes it, maybe even improves it."

"That would be a *new* one," Jerry said.

"Yeah," Mac went on, "but our own immune system adapts to fight thousands of foreign invaders every day—some of them brand-new. This could be a take on that mechanism."

Yanni shot Mac a skeptical look. "Okay, assumin' this is an organism we're talking about here—what does *it* get out of the deal?"

"Especially," Jerry added, "when you consider the seriously hazardous digestive system this 'what-zit' runs into after being ingested."

Mac considered the imagery for a moment. "Well, maybe some of it *doesn't* get digested. Maybe it can withstand the acid wash and enzyme rinse, pass through the walls of the digestive tract, and find a nice safe place to live and reproduce."

"And the more it reproduces, the more positive effect it has on the individual?"

"Could be."

Yanni shook her head. "Yikes."

Mac let out a loud whistle, and failed to notice the stares of the Morlocks as he continued his thoughts aloud. "Hendry was right. Back when Hitler dreamed of a master race, they would have needed generations. But with this kind of biological tool kit—damn!"

"That's assuming your hypothesis holds water," Jerry added. "I'm wondering how these individual changes get passed on to the next generation?"

Before they could bring their debate to the origin of Morlocks, the Morlocks themselves were pushing and poking again. As they moved forward, Mac began to suspect that their captors understood the rapidity with which the organism (if indeed it was an organism) produced its effect. It seemed to him that they realized their captives could be prodded along more quickly now. This added to a growing list of evidence indicating that the Morlocks were far from a pack of dull brutes who had stumbled into the ruins of someone else's lost civilization.

More archways loomed ahead, and beyond them still more galleries—forest cathedrals with walls supported by a dense meshwork of Jerry's "ice composite." In the distance a whole arboretum of columns and branching arches marched away into lurid shadows and phosphorescence.

They followed a long, narrow incline, which led, finally, down into the strangest space of all. Just how strange, Mac could not have guessed, at least initially.

"This thing is huge!" Jerry exclaimed. A fog appeared to have rolled in, completely obscuring the roof of the cavern. "Like something out of *Journey to the Center of the Earth*. The biggest cavern behind us could easily be lost in a small corner here."

"No more arches," Mac observed.

"So no more ceiling," Yanni said.

"Then we're outside," Jerry said, finishing the thought.

"I think you're right," Mac added.

"Could be the valley we were supposed to land in," Yanni suggested.

Mac managed a smile. "Now I think you're *both* right."

As they stepped out of the stony passageway, their feet crunched on a carpet of ground frost covering a surprisingly rich-looking layer of soil. Dusk and a thickening fog seemed to be closing in, limiting visibility to perhaps forty feet in any direction. Upon closer inspection, the incoming fog appeared to be a misty suspension of snow. Mac held out a hand and indeed some of the tiny crystals clung to it. Others, though, took the opportunity to demonstrate some very unsnowflake-like behavior by swerving away just before contact. As he watched spellbound, the pseudo-flakes, which MacCready now believed to be insects, resumed their mimicry, blending seamlessly into the frozen fog.

There were other amazements, and these were terrestrial in nature—loud, trumpetlike sounds coming from something unseen within the mist.

"Don't tell me, Yanni," Mac said. "Mini-mammoths with two trunks."

"Could be," Yanni replied. "But those calls are very different from anything you'd hear from an Indian or African elephant."

Much nearer than the unseen trumpeters, colorless plants were peeking up through the soil in clusters. The predominant flora reminded Mac of a drooping rosebud grafted on to the end of an asparagus stalk. Waxy and pallid, the plants stood just a little higher than Mac's knees. *No chlorophyll here, either,* Mac thought, as yet another set of bitonal calls, haunting and even mournful, emanated from somewhere behind the veils of fog.

"I think it's a type of corpse plant," Yanni said, having seen Mac's interest in the white clusters.

"That's pleasant."

"They're also called Indian pipes," she continued, in the lull between the presumed woolly mammoth calls. "They steal the energy they need from ground fungi."

"Parasites, huh?"

"Yeah, but compared to anything I've seen or read about, these specimens are on the extra-large side."

The botany lesson ended rather abruptly when the quartet of Morlocks pushed the trio of humans into a tight cluster, which they then immediately surrounded.

Even Alpha's getting into the act, Mac thought as the presumptive Morlock leader took up a position at the head of the formation and they set off along a trail that ran uphill.

At first the march reminded MacCready of three people simultaneously entering a revolving door, but the giants backed off a bit once their intentions became clear: the single-file line they had assumed in the mountains and through the subterranean cathedrals of ice had been replaced by a more compact grouping that would circumvent any thoughts the captives might entertain about suddenly breaking rank and tearing off into the frozen mist.

In reality, thoughts of running had not occurred to either Mac or Jerry, although Mac wasn't anywhere near as sure about Yanni, who seemed entirely enthused at the prospect of meeting up with some new pachyderm pals. Soon enough, however, the point became moot.

Approaching a field of ghostly white grass, the Morlock leader began shuffling his feet, kicking up clumps of frost and earth. In response, the carpet of ground cover before him began to part. Some of the blades scuttled off in high-speed inchworm style, exposing a narrow trail of bare soil bordered by frantic movement.

"Swell way to cut the lawn," Mac said, nodding to the Morlock leader. But the look on the creature's face revealed that he considered the proceeding to be anything but humorous. Instead, it was clear that Alpha was uneasy about the strange new path, and his enormous associates appeared even more wary.

A second revelation was olfactory in nature: the unpleasant, musky odor the Morlocks gave off had been ramped up to borderline nauseating. Further intensifying the stench, all four of the creatures began moving their arms up and down, as if performing jumping jacks.

"That's a nice touch," Jerry said, joining Mac and Yanni in what had turned into a group wince.

"I think that skunk scent they're giving off repels these grass mimics," Mac said, watching as the blades nearest the Morlocks beat an even hastier retreat.

The lead giant then turned to his captives, wordlessly calling for their attention, before withdrawing something live and squealing from a fur pouch it had evidently been carrying. Mac recognized one of the rodentlike creatures he had seen earlier. It resembled an eyeless albino squirrel but before he could get a better look, the Morlock casually flipped the animal into the field of white blades. The "squirrel" let out a series of yelps, cut off by a flurry of motion as the tiny troglodyte was stripped to the bone. Seconds later there came a new sound, a disquieting crunching communicating that the bones, too, were being consumed.

The message was simple: *This can happen to you.*

"So noted," Mac acknowledged.

The group moved slowly along the trail, whose boundaries seethed backward, then ever so threateningly forward—giving every indication of being held barely in check—before closing in behind the last (and indeed the most nervous looking) of the Morlocks, only seconds after it had passed by.

MacCready was drawn back to the Old Testament and what he'd always considered to be the most cinematic of biblical tales. The imagery was unavoidable once he saw the "grass" creeping in hungrily behind them. Now the trio of humans drew deliberately closer to their captors for the very first time—despite the inherent threat they posed and despite their god-awful smell. Glancing back, R. J. MacCready watched the turbulent swarm flowing around the Morlock footprints and closing off the path they'd traveled. He recalled an ancient description of the Red Sea rushing in to wash away the footprints left by Pharaoh's troops and carrying off the terrified men who had made them.

"They'll need to do that one in Technicolor someday," Mac muttered to himself.

In the Valley of the Cerae
May, A.D. *67*

G aius Plinius Secundus came to the realization that any concerns about the Cerae looking upon him as a potential meal
might have been unfounded—at least for the moment. The curiously lithe race he called "architects" seemed so focused on their
work that if they glanced in Pliny's direction at all, they regarded
the odd-looking strangers with contemptuous indifference.

"Who *are* these people?" Proculus asked, yet again. "And what
will they want with us?"

"I don't know," Pliny said. "At this point, the only certainty is
uncertainty."

A strangely high-pitched growl in three syllables and a sharp
thump from behind communicated that there was to be no further talking. It did not matter. In this strangest of strange lands,
Pliny found that there was little left to say. What he could not
shake, however, was the guilt that his mind should choose to be
more dominated by a sense of wonder than by the all-too-recent
loss of more than sixty men.

The structure toward which they were being ushered was a
dome, built on a scale Pliny had never seen—even in the most
imaginative architectural designs. At the base of the dome's nearest arched buttress, a wall was being constructed. Blocks of ice
were being broken out of molds and set into an interlocking arrangement.

Those Cerae doing the building were strikingly different from
any of Pliny's brutish captors. The "architects" had longer, more
spidery arms and legs than the others, larger eyes, and higher
foreheads. Now that the Romans were being led directly beneath

them, one of the workers finally seemed to take notice. Without thinking, Pliny raised a hand, as if greeting an acquaintance. Standing amid a pile of recently poured and frozen blocks, the creature seemed to disappear before his eyes. Pliny squinted into the shadows.

Can it move that quickly? he wondered.

The answer came to him as the architect reappeared just as suddenly in the exact position and pose it had occupied a moment before, staring back at him again in open daylight.

It's playing some sort of game with me—trying to frighten with a demonstration of muscles and reflexes so powerful that it can indeed move in a blur.

Pliny reminded himself that he had, at almost every step, continued to underestimate the Cerae and that every one of his assumptions about them was probably wrong.

Failing to ask the right questions.

He supposed there were enough new questions to be discovered just outside the threshold of the great dome to keep him busy through the next two or three imperial reigns. But there was no time even to begin working on the first few questions before he and the other two captives were shepherded inside.

But inside of what? Pliny asked himself.

Under the dome, tiers of arched supports had been grown, rather than built. A colossal and unfamiliar form of vegetation, looking like a cross between a paper birch and a mushroom stem, was being carefully directed in its growth by the Cerae. They had managed to guide these buttress trees with far greater knowledge of nature than any *vinetarius* ever applied to guiding grape vines along trellises.

The interior was illuminated by millions of ice-refracted glimmers from the setting sun. Pliny's mind, too, was illuminated—

asking the right questions now: *Are these Cerae animals that think like men, or men who look like animals?*

Proculus paid less attention to the Cerae, but their architecture seemed to hold him completely in its spell. He was a cavalryman, and under Roman law, every equestrian or equestrian candidate was required to achieve an expert rank in at least one trade. Before Pliny had begun his mentorship of Proculus, he had already watched him advance at a very young age from gifted artist to designer, specializing in the rapid construction and dismantling of boats and bridges. Pliny knew this was the reason for their shared appreciation of the skill necessary to raise structures such as these. He had noticed a similar genius and hunger for adventure in Severus, and had carefully mentored him as well.

"I suppose you both think this is a good place to die?" Severus asked.

"Better than most," Pliny responded.

"Then find me a sword," the centurion said. "So that I can die like a soldier."

"Go easy, my friend," Pliny said. "Were you to reach for anything remotely resembling a weapon, you would die here and now—but with no purpose."

Pliny thought that Proculus was about to say something but instead he lost his footing and stumbled against him. Blood continued to seep from his leg wound, pooling beneath his left foot.

Alarmed, they eased him down into a sitting position.

"I'm fine," Proculus said, attempting unsuccessfully to regain his feet.

"Remain seated," Pliny commanded, observing how difficult it had suddenly become for Proculus to fill his lungs.

As if in response, a score of hirsute brutes appeared, quickly surrounding the Romans with their bodies. As the Cerae encircled them in a living fence of flesh and fur, Pliny felt as if he were being enclosed in a corral.

"What now?" Severus asked.

Three of the newly arrived Cerae stepped into the circle with such suddenness that Pliny scarcely had time to follow their movements before Proculus was lifted to shoulder height. Just as swiftly, two more creatures, white-furred and noticeably lankier than the rest of their kind, sprang like acrobatic children onto the backs of the individuals securing the wounded man. Advancing with quick precision, they began probing and examining their prisoner. All the while, three pairs of hands clamped Proculus's arms and legs, rotating his body beneath the inquisitive new arrivals as Pliny and Severus watched in confusion and amazement.

The two examiners—Pliny immediately identified them as female—ran their fingers over Proculus's chest, back, and legs as he was rotated for their inspection. Thoughts of being consumed crept into Pliny's mind because he found it impossible not to think of a pig being slowly turned on a spit over a cook fire. Thankfully, the thought was fleeting, as it suddenly occurred to him that the more thickly muscled Cerae (*a warrior caste?*) were acting in tandem as a form of living medical instrument, allowing the two physicians to clamber around and examine their patient in the most efficient means possible.

Proculus's two examiners had more elongated faces than the other Cerae, a characteristic that gave the impression of being less brutish and more civilized. Pliny classified them as "a physician race." He noted that their more enlightened countenance was counterbalanced by short white fur covering the entire face (while the facial skin of the other Cerae he'd encountered was bare and leathery). Oddly, even the lids of the "physician" eyes were furred, and Pliny hypothesized that, out in the snow, the covering might be needed to protect and camouflage the eyes themselves, which were disquietingly large and intense. Similarly striking were the great manes of hair that framed their faces—combed and, curiously, either dyed or dusted in unnaturally dark hues.

Initially, Pliny wondered how these particular markings tied into their penchant for camouflage, until he realized that the dark streaks would resemble natural features of the landscape had they been set against snow and rock.

Despite the distinctive and terrible odor their bodies gave off, along with the inescapable sense that from certain angles they looked more animal than human, there was something dreadfully beautiful about the big-eyed physicians, who were currently smearing a yellowish waxy substance into Proculus's leg wound. Pliny observed that it seemed almost immediately to halt the seepage of blood and he wondered if it had squelched the man's pain just as instantly. One of them, keeping a hand planted firmly upon the cavalryman's chest, produced a small leathery pouch with a nozzle, through which she squirted a black, molasses-like substance into his mouth. That quickly, the refreshment the patient received from each intake of air was improved enormously.

"What form of magic is that?" Severus exclaimed.

"Real phenomena, poorly interpreted," Pliny said, quietly. "It's not magic. It's medicine."

For a while longer, the two physicians commenced to run their hands over every part of Proculus's body, monitoring his responses to their salves and elixirs. One of them flashed her patient an expression that in Pliny's view was a disquieting smile. *As if she enjoys the feel of his smooth bare skin.*

Proculus, for his part, reacted with disgust, deciding to focus his attention elsewhere by looking away from his caregivers. As his breathing became progressively easier, he was lowered to the ground. He stood, shakily at first, then seemingly recovered to a degree that Pliny would have found difficult to comprehend, even if his thoughts had not been interrupted by attention from the physicians. Thankfully he received a quicker examination than Proculus—which concluded with one of them squirting the same black elixir into his mouth. It was horribly bitter but almost immediately he could feel his breathing improving.

Finally, Severus was snatched up and raised high for inspection. As the centurion was being rotated and examined for wounds, Pliny noticed that the physician who had earlier taken an inordinate interest in Proculus's almost completely hairless skin was now demonstrating an even more unsettling interest in the Roman officer's well-muscled arms and legs.

Pliny observed that Severus did not seem at all unsettled by the prolonged physical inspection. In fact his attitude was undergoing a puzzling reversal.

Proculus, his color having returned to normal, sidled up to Pliny and together they watched as the Ceran physician brought her face close to the centurion's, brushing one side of her mane across a cheek. She stared directly into his eyes and he returned the stare.

Pliny nodded toward Severus and spoke under his breath. "He seems to have snuck in a weapon after all."

Proculus managed a smile. "His short sword, apparently."

In the Valley of the Morlocks
July 10, 1946

I s it me or do you feel like we've just landed on another world?" MacCready nodded absently at Jerry's comment, having been thinking something along those very lines.

Major Patrick Hendry had once brought up the topic of what

might happen if the aliens from an Asimov or Heinlein science fiction story ever landed on earth for real.

"Maybe they'd be friendly," Mac had suggested.

Hendry shooed away the comment as if it were a fly. "It wouldn't matter how friendly they were."

"But—"

"Just look in the mirror, Mac. That'll tell you all you need to know about what our reaction would be. People are people."

"So what do *you* think would happen?"

"Look, if Orson Wells's Martians landed in New Jersey and tried to cross the Hudson, they'd be on the daily 'Specials Board' at the Fulton Fish Market by noon. And if by some luck they happened to taste like crap, they'd be peering out from behind bars at the Bronx Zoo."

Mac forgot the rest of the conversation (*something about hating calamari*) but the bottom line was that he himself had some serious reservations about how humanity would react to an alien encounter. And now that they'd met the Morlocks, the closest thing to an alien civilization anyone had ever seen, he was even more skeptical.

But who must be more alien to whom? he wondered. It was a trio of humans, after all, who, much like Wells's Martians, had fallen into *their* world aboard a flying machine. And just as the fictional Martians coveted the earth, Hendry's "bigwigs in D.C." coveted the organism Morlocks (or their ancestors) presumably used to shape life. MacCready supposed it spoke volumes about Morlock temperament that upon capture, he and his friends were not treated immediately to Major Hendry's fish market solution. Instead, they were escorted through a sea of carnivorous grass to an igloo-like structure that apparently served as the local version of a county jail.

Their "cell" was undergoing some final assembly by a pair of Morlocks. The last of the freshly cut blocks were being set into place atop the nine-foot-high dome—which glistened through the mist and the shifting tide of snowflakes like an improbably large gemstone.

Mac looked around thoughtfully as they reached the arched entrance. The inchworm grass seemed to be keeping its distance, which he counted on the plus side. Yanni was listening intently to something out there in the mist, and though Mac and Jerry tried to listen in with her, neither of them was able to detect anything more than a barely perceptible, low-frequency murmur. They both shot Yanni a quizzical expression. "Whatcha got?" Mac asked.

"Those ain't Morlocks," she whispered.

R. J. MacCready managed a smile, having flashed once more, in his imagination, to the skull they'd shown Charles Knight back at the museum—the midget mammoth with its strange mutation hinting at two elephantine trunks. More interesting by far, he thought, was that the "mutation" suggested the possibility of *two* manipulative limbs, serving perhaps the same function as human arms and hands.

Yanni made a low-frequency sound that caught the sudden attention of all four of their captors.

What could be more fantastic? Mac wondered, watching Yanni as she called to the unseen mammoths. But before he could say a word, he had become airborne.

Flung through the igloo entrance, Mac thrust out his hands to avoid plowing face-first into the floor.

What the hell?

Jerry and Yanni were similarly tossed into the structure, landing beside and on top of him. Within that same second, one of the Morlocks pushed a slab along a groove at the threshold of the arch, sealing the prison door.

Rising to his feet, Mac observed that the portal was crystal clear, and so precisely cut that it fit perfectly into the curve of the dome.

"That doesn't look very secure," Yanni said, gesturing toward the now closed doorway. "Can't weigh more than a coupla hundred pounds."

"I'm thinking they put it there to keep the grass off the people—if you know what I mean," Mac said.

"You're right," Jerry added. "These monsters probably couldn't care less if we did decide to stage a jailbreak."

As indeed they could not.

This became as crystal clear as the ice door itself. Seconds after sliding it into place, the Morlocks simply walked away, leaving no guards behind.

Dusk descended quickly, and in response the local "streetlights" came on. Fungi glowed in the loamy soil, and bioluminescent plants and animals were active as well. But beyond a range of forty or fifty feet, every detail was hidden by the fog—which absorbed and scattered the phosphorescence.

Where dusk ended and where nightfall began had been difficult to define. Through the ice and not more than two yards away, they watched the lawn trying to close in—repelled by the scent, spread by the jail's architects over their prison's ice blocks. As the carnivorous blades continued testing the chemical boundaries of the igloo, a fist-sized, crablike creature burrowed up out of the ground. After flicking off a few shreds of shimmering plant matter, it began emitting a blue phosphorescence, then skittered toward the igloo's outer wall. A breakaway swarm of grass followed it, closing in quickly.

"This is gonna be ugly," Mac muttered, but he squatted down anyway to get a closer look. *Watch out, little guy.*

The crab scurried to within a foot of the structure, the blades continuing their hot pursuit of the pulsating blue light. *If anything,* Mac thought, *it's attracting even more of them.* Suddenly the crustacean flashed a stunning strobe of white.

"What the—" MacCready cried, snapping his eyes shut—too late.

"You all right?" Yanni said, moving in beside him.

"Just swell," he replied, shaking his head. A circular green afterimage burned brightly in his right eye. "Did you catch that?"

"I think so," Yanni said, watching as the former predators inchwormed their way backward in double-time fashion. Apparently, though, not all of them were successful, since the crab was now casually munching on one of the creatures, spaghetti-style, while brandishing several more, clamped tightly in a second claw. As the vanquished lawn mimics made an uncomfortable transition from hunter to main course, the crab continued to glow—blue to deep violet to blue again.

"Gotta admit, this prison has a coupla interesting features," Yanni said.

"*And* practical," Jerry added. "Who needs guards when the local grass can cut *us* down?"

"Unless, of course, you happen to be a light-emitting crustacean," Mac countered.

"I'm tellin' ya, this place is amazing. Beautiful, too," Yanni gushed. "So why the hell would we want to run?"

Jerry started to answer but Yanni turned to Mac. "Would *you* run? If we could get out of here?"

Mac shrugged his shoulders. He knew exactly how his friend would respond and she did not disappoint.

"Look, maybe you two are scheming to take a powder, but I plan on leavin' with a whole lot more knowledge and with my— you know—" She got stuck on a word.

"Dignity," Mac finished for her.

"Right," she said. "We're explorers, aren't we? And there's so much to learn here. So much to *do*."

Jerry gestured toward the walls of their prison. "If we weren't locked in an icebox."

Yanni turned toward the color-shifting crab outside—which seemed to have finished its meal. Jerry and Mac followed her gaze, watching as the creature sank back into the frost and earth, its light diminishing to a dull blue glow before blinking out.

"No argument there, Yanni," Mac said. "That was certainly an interesting little floor show. I'm guessing the blue color serves as an attractant while that flash functions as an offensive weapon."

"How do you figure?" Yanni asked.

"You ever heard of William Beebe?"

"Sounds familiar," she replied.

"He used to be a curator at the Bronx Zoo. Birds."

"Neighbor of yours, too," Jerry added, and Yanni shot him a quizzical look. "Brooklyn boy."

MacCready continued. "'Bout twelve years ago, Beebe and another guy took a diving bell down to three thousand feet. One of the things he described was a fish that used a phosphorescent lure to attract its prey."

"Which is certainly the *obvious* explanation for what we just saw," said Jerry.

Mac raised an eyebrow. "But?"

"But I'm starting to think that calling anything around here *obvious* is the first reason we should doubt it."

"Speaking of which, I don't know if you've noticed," Yanni announced, "but the lights are shuttin' down."

She's right, Mac realized. *It is getting darker.*

"Well, there ya go, Mac," Jerry said. "So much for any similarity to William Beebe's strange fish. When it's darkest, bioluminescent life should be at its brightest."

Mac peered into the mist and knew that his friends were right. At first, shortly after the last cloud-penetrating rays of sunset had retreated behind mountains and heralded dusk, the mist shimmered brightly from every direction—more brightly than the twilight itself. Now some lurid and heatless fire still burned out there, providing scarcely more illumination than a clear, starry night far from the city.

Outside, shadows held sway over the world, and these alone—whether imagined or not—became the real inhabitants of the Morlock's lair. Mac believed he observed a large figure moving in the distance, against the barely perceptible light, but he became reasonably certain that it had been something no larger than a cat, prowling only fifteen or twenty paces away. Surely it must have walked among the grass mimics, and he wondered what defense *it* might have evolved to avoid being eaten by the lawn.

"You know, if you think about it, it kinda makes sense for the local biolumes to feed at dusk, then shut it down in the evening."

Jerry thought about it for a moment. "Biolumes, huh?" Then he gave the name an approving nod. "So how do you figure, Mac?"

"Well, it's no stretch that there are probably aerial predators out there, doing their night-owl act over this valley. And if so, then anything illuminating up through these clouds at night could go from being hunter to hunted before you can say, 'Talon time.'"

"And so . . . they dim their lights," Yanni said.

Jerry stared out through the panoramic "window," lost in thought for several seconds. "All right," he said at last. "I'll give you that. So the little bit of shadow glow that remains must be completely invisible from above the fog."

Mac nodded. "Ding. No more calls."

Jerry, though, hadn't quite finished with their exercise in hypothesis building. "Also seems to me that shutting off the lights when it gets *really* dark preadapts the local wildlife to avoiding nighttime eyes of another sort."

"You mean, human eyes?"

"Yeah, nighttime recon from the air."

Mac found himself agreeing with his friend once again. Unlike the far more luminous world they had seen in the underground cathedrals, the denizens of the valley had no light-blocking layers of rock overhead. And neither was the snowy fog dense enough to completely block out bioluminescence. Without a carefully timed cycle, the lake of mist would glow as brightly as the twilight sky itself—easily seen from the cliffs above, *and nowadays by passing aircraft.*

"It's either a preadaptation or one hell of a coincidence," Jerry said. "I suppose—"

Yanni jabbed him in the side with an elbow. "Did you see that?"

"I saw it. But what's with the elbow?"

"Keep looking," she replied.

Mac stifled a laugh, knowing that part of the reason she'd thrown the jab was to prevent another round of *Who knew more shit.* Staring through the broad lens of ice, he saw nothing. "I missed it. Whatcha see?"

"A shadow about the size of a horse," said Jerry. "But it was gone in only a second or two."

"Out there with our chompy-grassy pals? You sure?"

"That's what I saw, too, Mac," Yanni affirmed.

If the prison's internal temperature being down near freezing was not enough to make them step away from the ice window, phantasms on the other side decided the issue.

They retreated to the center of their cell and sat back-to-back on the floor, each facing outward to cover one-third of their 360-degree view through the ice. The darkness, and fleeting glimpses of the mysteries it concealed, should have made sleep impossible, but their minds had been in a state of information overload all day, and now, even as their breathing had become easier with each passing hour, they were exhausted. And so one by one they began to slump and doze off.

May, A.D. *67*

After the acrobatic doctors were finished examining the three Romans, after sunlight had ceased filtering down through the dome's crystalline panes, the living corral of Ceran guards opened up on one side and the trio of humans were shepherded uphill. They were moved toward a central, spiral horn of strong, fiber-infused ice. It was crystalline art, a tower in which perhaps hundreds of Cerae dwelled. Pliny and Proculus were led across a broad balcony to an open-air room, with bowls of warm food laid out beside comfortable-appearing animal pelts. One of the little doctors separated Severus from his friends and two of the race Pliny had begun to call the "warrior caste" ushered Severus along behind her. Without any chittering, any words, or any fuss at all, she disappeared with him into an adjoining chamber.

Pliny puzzled over this for a moment, then looked around.

Where are we?

On the landscape below, only three or four small fires had been lit after sunset, yet Pliny could see clearly. A heatless, opalescent light gradually brightened the interior, highlighting the artistry of the grown arches, and the world over which those arches towered. Aside from a handful of multistoried structures (*indecipherable as to their purpose,* Pliny decided), most of the dome's interior space appeared to be devoted to a concentric arrangement of presumably agricultural gardens. Their captors farmed ghostly white plants varying greatly in height, all of them unfamiliar to the naturalist. A thin, waist-high mist hung over the gardens of the Cerae, filling the air with an underscent like rotten eggs.

The light grew almost bright enough to read by, then brightened further.

"Where are we?" Pliny asked again—this time aloud.

Proculus did not answer him. He had just discovered that some of his flesh was falling away.

For as far back as anyone could remember, the young man's face was marred by warts—most of them blacker than his Nubian skin, others alarmingly shifting toward an ugly, reddish purple. During the past year, Proculus had come to peace with the dawning reality that some of the growths had been worsening into a condition commonly called "the rocks." To a few, though, the mysterious affliction was known by another name. Pliny knew that, centuries earlier, when Hippocrates had examined victims, the pattern of veins on the solid, malignant tumors reminded him of the legs and claws of a crab. Accordingly, the physician named the condition after the Greek word for the creatures—*carcinos.* Recently, Pliny heard the condition called by the Latin word for crab—cancer.

Proculus scratched at a growth near his lip that had lately begun bleeding. But now, like the large warts that had simply fallen from his cheek, the mass of hardened flesh also came away, leaving behind only the faintest patch of scar tissue.

Surprise and disgust creased the cavalryman's face, and Pliny returned it with his own look of astonishment. "Amazing. And how are you recovering from those smashed-out teeth of yours?" he asked.

He ran the tip of his tongue over the gap in his smile, pressing hard. "Painless," Proculus replied. "Completely painless."

"I would not be surprised to see those teeth trying to grow back," Pliny said, failing to notice that two physicians had mounted the balcony ledge, far more stealthily than any leopard.

"If we can learn *how* they do this, and bring it back to—" Proculus began to say, but cut his words short.

Both men had heard the sound—if only barely—*like parchment shifting in a breeze.* They turned toward the ledge and were startled by the presence of the statue-like visitors.

Pliny wondered if the Cerae had captured additional Westerners over the years. *And if so, might these creatures understand some measure of Latin?*

"It's nice to see you healing so well, Proculus," he said. "Now rest your mouth and speak no more."

The cavalryman looked puzzled for a moment but then nodded.

Yes, Proculus, Pliny told himself. *There is a power here. And a wealth any emperor would envy.*

His new hope was that the Cerae could not read his mind.

Predawn, July 11, 1946

Not even a shove from the alpha Morlock could have been more startling than the sound that awoke Yanni. It seemed that the very sky had called out to her, first as a low-frequency drone, followed quickly by trumpeting and moaning and clicking.

Jerry, looking alarmed, was on his feet in seconds, staring up at the manhole-size vent in the ceiling.

"What's happening, Yanni?"

"Elephants," she said, noting that while they sounded similar to the unseen animals they had heard upon first entering the valley, these calls were louder and more beautiful. Yet it was also a mournful beauty.

Jerry shook his head. "Elephants can make a sound like that?"

"These can," she said, before gesturing toward the hole at the top of the dome. "Give me a boost, huh?"

The men responded instantly and the lithe Brazilian was soon standing on their shoulders, an ear tilted toward the circular opening.

"Whatcha hear, Yanni?" Mac asked.

"Shhhhh!" she replied, then said quietly, "The calls are bi-tonal. Each individual can sing the melody and harmonize at the same time."

"Guess it pays to have two trunks," Mac said.

Jerry shook his head. "And these are the same little guys Hendry showed you two at the museum?"

"Yep, miniature mammoths," Yanni replied, impatiently. "Now will you pipe down already?"

The calls were certainly very different from anything Yanni or any other human being had heard, yet at the same time they would have been eerily recognizable to anyone familiar with elephant vocalizations. She was still trying hard to decipher the chorus when the calls changed suddenly before fading away, leaving behind only silence.

Yanni, who had been craning to hear the sounds through the

partially open ceiling of the igloo, slowly sank down into a sitting position—the reason readily apparent to her friends.

Even Jerry, who knew little more about elephants than the typical New York City denizen, seemed to recognize the final notes of this opera. Like a dirge, they communicated the low, painful lamentations of slaves.

R. J. MacCready was about to move in to comfort his friend when, simultaneously, the lights began to come on again outside their prison. Yanni, ever the fascinated visitor to an increasingly strange world, put aside her sadness, if only for a moment, and watched.

Bioluminescent life was preparing to greet the morning twilight.

S oon it was nearly as bright as a full moon outside, bright enough to give depth and shape to shadows moving to and fro in the night. The Morlocks were awake now—if in fact they ever slept at all. One or two of them occasionally came into view, seeming to leer at the prisoners. The combination of their utter alienness and the unusual optics of the ice blocks made it impossible to really know whether their expressions conveyed anger or curiosity—or possibly both. They simply tended to show up on the other side—silently, without any warning or fuss. After a second or two, they vanished like creatures in a dream.

Eventually one of them showed up and did *not* go away. Mac believed it to be the same individual he had come to call Alpha. It slid the door seal effortlessly to one side and entered carrying something.

A few moments later their jailer laid down crudely hewn bowls full of cold soup with generous helpings of the same stringy white fungus that they had been served the day before. In addition, there was a single slab of tough-looking red meat, served on a thin stone platter.

"What, no steak knife?" Jerry asked the giant, who was standing beside the door, arms at his sides. "Jeez."

Mac managed a laugh. "Yeah, why don't you ask him to leave us a pistol, too?"

Jerry shrugged his shoulders before taking a sip of the fungus soup. Moments later he was gulping it. "This is even better than yesterday's," he announced.

Mac's attention, though, was on Yanni, who was clearly gearing up for another of her patented attempts at interspecies communication. As usual, she did not disappoint.

"Rrrr-rhea," Yanni half-said, half-trilled—the same whistling note with which she had exasperated Alpha in the caves.

The Morlock turned its full attention on Yanni. "Rrrr-ah-rhea," it replied.

Yanni nodded, and after only two more attempts she echoed it perfectly.

"That's amazing," Mac said, quietly.

"Yeah, thanks," Yanni replied proudly.

"What's it mean?"

She shrugged her shoulders, all the while keeping a smile directed at her hirsute instructor. "I have no idea."

What Mac *did* understand was that the level of tension in their igloo prison had dropped several notches.

Yanni, eager to continue the lesson, pointed to herself and pronounced her name.

Alpha repeated it.

Not bad, Mac thought. Then, as he watched, the creature

pointed at its own chest and sang out something that seemed far too long and cumbersome to be a name. *Perhaps,* he guessed, *it's a recitation of ancestry?*

Yanni stifled a laugh at the unpronounceable string of warbles and quickly decided to steer the linguistic exchange in a different direction. She passed her hands over the bowls and the meat, all the while smiling and keeping her movements slow—avoiding anything that might suggest dominance or aggression.

"Food," Yanni said, the giant still watching her intently. Then she bowed her head slightly for a moment. "Thank you."

Once again, Alpha appeared to consider her combination of gesture and sound before pointing toward the soup. He chirped a few syllables and Yanni began to repeat. Then, without pausing, Alpha gestured toward the meat and pronounced a word, distorted by high pitches that barely passed for syllables. Still, Mac noticed something surprisingly familiar despite the language barrier.

"Alapas?" Yanni repeated, wrinkling her nose questioningly.

"Alafas. *Alafas,*" the Morlock said, then turned and departed.

Yanni looked to Mac, noticing that he was suddenly less enthusiastic about the prospect of a linguistic breakthrough than he'd been only moments earlier. "Why the puss, Mac?"

The expression MacCready returned told Yanni that something was definitely wrong. "I think that last bit was Latin."

"Latin?"

"Yeah, a sort of big, hairy, bastardized Latin."

"Alafas," Yanni repeated, slowly, but this time the excitement drained from her voice.

"Well, whatever it is," Jerry announced from behind them, "*this* stuff tastes better than beef."

"I think he was trying to say *Elephas,*" Mac said, quietly.

Jerry had a flash of recognition and dropped the meat as if it had stung him.

"It's the little elephants," Yanni whispered.

MacCready suspected that something in the late afternoon soup the Morlocks had brought slowly converted tension and exhaustion into an overpowering sense of relaxation, making it impossible for him to remain alert. The rest of their second day in the igloo prison passed without their captors showing themselves at all. Mac was not quite finished digging a latrine when sleep overtook him. Hours after midnight, with a faint glow from the setting moon filtering down, he and Jerry awoke to find Yanni staring out into the ever-present mist.

"I'll tell you one thing," Jerry said, with as much nonchalance as he could muster, "I'd give just about anything for a smoke and a cuppa joe."

Yanni said nothing. Both she and Mac were members of a minority who did not smoke cigarettes, although neither of them would have turned down a steaming mug of coffee.

Outside, the strange air-suspended snow had thickened, and though there was no wind, some of the flakes moved with a life of their own, swirling like plankton.

"Snowflake mimics," Mac said, to no one in particular. He rose and took up a position several feet from Yanni, close but not crowding her. "Ya gotta wonder what percentage of this snow is actually alive?"

Mac had thrown out what he hoped would be a distraction, however brief, from the recent revelation about their breakfast, the remains of which he had hidden out of sight.

They stood together for a long time, even after the moon had gone down and there was nothing left to see. Like clockwork, as dawn approached the sea of fog, the world gradually filled with phosphorescence, then dimmed its lights with daybreak. Soon there would be only the dull, silvery glow of fog-obscured sunlight.

The sounds of the mammoths were back as well. Coming from somewhere beyond the carnivorous grass, they rose to a slow and steady murmur.

Like a communal moan, Mac thought, but did not say.

Yanni had a similar thought, and occasionally she was able to snatch glimmers of meaning from an individual call. "It sounds to me like most of them are being put to labor," Yanni announced. "Others sound like they're grieving."

"Grieving?" Jerry asked. "How can you tell?"

"Jewell."

"That's the old elephant in Central Park—the one you worked with, right?"

"She died recently," Yanni said, in a disturbingly uncharacteristic monotone. Then, after a pause, "These calls are like the ones Jewell made when she was reminded of her sister."

Jerry looked puzzled, but said nothing.

"Jewell's sister was put down right in front of her," Mac explained quietly.

"And these mammoths are using the same language?" Jerry asked. "Fascinating, given their geographic distribution."

"Well, sort of," she responded, seeming to recover a bit from her gloom. "These calls are more complicated and more—*subtle*—like songs of mourning."

The two men remained silent, allowing Yanni to finish her thoughts.

"And the Morlocks breed them like cattle," Yanni continued, her anger now rising to the surface. "How very *human* of them."

Mac tried to think of something to say that might soothe his friend, but he found it impossible to get the words out. Yanni wasn't someone who cried easily, but she was on the verge of tears when Alpha returned.

The Morlock was looking none too happy himself, upper lip drawn back to expose a pair of no-nonsense canines, body hair erect and bristling.

This form of communication required no words. It was a language as ancient as the meeting of predator and prey. *Hair-lifting arector pili muscles in full contraction. Fangs bared in a message straight from the sympathetic nervous system.*

Mac did not have to look at Yanni to know that she was experiencing a similar array of involuntary responses—now, thankfully, held in check.

As apparently unconcerned as he was unaware of Yanni's current mental state, Alpha tossed a piece of multigeared machinery at their feet. The metal parts showed no signs of wear and still bore portions of paper tags affixed with a bit of wire.

"Let me guess," Jerry said. "He wants to know who left a mess at the crash site."

"Not quite," Mac added, "although that *is* a spare helicopter part."

"What? They scavenging our bird now?"

Mac shook his head, then moved in and prodded the device with his foot. "That ain't from ours."

"Well whose is it, then?"

CHAPTER 6

Yeren

Whatever we believe about how we got to be the extraordinary creatures we are today is far less important than bringing our intellect to bear on how we get together now around the world and get out of this mess we've made. That's the key thing now. Nevermind how we got to be who we are.

—JANE GOODALL

We become what we do.

—CHIANG KAI-SHEK

Shennongjia Forest, Northwest Hubei Province, China
June 16, 1946 (Four weeks earlier)

A gust of warm, humid air rushed up from the valley floor—from five thousand feet below the overlook on which Wang Tse-lin had set up his tent. It was well past midnight, and once again the biologist was having a difficult time falling asleep. On most nights he could blame his insomnia on the forest sounds—the breeze rustling through stalks of dead bamboo, the high-pitched chatter of bats, or the incessant call of insects he could not identify. But tonight a new sound came to him—and so he sat up in his low cot, cocked an ear, and waited.

With his eyes acclimated to the dark, Wang realized that the canvas flap at the foot of his pup tent was closed, although he distinctly remembered tying it open before he lay down.

Beyond the confines of the tent, from the direction of the small pit of embers where he'd earlier roasted a hare, came a faintly whispered "eh" sound. It was followed by something he made a mental note to record as "a short guttural growl." A response came from a different direction, high-pitched and composed of but a single brief note.

Wang had been in the forest for nearly five weeks now, relocating his campsite every three or four days and only occasionally crossing paths with another soul—usually a villager or a hunter, eager to take him up on his offer to buy the skins and skulls of the strange and unique creatures that inhabited the pristine Shennongjia wilderness. One of the endemic mammals was the *takin*—a large goat antelope whose thick blond coat was said to have inspired the legend of Jason and the Golden Fleece.

The *real* prize, if it existed, was the white bear. Some of Wang's colleagues believed that it existed in legend only, while others suggested that it was an albinic form of brown bear, pointing to the fact that there seemed to be an inordinate number of albino species in this particular forest. Wang, however, hypothesized that the bear was neither legend nor mutant but rather a separate species of *Ursus*. This, of course, would be a major coup for anyone who could provide physical evidence—*especially* if that someone was a young university faculty member like himself.

Now, however, his night visitors seemed a real and present obstacle. Though Wang's bounty for the skin and skull of a white bear was the highest he had offered for any specimen, experienced hunters would not likely have entered his camp at night. And in these parts, few (even if well armed) would have dared move too deeply into the forest after sundown.

Locals, he thought, *desperate to steal my supplies.*

Wang swung his feet toward the tent opening and, having slept in his boots, he reached for the bayonet he'd recovered from a Japanese soldier, dead now for just over three years. The sounds outside his tent had stopped but somehow he could still feel the presence of someone creeping about the campsite.

Who else could it be? Can't be my coworkers, he told himself. None of his three colleagues in the Yellow River Irrigation Committee would have ventured this far into the mountains. Immediately realizing his mistake he shook his head. *Make that two colleagues.*

"The River of Sorrow Flood Committee," is how one of his coworkers had jokingly referred to it on the day the team of four was to depart by boat from the city of Yi Chang. On that same day, the unfortunate jest rendered his colleague a "former asso-ciate," reducing the survey team to a trio. Wang knew that there was no way to make even an educated guess at how many friends back home might now be under arrest or had simply disappeared for committing lesser infractions.

The great moment of freedom from the yoke of Japanese oc-cupation lasted precisely that long—a mere moment, so quickly did liberators become oppressors. Men known to Buddhist and Christian survivors as "sainted ones" were vilified each day. Fear-less acts that saved lives during the war could be transformed, without warning, into examples of "social incorrectness" or even criminality. The fact was that whoever or whatever happened to be prowling his campsite could induce no more terror in Wang than he himself had already seen in postwar Peking and Shang-hai. As civil war raged across China, men and women of every age were rounded up in the night, for any reason at all, or for no reason at all.

The Second Sino-Japanese War had left Wang Tse-lin's country clinically insane. As a scientist, he had concluded: *A human creature driven crazy is a most frightening sight in itself. But when we go crazy together, we are the most terrifying power in all of creation.*

Military and paramilitary mobs now roamed well-paved big city streets and muddy backwater villages, given free range by whatever gifted abomination of an orator happened to be in command at any given moment. There were intimidating, openly circulated stories about whole families executed, with the parents granted the mercy of death only after watching their children precede them.

Which should I fear more, the rabid mobs or what might lurk right outside, among the rattling bamboo?

For Wang (himself a Ph.D. recipient at Northwestern University in Chicago), a months-long assignment in a primeval deciduous forest was a blessing, specifically because it took him far away from the madness that had so tightly gripped much of his country.

Could my visitors be soldiers sent to arrest me? he wondered, his body reacting to the question with an involuntary shudder. Pulling aside the tent flap, he stepped outside and stood, holding the bayonet.

The River of Sorrow—not a misnomer, Wang Tse-lin had thought upon hearing his coworker's joke, though his own response was stony indifference. He knew that the accumulated sorrows of more than two millennia occurred at the whim of the Tibetan Plateau's glaciers and vast underground springs. Although these were hundreds of miles to the west, without warning they frequently changed the Yellow River from a muddy stream into a flood-blasted channel.

Currently Wang's two remaining colleagues were stumbling around in the humidity and heat of the river valley below.

"What a waste of time," he told himself. *Drafting details of riverbank profiles that might disappear even before those maps can be sent home—only to be ignored by bureaucrats more concerned with not joining "the disappeared" than with the lives of those living along the river.*

Nonetheless, Wang knew that it was important for him to keep the charade going, for to place scientific reality or good sense above political reality could be just as fatal as a coworker's casually tossed joke.

Wang Tse-lin looked in every direction around the campsite, noticing at once that it was completely fogged in. The full moon, which would have been only intermittently visible through the canopy, was covered in thick gray gauze. Even the night sounds seemed to have been swallowed by the heavy wet mist.

No one here, Wang thought. *Maybe it was my—*

The sound of a misplaced footfall on a dead bamboo stalk stopped the thought and he spun in the direction of the disturbance. Flicking on a battery-powered lamp, he aimed the beam into the forest. The fog consumed most of the light before it could reach the source of the sound; it threw the rest of the rays back at him, producing a shapeless white glare.

Villagers, Wang told himself again, though he was inwardly certain that this was not the case. As if to confirm his suspicion, he noticed something else—a musky smell that had not been there earlier. And though he would never come to understand how, it was a scent that chemically circumvented any inclination he might have had to head off into the forest in search of his visitors.

Ten minutes later the biologist was back in his tent, and despite the musky night visitor, and the discomfort that a sheathed bayonet made for a bedmate, physical and emotional exhaustion had done their work. He was soon fast asleep, and at peace.

It did not last—could not last, in a time and place such as this.

Before the moon had moved halfway across the sky, he was awakened by a single gunshot. The blast echoed up the canyon like a reverse thunderclap. It was followed several seconds later by the distant baying of dogs—incessant and aggressive. *They smell blood,* Wang thought, a moment before another sound pierced the night. It was an almost human cry—high-pitched and conveying fear. Simultaneously muffled and echoed, magnified and distorted by the combination of fog and valley walls, the shriek passed through his campsite like a ghost. The reaction from below to this sound was completely different from the response to gunfire. It was as if someone had flicked a switch—the forest and indeed what seemed to be the entire canyon went completely silent: no dogs, no bats, and no insects. Even the windblown clacking of the dead bamboo seemed to have stopped.

At dawn, Wang quickly broke down his campsite and began a descent toward the nearest village, in the direction of the previous night's gunshot. As usual, the hike was treacherous. The Silurian karstic limestone that made up the Daba Mountains was riddled with cavities ranging from finger length to cavernous—nearly all of them hidden by dense scrub and a thick layer of humus. One false step could easily lead to a broken leg—which in these regions was often indistinguishable from a sentence of slow death. An even faster route to the afterlife might be found in a crash through the thin ceiling of an uncharted cavern system—a spectacular but final discovery for an unlucky explorer.

Even before he reached the village, Wang Tse-lin could see the smoke from its morning cook fires. Though the settlement, a half-dozen bamboo huts with thatched roofs, defined remote, there was no fear of being treated as an intruder. Having visited before, he entered the clearing and found slightly more than a dozen people standing together.

Nearly the whole village.

They were gathered around something on the ground. The men crowded in close—the women and children on the periphery. As Wang approached, heads turned in his direction. Recognizing their strangely dressed visitor, the tight cluster of men parted, allowing him a first look at what appeared to be a body lying prone and wearing an elaborate ceremonial costume. Raising a hand in greeting, Wang nodded and advanced.

His first revelation was that the figure lying before him wasn't wearing a costume at all. It was in fact covered from head to foot in dense, grayish-red hair. And, although the body was clearly bipedal, it was definitely *not* human.

"Yeren!" the leader of the village cried. He was a wiry-looking man, with a bowl haircut. Immediately the others followed with their consensus opinion: "Yeren! Yeren!"

Wang dropped his backpack and knelt to examine the creature, lying facedown on a patch of wet earth. A fist-size hole in the lower back showed how it had died—its spine severed by a single gunshot and most of the abdominal organs blown through.

He estimated it to have stood around six feet tall, perhaps a shade taller. Extending a hand, he touched one of the elongated arms—which had been thrown forward, completely obscuring the face.

The body is still supple, Wang realized, before being startled by what he thought was the heavily muscled limb beginning to move. His momentary alarm gave the assembled crowd a good laugh, and he quickly realized that two of the men were turning the corpse over to get a better look.

Later, Wang Tse-lin wrote in his field notebook:

The creature turned out to be a mother with a large pair of breasts, the nipples being very red as if it had recently given birth. The hair on the face was shorter and the face itself was narrow with deep-set eyes, while the cheekbones and lips jutted out. The scalp hair was roughly one foot long and untidy. The appearance was very similar to the plaster model of a female Peking Man.

After examining the body, Wang questioned the villagers, who told him that the Yeren had *always* lived in the forest and that two of them, a male and a female, had been in the area for over a month. The creatures were reported to have great strength and "were very brisk in walking," with the ability to move as rapidly uphill as on a plain.

"This," the chief explained, "makes it difficult for normal people to catch up with them."

The biologist nodded and forced a smile. *Unless those normal people have rifles,* he thought, but left unsaid.

"They do not have a language," the head local assured the biologist, with his "expertise" regarding the Yeren beginning to wear a bit thin. "They can only howl."

Wang requested and was granted a meeting with all three of the village leaders. He presented his university ID card again, reminding the men that he was on a government-sponsored mission and that his superiors would certainly express their gratitude for the sale of the Yeren's body, though the payment could be no more than he had previously offered for a specimen of white bear.

"These are hard times," Wang added in a grave tone. "And there is little funding for this sort of work, especially since we have several similar specimens donated by villages in the western portion of the district." This last part was, of course, not true but it quickly produced the desired effect.

"Of course you may have the wild woman," the chief said, with the wave of a hand and a gap-toothed grin. "The forest has plenty of game and there are plenty of Yeren."

Though Wang was puzzled at the mention of game, the thought was soon forgotten in the excitement of having so easily procured a specimen of such monumental scientific importance. The chief even volunteered to provide him with the salt necessary to dry the "Yeren's" pelt and the services of a pair of stout villagers who were said to be "the finest skinners in the region." Wang expressed his gratitude, then insisted on paying extra for an oversize clay jar half-full of the potent local home brew, into which he intended to preserve as many samples of the organs and other soft tissue as he could.

The day proved to be very long and very bloody and by the end of it Wang was not only exhausted but also covered in gore. The amiable chief, noting the weight of the now specimen-filled jar, assigned two porters to transport it—first to the river, then by canoe to the town of Yi Chang.

"When you arrive, you can tell your bosses about us!" the chief suggested enthusiastically. "How generous we were."

"Your people are indeed generous," Wang said, "but telling my supervisors might send the wrong message." He paused, thinking about the coworker who disappeared after having uttered a single, harmless joke. Wang could see that the chief was confused, so he continued. "What if . . . more and more *guests* arrived . . . trapping your forest animals, killing the Yeren?"

The local nodded, solemnly. "That would be bad."

By nightfall, the specimen had been completely packed, as had an array of sharp, newly washed instruments used to skin and prepare the creature. Wang bowed deeply, thanking the chief for his generosity before presenting him with a brass pocket compass that he'd owned since childhood.

Shortly before dawn, the biologist and his two porters began their descent out of the Shennongjia Forest. Although there would be no specimens of white bear to study and describe, Wang Tselin knew he would be returning to civilization with something of *far* greater value—the salt-packed skin, alcohol-preserved entrails, and partially disarticulated skeleton of an unknown primate—a creature that by all appearances had evolved along a branch somewhere between humans and apes. In all likelihood it would become one of the greatest scientific discoveries of the twentieth century. But while this was certainly a cause for celebration, another emotion was creeping into his consciousness. These days, even in the presence of a discovery that put his greatest childhood dreams to shame, darkness lurked beneath the excitement—a sense of fear and dread that would not go away.

The inland port city of Yi Chang
Western Hubei Province, China
June 20, 1946

A trip from the Shennongjia Forest to Yi Chang required four full days. During the second day, Wang and his escorts arrived at a larger village where he was able to hire a motor launch. He also contacted his supervisor at the Irrigation Committee as well as his university department chairman. The former instructed him to check into a hotel in Yi Chang and wait for further word. The latter, after determining that Wang had not lost his mind, urged him to "safeguard the specimen at all costs."

"Someone will meet you," he was assured, "when you disembark at the Yi Chang's central harbor."

Two days later, as his boat approached the crowded dock, he saw a line of ten or twelve soldiers, standing at attention behind an impatient-looking army officer.

"Are you Dr. Wang Tse-lin?" the man called.

"I am," the biologist replied.

The officer gestured to one of his men and immediately the soldier stepped forward to receive the bowline from the frightened-looking boat pilot, who immediately retreated and checked the fuel level of a gas tank he had planned to refill after getting paid.

"You and your specimen must come with me," the officer snapped at Wang.

"Yes, but—"

The military man held up a hand. "Enough talk!" With that, he signaled for his men to remove the scientist, his bags, and the containers containing the Yeren from the vessel. "Take them to the trucks."

Within minutes, Wang was sitting in the back of a seven-passenger, armored scout car. He knew that the Americans had been supplying Chiang Kai-shek's National Revolutionary Army with outdated and sometimes barely functional vehicles and equipment since 1942. The scientist noted that the interior of this particular model was so poorly ventilated that the engine fumes became almost immediately nauseating. Of more concern to Wang was his precious Yeren specimen—which had been loaded into a second vehicle. Now, as both truck drivers gunned their engines, Wang glanced back to see the motor launch pilot do-ing exactly the same thing—rapid departure. Their vehicles were now speeding in opposite directions, throttles open. What disturbed him most was that the boatman had never even bothered to collect his fee.

Less than a half hour later, the two trucks slowed down at a checkpoint outside the Yi Chang airport. The guards there quickly ushered them through and the vehicles made their way toward the runway. Wang could see that the few planes present had been shifted to one side, and the reason for this was immediately and perplexingly apparent. Three of the strangest-looking helicopters he had ever seen—or imagined he would ever see—were arrayed along the blacktopped runway.

They look like enormous bananas, Wang thought.

CHAPTER 7

A Hitch in the Plan

Civilization is like a thin layer of ice upon a deep ocean of chaos and darkness.
—WERNER HERZOG

I see technology as a Trojan Horse.
—DANIEL GREENBERG

Trojan is a horrible name for a brand of condoms. Why name it after something that, after penetrating the wall, broke open to let [an army] of little guys pour out and [mess] things up for everyone?
—ANON.

Metropolitan Museum of Natural History
Theodore Roosevelt Auditorium
July 12, 1946

Did you know that Selznick cut ten minutes out of that Dalí dream sequence?" The film director had used a slight pause in the musical program to inform Charles Knight of this seemingly important fact about his most recent motion picture.

"Really," Knight whispered back, hoping his guest would keep his lugubrious, and soon-to-be-world-famous, voice down.

Onstage, composer Bernard Herrmann had just finished conducting a full symphony orchestra in the *Prologo* to what would become his only solo opera, *Wuthering Heights*.

"Now this is what I've *really* come to hear," said Alfred Hitchcock.

With the aid of an assistant, a young musician carried something that more resembled an odd piece of cabinetry than a musical instrument, to a spot adjacent to where the conductor stood.

Herrmann, already famous for scoring *Citizen Kane,* and *Jane Eyre,* basked in the applause of a sold-out audience before introducing the newly arrived musician with a wave of his hand.

"It's a theremin, my dear man." Hitchcock continued his monologue, every syllable given its own moment, even as the rest of the auditorium went silent.

Knight flashed a tight smile, then turned quickly toward the stage.

"Miklós Róza used one in *Spellbound.*"

Someone in the row behind them shushed the director, who immediately pivoted in his seat. Appraising the considerable size of the "shusher," whose biceps seemed a serious threat to burst his tuxedo jacket, Hitchcock chose survival, turning back again toward the stage himself. "Riffraff," he mumbled.

From her seat on the other side of Charles Knight, Patricia Wynters quietly let out a breath she felt like she'd been holding for several minutes. As she breathed in again, sounds that might have come from a ghost orchestra filled the auditorium, although oddly, the musician producing the notes was not even touching the instrument—instead passing his hands in the proximity of a pair of metal antennae.

How chillingly wonderful, she thought, watching as the "thereminist" (as he would later be introduced to her) seemed to wring eerie swoops and flutters from the very air.

H is majesty awaits," Knight warned Patricia, in a whisper. Patricia had grown accustomed to giving tours of the museum's Vertebrate Zoology Department. What she found most amusing was the fact that dignitaries of every ilk, in addition to all manner of the rich and famous, reacted in precisely the same way—leaving their titles and self-importance in the elevators as they stepped onto the museum's legendary fifth floor. Once there, each of them was a child again—from kings to stuffy British directors—and each was thrilled by the opportunity to visit a part of the museum they knew few people would ever see.

And tonight is no different, Patricia thought, unable to suppress a smile. For while Alfred Hitchcock was being given a personal tour of the paintings and dinosaur statuary in Charles Knight's office (by the artist himself), "Call Me Benny" Herrmann was demonstrating a theremin (which had recently been gifted to Knight) for an uncharacteristically bemused Major Patrick Hendry. Choosing to avoid the aural torture that soon followed—as the major initiated a series of rude-looking contortions in a vain attempt to play theremin "Chopsticks"—Wynters and the composer wandered over to where Hitchcock was admiring Knight's *Tyrannosaurus rex* model.

"There's something terribly familiar about this creature," the director said, stretching the sentence out so that it seemed like a paragraph.

Knight laughed. "I agree. My colleague Edwin Colbert thinks

they're birds, or rather that birds are dinosaurs. A fascinating concept, no?"

Bernard Herrmann nudged his corpulent new acquaintance. "Alfred, can you imagine these horrors running wild across the earth today?"

The director said nothing, apparently lost in thought, so Knight responded, "I guess we should be thankful the modern versions have lost both their size and their teeth."

"I'm not sure that would matter, my dear Charles," Hitchcock replied. "They do have numbers on their side."

Patricia was just about to chime in when the sound of a crash from across the room caused them all to jump.

Four pairs of eyes turned toward the commotion, which found the redheaded Army officer holding his hands up as if in surrender. The theremin lay tipped over and splintered on the floor, emitting a thin trail of smoke and a brief sizzle before it died.

"I barely touched it," the major exclaimed, defensively.

At that very moment, in a small dark room less than a block away on Central Park West, a man screamed and fell backward off his chair, tearing at the headphones he had been wearing and kicking over a monitoring device—which flew in the opposite direction.

"Are you out of your mind, Julius?" came the loud whisper of a second man, spoken in Russian.

The man on the floor moaned and rubbed his ears.

"I assume you've lost contact," the other man said.

"*What?*" the man on the floor said, in a voice that was far too loud considering where they were and what they were doing.

Suddenly, a bang on the wall, followed by an only slightly muffled voice, "Hey! How 'bout shuttin' up in there?"

"Yes . . . sorry," the man who was standing called back in un-accented English.

"My kids are tryin' ta listen to Fibber *fucking* McGee and Molly!" the plasterboard explained.

"Okay then. We are just fine in here," the man reassured the wall. "Thank you." Then, when there was no further response, he turned to the man on the floor. "You see what you have done?" he hissed in Russian. "Wait until Comrade Theremin hears how you've destroyed his prized bug."

The man on the floor nodded but then quickly shook his head. "*What?*"

CHAPTER 8

Foreign Parts

Time destroys the speculation of men, but it confirms nature.
—MARCUS TULLIUS CICERO

In waking a tiger, use a long stick.
—MAO ZEDONG

South Tibet
July 12, 1946

R. J. MacCready held up his hands "peaceful-guy" style, waited a beat to gauge Alpha's response, then knelt beside the machinery that the Morlock had dumped on the ground.

"This looks like part of a helicopter transmission," he said, shifting the object onto its side. "Definitely American made."

Yanni moved in beside him. "How can you tell?"

"Serial numbers are in Arabic numerals. But take a gander," he said, pointing to a flat section of metal with a set of characters stamped in red.

"Well, that's definitely *not* American," she replied.

"Chinese, from what I can tell."

"It *is* Chinese," Jerry confirmed.

Yanni shot them a confused look. "But how did the Chinese get their mitts—"

"Lend-Lease," Mac said. "Back in '41, we started sendin' shitloads of supplies to the Brits, French, and Soviets—trucks, railroad equipment, helicopters, and the like. Some of it went to China."

The Morlock, who had been standing by silently, now took the opportunity to emit an impatient-sounding growl.

"I guess somebody needs to explain that to Alpha here," Jerry suggested, doing his best imitation of "the least threatening human in Tibet."

Mac pointed to the machinery, shot the creature a quizzical look, and then shrugged his shoulders. "No clue, big guy," he said.

The Morlock emphasized his next growl with a facial display that caused Mac to momentarily imagine being driven into the ground like a screaming, six-foot-long tent peg.

Sensing calamity, Yanni stepped between her friend and the giant. "I've got this one," she said to Mac and Jerry. Rather than speaking to the creature, or even looking it directly in the eye, she knelt down and smoothed a section of the dark loamy soil into a sort of canvas. Then, using only her index finger, she began to draw.

The figure was clearly meant to depict the face of a Morlock. Mac noted that Yanni correctly portrayed the long hair but had decided to leave out the snarl and the canines.

"Nice touch with the smiley kisser," Mac said quietly, and by way of support.

Yanni did not bother to respond. Instead she pointed to the portrait and then to Alpha. She repeated the move, checking to make sure that the Morlock had made the connection. Apparently he did.

Next, she drew a rather decent facsimile of MacCready's face and reenacted the pointing-from-picture-to-object pantomime, while Mac tried as hard as possible to resemble the caricature. Finally, she drew a third figure, this one with what appeared to be exaggerated Asian features. Completing it, she pointed at helicopter parts and then to the last section of her artwork.

The response by the Morlock, whose initial transition from jailer to art critic seemed to have diminished his anger, took an unexpected turn. With canines in full threat display again, the giant moved forward and used its foot to stamp out the last figure.

"Serr-rah!" Alpha growled.

"I'm guessing he's not a big fan of Impressionism," Jerry muttered. Mac and Yanni followed up by flashing him a matching pair of *shut the hell up* looks.

"SERR-RAH!" Alpha emphasized, in a tone that was simultaneously a roar, yet part of a curiously birdlike language.

"Sarah?" Mac wondered out loud. "Sure doesn't sound Chinese."

"Jesus," Jerry said. "I don't think he's saying Sarah."

"SERR-RAH!"

"Lemme guess," Yanni said. "More bastardized Latin."

"You got it. *Sere* is the Roman word for Chinese."

"But how the hell do the Morlocks know Latin?"

The trio exchanged glances, each of them sharing the same thought: *Pliny*.

May, A.D. 67

For a creature of such short stature, the little doctor was astonishingly strong.

Moments after the female Ceran physician separated Severus

from his two friends and led him indoors, she pushed him to the ground. Then she brought her face close to his—holding him spellbound, as if by the stare of a cobra. Severus found it impossible to determine, from the Ceran's expression, what to expect. All he knew for certain was that, at any chosen instant, she could strike him dead.

Pliny, what did you get me into this time?

"The only certainty is uncertainty," Pliny had said. Severus, however, was not so sure. One certainty *did* gnaw at him: that he was losing, forever, everything that his family had built for him back home. It occurred to the young Roman that Pliny had planned to seduce him away from art and engineering, into doomed expeditions such as this. By the time the voyage was planned, his family owned the Bay of Naples's most educated and artistic slaves. They counted themselves among the city's wealthiest architects and engineers.

All those carefully planned connections and all that hard work—wasted.

Looking back, he could see that once Pliny caught sight of an explorer's uneasiness in him, he had begun stoking the fires of confusion. The older man had recognized in Severus a student torn between wanderlust and the desire to design great machines. Eventually Pliny convinced him that there was no need to choose one love over the other. Like a half-dozen others in the hand-picked expedition team, Pliny had deceived him into believing that he could live out all of his dreams.

And how have those dreams rewarded me? Severus asked himself, and tried to avert his eyes from the beastly physician. But she would not let him turn his head away. *I'm dead,* the centurion thought. And for a single, nightmarish moment, true fear welled up like a punch against his heart. By the time the Roman shook aside that emotion, two other physicians had descended into the dwelling. They flitted in with such fluid and silent motion that he failed to notice their presence, or their exit. He simply realized, with a start, that someone else had draped a warm robe over his shoulders—incomparably soft to the touch and woven from a delicate fiber that was neither wool nor cotton.

Perhaps I will not be joining our honored dead quite yet, he thought.

He had no sooner realized how hungry he was when the physician who had apparently chosen him as her own personal captive produced a bowl of hot broth. Surprisingly tasty, it contained generous helpings of a strange grain that defied identification.

"*Gratiam,*" Severus said, thanking her in Latin.

The Ceran locked her large, almond-shaped eyes with his again, trying unsuccessfully to imitate the sound he had just made. She studied his expression, then raised a hand and shoved him hard on one shoulder.

Message received, Severus told himself. *Repeat.*

"*Gratiam,*" he said.

"*Graaa-tee-yum,*" she shot back at him, though far more accurately this time—even down to the parroting of his accent and the slight speech impediment that served to further bastardize his Latin. Again the physician struck his shoulder with the "repeat" signal.

He said the word again, slowly raising the bowl and sipping from it. This time she pronounced it even more precisely, though Severus wondered if the physician believed herself to have learned his word for the bowl of soup, or the thanks he had expressed for receiving it.

She motioned toward her eye and uttered a long, trilling whistle. After his third try at parroting it back to her, he began to realize that the word—if it was a word—contained multiple whistled inflections in *more* than six syllables. He tried . . . and failed. Then failed again. He hoped their words for a simple "yes" or "no" would prove easy enough to at least start something like a conversation. They were—just barely.

After mastering a handful of Latin words in only a few tries, it became clear that whatever passed for Roman language was far simpler (and perhaps more primitive) than the Ceran tongue.

The lessons continued until dawn. By then, only occasionally did she attempt to teach him her own words, and each time, he failed. At one point Severus became vaguely aware that the stench from the one he would henceforth refer to as "Teacher" had become a nearly tolerable background odor. As daylight began flooding in, Teacher's cobra stare was still horribly apparent, yet not quite so threatening as it had seemed to him at sunset. Now he noticed that when the pupils of her eyes narrowed, they revealed irises like those of an alpine wolf, flecked with speckles of blue-green. Those eyes, and the dyed stripes of the creature's mane, were the only signs of pigment on her entire body.

Belonging to a people who could deliver death with both speed and cunning, Severus knew that this rendered Teacher was as fascinating as she was dangerous. He saw in her a being who was at once amazing and obscene, terrifying and wonderfully mysterious.

CHAPTER 9

The Missing

What seest thou else, in the dark backward and abysm of time?
—WILLIAM SHAKESPEARE, *THE TEMPEST* (ACT 1, SCENE 2)

South Tibet
July 12, 1946

This is some seriously perplexing shit," Jerry said, after Morlock "Alpha" singled out and obliterated the last of the three caricatures Yanni had drawn in the soil, then left with the Chinese helicopter parts.

"What's up?" Mac said, though clearly preoccupied with his own thoughts.

"I'm still wondering what they've got against the Chinese."

Mac shrugged, and looked through the curved wall of ice at the swarming field of inchworm grass just beyond. Distracted by it, he thought aloud, "Some sort of hive organism—like wasps."

"Huh?" Jerry said, puzzled. Then he turned his gaze to the seething, carnivorous lawn. "Oh, them. Gotcha."

Together the two men watched silently, lost in thought, until Jerry spoke. "So here I am, Mac, thinking you've already been through enough strange shit to last a lifetime. Like that little adventure you had in Brazil."

"And?"

"So do you ever get the feeling that we're being dragged down Alice's rabbit hole?"

MacCready paused for a moment. "I suppose it feels like that sometimes, although that 'adventure' in Brazil was certainly no fantasy." Then he gestured to the activity taking place just outside. "And neither is this one."

"I guess what I mean is . . . do you ever get *used* to it?"

MacCready thought about it for a moment, and then for another. "I don't know if 'get used to it' is the right phrase," he said at last. "You travel to incredible places—dangerous places—and too often you don't come back with as many people as you went in with. But somehow you feel honored to be there."

"Even though the story can end badly," Yanni added, before falling into stony silence.

Mac knew that her thoughts were drifting back to another time and another place.

Ashamed that he'd done something to upset the only person in the world he *never* wanted to upset, Mac backpedaled. "Jerry, have I told you about Bob Thorne's diaper invention?"

Jerry, who also noticed what had just occurred, shook his head.

"Sparties!" Yanni blurted out, with a laugh.

Now Mac's face broke into a wide grin. He supposed that this might have been the first time since Bob's death that Yanni could recall something about him more with laughter rather than pain.

"Sparties?"

"Yeah, Jerry—a diaper you only have to change every month!" Mac announced proudly.

"The Spartan thirty-day diaper," said Yanni, picking up the story. "The baby fits inside—"

"—except for their head," Mac added, with a laugh.

"Right," Yanni continued, "and you kind of secure it around the kid's neck." She made a string-tying motion around her own neck. "Done!"

Jerry threw his friends a skeptical look. "Then what?"

Mac continued the pitch. "Then thirty days later, you take Junior out of his diaper, hose him down, and leave 'em out in the sun to dry."

Yanni finished up, "Then ya stick 'em into a new Spartie and he's good to go."

Jerry laughed before shaking his head at the imagery. "Sparties, huh? Sounds like your Bob was a real hoot."

Yanni nodded, and gave Jerry a rare compliment, a showing of respect that would have gone over the heads of most outside observers. "I'm sure you two woulda become great friends," she said. "I'm startin' to think you're our kind of stupid."

The trio lapsed into silence as the here-again, gone-again white shapes they had been watching converged menacingly outside the igloo.

The ice-sculpted door slid open. This time Alpha and two other giants entered without uttering any sounds. Each took a prisoner under an arm, exited, then started off at a fast jog—the sea of grass mimics parting before the three Morlocks. Mac glanced around in every direction, trying to get his bearings. His best guess was that they were headed back toward the cave system they had passed through earlier. He tried to take in more details but "the armpit express" was moving with such haste that there was time enough only to *think* he had seen something large and white foraging in the mist—but the moment passed so quickly that now he could not be sure.

Soon they were once again in among the tunnels and cathedral-like caverns, the supporting ribs and buttresses lit brightly by heatless fire. After passing through a chamber system so large that St. Patrick's Cathedral could easily have been contained in one of its side branches, the prisoners were taken into an alcove and unceremoniously dropped to the floor.

What Mac saw confirmed beyond all doubt that the Morlocks had been the architects of this undiscovered realm. But of morality and wisdom, no matter how intelligent these beings might be, they could easily match humanity's own savage impulses, black for black. The stalagmites told it so—row upon row of polished ice columns.

No, Mac reminded himself. *Not merely polished—planned and constructed.*

From the floor up, it was an atrocity of rare design. In this most brilliantly illuminated of subterranean chambers, the pinnacles spoke, in crystal clarity, of the savage brain. There were hundreds of the artificial stalagmites, each cut into a perfect cylinder, each enclosing and preserving one or more "specimens." Some were zoological, some were botanical, while others were clearly man-made. But by far most of the shapes entombed in ice were human—sometimes dozens of people in a single enormous column.

"Like—"

"—flies trapped in amber." Yanni completed Mac's thought.

The Morlocks prodded their three human captives, as if to say, *Go and see.*

And so they did.

"Holy shit!" Jerry blurted out. "Their equipment is here, too!"

"Who?" Mac asked, trying to keep up with Jerry as he ran from one pillar to the next, barely pausing at each for more than a glance. To Mac it seemed as if his friend was trying to fill his mind with everything he could glimpse before the Morlocks stopped him—and he looked that way because, in fact, he was. Jerry finally came to a momentary halt at one of the tallest cylinders. Inside, no fewer than twenty soldiers were arranged in a semicircle amid broken pieces of military equipment—artillery, firearms, and swords.

Mac could see, in at least a dozen of the pillars standing nearby, that all the bodies encased within were wearing the same uniforms.

Jerry, who had resumed his flitting back and forth between columns, followed silently by the trio of Morlocks, finally came to a stop.

"Chinese," he said, pointing to one of the icy displays, then turning to his captors. Their expressions seemed to be wavering somewhere between mild amusement and annoyance, but Jerry appeared unconcerned. He repeated the word, then shrugged, clearly hoping that the gesture conveyed three truths to the Morlocks: confusion, surprise—and finally, a message: *We are not Chinese and we are not your enemies* (the latter Jerry emphasized with some hand-waving that reminded Mac of an interpretive dance).

Jerry turned to his friends. "Ever heard of the Yangtze disappearance?"

Mac and Yanni both shook their heads.

"You mean the Nanking disappearance?" Mac asked.

"No," Jerry said, quite unable to hide his excitement. "Although it did happen around the time Nanking fell to Japan back in '37."

"And?"

"And there's even less known about this one. Nothing but rumors, really. What we *do* know is that the Chinese sent a large force up into the mountains, beyond the source of the Yangtze. Tremendous undertaking—with all sorts of equipment. Huge generators. Cannons. They hauled it all up there."

"The proverbial 'force to be reckoned with,'" Mac said.

"Exactly. Something like three thousand men. Anyway—"

Mac held up his hand. "Jerry."

"Yeah, Mac?"

"Take a breath."

"Oh, right," Jerry said, looking slightly embarrassed. "At any rate, from the way Alpha responded to Yanni's drawing, I'm guessing these Yangtze guys must have killed more than a few Morlocks before they fell."

Yanni looked around. "And there were three thousand of 'em, huh?"

"I know what you're thinking," Jerry responded quickly, and, as Mac and Yanni exchanged glances, he made a quick recount of the Chinese-laden columns. "There's not nearly enough bodies here, right?"

"War trophies?" Yanni suggested.

"Or maybe museum pieces?" Mac said with a shrug. "Who can tell what's really going on here?"

"*They* can," Yanni said, gesturing toward the Morlocks. "If we can learn to speak their language."

She paused at a particularly gruesome pillar that seemed to tell the fate of a similarly armed group, though these were wearing different uniforms. Young men had been tied in a circle with their feet at the axis—and above them, another layer had been tied likewise, with their heads facing outward. There were twenty such layers, encased one upon another within the column of ice. Yanni could see that those on the lower layers had the life crushed out of them by the layers above. A Japanese war flag left no mystery as to their origin.

Yanni pointed to the banner. "Maybe these guys tracked the Chinese up into the mountains?"

"And ran into quite a surprise." Mac finished the thought.

Jerry continued moving forward into the forest of crystalline display cases. Yanni followed, then Mac, without any discouragement from the Morlocks.

He halted at a display of what was apparently a lost German expedition, pre–World War II. "I'd say your Morlocks have been playing this gig for a long time."

Mac found himself overwhelmed by the sheer variety of organisms, tools, and people on display. The chamber really did remind him of a museum—full of historical clues, and with nothing random about it. In fact, the deeper they walked from the alcove entrance, the deeper they traveled backward in time.

"Holy mackerel. Will you look at that," Jerry exclaimed. "I mean, who knew that Templars made it this far?"

R. J. MacCready nodded, his puzzlement giving way to something else. He had sometimes felt inadequate against the broad canvas of Jerry's knowledge—which seemed to span every arcane subject and, by comparison, often left the zoologist feeling a little too specialized in his own field. This was hardly a cause for despair. Mac hoped, as any true teacher or explorer hoped, that Jerry and others who followed would surpass him.

Only a few short paces from the Templar knight, Jerry paused at a display of men and their horses. They seemed to have died together, in twisted agony, within the ice itself.

"Khan's men," Jerry announced.

Mac peered through the ice. "So Genghis lost an army, too, huh?"

"His grandson Kublai did. Or so say the legends," Jerry replied.

"Well, they might be from the right time, in this sequence, but they certainly took a wrong turn somewhere."

Jerry led Mac and Yanni farther down through the centuries until a carved golden eagle, encased in ice, brought him to a stop. Behind the winged symbol of Rome, the rest of the column contained a tangle of bodies.

"Those Pliny's men?" Yanni asked.

"I don't think so," Jerry said as he moved in for a closer look at the eagle. Turning to Mac, he said, "You've been boning up on your Roman history. Who do you think they are?"

There had been damage to the inscription beneath the talons of the sacred icon, but even through the distorting lens of ice, Mac was able to read enough. "Not Pliny's Romans, that's for sure."

"You give up?"

"I think it's the Ninth Legion."

"Excellent!" Jerry said. "The *Legio nona Hispana*."

"Show-off," Mac said, under his breath. "Jeez, that would be about what—forty years *after* Pliny?"

Jerry replied, with a smile. "Yeah, something like that—forty, fifty." He was about to place a hand on the ice containing the Romans but a glance at the Morlocks made him stop. "This one's a real head-scratcher though."

"How so?"

"I sure as hell wouldn't have expected to find the Ninth Legion anywhere near Tibet."

"So how'd they get here?" Mac wondered.

"Dunno," Jerry said. "According to historians, the Ninth was either annihilated in northern Britain by Celtic tribes or they were transferred."

Yanni moved in for a closer look. "I'd vote for number two. But transferred where?"

"Possibly to the Jordan Valley," Jerry said, continuing the tale. "One rumor has them moving east from there into India."

"And what were they doing in India?" Yanni asked.

Mac shrugged and turned to Jerry, who shook his head. "Who knows? Like I said, it was pretty much just a rumor, sung by ancient poets. What is clear is that there's no trace of the Ninth after A.D. 120. After which they *did* pick up a new moniker."

Jerry waited, but the pair remained silent.

"Go on," Mac said at last.

"Rome's Ghost Legion."

"So they just up and disappeared?" Yanni asked.

"All five thousand of them, poof—gone."

Yanni gestured toward the columns. "Until now." She knelt down near the base of the pillar, where a Roman leg had been thrust close to the surface of the ice—thrust at an angle so awkward that she supposed it would have been extremely painful were he alive in that final moment. Dozens of yellowish strands seemed to have sprouted out of the leg, tearing at the flesh before he died.

"Talk about your shitty transfers," Mac chimed in.

Yanni squinted at the bizarre wounds. "What are those things?"

A shove at Jerry's left shoulder blade communicated that Alpha was finally becoming impatient with the conversation. Obediently, the trio moved in the direction indicated by the shove, down through the second century B.C. into Hannibal's time. Far ahead, Mac could see bodies whose faces were pressed near the outer surface of an ice pillar. They displayed distinctly Asian features but their hair was bright red.

Mac was certain that the Morlocks' collection went back at least through the Bronze Age—past the incongruous-looking redheads and beyond the first dynasties of emperors and pharaohs alike. "Jerry," he asked, "you've heard of Howard Carter, right?"

"Sure, Mac. Why? He sure as hell didn't get this far."

"No, but I was just thinking that discovering Tutankhamun's tomb completely intact might take a backseat to a thirty-foot walk in any direction down here."

Jerry was about to respond when his attention was suddenly diverted by something near the very center of the chamber. The Morlocks allowed him to sidetrack past a display of Jin Dynasty infantrymen and their rockets, toward the tallest and widest of the pillars they had encountered thus far.

It stretched high above the backs of the elephants entombed within—and in fact four of the neighboring pillars also contained elephants, along with their drivers. The frozen pachyderms were outfitted in protective plating and the warriors astride them also wore battle armor and thick furs. Mac was just telling himself that the soldier nearest to him looked either Chinese or Cambodian— and possibly female—when Yanni distracted him. She had knelt down beside one of the entombed elephants. Clearly, she was deeply immersed in her own thoughts.

Despite the distinct possibility that the remainder of their lives would henceforth unfold under the whim of the Morlocks, and despite certain grim details of their immediate surroundings, Mac had at least some small measure of success in convincing himself that being here was an astonishing turn of good luck. For now, even Jules Verne's fictional Captain Nemo and his discovery of the ruins of lost Atlantis could not compare to this.

"Hannibal's army?" Mac spoke, not quite believing his own question.

"I don't think so," Jerry replied, when Alpha's call startled them both.

The Morlock had been watching intently as Yanni sketched yet another figure into the earth—this time it was an elephant's head. And after emitting a rather loud call, the giant was kneeling down beside her, using an index finger to draw his own version of the figure.

He looks almost enthusiastic, Mac thought.

"*Alafas,*" Yanni said, then quickly sketched one of the two-trunked mammoths Knight had described back in New York.

But the Morlock did not respond to Yanni. Instead, Mac saw that Alpha's attention was drawn to the pair of Morlocks who had been standing by silently. One of them displayed what had been a seriously deep and recent wound, running from above his left temple down to the jawline. Now almost completely healed, the wound was discernible mostly as a line of slightly mismatched fur. Alpha and "Scarface" had both begun uttering low-frequency growls.

The pair exchanged a series of whistles and canine-flashing grunts that concluded with Alpha looking frustrated and even angry. Turning back to Yanni, the creature erased the drawing of the bi-trunked *Elephas* before lifting her up gently. Then, as swiftly as she had been carried into the chamber of ice and lost souls, Yanni was whisked away from its center, and up again through time.

The two men exchanged frantic looks before MacCready turned and caught a last glimpse of Alpha retreating out of the chamber. Their own escorts approached quickly, each of them hefting their human cargo before setting off at a trot. To Mac, however, it seemed as if they were being handled more roughly this time.

"Where do you think he's taking her?" Mac asked, straining in vain to see around the Morlock's bulk.

"Search me," Jerry responded, "but she'll be okay, buddy."

Something's up, Mac thought. And now he realized that it had been Alpha's reaction to his own brethren that he'd found most disturbing.

Near the chamber threshold, among what they had determined to be the youngest pillars, Mac saw that a new pedestal of ice, wood, and rock was being constructed adjacent to a column containing what appeared to be a British explorer and his Sherpa guides. A pair of Morlocks looked up from their work.

Jesus Christ, Mac thought, but kept to himself.

"Hey," came a concerned voice, "I don't like the way that one guy is—"

There was a crack—loud and unmistakable, and Mac reflexively turned toward the sound. The Morlock who was carrying Jerry had dropped him to the ground. His friend's eyes were open—wide open—and Mac immediately felt a sickening feeling in his guts.

R. J. MacCready had just begun to scream when a hand clamped over his mouth and nose.

His world went black.

CHAPTER 10

The Gathering

With man, most of his misfortunes are occasioned by man.
—PLINY THE ELDER

Only two things are infinite: The universe and human stupidity. I'm not sure about the former.
—ALBERT EINSTEIN

Yi Chang Airport
Western Hubei Province, China
June 20, 1946, 11:40 A.M. (22 days earlier)

"W here are you taking me?" Wang asked the army officer. The man, who appeared to be about forty years of age, had a long scar that ran from just below his right eye to the point of his chin. He said nothing but responded by gesturing to the first of three strange-looking helicopters tethered to the tarmac.

Climbing down from the armored scout car, Wang noticed that their arrival had set off a flurry of activity at the airport. Members of the ground crew were sprinting from a rust-stained hangar toward each of the aircraft. They were followed by three pairs of serious-looking men in flight suits—*pilots,* Wang assumed—who began double-checking the outsides of their respective machines. Each of the helicopters had a pair of rotors—one centered on the roughly fifty-foot-long fuselage, the other mounted at the rear, atop a section of the body that curved upward to an angle of approximately 40 degrees. The front of the craft was roughly triangular in shape, with large windows. Approaching the open aft cargo door, Wang noticed with a sense of alarm that the ship's outer shell appeared to be made of nothing more substantial than fabric that had been stretched over a thin tubular frame.

After a prod from behind, the zoologist entered the craft, the officer and his men following through the same cargo door.

Wang shuffled forward, carrying his backpack, and took a window seat near the cockpit. Behind him, the earthen jar containing the Yeren specimen was loaded into the cargo hold, along with the small wooden crate containing the creature's skin. The skull sat at the bottom of Wang's backpack, cushioned by clothes.

As the pilots strapped themselves into their seats, and just before the noise from the dual engines rendered any conversation impossible, Wang turned to the army officer, who was seated across from him. "Is this trip related to the specimen I found?" he said, pitching his voice above the increasing whine. "The Yeren?"

At the mention of the creature, the officer's eyes widened in a momentary flash of anger, but just as quickly his face returned to its previously passive state. Then, in a gesture that only served to increase the unease Wang had felt since his arrival in Yi Chang Harbor, the military man turned silently and faced forward in his seat. Glancing aft, Wang began to see that every step he had taken was degenerating into a string of poorly chosen actions. All conversation between the soldiers had stopped, but it was clearly

more than the rise of engine noise that silenced them. Each of the
men was glaring at him. Like the officer, Wang turned and stared
straight ahead, letting out a deep breath.

Underfoot, river and forest gave way to more rugged terrain.
After several hours, the helicopter began a descent and Wang
could see that they were approaching a field of well-irrigated
farmland, located on the outskirts of a small village. The great
peaks had been looming ever larger as the trio of aircraft flew
steadily southwest but now, descending into a landscape lit by the
last rays of the setting sun, the vast mountain range dominated
the entire western horizon. Directly below, Wang watched three
torch-waving figures arraying themselves across a field of ripening
crops. As the helicopters made their final approach, each of the
torchbearers scrambled out of the way, just before the downwash
from the six enormous blades destroyed a month's supply of the
village's squash crop.

Wang was escorted hastily to a small yurt and he was thankful
to see that it was equipped with a chair and a little table, upon
which sat a lantern. There was also a straw-filled mattress, and
after setting his pack beside it, he lay down. Exhaustion had come
upon him like a wave.

Only for a moment, he thought, closing his eyes. *Only for a—*

He awoke to the sounds of men singing—a drunken chorus,
as near as he could tell. Crossing to the open doorway, Wang saw
soldiers gathered around a sizable campfire. Some of them were
dancing and all of them seemed to be making quite a great time
of it. He caught the glint of bottles being passed around and the
smell of meat cooking. The villagers were watching the festivi-
ties as well, but they stood grim-faced and silent. *This is not their
party.*

Afraid that someone would see him, he withdrew quickly, closing off the doorway, then lighting his lamp. Retrieving the Yeren skull and his notebook from the backpack, he sat down. Examining the anterior aspect of the skull, he began to sketch. His descriptions of the incredible find filled ten pages by the time a knock on the door frame interrupted him and an officer entered, carrying something.

Captain Mung Chen placed a plateful of food beside the notebook. He waited for a lull in the alcohol-fueled din taking place just outside. "You should eat something."

"Captain, why am I being held prisoner?" Wang asked.

"You are *not* a prisoner here," the officer responded, his voice calm and measured.

Wang then managed a smile, before gesturing toward the plate, which contained rice and vegetables. "If that is as you say, then why am I not being fed the meat I've been smelling—fed like the other men?"

Captain Mung had already turned to leave but now he stopped to address the scientist again. "Because, Wang Tse-lin, I did not think you would enjoy eating your specimen. My men, on the other hand, *are* enjoying it. They'll be stronger now. And where we are going, they will need strength."

Wang stood. "But—"

The captain held up a hand. "Of course they had no idea that we were carrying the flesh of the mountain ogres with us—until you told them. So before you say another word, know that *you* did this."

Wang's mind flashed back to the helicopter and the careless words he had spoken just before takeoff. Then he slowly lowered his head into his hands.

"You did this."

Wang Tse-lin had been sitting in stunned silence for many long and uncomfortable minutes when the officer reappeared and took a seat at the bamboo-framed table. He gestured toward the skull. "Tell me more about how you tracked the Yeren."

The scientist's worried expression shifted to puzzlement. "Tracked? I don't understand."

Captain Mung crossed his arms. "It's no secret. Your university colleagues couldn't stop talking about you—how you had tracked the Yeren across the mountains. How you followed it into the Shennongjia wilderness."

Wang sat silently for a moment, then shook his head. "Who was it? Dr. Yi?"

Mung said nothing but reacted as if the chair had suddenly become uncomfortable.

The scientist managed a wry smile. "It *was* Dr. Yi."

"Explain yourself," Mung commanded.

"My work was to survey the valley. I used the opportunity to collect zoological specimens. I was hoping for a white bear but instead—"

"But instead you killed a Yeren?"

"The villagers killed the creature. I tried, as I said, to . . . purchase it."

"You *bought* it?"

"They gave it to me."

Captain Mung sank back into the chair, closed his eyes, and let out a deep sigh. A minute passed, but to each of the men it seemed far longer, until a burst of drunken laughter outside brought them back to present reality: a damp hut in a nameless village.

Finally, the officer spoke. "My family came from a settlement not much bigger than this one," Mung said. "Outside Harbin."

Wang winced involuntarily at the name.

"You've heard of it, I see," the captain said, briefly wearing a humorless smile.

"To my sadness, I have."

"My wife was killed there, as was my youngest child."

Wang bowed his head.

The officer continued. "My two remaining children are sick—poisoned with candy. Can you believe that? Candy."

"I am sorry," Wang said, quietly. Like many people, he was familiar with the rumors about what took place at Harbin during the war—rumors whose details became far too specific to have been made up. The Japanese invaders had constructed a vast complex of buildings—"a lumber mill," inquiring local leaders were told. Then the walls went up—razor wire and guard towers—the perimeter patrolled by soldiers and vicious guard dogs. Stranger still were reports of a ceaseless rumble of trucks moving into and out of the facility in the dead of night and long after construction was completed.

Through it all, and in what would become the most disturbing development, was the oddly charitable nature of the Japanese occupiers—who provided regular deliveries of food to the perplexed and war-starved locals: fresh vegetables, meat, even cookies and candy. Soon after, many of the villagers became horribly sickened and most of them died. The few who survived were taken in the night by teams of men who arrived and departed like phantoms, men clad from head to toe in strange suits.

The officer had gone silent, his attention seemingly focused on a cockroach that was making its way down one of the hut's wooden support beams.

"But why are you here, Captain? What do you and your men want with me?"

Mung stared at him, severely. "It seems we were sold a rather inaccurate bill of goods."

"How so?"

"Your colleagues exaggerated your role in the discovery of the Yeren."

"Out of fear, I am certain," Wang said, trying not to appear too defensive.

Mung paused for a moment, then gave a slight nod. "A logical suggestion."

"And so what will become of me now?"

"Now, Wang Tse-lin, to survive you must play the game. And no matter how little you *do* know about the biology and habits of the Yeren, you must quickly become an invaluable expert on the topic."

"But, Captain, why are you so concerned with these creatures? Why all the soldiers? Why the helicopters?"

"It seems physicians in Peking have concluded that the stories passed down through the centuries about the Yeren are true."

"Which is why your men ate my specimen?" Wang responded, his anger surfacing for only a moment.

"Precisely," the officer said. "In this case, to increase their strength."

The scientist looked perplexed. "But why 'in this case'?"

"Because the flesh of the Yeren is also said to have unsurpassed curative powers."

"Surely you don't—"

Mung held up his hand. "I *do* believe it. I believe that the flesh of the Yeren can cure the sick. That it can cure my children and others like them."

"But if this is true, then why aren't you combing the Shen-nongjia valley for more Yeren?"

"The reason, Wang Tse-lin, is that the forest ogres—like the one I mistakenly presumed you had tracked and killed—are far too rare. The Shennongjia population is small and scattered, and soon it may be extinguished."

"Then with all respect, Captain, I'm confused as to why you allowed your men to consume such a rare find."

The officer rose and moved slowly toward the door, unable to hide his fatigue. "Because you have changed everything," he said. "None of us ever believed in legends told by the khans about the Yeren—or that any Yeren could actually exist—until you made belief possible. I allowed my men to eat your specimen because, where we are going, there should be many more of them—each one composed of life-giving flesh, and in possession of secrets that can cure every affliction."

CHAPTER 11

Things We Lock Away

When we think we have been hurt by someone in the past, we build up defenses to protect ourselves from being hurt in the future. So the fearful past causes a fearful future and past and future become one.
—ALFRED HITCHCOCK

South Tibet
July 12, 1946

After leaving the cavern and its strange museum of the dead, Alpha carried Yanni down a snowy incline. She craned her neck, hoping to see Mac and Jerry, tucked under the hairy arms of their own escorts. But there was no one following them and soon the cave opening was obscured by mist.

Yanni's sense of unease increased further when, instead of being returned to the igloo with her friends, Alpha had set off in a wholly new direction. Stopping several minutes later at the edge of a corral-like structure, they were met by two female Morlocks.

Even as Alpha gently set her down outside the "fence," she could hear the mammoths, somewhere beyond the veil of perpetually suspended snowflakes. The enclosure (as much as she could see of it through the mist) was a series of chest-high, semi-rectangular granite columns, connected by thick cords of something resembling woven silk. The material was drawn piano-wire tight, and the carved granite had become weatherworn long ago. The calls of the creatures within the enclosure grew louder with their approach—clearly elephantine, but unique and more complex. Though still wondering about Mac and Jerry—back in the "Trophy Room from Hell"—Yanni prepared her mind for the approach of yet another first-contact situation.

Her initial view of them was shadowy—the shifting of ghosts in the mist. But as the phantoms stepped forward and out of the snowy cloud, they resolved themselves into a dozen white-furred mammoths. None of them stood higher at the shoulder than a Shetland pony, but one, slightly taller than the rest, lumbered cautiously toward the edge of the corral.

Yanni's initial impression was confusion. *This can't be them,* she thought, as the largest animal approached. *They've only got one—*

As if to allay her concern, the creature slowly extended its trunk toward her, and, as it did so, the appendage began to split from tip to base.

—*trunk.*

Then, as the appendage's right-hand section gripped a horizontally arranged cord with its digitlike tip, the left-hand section reached out and came to a pause inches above Yanni's shoulder. The entire movement was as graceful as any dance move Yanni had ever seen.

Her second impression, during the first moments of the encounter, was that their limbs were clearly built for agile locomotion. *You'd never know it, though,* Yanni observed, from what appeared to be an almost deliberately lumbering gait. *The Mor-*

locks may have superior numbers on their side, but the mammoths are clearly hiding something.

"Yasss, tang-gerr," one of the female Morlocks said, in its bastardized version of Latin. The words were accompanied by a hand signal, and Yanni was immediately reminded of the trainers at the Central Park Menagerie.

The mammoth, a male with beautiful brown eyes, reacted to the command by resting the tip of one trunk gently on Yanni's shoulder. Its tusks were noticeably stubbier than those of the other individuals, and one eyelid appeared to be healing, from some sort of tussle.

"You don't look like a bruiser," she said, her voice calm as she stroked one of the muscular and lightly furred trunks.

"Conversssa-can-tah-bo," the Morlock commanded, using yet another hand signal. Yanni was able, just barely, to decipher something specific from the directive.

Was she trying to say, Conversa? Yanni wondered. If so, a word that meant "conversation" among the miners of Brazil and *cantar* in the Brazilian dialect of Portuguese was the Latin-derived word for "sing."

The mammoth's response left no room for doubt as it began to vocalize in a strange bitonal language. Four others of his kind followed his lead.

Presently Yanni realized she might have an easier time understanding Morlock-Latin than the language of the mammoths. Still, the miniature pachyderms were effortlessly conveying emotions in their tones, in much the same manner that a talented violinist conveyed moods without words. And likewise, they were doing it to equal or greater effect.

No one who hears this will ever forget the sound, Yanni thought.

The low notes and the high notes swooped down and spiraled

up in a lament that vibrated through her ribs as if they were tuning forks. Yanni did not fully comprehend that the heritage of more than two thousand years was being recalled and sung out to the mists, much of it, she suspected, below the range of her own hearing. She felt the emotions within the tones but could not quite decipher the cries of loves lost, of freedoms lost, and all the loneliness of slavery.

Yanni could not know that the composer, who paused to rest a pair of trunks gently on her shoulders, was reaching across broken foundation stones from the great tower Pliny had seen protruding above the sea of mist. The tower was now a roughly circular ruin, converted into a corral. Its actual dimensions were difficult to determine, the far reaches of the enclosure remaining obscured by the ever-present flakes and the fog.

She tried to communicate back to the mammoths, in tones of her own, but she felt wholly inadequate. As the twelve slaves stared back at her, there was no escaping a clear sense that minds the equal at least of men and Morlocks lived behind those gentle eyes. The mammoths responded encouragingly to her effort, and the Morlocks seemed as curious as she was about the encounter.

The song continued, a dirge that belonged to the white mammoths, and to the white mammoths alone—the incomprehensible song-story of generations long ago lost yet preserved in memory. Yanni was beginning—and only just beginning—to perceive the depth of detail, but the mammoths looked up suddenly and the lamentation died in the mist.

She started to raise a hand toward an outstretched trunk and was about to say something when a growl from the other "elephant keeper" sent the creature back several steps. The mammoth let out a low-frequency hiss as it withdrew.

"No need to translate, kiddo," Yanni spoke quietly to the retreating mammoth. Its companions spread their ears wider and looked past her, with a new and sudden concern.

The Morlocks heard it, too, then Yanni.

A helicopter was approaching.

"Mac," Yanni said to herself. "Where the hell are you?"

In the Igloo

S he'll be okay, buddy."

"Yeah, whatever you say, Jerry," Mac replied, squeezing the head of an inchworm blade up through the skin of his leg like a pimple. He watched his friend pulling evenly and gently along the remaining two-inch length of the creature's body.

Despite the reassurance, and through the pain, Mac's thoughts were with Yanni and her sudden departure from the cave with Alpha. Meanwhile, Mac's own escort had apparently all but killed him during a particularly rough ride back to the igloo and through the field of bitey grass mimics. One of the creatures had latched on and was stubbornly resisting eviction from its new home—Mac's calf.

"Are you making a career out of this, or what?" Mac asked his friend, impatiently.

"Mostly *or what*—especially if I break this critter off inside of you."

Once again, Mac's mind wandered, and for at least the third time Jerry seemed to read his thoughts. "She'll be okay, buddy."

Mac nodded, less than entirely convinced.

"You *know* Yanni," Jerry continued, "and the effect she has on animals."

"Yeah, that'd be fine," Mac said, squeezing harder against the creature under his skin, "if the Morlocks were animals."

"Nah, come on. She's probably got Mr. Alpha wrapped around her little finger by now."

"Do ya . . . *ow!* . . . think?" Mac said, as the creature in his leg came out another fraction of an inch, bit at him, was drawn out a little farther, bit again. "Shit!"

"Sorry!" Jerry said. "And just in case you haven't noticed, Yanni is already working on them. I mean, compared to the way they treat us, they're treating her like royalty."

Mac gritted his teeth. "I suppose . . . they have been giving her the kid-glove treatment. Not like that hammering you took back there in 'Lost and Found.'"

"What are you talking about?" Jerry replied, calmly. "You're the one they smothered half to death—and that was *before* you picked up your little passenger on the return trip."

Mac vaguely remembered being hauled back to their igloo jail like a sack of potatoes, and he remembered pain. Evidently, the Morlock had also been somewhat less than efficient in clearing a path through the inchworm grass and one of the miniature predators had managed to gain purchase. Its mouthparts, having pierced skin and muscle, felt like a thorn dipped in electric fire.

Somehow this all made sense, except for Jerry's comment about being suffocated—Mac had no recollection of that at all.

"I think Alpha's taken a real shine to her," said Jerry, *still* trying to sound cheery—a tone that was definitely starting to piss Mac off.

"Yeah, well, just keep that shit to yourself, okay. Now about that smothering they laid on me, I'm wondering why— *Ouch!*"

The head of the little monster, which had dug deep into the muscle of his thigh, was now almost out through the skin surface, and with its battle nearly lost, it felt like the thing was spitting more venom. Mac already had an advanced education in pain, but this creature was helping him to write a whole new thesis.

"So, why *wouldn't* Alpha be smitten?" Jerry said, in a further attempt to distract his stricken friend. "He sorta reminds me of those Brooklyn musicians you're always complaining about—only with more hair and no guitars."

"Stop trying to make me laugh!" Mac replied. Jerry was one of the only people he knew who could pry something funny out of even the gravest situation, who could laugh and be afraid at the same time.

"And stop trying to change the subject!" Mac added. "Tell me what happened—back there."

Jerry feigned an offended look. "Okay, Mr. Sensitive. Now just hold on. This bugger's almost out."

Mac felt another surge of venom and his subconscious seemed suddenly more in control than his conscious mind, seeking out a lighter place—a place he hadn't thought about in—

"Well, it's about time, Yanni," Mac said, absently. He had been pressing a handkerchief to his wounded leg but started dabbing clumsily at the air several inches above his knee. "Whoops," he said, flashing a lopsided grin. "Missed."

"Say, you're looking a little pale there, Mac." Jerry's voice seemed to be coming from far away.

Mac felt as if he were being lowered into a prone position, strangely relieved to be drifting off, as a heretofore-unknown chemical compound did its work. Semiconsciousness allowed worry to slip away and into the distractions of random and sometimes absurd details, bubbling up from the subconscious—*Long Island . . . Fresh bagels! . . . the smell of Mom's perfume . . . Tamara . . .*

Mom's grave.

"Stop."

He drove his thoughts away from his mother and from loss—wondering for a moment what force of natural selection had led to the evolution of grief and regret.

"Stop!"

Instead, Mac latched on to the now barely felt but nonetheless paralyzing sting. He wondered why an animal that could so quickly swarm over and strip its prey down to the bone, before consuming those very bones, needed a toxic bite as well. Thus far he had only seen the inchworm grass consuming small game—the "squirrel" Alpha had used for demonstration purposes.

Perhaps something special for larger prey, he guessed, *like us.*

The blade pulled out another fraction of an inch and Mac struggled to focus his thoughts on helping Jerry to remove the grass mimic.

"Jeez, this sucks!" Mac called out, against a sharp, acidic sting, followed by relief at the final withdrawal of his tormentor.

"She'll be okay, buddy," Jerry said, holding the creature as it snapped and contorted into fantastic S-shapes—trying unsuccessfully to latch on to a new prey item.

"Huh?" Mac asked. "What'd you say?"

"She'll be okay, buddy."

"Pally, you are startin' to sound like a broken record," Mac said, feeling the venom-induced fog beginning to lift rapidly.

Jerry put an end to the creature's relocation attempt by crushing its head between his thumb and forefinger. Then, as Mac watched, his friend took a sniff of the dead animal.

"Smells like antifreeze," Mac told Jerry, while another part of his brain recognized, *Something's wrong.*

MacCready realized that what he had just experienced was like watching his friend down a tumbler of Jack Daniel's, but with *Mac* being the one who tasted and felt the effects of the whiskey.

She'll be okay, came a voice in his head, startling him.

Mac stared down at his own thumb and index finger. *They* were covered with the blood of the grass mimic.

Fully conscious now, he glanced frantically in every direction. The igloo had gone completely silent and he was alone.

"Jerry? *Jerry!*"

Mac lurched up and tottered over to the ice wall. Recollection and realization were slow to emerge. When they did, he knelt down hard—mentally groping for retreat into a private world of denial.

He failed.

Instead, Mac relived over and over again the awful crack of Jerry's neck breaking.

He's still in the trophy room.

Outside the ice prison, a great shadow passed overhead, making a mechanical commotion.

R. J. MacCready did not perceive it, over the sound of his own weeping.

CHAPTER 12

Dracunculus Rising

One death is a tragedy; one million is a statistic.
—JOSEPH STALIN

Extinction is the rule. Survival is the exception.
—CARL SAGAN

Somewhere above the south Tibetan Labyrinth
July 12, 1946

"Should we be doing this, sir?" the Chinese helicopter pilot called back to the officer standing behind him in the cockpit.

The pilot, whose name was Po Han, was gradually easing the "Dogship" toward a sea of mist that seemed to rise threateningly, filling more and more of his visual field.

"You have your orders," snapped the officer, a lieutenant named Lee Song.

"But, Captain Mung told us—"

"These orders did not come from Captain Mung."

"Of course, sir," Po Han said, wondering only briefly *who* was giving the orders now. What he did know was that he had already developed a strong dislike for this particular helicopter. And then, as if those in charge had not already pressed far enough into the limits of crazy, he was being asked to push the craft—an American prototype known as a Harp—beyond what any sane person would consider to be safe limits.

Safety, though, appeared to be the last thing on the lieutenant's mind. The original orders had been simple: drop off additional equipment and fuel at a previously established supply site near the labyrinth's edge. The plan fell apart, however, once they discovered that someone had ransacked the initial cache of fuel and spare helicopter parts. But instead of returning to the village where they'd established their primary base camp, the officer on board had taken a sudden interest in tracking down the perpetrators—especially after their guides insisted that the thefts were the work of the Yeren.

"I see where they've gone," the lieutenant had said, pointing to what he believed was a trail through the mountainous terrain. Po Han and his copilot had serious doubts but the officer left no room for discussion. The new supplies were dumped hastily into the already compromised site ("to lighten the ship and extend our range for the hunt").

This makes no sense, Po Han thought. *Heading deeper into the mountains is madness.* For a while he was certain they were following imaginary trails—*shadows in the stone*—and then the helicopter crested a ridge and the earth fell away into a wide valley, the bottom of which was completely obscured by dense mist. The officer ordered them to fly toward the center of the valley and so, reluctantly, they did.

Within minutes, the mist was rising all around them, and as the rotors pulled down dual columns of clear air from above, the pilot was expecting to see solid ground, but there was none. "It looks bottomless," he said, grimly.

"Keep going," commanded a voice behind him.

"Sir, we need to put a man in the doorway right now. And tell him to start shouting the moment he sees the valley floor."

The officer shouted an order back to one of his soldiers and moments later two others wrestled open the aft cargo door.

Po Han took the helicopter down, skillfully, a foot at a time. The rotors were no longer bringing down clear air. The world was a white blur, with nothing ahead and below except fog. "See anything?" he shouted back into the cabin.

A moment later the officer scrambled forward. "There's grass!" he cried excitedly. "You've got a spot for your landing, now take us down!"

Po Han nudged the helicopter lower, and for a change, he thought, the craft handled smoothly. *No wind at all down here.*

With the lower portion of the cockpit now hovering a mere six feet above the ground, Po Han could see that the officer had been right about the landing zone. It was a flat field, covered in frost-laden grass but otherwise unimpressive. He eased the helicopter even lower, relieved as the tricycle landing gear contacted the ground and at the near certainty that whoever the officer might have been chasing would have been long gone by now. These thoughts had barely registered when, remarkably, he saw three tall figures standing at the extreme edge of visibility. At first the pilot thought they were wearing strange costumes.

"Do you see what I'm seeing?" he asked his copilot, even as the shadowy figures seemed to disappear before his eyes.

There was a pause, followed by a stunned, one-word reply. "Yeren."

Though the word brought a deep churning in his bowels, it was a shriek from behind, louder even than the considerable engine noise, that shifted Po Han's fight-or-flight response into overdrive. The lieutenant's voice rose above the commotion—strangely high-pitched and frantic: "Take us up!"

Glancing back over a shoulder, Po Han glimpsed the officer and the other five soldiers writhing in a tangled mass on the cabin floor—tearing at their own uniforms and at their own bodies.

Forward and below, through the Plexiglas, the pilot imagined he saw (and his mind told him that he *had* to be imagining) frost-covered grass moving toward him in a wave. *Like a school of ravenous fish.*

Reflexively, he throttled the engines up, desperate to get away from a landing spot that had become more like a descent into a hive of angry bees. But as the screams of the men in the cabin actually grew to rival any he had heard during the war, Po Han began to believe that landing in a field of hornet's nests would have been preferable.

The sudden throttle-up, and the rebound effect of the rotors' downwash against the ground during an abrupt change of both thrust and direction, suddenly revealed a design flaw that had rendered the "Dogship" undesirable to Americans and Russians alike—the hull was nothing more than canvas, stiffened with dried glue. The entire starboard side tore open and as Po Han instantly corrected the tilt to his right, the port side too was suddenly all open air. The ship's aft end bounced down hard but during the next instant, another throttle-up seemed to have them safely airborne again.

The pilot allowed himself to believe that they might still complete this cursed excursion and escape with their lives, but this belief was shattered the moment he heard (and felt, through his controls) the shreds of his ship's membrane being tornadoed into the rotors.

"We're going in!" Po Han called out, breaking radio silence.

As the aft section pounded down again and the rotors began to die, and as he tried to describe his location to anyone listening at base camp, it became all too horribly clear that more and more debris from the ground was being whirled into the cabin.

The screams behind Po Han continued to rise above the grind and whine of failing engine parts and as he glanced again over his shoulder he recoiled at what he saw. The men—all of them were covered in white grass turning red.

But it's not grass, he realized at last. *They're worms! And they're everywhere!*

The pilot kept his microphone open and broadcasting till the very end, even after he looked down and realized that the monsters had begun drilling into his own arms and legs and were swarming toward his face.

During the seconds in which Po Han broke radio silence, the helicopter windmilled out of control and slid in Yanni's direction. It was still a vague shape in the mist when it bounced to a stop, its rotors whipping her with a fierce gust laden with soil and something else—something alive.

It took only another moment for Yanni to fully realize what was happening.

Grass mimics!

Throwing both hands up to protect her face, Yanni fell backward against the corral's fence. Alpha, seeing immediately that something had gone terribly wrong, stepped in front of her, forming an effective but incomplete wall against the flying debris and hungry predators. Yanni could smell the musk he was releasing but the inchworms were already crawling along the shoulders of her parka and becoming tangled in her hair.

At the moment in which she was about to scream, a familiar sound came from behind and she turned toward it. Yanni's cupped hands obscured her view but she knew there was nothing else keeping the ravenous biters away from her eyes.

Suddenly, twin blasts of liquid struck her shoulders from separate directions, then her head and hands were similarly sprayed. When Yanni realized that she could no longer feel the grass wiggling toward her scalp and her face, she spread her fingers slightly, peeking out between them. Two of the little mammoths had come up behind her. She felt a series of tugs as some of the grass mimics were blown out of her hair while others were flicked off by the fingerlike projections that tipped the muscular bifurcated trunks.

Get them all. Every single—

The thought was interrupted by two more blasts in the face with the foul-smelling liquid. Yanni became aware that the last of the white blades were springboarding off her neck and fleeing. She exhaled, unaware of the breath she'd been holding.

Saved by the mammoths, she was dismayed that two of their Morlock keepers were already herding them away, tugging on leashes attached to what appeared to be woven choke collars.

"Thanks, guys," she said quietly, as they disappeared back into the mist that hid the rest of the corral.

Turning again toward the downed helicopter, Yanni was prodded forward, now surrounded closely by Alpha and two female Morlocks. Their musk was stronger than she thought possible and the inchworm grass reacted predictably, moving apart and forming a barren trail in the debris-strewn soil.

Once the helicopter rotors stopped spinning and breaking, the machine had apparently keeled gently over to one side, its membranous outer covering in tatters. A figure tumbled out, screaming weakly and wrapped in what appeared to be a cape of inchworm grass. The man's cries did not last much beyond the moment one of his arms broke off near the shoulder joint. The horde of now red-tinted blades seemed to vie for possession of the limb, its previous owner even making a desperate grab for it before falling face-first into the welcoming carpet.

An eerie quiet began to settle over the valley.

Lifting Yanni and carrying her with them, the Morlocks approached the dead machine and its dying crew, but they clearly refrained from moving near enough for their scent—which shepherded the inchworm grass before them—to repel the predators from their prey. With nothing to interrupt their feast, Yanni heard new sounds—faint and horrible—like corn being milled with a grinding stone. And now, as a distinctly queasy feeling crept into her, the grass mimics penetrated humerus, femur, and brow and continued to gorge themselves.

Alpha broke the spell, giving Yanni an uncharacteristically rough shaking and uttering a familiar, mispronounced exclamation in Latin, "*Serr-rah.*"

"Serrah," Yanni repeated, under her breath. "Chinese," she whispered.

Alpha followed with a more primal form of body language that left no room for misinterpretation. He snarled at the disintegrating men.

Though it ranked with some of the most horrible things she had ever seen (and perhaps because of this), Yanni was unable to turn away.

As a chill ran up her back, Yanni swept her gaze around as far as the fog allowed, searching for warning signs of a second, shadowy wave of carnivorous grass—but none appeared. The combination of Morlock and mammoth stench was evidently maintaining its repellent effect.

But for how long? she wondered.

Nearby, the skeletons of the Chinese intruders caved in like children's sand castles and were swept swiftly away by the hungry blades.

Metropolitan Museum of Natural History
Fifth Floor

A nd how old is this Lost Codex supposed to be?" said Dr. Nora Nesbitt. She was the invertebrate zoologist Wynters and Knight had requested, now officially and freshly approved by Major Hendry. She was also one of the Metropolitan Museum's rising stars.

"It dates back to not very long before Vesuvius buried Pompeii," replied Patricia Wynters. "Now is that a humdinger, or what?"

Nesbitt, who had been examining a grainy photograph of the ancient text, peered over the top of her stylish horn-rimmed specs. "*Definitely.* Too bad these photos are for shit."

Wynters glanced at the closed office door, then flashed a wry smile. Today Charles Knight was off exploring the museum with his granddaughter, which meant that in all likelihood he would not be back until after lunch. "Want me to show you the original?" she said, with conspiratorial glee.

Nesbitt, an attractive thirty-something brunette, returned a wide smile of her own. "Sure thing."

Wynters led her thoroughly amused guest to a map table. Opening the top drawer, she carefully sorted through a saga of yellowed and browned pages that had been skillfully mounted between acetate sheets. "Here we go," she said, selecting one, then handing it to the biologist. "This work a little better for you?"

Nesbitt studied an ancient illustration—which showed a human figure pulling what appeared to be a strand of spaghetti out of another man's foot and winding it onto a spool. The second man seemed to be in great pain. "Is that supposed to be a nematode?" she said, at last.

"That's above my pay grade," Patricia replied. "You tell me. Charles thought that maybe these guys were doing some strange knitting."

Nesbitt flashed a *you've got to be kidding me* expression, then saw that indeed Wynters *had* been. She squinted at the codex. "It looks a lot like *Dracunculus*."

"Lovely!" Patricia replied. "That's a worm, right?"

"Yes, a guinea worm."

"Well, Pliny *does* mention worms quite a bit."

Nesbitt nodded toward the ancient text. "Which is, I suppose, the reason you called me in."

Patricia responded with a wry smile.

Nesbitt continued. "Europeans named these critters for the Guinea coast, where they first encountered them in the seventeenth century. You gotta like the Latin, though—'little dragons.'"

"That *does* sound pleasant. And what's their deal?"

"It's more of a horror story, really. *Dracunculus* is a parasite. You pick it up by drinking water containing copepods—tiny crustaceans."

"You mean those little one-eyed critters they call Cyclops?"

"Exactly."

"Yum," Wynters said, scrunching up her face. "Let me guess, the copepods carry the *Dracunculus* larvae?"

"You got it," Nesbitt replied. "And by the way, Egyptian physicians described dracunculiasis in medical papyri dated to thirty-five hundred years ago."

Patricia repeated the disease name to herself. "Interesting. What are the symptoms?"

Nesbitt grimaced. "Well, here's where things get a little grim. The larvae are released when the ingested copepod dies. Then they penetrate your stomach and intestinal wall, and mate in your abdominal cavity."

"And how do I feel about all this?"

"Not so good—fever, nausea, vomiting, diarrhea."

"Oh my."

"But after the nematodes have their little honeymoon—that's when the real party begins."

"Do tell," Patricia said, clearly enjoying the narrative.

"The females start to migrate, burning a path through your soft tissue, and following the long bones out to the extremities. Eventually they make their way to your feet, then up through the skin, where they form a blister—which happens to burn like hell."

"Ah," Patricia exclaimed. "Hence the term 'little dragons.'"

"Exactly. And of course you are now looking for any relief possible, so—"

"—so I dip my dragon-scorched piggies in a cool stream."

"Now you're cookin'!" Nesbitt exclaimed. "Eggs get laid, little swimming Cyclops gulps them down—"

"Water gets drawn by some unsuspecting human, and the whole shebang starts up again."

"Bingo."

"But what does this have to do with what a Roman expedition found two thousand years ago?" Patricia wondered aloud. She returned her attention again to the codex, sorting carefully through several mounted leaves, until she came to and withdrew a page she had been seeking. "Okay, what do you make of this one?" she said, and handed it to Nesbitt.

The zoologist examined the figure for half a minute but remained silent. The badly damaged papyrus depicted what looked like a hair-covered and vaguely human arm, using a stick to hold a coiled mass of spaghetti above a shallow pool of water.

"Beats me," Nesbitt said at last.

"It looks like whatever this creature is, it's harvesting guinea worms, no?"

Nesbitt looked more closely at the codex, then shook her head. "If that tangle at the end of the stick is supposed to be *Dracunculus,* then what we're seeing here is the adult stage—which can get up to forty inches long."

"So . . . you're saying these things wouldn't be coming *out* of the water?"

"Right," Nesbitt agreed.

They exchanged puzzled looks, then turned back to the ancient, humanoid figure. It was Nesbitt who spoke first. "Then why's Mr. Fuzzy here placing parasites *into* a pool of water?"

Patricia thought about the question, then shrugged her shoulders. "Maybe he's breeding them."

"Breeding them? Jeez, for what?"

Wynters shrugged. "I have no idea. But Pliny does go on about shaping the substance of life. Now what if these Cerae were shaping the guinea worms?"

"Why on earth would they do that?"

"What if they were designing a weapon?"

Both women gave a start at the creak of the office door opening. It was Charles Knight, with his little blond granddaughter in tow.

"Patricia, I thought you might want to accompany us—" He stopped, realizing that she had a guest. "Ah, Nora," he said, but with a glance at the codex she was holding, the cheer drained from his face. The pair had obviously been doing quite a bit of work without him.

"Charles, we'd *love* to go to lunch with you," Patricia chirped. Then she bent over and gave the child a welcoming smile. "Well, hello. This is Dr. Nesbitt. She studies animals with no backbones."

"You mean invertebrates—like insects and worms," the girl replied, with an assurance that belied her age.

"Absolutely," Nora responded, cheerfully. "Now, who's ready for lunch?"

"*I am!*" the girl cried happily. "I'm starving!"

"Me, too," Nora said. "Thank you for the invitation, Charles."

Knight turned to the trio, his demeanor apparently restored. "So, ladies, what would you like to eat?"

"Anything but spaghetti," Patricia replied.

An unnamed village on the Tibetan Plateau
July 12, 1946

As Captain Mung left the hut that held their shortwave equipment, Wang thought he resembled someone who had just suffered a swift kick to the solar plexus. Since their arrival at the Tibetan village six days earlier, the officer had opened up to him even more, about the mission and even about his family. Aside from the haunting memories of diseased children, the unusually large and complicated expedition had been progressing quite smoothly. The relay of supplies to and from this western-most outpost was not even an hour behind schedule. But now Mung stormed past the scientist, jaw set and silent. After clapping his hands twice, his path was quickly intercepted by two of the three junior officers who had accompanied him from Yi Chang. As Wang watched, the captain spoke quietly to the men—who, moments later, ran off in opposite directions.

Mung stood perfectly still, arms at his sides, then turned and motioned for Wang to approach.

Something has happened to the other helicopter, Wang thought.

"Captain Mung, what is it? How can I help?"

"They were ordered to drop off supplies," the officer said quietly. "That's all. Drop off supplies and fuel, then return."

"But—"

"But this time they went off course—far off course, according to the distress call."

"And why would your men do that?" Wang asked.

"Apparently, they received orders that superseded my own."

"But who would have—"

"That's not important now. What is important is that they discovered a valley—fogbound. For some reason they either de-cided to land the helicopter—or it crashed. Then they were . . . attacked."

"By the Yeren?"

"No," the captain said, then hesitated. "By the earth, or the ground—or something *on* the ground."

"By the earth?" Wang repeated, to himself.

"Only parts of their message came through," Captain Mung said. "It's difficult to know what really happened."

"But maybe they—"

"They could not have survived what I heard."

Wang bowed his head but said nothing.

"We will be leaving this place," Mung said. His voice belonged to a commander who had just lost seven of his men, including a pair of pilots. "And we will find out who or what attacked them."

CHAPTER 13

The Taken

*You need the ability to fail. . . . You cannot innovate unless you
are willing to accept some mistakes.*
—CHARLES R. KNIGHT

In the igloo
July 12, 1946

R. J. MacCready never heard the tandem-
rotored helicopter until it crashed somewhere in the distance. Even muffled by
snow and fog, the smashing of steel framing against rock and
earth was unmistakable. It also provided the minor favor of allowing him to concentrate on something else—anything else.

Mac flashed back to their own crash only days earlier. Given
everything that had transpired since then, the event felt oddly
distant—as if it had happened to someone else.

But it didn't, he thought. *I'm the one who got us stuck here. And
now Jerry's—*

"All right, cut!" Mac said, shaking his head as if to clear it of
the very thought. The cold, hard fact was that Jerry was gone—
having done nothing at all that might have provoked his captor.

The Morlocks are completely unpredictable, he thought, realizing that now there could be only *one* concern—*finding Yanni and getting her the fuck out of here.*

But is she even alive? Mac wondered. *Or are they both gone?*

"She's alive," he told himself.

Mac moved across the silent interior of the igloo and pressed his hands against the freezing walls, trying in vain to see beyond the mist.

"So whose chopper was that?" he asked himself, before mentally reconstructing what he'd just heard. *Six sequential blows— six blades, two rotors.* Mac knew the sound of a double-rotor set was consistent with the spare chopper part Alpha had thrown down at their feet. *Probably Chinese,* he thought, remembering the stamped metal and Hendry's warning that those guys were swarming over the region like hornets.

What *wasn't* swarming, he noticed, were the grass mimics. In fact the entire white horde that seemed to be permanently camped outside the igloo was gone.

Mac approached the slab that served as a door, squinting through the thick, polished ice as he went, but he could detect no movement at all. He put his shoulder to the portal and immediately felt it begin to move. *I can do this,* he thought, now giving serious consideration to pushing it open and taking his chances outside. The more rational part of his brain decided to wait *a few minutes more.*

"But where the hell is—" Mac said, his question interrupted by sudden movement. It came from deep within the mist, which swirled upward, displaced by a new wave of grass mimics. *There's something different about them,* Mac thought, straining to determine exactly what that could be.

It's their color, he realized, aware now that many of the blades rushing toward him had a distinctive crimson tint. Mac felt his insides beginning to twist in an all-too-familiar manner. *Is that Yanni's blood?*

The answer arrived barely more than thirty seconds later, but for R. J. MacCready those seconds were longer than any hour.

Out of the snowy mist strode one of the Morlocks. It was the same individual, the one they'd been calling Alpha, who'd prevented Yanni from seeing what had taken place in the cavern. Now the grim-faced creature was carrying her on his shoulder.

"You are shittin' me," Mac muttered, to himself.

Predictably, the sea of white and red pseudo-grass parted before the Morlock as he advanced toward the igloo entrance, simultaneously closing behind once the giant had passed.

Stopping just shy of twenty feet from the ice prison, Alpha set Yanni down gently and gave her a slight nudge forward. Yanni glanced back for a moment, as if to confirm what she was being asked to do. Then, seemingly without giving it another thought, she began walking toward the igloo.

Mac pounded against the ice—screaming out against the realization that she was being forced to walk into her own execution.

"No!"

Looking quite calm, Yanni responded with a wry smile and a wave of her hand. Then she stepped away from the Morlock and into the seething carpet of grass mimics.

Mac cursed, throwing his weight against the door and pushing for all he was worth. The slab fell forward. By then Yanni was so close that she had to jump back a step to avoid getting her feet crushed by the ice.

Mac threw his arms around Yanni and spun her toward the opening. She responded with a look of surprise at what turned out to be his unnecessary attempt to use his body as a shield. The zoologist had failed to notice that the grass had parted before Yanni, fleeing in such haste that not a single mimic stood within ten feet of them.

"Mac, what on earth are you doin' out here?"

Before he could reply, a shove from behind sent them both tumbling into the igloo and immediately the Morlock reset the door and slammed it back into place.

"I . . . I thought he was trying to kill you, *too*."

"What? I was perfectly safe," she said. "Take a whiff. I call it *Eau de Elephas*."

Mac responded to her joke with unexpected silence.

"Mac, what did you mean 'kill me too'?" Yanni said, amid a very sudden realization that they were no longer a trio.

Mac turned away from her.

Normally, the friends would have talked for hours about Yanni's twenty minutes at the corral. Instead, in utter silence, they thought only about Jerry.

1,500 feet above the south Tibetan Labyrinth
July 13, 1946

D o you see that ledge ahead of us?" the Chinese helicopter pilot asked. He was pointing to the exact spot that Yanni had indicated to Mac, on the day their trek began.

Captain Mung Chen took off his aviator glasses and squinted through the cockpit window. "Yes, take us down lower."

As the shelf came nearer, the copilot contacted the crew of the second chopper, who put their ship into a slow holding pattern circuit as Mung's craft went in for a closer look.

The resulting flyby revealed the same low wall of stones that had prevented Mac and his friends from tumbling off the ledge.

This time, however, the rocks and snow gave silent testimony to more than the work of a past civilization.

"There's another helicopter down there," the pilot said. "Or at least part of one."

Once again, Captain Mung strained to see, but this time he shook his head. "Where? I can see nothing but those low ridges."

"Lying at the base of that rock wall flanking the terrace," said the pilot.

"Nature hates straight lines, sir," the copilot added. "Those two long shadows in the snow appear to be rotors—and over there, maybe a wheel assembly."

Now Mung saw them as well. "Ours?"

"Impossible to say from here," the pilot responded.

"Can you put us down, *safely*?"

The pilot flashed a brief but confident smile. "I think there is just enough room for both ships, sir."

"Good. Inform our sister ship, then take us in."

Only after Mung had returned to his seat in the cabin did the two flyers exchange looks. "*Both* ships?" the copilot repeated, somewhat incredulously.

"He was just about to ask us anyway," the pilot responded. "And you . . . 'Nature hates straight lines'? Who said that? Certainly not you!"

The copilot shrugged. He knew it was either Buddha or some long-dead English landscape architect. Though he could never quite remember which.

July 14, 1946

The pair of prisoners from New York never heard the new arrivals. The Chinese were a long way off, miles beyond the maze of underground passages and high above a sound-muffling sea of snowy fog.

What they *did* notice, just before nightfall on the second day after Jerry's death, was an increase in the activity outside their prison.

"What do you think they're up to?" Yanni asked.

Mac shrugged his shoulders but remained silent. She had yet to draw anything like a normal response from him.

"Mac?"

Silence.

"You really should eat something," she followed, although even she had left her food mostly untouched and neither of them had slept.

"Please leave me alone," Mac said at last. Then he curled up on the ground with his back turned.

Previously, the three prisoners had reluctantly begun sleeping in what Mac referred to as "a thermodynamically efficient position." Yanni had actually preferred Jerry's term, *spooning*, although they were careful not to use that description around Mac.

Yanni approached her friend and lay down behind him. She could sense his shoulders tensing up and he inched himself away from her.

"Good night, Mac," she said gently. Then, moving to fill the space between them, she placed a hand on his shoulder. Mac allowed it.

"He's gone, Yanni," he whispered.

"Shhhh," she whispered back. "Good night, Mac."

M ac supposed he should have dropped off into sleep from sheer exhaustion, but it seemed unimaginable to him that his thoughts could stop racing for even a few seconds. He had become so accustomed to stepping into and out of improbable shit storms with Jerry that it had become possible for both of them to let down their guard—even here, among creatures no more predictable than tigers.

Yanni had only recently accepted Jerry as "our kind of stupid," but she did not know the half of it. Their first mission together had begun in the Pacific, after Jerry received word that "Captain America"—actually a lieutenant jg—and his crew *might* have survived the total destruction of their torpedo boat. No one at the time seemed willing to believe it. The "proof of life" was a message found by a local fisherman, carved into a coconut. Against a "no-go" decision from their superiors, Mac and Jerry went into freelance mode, eventually stealing a canoe from under the noses of ten thousand Japanese soldiers stationed on the nearby island of Kolombangara. Following a set of cryptic directions and a familiar surname carved onto the shell, they found the grateful lieutenant and most of his crew on a tiny island that Jerry had aptly described as "a pile of sand with visions of grandeur." Ultimately, Mac took a spearhead in the leg for his troubles—from a friendly native.

"You definitely can't make this shit up," Mac later told a less-than-pleased senior officer. Eventually it took a personal call from Captain America's father to get him and Jerry off the hook for disobeying an order.

Jerry was also present when, during an interlude between missions and while the spear-pierced muscles of his leg healed, Mac met a youthful genius named Tamara, who saw in ants and bees the intelligence of "superorganisms," and who would certainly have been helpful in figuring out inchworm grass and Morlocks. Mac had noticed only during their first two minutes together that

Tamara bore the childhood scars of smallpox. From the instant they began speaking, he could remember only her unforgettable grace, her kindness, her brilliance.

And Jerry was there with him, in that place of tropical beaches and grief, wonder and loss, beauty and regret. He was at Mac's side when he no longer needed a crutch to walk, was healed to the point of "mission ready" and sailed away, vowing that he would return to the island.

Only three weeks later, the beaches and the forests belonged to carrion-feeders, the island having been overrun by the enemy. Tamara, her family, and more than two thousand civilians disappeared, with less mystery but even more all-embracing thoroughness than Rome's Ninth Legion.

Jerry had been there to console him.

"Tamara—"

Mac's arm thrashed involuntarily, just as he began to doze off. "Shhhh," Yanni whispered again. "It's all right."

He'd never spoken to Yanni about Tamara. Back then, he scarcely had time to grasp the fact she was gone when he received word that another of the war's evils had claimed his mother and sister. Jerry had been there for that, too.

In one way or another, bit by bit, the world had taken everyone Mac loved. There seemed little left to do about it, except to keep everyone else at arm's length and attend to the job: *Save lives, where you can. Keep exploring and writing, exploring and writing.*

"Some men *can* be, and maybe *should* be, islands," Mac had recently told Jerry.

Slow to trust and emotionally emaciated, Mac came to regard himself as the human equivalent of a remote island—a place where nature itself veered off into different and unexpected directions. His way of thinking had likewise evolved along its own directions, and perhaps even flourished. It was, he suspected, what had turned him into a think-outside-the-box type of explorer, and so useful to the military.

"*Jerry*—" Mac's arm lashed out, awakening Yanni again. She was still there, trying to console him.

"It's okay, Mac. Try to rest."

I can't, he thought, and wondered if it would be possible ever to rest again. He let out a deep breath and felt Yanni's hand on his shoulder. Somehow Mac knew that she would not remove it. And she did not, even after sleep eventually reached out and took him into its house.

Long past midnight, yet before the phosphorescent world outside came alive, Mac and Yanni were awakened by the loud arrival of several Morlocks outside the igloo.

The pair sat up as the ice door was pulled aside. They saw a blur of movement in the dark and something large was flung onto the ground. Landing with an audible grunt, it became immediately apparent that this late-night delivery was another person, and as the ice door slid closed, the fur-clad figure sat up and shook his head—as if trying to convince himself that what he had just experienced was simply a bad dream.

The man turned to the two silent figures sitting on the floor. He spoke a few words in Chinese, seeming to ask a question.

MacCready, who had only a rudimentary knowledge of the language, tugged at an earlobe as he tried to work out the dialect and the translation. He replied at last, with a short phrase of his own.

Yanni nudged Mac with an elbow. "What'd he say?"

"I think he wants to know where he is."

"And what'd ya tell him?"

"I *think* I told him 'Up Shit Creek.'"

"That's helpful, Mac," Yanni said, with a head shake, although she did consider the first sign of a "Mac-like" response to be a welcome improvement.

Their guest needed a few seconds to rough out the meaning of Mac's slang. Then he sighed and lowered his head into his hands.

O nly a day before, the helicopter pilot (whose name was Li Ming) believed that he was prepared for anything. He knew that strange encounters had been part of the region's mythology for centuries, and after the carved-up remains of a Yeren were actually loaded aboard his craft he began to accept that the old stories about monsters in the hills were not merely warnings, contrived to keep people away. Yet when one of the mythical giants finally stood before him, Li Ming was taken completely by surprise.

In the end, they *had* been able to land both of the remaining helicopters on the challengingly small table of flat ground. After Captain Mung's initial plans unraveled with the disappearance of their third aircraft, Li Ming's commanding officer had decided to consolidate his remaining force of thirty men. They would explore the mountain pass, leading away from the landing zone—the very spot where an American helicopter had recently crashed, and where someone or something had attempted to hide the wreckage.

Captain Mung's men set up camp on the improbably located terrace, their tents hidden among the rocks and as far away as possible from the vertigo-inducing cliff. The pilot and four other men were selected to remain behind. They would safeguard the helicopters from intruders and from the engine-degrading effects of the harsh winds and temperature changes.

Li Ming's first sunrise at the base camp broke clear and relatively warm. Within an hour, Captain Mung, accompanied by twenty-three heavily armed soldiers, marched away from the landing site. Wang Tse-lin, the scientist Mung had evidently coerced into joining the expedition, went along as well.

The two flyers who had safely landed Captain Mung's "Dogship" watched as the last members of the expedition disappeared around a bend.

"Well, this is going to be fun," Li Ming mumbled after briefly touring the perimeter of their new home base.

"Would you rather be going with them?" his copilot countered.

The pilot shrugged. "At least we'd be doing something exciting, instead of babysitting a pair of Russian bananas."

The copilot was just about to express his preference for bananas when Li Ming gestured toward the helicopters. "Which reminds me," he said, "you should check those safety tethers. I'm sure Captain Mung wouldn't be pleased to find that a sudden gust caught us unprepared, and that his ride had left without us."

The copilot nodded and trudged off toward the nearer of the two aircraft, then stopped and shot Li Ming a quizzical look. "*Me* check the safety tethers? And what are you going to do, stand around here and brood?"

"No," Li Ming said, pointing to a rock near the base of the sheer wall. "I'm going to stand over *there* and piss."

During the next three minutes, and with disorienting rapidity, the air shifted from dead calm to snow-driving gusts. The copilot, meanwhile, had double-checked the straps that secured the two helicopters' landing gear to a set of thick pegs, driven into solid bedrock. He was annoyed to find that he actually had to tighten one of them.

"Nice job those two did on this thing!" he called out to his friend.

There was no response, so he called again, walking through knee-deep snow to the beginning of the footprint trail left by his partner. The trail ended at a puzzling pattern of markings and fresh-frozen urine, *as if he had started pissing against the base of a boulder that was no longer there.*

Perplexed, he glanced to a spot just beyond Li Ming's trail before letting out a frighteningly childish cry that echoed along the full length of the rock wall.

It took a fellow copilot and two other men a good five minutes to calm him down. By then they had all seen the footprints in the snow—far larger than those of any human and with an oddly placed big toe.

Approximately three hours into their trek down the mountain pass, Captain Mung and his group came to a dead end. An enormous wall of stone and ice stood blocking their path.

Wang stared up at the imposing formation, then took a peek over the edge of the "trail"—which fell off into clouds and vast open space. "Do we go back?"

"No," the officer replied, "we go up."

"But—"

"Get those climbers up here," Mung called out. "Everyone else form a defensive perimeter. Be ready for an attack at any moment."

Instinctively, a part of him already knew that the enemy would choose its own ground, its own striking distance, in its own good time. He also believed that a difficult cliff ascent, led by climbers burdened with coils of rope, harnesses, and an array of strange-looking gear, might bring the Yeren out. But after four hours, the twenty-five men and their supplies had made it uneventfully up the sheer wall and onto flat ground.

Mung was able to plot another trail almost immediately, and there was even a broad "tabletop" formation along the wall, where they could pitch their tents and spend the night.

As Wang began to unpack his one-man pup tent, the officer approached, shaking his head.

"I want you to set yours up there," he said, pointing to a patch of ground away from the cluster of soldiers' tents, and slightly up a "trail" that was now mostly obscured by lengthening shadows.

"But why?" Wang asked, clearly unnerved.

"Some of the men think your presence here is bad luck," he responded, though far from convincingly. "Just do as I say."

The scientist glanced over at the others. None of them appeared to be paying the slightest attention to him. Knowing that it would be senseless to argue, he picked up his pack and trudged away.

"And stay in your tent, once it gets dark," the captain called after him. "Until I tell you to come out."

By way of affirmation, Wang gave the officer a wave without turning around. *Wonderful,* he thought. *And here I was planning on a midnight tour of the place.*

About twenty before midnight, and as a nearly full moon was setting, Wang Tse-lin dreamed he went again to the Shennongjia Forest.

His dream of Shennongjia night began with the metallic clamor of insects that he could not identify, and the barely audible high-frequency calls of the bats hunting them. Then the night sounds died—as if someone had turned off a switch. For a while all that could be heard was his own breathing, until something began rustling through the brush, just outside his tent—something strangely familiar. This time, when Wang tried to sit up, he discovered that he was trapped inside a canvas-covered cage. Straining to hear what might be happening beyond the tent, he suddenly wished that he could not hear at all.

Outside his cramped prison, the gentle rustle of stealthy movement had been transformed into the slurping and crunching of a bestial meal. Growing louder and more disturbing with each passing second, the merriment of a ghoulish feast quickly became terrible beyond words. Wang started tearing at the canvas and screaming. The sounds did pause, as if in response, but for some reason Wang found this even more disturbing than the dark banquet. Slowly, someone dragged the tarp away from his cage. The scientist could see figures huddled around a campfire now, their bodies naked, slick with grease and blood. One of them was holding a severed arm, and as the reveler stood and shambled toward the cage, his face broke into a hideous grin. The other monsters began to rise and—

An explosion jolted Wang into semi-wakefulness and he struggled to free himself from the hungry embrace of the revelers. By the time the second blast came, the captive knew that he had been wrestling with his own sleeping bag. Freeing himself, he threw back the tent flap and stumbled outside. Beams of light alternated between his tent and the trail, one of them sweeping upward and hitting him square in the eyes.

"I ordered you to stay in your tent until I called you out!" said Captain Mung. Then, in what had quickly become the conscious extension of his still-vivid nightmare, the voice and the light were gone, leaving Wang momentarily blind.

Another man rushed past him without stopping.

"*But I—*" Wang called after the officer. As his eyes adapted to the haphazard sweep of flashlight beams, he could see Mung and two of his men, each holding rifles and staring down at a large figure on the ground. Eventually, three separate beams converged on the kill—which glistened wetly under the flashlights. Wang squinted and stepped closer. His first impression was that someone had just shot the largest bear that he had ever seen. But he already knew that this was no bear.

"These are not your grandmother's Yeren," Mung told the crowd of soldiers, as they gathered three deep around the body.

The officer went down on one knee and used both hands to lift the creature's head out of the spreading puddle of blood. Mung turned the fur-covered face toward his men. For a few seconds more, it continued to pulse blood through a gaping hole where the right eye had been. The left eye seemed to have been following the movements of Mung's electric lantern.

A trick of the light, perhaps? the scientist thought.

But now Wang was able to see clearly (too clearly) the moment the life went out of that eye.

"*This* is what we are up against!" the captain said.

As Wang Tse-lin watched, and as the officer continued to address his men, several facts were becoming apparent. First, Mung had not hesitated to use him for bait. But, as unnerving as this was, it also made perfect sense. *He needs warriors to carry out his mission. My presence here is an afterthought.* Second, the officer had been *expecting* a visit from the Yeren. The two marksmen Mung had assigned to lie in wait were all the proof he needed of this. Despite his being set out as bait, Wang's respect for Captain Mung's tactical and logistical skills had actually gone up a notch. The third realization concerned the Yeren themselves, for Wang could see that while there were certainly characteristics shared by this creature and the Shennongjia specimen, it was like comparing a howler monkey to a gorilla.

By the time the captain had finished his examination, Wang Tse-lin knew that these beasts were *not* the mischief makers of deep-forest lore. This species was the supremely adapted denizen of a dangerous and unfamiliar world. It was also a world in which the scenario for any meaningful contact was now completely redefined. In the eyes of the Yeren, he, Captain Mung, and all of the others had been transformed from intruders into murderers.

In the Valley of the Morlocks
4:00 A.M., July 15, 1946

H e says he's a helicopter pilot," Mac told Yanni, as they sat across from a disheveled-looking Asian man dressed in an insulated flight suit.

"Can you ask him what he's doing here?"

Mac resumed his duties as a reluctant translator, first trying to work out the question, then listening to the rapid-fire response.

"No dice," Mac said with a shrug, before deciding to take another tack. "Yanni, could he have gotten out of the chopper that came down in the valley?"

"No way, Mac," Yanni said. "I told you what happened to those guys. *All* of them."

"Then our friend here got snatched from a separate group—Chinese army, from the looks of it."

Yanni gestured to the new arrival, who looked not quite thirty years old. "How 'bout we lay off him for a while? Ya gotta figure this guy's just gone through some serious shit."

"Serious shit," the man repeated.

Two sets of eyes turned toward the pilot.

"You understand us?" Mac asked.

The man nodded. "I go to flight school in Hawaii," he said, in heavily accented but perfectly understandable English. "Before war."

"What's your name?" Yanni asked.

"Li Ming," the man replied, and gestured toward a gourd sitting on the floor. "Water, please."

Mac passed him the container, then watched as the man gulped down the contents. When he finished drinking, Mac held out a wad of foil, filled with the crushed remains of a chocolate bar he had been saving for a "special occasion."

"And how did you wind up here, Li Ming?" he asked, nonchalantly.

Instinctively, the man reached for the candy bar, but he then hesitated and pulled back his hand. "Would you disclose your mission . . . if *you* are sitting here instead of me?"

Mac smiled. "No, I wouldn't." Then he gestured for the man to take the chocolate anyway—which he did, unfolding the wrapper.

"How did *you* . . . wind up here?" the pilot asked, between bites.

"You're kiddin', right?" Yanni said, stepping forward.

"Helicopter," Mac responded, surprising her.

"Not so much a good hiding job," the Chinese pilot responded quickly—*too quickly*.

"So your men landed up there as well," Mac said, though it was clearly not a question.

Li Ming immediately realized what had happened. Turning away, he directed his stare to a point beyond the igloo's wall of ice.

Mac flashed Yanni a short, knowing nod.

She returned it with a nod of her own, then moved in to stand beside the downcast newcomer. "Don't be so hard on yourself, Li Ming," she said. "Mac's a professional ball-breaker."

Li Ming did not respond. His only concern appeared to be the three white-furred giants that had suddenly appeared out of the snowy mist, and who were now striding toward the igloo door with what seemed to Yanni to be a lot like grim determination.

CHAPTER 14

Strange Days

I learned from my dog long before I went to Gombe that we weren't the only beings with personalities.

—JANE GOODALL

We misuse language and talk about the "ascent" of man. We understand the scientific basis for the inter-relatedness of life, but our ego hasn't caught up yet.

—JILL TARTER

Pliny's chamber
June, A.D. *67*

Long before the first rays of dawn began slanting across the floor of the Ceran dome, Severus's language-teaching physician entered the living quarters and roused the groggy historian. As Proculus stood by, trying to assess what was happening, she forced Pliny's mouth open and squirted the contents of a small, wine-bag-like pouch into his throat. Another Ceran entered carrying a bowl of thick, stringy soup and the physician gave Pliny a wordless prompt to consume it. Proculus noted that this time

there would be no force-feeding, though the Cerae stood by anyway, as if to ensure that Pliny would finish every drop.

Within an hour, Pliny came to realize that whatever Ceran
medicines had healed Proculus's wounds and caused the tumors
to fall from his face were vastly improving his own breathing.
The sinus pain and asthma that had begun troubling him before the voyage and worsened with increasing altitude were now
gone seemingly beyond recall. He longed to record these amazements in ink and papyrus, but even the absence of such materials
seemed no cause for despair, since his normally sharp memory
had suddenly become noticeably sharper.

After sunset, when he stepped out onto the balcony with Proculus, Pliny discovered that even his vision had improved enormously. He was now able to discern new details in the luminous
vegetation—as diverse in its abundance as it was in variety.

At dawn, on the third day of their imprisonment, three attendants brought bowls with combs and washcloths soaked in warm
water. One of them began tugging at the back of Pliny's head,
and it occurred to him that she not only wanted to comb his
hair but to braid patterned fur into it. She had long, agile arms
and a far more slender body shape than the brutish warriors.
Yet somehow he knew that she did not belong to the physician
caste.

"*No!*" he heard Proculus shout, and as Pliny gently pushed
away the hand that held a comb near his head, the attendants apparently got the message that neither man wanted his hair pulled
or braided with camouflage. The three Cerae backed off, made
something vaguely like a polite bowing motion, then sat on their
haunches and stared at the two Romans.

After Pliny was handed a fresh serving of the soup and began
to eat, a moan reached him from the adjoining cell.

It sounded as if the language lessons next door had continued throughout the night again—that, and apparently much more.

The attendants heard it too, and, aroused momentarily from their sphinxlike silence, they chittered back and forth in what could easily be interpreted as knowing, mischievous laughter.

Pliny could not shake the imagery from his mind, so he attempted to steer his thoughts elsewhere, wondering about the fate of his *medicus* and the other survivors they had left along the trail. *They must be in a safer place than up here,* he assured himself. Another grunt sounded from the other side of the black ice wall and Pliny tried to imagine what his *medicus* would make of Severus's current "entanglement."

"He'd think you're possessed, Severus," Pliny muttered to himself.

A high-pitched scream gave the historian an involuntary start, and glancing over at a thoroughly unnerved Proculus, Pliny knew that he too was uncertain if the scream had been human or not, pleasure or pain.

P liny's *medicus,* Chiron, was not a betting man, but if anyone had told him at the time of Pliny's departure into the highest reaches of the snow line that his commander could still be alive, he would certainly have wagered against it.

Chiron and nineteen of his men had settled in and waited beside the ruins of a fortified wall overlooking the city of Pandaya— what was left of it. The fragment of wall, which survived above the surge of water and boulders, was equipped on one side with a stone tower. Atop its observation platform, the *medicus* shared guard duty with the other survivors. The task had become an exercise in boredom, primarily because, with the exception of weeds and cottonwoods taking over the ruins, none of those on watch noticed any signs of life—human or otherwise.

And for a short while, it remained that way.

On the third day of Pliny's captivity, Chiron struggled back to consciousness in the aftermath of an attack that began with silent foot soldiers and ended with a dozen elephants striding forward, two by two. Adorned in elaborate body armor, their tusks had been outfitted with swordlike blades. But even beyond this menacing sight, it was the appearance of their fearsome riders that stunned the battle-tested *medicus* and his men. These warriors were the last thing he saw before a blow to the back of the head flashed his world to black, and they were the first thing he saw when someone pulled him brutally to his feet. With long ebony hair streaming backward, the wild-eyed elephant riders had removed most of their body armor to display an array of tattoos and self-inflicted scars. Their forearms and hands bore grotesque wounds as well—*oddly similar,* he thought—until a sudden realization solved the riddle. The brutish cavalrymen were wearing gauntlets fashioned from human flesh.

Ten of the *medicus*'s men had survived, and stood bound with him.

He could see that the foot soldiers were creating a bed of coals that now glowed bright enough to drown out the starlight. The entire area around the fire pit was crowded with the strangely garbed invaders. They reminded Chiron more of hyperkinetic insects than soldiers—some gyrating wildly against the shadows of dead Pandaya, others simply bashing into their brethren. All appeared to be intoxicated but nothing about their actions resembled conventional drunkenness. There were guttural chants and the sounds of a strange language coming from all around. Though it hurt to look up, Chiron could see that there were figures all along the top of the wall. Several fell and smashed to the ground amid wild laughter, only to be replaced by a constant stream of revelers pouring out of the former observation platform.

Then, in what Chiron could have sworn was a simultaneous action, the entire crowd went silent, the wild gyrations transforming into frightful whole-body vibrations that ran back and forth through the sea of human figures like a wave. The wave parted and six of the elephant riders, all of them women, advanced upon the Romans. Chiron squinted, not quite believing his own eyes. Each of the women had but a single breast. Where the one on the right side had been there was instead a hypertrophied pectoral muscle bearing the unmistakable scar of an old cautery wound.

"They burn away their breast to make themselves better archers," said the man next to Chiron.

"How do you know this?" the *medicus* asked, under his breath.

"They're Scythians," he said, and then, noticing that many of them had Far Eastern features, added, "or some strange offshoot."

"Scythians? I thought they were as extinct as the Babylonians."

The cavalryman nodded toward three of the approaching female warriors. "Maybe you can ask them about that."

CHAPTER 15

Fear of Pheromones

Each piece, or part of the whole of Nature is always an approximation of the complete truth, or the complete truth so far as we know it. In fact, everything we know is only some kind of approximation because we know that we do not know all the laws yet.
—RICHARD P. FEYNMAN

Evolution is opportunistic, hence unpredictable.
—ERNST MAYR

Metropolitan Museum of Natural History
New York City
July 15, 1946

D r. Nora Nesbitt believed no astronomer discovering a new planet beyond Pluto could have been filled more with a sense of wonder than she was every time she translated a newly puzzled-together page from Pliny's Omega Codex and made a connection no one had made before.

"This is pretty strange," she said, pushing her chair back from the lab bench where she had been working with Patricia Wynters. "*Too* strange."

"Compared to what?" asked Patricia.

"So, you know this apish doctor Pliny mentions?"

"You mean, Severus's favorite member of the Physician race?"

"That's the one. What if she infected our centurion with a mind-controlling parasite?"

"Severus?"

Nesbitt nodded, then they both stared in silence at a particularly well-preserved Pliny sketch depicting the Ceran version of a *medicus*. Although nearly half of the papyrus sheet had been lost to ancient disintegration and modern mishandling, the pair could make out enough to sum the portrait up in a few words: *bestial* was one they both agreed upon, and yet they also perceived a strange beauty in those barbaric eyes.

According to Pliny, even he eventually had to resist an inexplicable attraction to the little doctors. In one part of the codex, the famed historian/naturalist had dedicated nearly a half page of his near-microscopic penmanship to descriptions of their uniquely disgusting odor—"difficult to relate, how strongly it emanated from sweat-slicked fur." In a later entry, Pliny recalled that the cavalryman Proculus had developed a tolerance to it, while he himself had first become accustomed to the stench, before claiming to have actually come to like it. To Nesbitt, though, poor Severus seemed hopelessly bound to the musk of a very specific physician, and perhaps even addicted to it.

"Have you ever heard of the cat-rat paradox?" Nesbitt asked at last.

"No, but do tell."

"Well, you know how much I love protozoa?"

"Don't we all?" Patricia answered, without a hint of sarcasm.

"So, one of my recent favorites—*Toxoplasma gondii*—seems to have evolved a particular talent for toying around with the wiring of rat's brains. Normally, it's no stretch to infer that rodents must be born with an instinctive fear of cats, and all the smells associated with them."

"Okay."

"But in rodents infected with *Toxoplasma*—"

"Let me guess," Patricia interjected. "The rats end up being attracted to them."

Nesbitt smiled. "Yes, though it's more than just an attraction. Once infected with the parasite, male lab rats respond to cat hair, dander, skin oils, and even urine in the same way they respond to the pheromones female rats release to attract mates."

"That's interesting. Go on."

"And in my lab we've even seen the *Toxoplasma* parasite make the rat run *toward* the cat."

Patricia looked at the Pliny drawing with increasing amazement. "So . . . you're saying Pliny's man Severus became the lab rat in this equation."

"Could be," Nesbitt replied.

Patricia, who was clearly excited, continued the mental exercise. "Then the lab rat gets eaten, right?"

"Yes, and—?"

"And the parasite reproduces in the cat."

Nesbitt nodded. "It certainly appears so."

"Incredible."

The invertebrate biologist continued: "I'm beginning to think Pliny's Cerae were doing something similar, but of course operating on an even more complex level than a microbe infecting lab animals."

"You mean, the Cerans were consciously altering the responses normal humans *would* have had to being in close contact with them?"

"Right," Nesbitt said. "Maybe this Ceran version of a similar parasite started switching circuits in regions of the human brain that control emotions like fear or anxiety—or even sexual attraction?"

Both of the researchers took another look at Pliny's figure of the physician, and winced simultaneously.

"Do you realize how nutty this is beginning to sound?"

Nesbitt nodded. "I know, but just because this little hypothesis *sounds* crazy doesn't mean it's not crazy enough to be correct."

"Scary to imagine, really," Patricia replied. "A tiny invertebrate puppeteer, pulling Severus's and Pliny's strings—yuck."

"Yuck is right. Like I said, though, for now it's hypothetical. But the closer you look at our world, the more apparent it becomes that we live in a dancing matrix of hosts, parasites, and symbionts. And if Pliny wasn't just penning a fantasy, if this codex is more than some ancient myth—"

"You mean the part about a race that could 'mold life the way we mold clay'?"

Nesbitt took a moment to consider Pliny's quote again—important enough for him to have repeated at least a half-dozen times up to this point in the manuscript. She nodded her head slowly. "That does seem to be the line that got us into this mess."

Patricia stood silently for a moment before responding. "Pliny's physicians could have designed that response themselves—based on something learned from prior encounters with people or animals outside the valley."

Dr. Nora Nesbitt, who now wore a wry smile, gestured back to the rest of the codex. "So, what does Pliny say finally happened to the centurion?"

"Hard to tell," Patricia said, and shook her head. "That's the frustrating thing. The codex breaks away into five or six missing pages, just when that part of Pliny's story gets most interesting."

August, A.D. 67

D uring the weeks since the capture, Pliny noticed that Severus and "Teacher" had become more inseparable than he ever imagined possible—or healthy.

In any case, no matter how far Severus might have pushed long-held taboos, Pliny believed he owed a depth of gratitude to that very same relationship. He had no doubt that Severus and the Ceran physician were the reason he and Proculus were still taking in air through heads that had not been smashed flat against a pillar of ice.

Language-wise, for all of their efforts, the Romans had learned no more than a score of Ceran words. *It was,* Pliny thought, *a maddeningly difficult exercise.* Inexplicably, teaching the Cerae Latin was only marginally easier—even basic things like colors. *Did they even interpret them in the same way?* Pliny wondered.

On some levels, it seemed easy to understand the Cerae—as in their mastery of architecture. On other levels, though, Pliny believed he might have had greater success trying to understand the thoughts of a housefly.

For a time, the Romans were allowed to walk freely through the garden plots, tasting all of their fruits, grains, and meaty gourds at will—and there Pliny learned that the word for each plant seemed to have its own unique series of Ceran whistles and inflections. *Each individual plant has its own name?*

Pliny guessed that more than two or three weeks must have passed before he began to acclimate, emotionally, to the utter alien nature of this hidden world. The rough treatment—pokes and prods mostly—from their chaperones continued even after they were reunited with Severus. It served to remind him that this was not the tour of wonders he had once hoped for. There were, of course, wondrous sights to behold—the wall of mountains surrounding the valley, the tower of stone and ice rising with intimidating majesty from the center of the fog lake. Despite the often-boorish treatment by their captors, Pliny might have even found some serenity in the view—if not for a few contrary facts.

The Cerae were clearly disturbed about something. Scores upon scores of them were hurrying up and down through the mist layer. And, fewer than forty paces from Pliny's overlook, two men staked out for Ceran target practice had been reduced to little more than smears on the ground, their distinctive garb revealing them to be Scythians.

"Though horrible, it brought great relief, to see immediately that they were not my men," Pliny would write later.

There was little time, however, for relief or reflection. Teacher, two other physicians, and seven members of the race Pliny had come to call "the warrior caste" ushered them along a path that descended below the lake of snow fog. The historian noted that though they usually displayed little emotion, the Cerae now exhibited undeniable signs that indeed something new had intruded upon their well-ordered and strangely lit world—something next of kin to chaos. Briefly, they approached and then passed the base of the central tower.

"There's something wrong with it," Pliny thought aloud.

Proculus replied, "It looks like no one is home."

Pliny shook his head, trying to peer through the floating snow—listening for sounds of a population that was no longer present.

"Severus, ask your friend where everyone went."

The centurion hesitated.

"Go on," Proculus urged, employing a tone that Pliny found as surprising as it was lacking in respect.

Severus waved his hands and flicked his fingers in what appeared to be developing into his private language with Teacher, reinforcing hand signals with a series of high-pitched syllables that barely passed for Latin.

The Ceran made a sound that only Severus could begin to understand, accompanied by a sharp hand motion. Once again the officer hesitated.

"Well?" Proculus said, now openly displaying impatience toward his superior.

Severus returned a stern expression that had nothing to do with Proculus's insubordination. "We would heed well, all of us, not to speak unless spoken to."

This time both Pliny and Proculus obeyed the order. Neither man had any way of knowing what was really happening. There was too little information available, no basis on which to conclude that the great building's inhabitants were fanning out into the wilderness—that they were preparing for war.

Ten or twelve stadia beyond the tower, the group came to the edge of an unusually quiet river, from which warm mists were rising and crystallizing in midair. Pliny hypothesized that this process, here and at similar bodies of water, functioned to regenerate the snow fog.

Teacher raised a hand, signaling, *Halt*.

Two more of the physician caste arrived, along with one of the more spidery-limbed Cerae that Pliny had identified as architects. At Teacher's urging, Severus unraveled a maplike sheet of unusually flexible paper and spread it out on the ground. It bore a set of immediately recognizable designs, illustrated from multiple angles, and rendered in Severus's precise hand.

"*What?*" Proculus asked. "You're showing them how to build catapults?"

"*No,*" said Pliny. "This cannot be true!"

A glare from a Ceran physician put an end to the comments while the "architect" unfurled a second sheet on the ground. The Romans could see that this too had been drawn in Severus's hand. The creature ran her fingers back and forth over both sets, clearly making careful comparisons between the two drawings.

He's not only showing them how we build our weapons, Pliny realized, *he's improving the designs.*

"You treasonous dog!" Proculus cried, and lunged toward his commanding officer and former brother-in-arms.

Teacher appeared between them in a white blur and before Pliny could even begin to track her motion, Proculus was airborne—with his face bleeding and two more teeth flying out of his mouth.

Nightfall, July 15, 1946

Although Mac was still asleep—albeit fitfully—Yanni Thorne found herself in a state of hyperalertness. Something more than the loss of their friend Jerry kept her from eating or sleeping, but she struggled to determine exactly what her instincts were trying to tell her. Certainly, there were the many possibilities. High on the list were the three angry Morlocks who had removed the Chinese helicopter pilot. Complicating *this* particular issue was Mac's insistence that one of the giants, a beast he began referring to as "Scarface," was the same individual who had killed Jerry.

On the other side of their icy window, the Morlock world was an unending parade of strange inhabitants. Even now she was watching a flower-mimicking animal that appeared near the outer edge of the igloo wall. The newly arrived "what-zit" attacked one of the grass-eating crabs they had seen previously, trapping it in a net of glowing red petals. Only a few days earlier she would have looked upon the flower mimic with a sense of wonder. Now, though, her thoughts were dark.

Yanni looked away to where Mac was sleeping, and was reminded of the fact that just a single grass mimic possessed enough toxin in its bite to nearly kill him. *There's widespread lethality here,* she concluded, and wondered how many deadly organisms they'd walked by already without any concern at all—the stand of Indian pipes, the strange little creature that darted across their path in the cave.

Yanni understood now that she had been looking at the world of the Morlocks through innocent eyes, but the reality was, *There is no innocence here.*

Outside, as if to support her newly acquired view, the "flower" was suddenly writhing on the ground like a viper bitten by something even *more* poisonous. The little crab scuttled away, carrying with it one of the petals.

Yanni reasoned in passing that if evolution *were* being sped up here, then the arms race between predator and prey had also been sped up. *But were the Morlocks controlling any of this? Or had they somehow dropped the reins?* From their unease with the grass mimics to their relationship with the little elephants, Yanni believed that any control the locals might have once wielded was now tenuous at best.

In the center of the igloo, R. J. MacCready was finally awake—staring up at the circular opening in the ceiling.

"Did something just scream?" he wondered.

"Yeah, a flower," she replied.

"Oh, okay."

"How's that leg of yours?"

"Feels a lot better, actually," he reassured her.

Yanni did not continue the conversation. A sudden movement had drawn her attention outside, again.

The world tonight was so black that it was impossible to see beyond the limited range of bioluminescent speckles on the ground. No moonlight filtered down through the fog. Yanni could just barely recognize the shape of a Morlock walking out of the mist, eclipsing the little ground "stars" as it approached. It was Alpha and he was not alone. Trotting beside him were three of the bi-trunked mammoths, still wearing their choke collars but now without leashes.

Very quickly, and with deliberate stealth, Alpha slid the cell door aside and motioned for Yanni to come out. Mac hesitated, then followed her, expecting at any moment to be pushed forcefully back through the opening, but Alpha did not seem to care. The ground around the igloo was strangely free of grass mimics, though the harsh scent of the elephant-generated repellent Yanni had described previously provided an explanation for their absence.

There was no rumbling or snorting from the mini-mammoths, and no loud, whistling Morlock-speak, making it even more apparent that whatever the reason might be for this middle of the night visit, it was happening in secret. Alpha and the mammoths stood in utter silence and Yanni took the hint, signaling Mac to do likewise. Then the Morlock led her and the three little elephants to a spot some thirty feet away, for what R. J. MacCready supposed must be the strangest conference of all time.

Mac checked their surroundings—on the lookout for less friendly visitors. *One hairy son of a bitch in particular.*

On previous nights, at about this time, phantom shapes, wider than the stretch of his arms, had fluttered overhead. Tonight, he noticed, there were no flyers. In fact the only trace of nightlife, besides their mammalian visitors, was the "poisoned flower" Yanni had been watching earlier. Mac felt a sudden unease that its phosphorescent blush was returning and as the minutes passed, the creature had rekindled brightly enough to illuminate a broadening swath of the mist. The meeting participants seemed too busy to notice.

Not so fast there, son, Mac thought, before moving quickly toward the steadily strengthening glow and stamping the bogus flower flat, as a smoker might stamp out a cigarette on a sidewalk. Then he kicked some dirt on top of the glowing red bits.

"Evolve your way out of that one," he muttered to himself.

Mac's mind-set was "all mission" now and his only mission was to get Yanni out of this valley alive. He was also starting to hope against hope (something Mac did very rarely) *that Yanni's pals might have the very same thing in mind.*

Soon after Mac finished his novel impersonation of "lights out," the meeting ended. Yanni took a moment to give an approving nod to his handiwork before Alpha motioned them back into the igloo.

"What's going on?" Mac asked.

"Shhhh," Yanni whispered. "You're not gonna believe this."

They scrambled inside. The seal was closed silently behind them, and the four night visitors disappeared, in perfect silence.

"Okay, spill it," Mac said.

"Seems that Alpha wants to learn more about the mammoths— and he wants my help."

"Oh?" Mac replied, unable to hide either his skepticism or his concern.

"Yeah, well, apparently at least one Morlock has discovered that these little elephants are a lot smarter than they've been letting on."

"How smart?"

"*Very.* Maybe smarter than us."

Mac shook his head, amazed and incredulous at the same time. "And remind me again how you figured this all out, in what—five minutes?"

"I don't know how to explain it," Yanni said. "Trying to understand both of these species is kinda like pounding at a cement wall. At first you don't get anywhere. Then this little crack appears—and maybe there's a hint of feelings or a specific emotion. You keep hammerin' away and suddenly there's light shining through it. Now when you move closer to that tiny crack of light, you can start to see a whole lot, even stuff on the other side."

Mac remained silent.

"Like I said, it's tough to describe. But toss in the bit of Latin that Alpha and I share, and I just *know* what's going on now."

"But, Yanni," Mac said, then hesitated, "the Morlocks *eat* these elephants. And they—"

"And your point is what?"

"My point is, why all this sudden interest in cooperating with a menu item?"

"I think things are different with these individuals," said Yanni, firmly. "I get the sense from Alpha, *and* from those three mammoths, that they've been treating each other as equals."

"What about Alpha's brethren?" Mac added. "What about the asshole who—"

"I think Alpha's in this by himself," Yanni replied, cutting off

Mac's thought before it went any further. "I really believe he sees the outside world closing in. First us, now the Chinese are back again, this time in flying machines. I get the feeling he's looking at cooperation as a necessity—for both species."

Mac nodded. "Well," he said, grudgingly, "I suppose if anyone can help get you out alive, it'd be the Morlock *jefé* and his mammoth posse."

Yanni managed a quiet snort of a laugh. "Now *there's* a sentence I'll bet you never thought you'd be uttering."

With the stakes as high as they had become, Mac pushed the irony of their situation aside and decided to play the skeptic. "Look," he began, "what do we know for sure? These Morlocks are sentient creatures. Right?"

"Right," Yanni replied, quickly recognizing where Mac was taking the conversation.

"Well, then they can lie and deceive just like everybody else."

"Sure," Yanni said, "but if I missed the boat on this one, then Alpha's got the elephants fooled, too. And why bother doing that? They've already got 'em completely enslaved."

"All right, good point," Mac acknowledged, "even if their way of thinking should turn out to be completely alien to us . . ." He trailed off into thought for a while, adding up the facts. "Two wildly intelligent species," he said at last. "Existing side by side as master and slave for who knows how long? Can it even *be* changed?"

Yanni stared into the night. "Of Morlocks and mammoths," she said to no one in particular.

"It'll be tough," Mac added. "And even more dangerous with the third species elbowing its way in."

Yanni shook her head. "Yeah, the ones with rockets and atomic bombs."

Mac shuddered inwardly. "In a few years, the question won't be about masters and slaves. It'll be about whether this world of theirs exists at all."

"Or ours for that matter," Yanni added.

"Or ours," Mac conceded.

On the floor of Pliny's Mist Lake

August, A.D. *67*

The catapults were still under construction when Pliny and Proculus, now separated from Severus by members of the soldier caste, were led to what Pliny would later christen, for his codex, "The Pink and White Terraces."

He had never imagined, much less seen, the like. For many centuries, perhaps for many thousands of centuries, steaming hot water must have been rising from somewhere deep beneath the valley walls, trickling downhill and depositing pink and white minerals in tier upon tier of gently overflowing pools. It was, to Pliny, a stairway to the gods. He could not see the top of it.

But all thoughts of beauty were soon squashed as their own survival again became a matter of grave doubt. The abrupt transition occurred once Pliny saw what the Cerae had been cultivating in the pools, and once he realized what was being dragged out from beneath mounds of crushed ice. He closed his eyes, trying to calm his mind against the atrocity and taking several deep breaths before opening them again. When he did, the view became even more overwhelming.

Severus, what have you brought us into?

Against the haunting beauty of terraced pools, against strata of fog that obscured everything above and beyond the nearer pools and subdued a valley's usual level of noise, the area around the catapults was a scene drawn from the deepest and busiest level of Hades.

Pliny felt sick with anger, watching as pieces of naked Roman bodies were hauled from beneath mounds of crushed ice by Ceran physicians and elephants—each of which, though small, possessed a powerful trunk, more muscular than a physician's arm. The body parts were from his own soldiers, the ones who died all around him during that first afternoon at the valley entrance. Five of the so-called physicians were separating muscles from bones—peeling them into long strips, which were immediately scrutinized, as if the examiners were searching for gold.

One of them pulled something yellowish and stringy from a ribbon of curled flesh. The "string" was about the length of a man's forearm, and though still ice-chilled, the physician pinched it just hard enough to provoke a wormlike wiggle, verifying that the parasite was indeed very much alive.

Pliny looked away; but it seemed there was no direction in which he could turn his head and avoid a new vision of hell. The explorer knew very little about the pain-dealing guinea worms, little beyond a warning from his *medicus* that some of the men had apparently contracted them while on leave in Alexandria.

At the edge of a pink and white terrace, three more physicians had been spooling worms out of the water and onto the ends of long sticks. Although closely resembling the parasites Pliny had seen pulled from Roman flesh, these creatures were different— each equipped with a short, needle-like probe at one end. Judging from the caution exhibited by those doing the spooling, these worms were a far more aggressive and dangerous lot.

Pliny attempted to reason out what he was seeing, struggling to accept what he feared was the only logical conclusion. *Weeks ago, the Cerae must have begun extracting parasites from Roman bodies. Now they have succeeded in breeding them.*

Nearby, a familiar voice cried out, but Pliny never heard it. As the reality of what he was seeing invaded his brain, Pliny failed to notice that Proculus was no longer at his side.

"They're not just breeding these worms," Pliny said to no one in particular. "They've processed them into something new."

"May the sands lie softly on your grave, Severus!" came the familiar voice, and Pliny gave a start as if snapping awake from a nightmare. "So the dogs may dig you up!"

The historian turned away from the worm spoolers to face yet another vision from the depths of hell. Proculus, now bound hand and foot, was being dragged by two Ceran warriors toward a series of circular pits in the ground. Less wide than the span of a man's arm, each of the excavations was deep enough to hold a Roman soldier, up to the level of his chest.

"Spawn of Cretan whores!" cried Proculus, who, despite the dire circumstances, continued to roll out an impressive litany of curses.

At first the Cerans simply stood the cavalryman before a row of the holes. Then, in a move that surprised Pliny (at a time when he feared nothing could any longer come as a surprise), a particularly large member of the warrior caste rubbed Proculus's face in a fur-tangled armpit. It followed up this rude exercise by chest-butting the centurion back and forth between itself and another Ceran. Having anointed the Roman with a stench that could be smelled even at Pliny's distance, they lowered Proculus into one of the pits.

On either side of Proculus were similar holes containing bodies, though they did not appear to be Romans. Any further identification was impossible, because their heads, shoulders, and armor breastplates were cloaked in seething masses of what Pliny believed to be white ants.

"Remain *calm*," Pliny told his friend. "We've survived worse situations than this" (*even if I cannot think of one right now,* he left unsaid).

Then, naturally, the situation became worse. Three new prisoners were herded out of the snowy fog and dropped into pits. Spewing what were curses in their own tongue, Pliny was able to identify their tribal origins: *Scythians.* He observed that the pit-bound corpses flanking Proculus were also Scythians, a point made clear as the living veils of white fell away—revealing similar tunics and armor, draped upon bloodless husks. One of the dead's armor plates had been scavenged from a slaughter. It bore the crest of a Roman *medicus.*

Chiron . . . Pliny did not have time to utter the word. Proculus's movements suddenly became frantic and it was all so clearly too easy to know why. In that moment, a small part of him would have traded for a quick death at the mountain pass, if in the bargain he would never have lived to see this. Having fallen from their wraithlike former hosts, the veils of white ants now reappeared from below, streaming over the ground and toward Proculus. Pliny prepared himself to turn away at the last instant—but to his utter surprise, instead of pouring down around the centurion, the miniature horde hesitated, then began to retreat.

Any solace Pliny received from the realization that Proculus might live did not outlast the revelation that the miniature army was now advancing on his own position—with the only buffer being the freshly trenched Scythians. Pliny squashed growing panic beneath his ever-present urgency to observe and record. His latest revelation was that the "ants" had never been ants. They were in fact some form of tick, each no larger than his pinky nail.

This time, the same veil of parasites that had spared Proculus spilled like milk down the three Scythian pits. The Easterners strained erratically against their bonds. Their struggle was not an escape attempt. It was a combination of anger and what the historian regarded as an honorable defiance. Within only forty beats of Pliny's racing heart, the ghostly white swarm began rising from beneath the prisoners' armor—streaming out in waves and then coalescing into tentacle-like branches across shoulders, necks, and finally heads. As the seconds passed, the branches began to change color—from pallid white to pinkish white, then finally, red.

They have refused to let out a single cry of pain, Pliny dictated to his mind's expedition log.

A new commotion at the stalactite-lipped terraces—concentrated at a pool filled with dark water and white worms—drew his attention away from the pits. Three large sticks, their ends coiled round and round with glistening trapped worms, were withdrawn from yet another black pool by physicians, who brandished the worm sticks like spears and moved toward the already parasite-covered prisoners.

The addition of transformed guinea worms to the already incomprehensible hellscape removed all doubt: *The Cerae have forged weapons from life itself.*

By the time worms were introduced to the carnivorous mix, the three Scythians in the pits were not nearly so drained of blood as to be spared by merciful unconsciousness. The ticks seemed to invade only the skin; now with the worms added, their bodies were being invaded from within and without. The end did not come quickly. For too many minutes, the Easterners continued to burble and quiver.

Pliny knew what he was watching, but true understanding was difficult. The term *biological weapon* did not yet exist. But there was a term for the engineering prowess that had produced ball bearings, and the movable pattern printing press that was the pride of Neapolis (Naples), and which Pliny had known until now as "superior technology." *That* term, for the moment, served him.

At last, Pliny turned his gaze back toward the catapults, where shoulder-width casks were being carefully stacked and arrayed nearby—empty and awaiting the addition of their deadly cargo. But while the engineer in him admired the subtle design modifications to the machines, a far greater part of him was sickened by Severus's actions, clearly directed at enhancing range and accuracy to serve an enemy of Rome. More sickening yet were the raw materials—the worms—contributed by the flesh of his own men.

"Severus, what have you done?"

Severus did not answer. Despite his work on the catapults, he was seized by the Cerae, covered in their stink, and thrown into a pit just like Proculus.

The bastard deserves it, Pliny told himself. The worms and ticks, he was certain, would soon spill in upon Severus—weapons of biological alchemy, made possible by an elixir hidden in those hellish pools of black water. Pliny remembered Proculus's initial suggestion that medicines used by the Cerae to repair his body were a form of magic. Pliny was the first naturalist to observe how easily an advanced technology could present the stubborn illusion of witchcraft. In much the same way his fellow Romans had learned to control steam, forge iron, and make concrete, the Cerae had plucked something out of nature, studied it, and built a thing the world had never seen before.

At the moment Pliny believed he could understand what was happening, two physicians lowered him into his own pit. They spared him the humiliating smearing with their stink, to which Proculus and Severus had been subjected.

In another moment, he saw two more Easterners shepherded out of the fog and lowered into pits. They too were spared the greasy-fur-smearing. This time the weapons burrowed into the newcomers' bodies with such astonishing rapidity that Pliny supposed, if these Scythians worshipped gods, they did not survive long enough to pray.

Pliny became transfixed by the small line of ticks that climbed out of the killing pits and began moving steadily, and apparently still hungrily, in his direction. Another trail fell in behind it. Then another. And yet another.

Pliny's world was reduced again to tunnel vision. So completely was he focused on the approaching blood-feeders that if not for the grunt she emitted, he would have failed to notice Teacher's immediate presence.

He looked up at her, his eyes trying to convey defiance.

She responded to him with an incomprehensible trill. Then, hefting a jug filled seemingly to the brim with weaponized life, she strode off directly toward Severus—the man Pliny vowed would, in a just universe, be written down into history as the modern-day Brutus.

Now the puzzle pieces were lining up, but analysis of their meaning remained elusive. Four things, he noticed. First: The ticks were avoiding the Cerae and even the tracks made in the ground by their feet. Second: They were avoiding Severus (who was covered in the stink of the Cerae). Third: They seemed to be consistently avoiding Proculus (also covered). Fourth: They swarmed straight to the Scythians (not covered). This led Pliny to know a fifth thing he had not quite pieced together before: He was not covered; he was, like the Scythian enemies, unprotected by the stench of the Cerae.

More trilling drew him away from these thoughts. He saw Severus bowing his head and even managing a submissive smile as Teacher laid a hand gently on his shoulder. Then, suddenly and without any warning or expression of emotion, she emptied the contents of her jug over his head.

Finally, more thorough analysis became possible. *Even unprotected, I might live through this after all,* Pliny realized. There was actually a bizarre logic behind what he was witnessing. *They have a plan,* he told himself. And the implications for the future of man were terrifying.

CHAPTER 16

Adam Raised Cain

Things fall apart. The center cannot hold.
—WILLIAM BUTLER YEATS

Things do not happen. Things are made to happen.
—JOHN F. KENNEDY

Show me the man and I'll find you the crime.
—LAVRENTIY BERIA

In the Valley of the Morlocks
July 17, 1946

"Where's Alpha?" Yanni asked. Her words were uttered in surprise, underscored by alarm. She and Mac had been shepherded by three Morlocks to a hill, along a path clear of grass mimics. As deeply as either of them could peer through the fog-suspended snow, they saw no sign of the giant.

This was the third time in two days that they had been taken out of their icehouse jail for what, at least on its surface, appeared to be the start of another leg-stretching exercise routine. During each outing, they were encouraged and even prodded to run through knee-deep dunes of snow. And each time, Alpha had led the way—until now.

Today they were led by a Morlock Yanni had never seen before, and accompanied by another Mac instantly recognized by a distinctive irregularity in the hair along one side of his face.

"What's wrong?" Yanni asked.

"Scarface here," Mac said, "is the asshole who—" He stopped short, having just taken a hard jab to the kidney. *Do these things murder each other, too?* he asked himself. *Is Alpha even alive?*

Though this new dilemma was bad enough, Mac realized that something more subtle had been troubling him. While Yanni still reeked of Alpha musk, even from two arm lengths away, he'd noticed that neither of them stank quite so much as the day before, or the day before that. He glanced around, looking for grass mimics—thankful that the repellent was still working— *for now.*

Without any threatening sounds, without any warning at all, Mac was grabbed from behind and forced face-first down into the snow.

Within that same moment, Yanni was lifted off the ground and, turning toward Mac, watched as dozens of snowflake mimics swarmed away from his face, separating themselves from the real snow that only partially obscured his features. The Morlock who held Yanni let out a series of whistles that sounded to her like approval—as if some sort of test were taking place, the nature of which was utterly inexplicable. What had become clear was a feeling that their chances of ever leaving this valley alive had just descended deeper into what her late husband would have designated as "the shitter."

"Mac?" she called out, recognizing that his abuser was the one he had come to call "Scarface."

"Listen, Yanni, just roll with it," he managed, as the beast hoisted him up under one arm and set off at a jog.

The last thing Yanni wondered, before Mac and Scarface disappeared into the mist, was whether those would be the last words she ever heard from him.

R. J. MacCready knew exactly where Scarface was carrying him, long before the entrance to the subterranean world came into view. He saw few other Morlocks during the trek, but those that they did pass appeared to turn away.

Within the earth, and even before they approached the newest of the "trophy room's" ice columns, Mac felt an all-too-familiar churning in his guts. He caught a glimpse of Jerry's parka and closed his eyes tightly, forcing himself to think about something else—anything else. *A way out of here or at least a way to put a dent in this guy's day.*

MacCready's ride ended with a fling along the ground and he skidded into a violent shoulder slam against an object he already understood too well.

Refusing to look at the freshly constructed stalagmite, Mac sensed the approach of his tormentor. Defiant, he stared up at the beast, right in the eye. Although Mac always detested the habit many people had of anthropomorphizing, at that moment he would have sworn on a first edition of Darwin's *Origin* that Scarface was gloating.

"Yeah, fuck you, too!" Mac snarled, calculating that this would probably be his very last second of conscious existence.

The creature reacted with something approximating a laugh,

removing from Mac's mind any doubt that his sentence in Scar-face's court was about to be carried out. During another of his rare hopes against hope, he wished that Jerry and everyone else he had lost would somehow be there to embrace him, even if only during a near-death hallucination.

Yanked off the ground by one foot, Mac drew a bead on the creature's genitals and lashed out with his free leg. Scarface side-stepped the attempt and slammed Mac's body into the pillar of ice—just hard enough to hurt, but not with enough force to break bones or to kill. *Not this time,* Mac told himself, before he was flung again along the ground.

Shaking his head, the zoologist struggled to his knees, using the nearest column for support. He was unable to avoid the sight of a modern Chinese soldier in an ice pillar—recognizable only by his uniform. *One of Li Ming's buddies,* he thought.

There was also no doubt in his mind that Scarface was draw-ing a malicious joy from this new exercise.

With a speed that, despite everything he had already wit-nessed, caught Mac by surprise, his tormentor rushed forward and hoisted him into the air, this time by both arms. Again he kicked at the giant, who spun him around and brought his face within mere inches of a gaping mouth. The close-up threat dis-play of Morlock teeth was enhanced by a skull-vibrating roar, ac-companied by the hot stench of decayed meat.

"Jesus Christ," Mac roared back, fighting off dizziness. "A lit-tle Listerine wouldn't kill you!"

The creature ignored him, flipping his body around again like a rag doll before forcing his head finally to face, at close range, the ice column containing his friend. Mac looked past the familiar figure, doing everything he could to *not* see what they'd done to Jerry.

It did not help.

Beyond the ice-suspended body, his eyes focused on an open space in the cylinder—clearly meant for him. What took Mac to the very precipice of madness was not his own soon-to-be permanent niche, but what lay just behind it. The beast lifted him higher, to see it more clearly—a second unfilled cavity, meant for Yanni.

Now, held immobile and with a Morlock hand tightening around his neck, R. J. MacCready began to give in, for the first time ever, to a sense of utter hopelessness. Emphasizing the point, he heard the arrival of a second Morlock, accompanied by an even more skull-vibrating roar. Scarface reacted by dropping Mac to the ground and kicking him backward with a leg sweep.

As he came to rest beside the Chinese soldier's column, Mac looked up and beheld a suddenly tamed killer. He was reminded of a guilty teen kicking a risqué magazine under his bed. But instead of a shocked parent, the surprise visitor was Alpha, who rushed forward to confront Scarface.

Making certain that the Big Guy knew exactly what had been happening in the Trophy Room, Mac pointed at the space prepared for Yanni, struggled to sit upright, then gave up.

Even from his prone position, the zoologist could see that the changes in Scarface's stance and demeanor were as immediate as they were dramatic. Head bowed, the Morlock took a step backward, letting his arms drop to his sides.

"Subservient, my ass," Mac muttered, sensing even without Yanni's abilities that Alpha could not trust this particular beast. "Watch out for that one," he called to Alpha, saddened that he might just as well be warning him in Yiddish. Then he collapsed in exhaustion.

Alpha snatched up the human rag doll, tucked him under an arm, and carried Mac out of the subterranean maze.

Yanni had been nervously pacing the interior of the igloo when, at last, Alpha approached through the fog. She let out a small cry as she saw that he was carrying Mac—bloodied and seemingly in shock but very much alive.

Pushing aside the ice door, Alpha, with Yanni's assistance, eased Mac down onto the floor. The giant communicated something that approximated a sigh, then exited without any further attempts at communication. She watched him through the ice wall until he disappeared into the mist.

Yanni brought Mac some water and squatted down to help him drink.

"I'm all right," he said, noting the look of concern she wore.

"Oh, yeah," Yanni replied gently. "You look great."

"Really," he said, stopping when she put a finger to his lips.

Mac looked past her.

What did you see out there? Yanni thought, but could not bring herself to ask. MacCready's entire body seemed to shudder for a moment, then he closed his eyes, very tightly.

Whatever it was, she told herself, *it sure as hell wasn't in Pliny's codex.*

Metropolitan Museum of Natural History

The weak never become top dogs. This is an unbreakable rule. Be they Roman, or Ceran, or Easterner, any people capable of building a civilization will be highly intelligent, vigilant, and (when necessary, from their point of view) thoroughly ruthless. Thus, their survival will always be more important than our survival. And in the end, we must remember above all else, that when we encounter any foreign civilization for the first

*time, their people will know that these same unbreakable laws
define our way of thinking about them.*
    —PLINY THE ELDER (AS TRANSLATED BY
    PATRICIA WYNTERS, MMNH)

S o began a concluding chapter of Pliny's hidden codex. Patricia Wynters knew that the collision of three civilizations had led the historian to believe that whenever Rome or one of its descendant cultures met another so alien as the Cerae, "the very few things that can be predicted for certain, render the outcome certainly unpredictable."

"Sheesh, this guy rambles on like nobody's business," Patricia told Charles R. Knight. "It's all pretty obvious nowadays but I guess two thousand years ago, this might have been an example of hitting the nail square on the head."

"A few things never change, I guess," Knight replied.

"But most things do," she added, her friend sensing more than a hint of sadness in her voice.

The Kremlin
July 17, 1946

I have called this meeting," Joseph Stalin began, "because the young man in charge of decoding transmissions from our people in New York has something important to tell us."

A young electronics prodigy named Anatoly handed out transcripts to the other two men who had been called into the office.

"Our problem is named MacCready," Anatoly said. "The same MacCready sent to the wilds of Brazil in '44 by this Major Hendry. The theremin device transmitted at least two references confirming this fact. There was no mention of what he did there, but we feel he was somehow involved in the destruction of a missile base—but not before a high-altitude rocket launched from there dropped bacteria bombs on our troops in the Ukraine."

"And what is his job now—this MacCready?" Stalin asked.

"Officially, he is a zoologist," Anatoly continued.

"And *is* he—a zoologist?"

Anatoly's boss, a bespectacled man, stepped forward and cleared his throat. Although he would have looked at home stacking canned goods in a market, Lavrentiy Beria was more feared in his country than Stalin himself. Only three years earlier, he had been introduced to President Roosevelt by the Soviet leader as "our Himmler." It was a designation that had much to do with the fact that Beria not only oversaw Stalin's dreaded secret police, but was also in charge of the gulag labor camps.

"Recently, this American was planning a return to Brazil—to look for prehistoric horses. At first, I believed it to be just a stupid cover story—but there is a solid paper trail."

"Go on," Stalin said, gesturing to the transcript.

Beria continued. "The man—MacCready—wherever he goes, is a human lightning rod for trouble."

Anatoly nodded in agreement. "The incident two years ago killed thousands in the Ukraine—and, in the end, the Nazis trapped there were able to break out of the encirclement our brave comrades had fought to create."

"I know all about this disgraceful incident," Stalin bellowed. "One in which our 'brave comrades' *failed to carry out their orders!*"

"Of course you're right, sir," Anatoly said, with a submissive bow.

Stalin continued, his voice noticeably slurred by alcohol: "And did anyone take the time to examine these dead *heroes*? To determine just what killed them?"

There was an uncomfortable silence until Lavrentiy Beria cleared his throat yet again. "No, Comrade Stalin, but those responsible for this oversight have already been . . . *reassigned.*"

Anatoly followed up. "I believe that this American was sent into Brazil to find something and to stop the attack."

"Well, then obviously *he* failed, too," Stalin said, with disgust.

"Unless of course, he did *not* fail," Beria said, pausing for effect.

"Go on," Stalin said, with impatience.

"Unless the American *wanted* the attack on the Mother Country to succeed. Who can forget their General Patton, who said—"

Stalin held up a hand. "I know exactly what that presumptuous asshole said: 'After Hitler is dead, if FDR wants Moscow, I can give it to him.'"

Once again, the room went uncomfortably silent.

Stalin seemed to wave off the thought, then poured himself another glass of "water." "And we all know what happened to Patton," he muttered to himself, before turning to Anatoly. "Do you think MacCready could have been ordered to let this attack occur—maybe even to *help* it happen?"

"Difficult to tell, sir," Anatoly lied. The man was clearly trying *not* to let his response sound like a contradiction to Beria's suggestion. "According to the information we were able to gather, through Comrade Theremin's 'gift,' MacCready is, as the Americans say, a loose cannon."

"But they do find him to be a valuable asset, yes?" said Beria, before finally turning to the fourth man in the room. "So, Nikita, you were assigned to read everything this MacCready has published. Have you any predictions? What do you think is on his mind?"

An inordinate interest in horses and bats, Nikita Khrushchev thought, and decided to keep even this observation to himself, because it was clearly far safer to play the bumbling, uncivilized half-wit only recently recovered from an extended (and nonexistent) bout of pneumonia. Khrushchev never suspected that the facade would ultimately leave him the last man standing in the Kremlin, as history hurried him along toward a game of nuclear poker with an American president. Presently, his only concern was to avoid taking his place beside those who had spoken the wrong words (or any words at all)—and who now lay buried under Beria's rose garden.

Khrushchev stammered.

"Out with it!" said Stalin.

"I . . . I don't believe I can predict anything," he said quickly. "I don't know."

Beria shook his head in an exaggerated manner. "I don't believe you know anything, either. Or that you ever will." He glanced over at young Anatoly, who laughed obediently.

Beria continued. "As *we* now know perfectly well, the Americans uncovered an ancient Roman expedition log indicating the existence of certain biological monstrosities, out there in the wild. And—"

Stalin interrupted. "And now this same MacCready is on this ancient trail like a bloodhound."

"A brilliant deduction," Beria said, seemingly making a second career out of constantly redefining the word *obsequious*. "And if what we've overheard during the translation of this 'Omega Codex' is true—" He turned to Anatoly.

"I believe it is," said Anatoly.

"Then you will assemble a team immediately," Stalin decided. "Priority one—find this MacCready and bring me whatever it is he is searching for. It must be important for the American military to have risked sending him in there."

"And priority two?"

Stalin smiled an undertaker's smile. "Bring me this loose cannon—or silence him for good."

What about the Chinese? Nikita Khrushchev asked himself. *What will they think of this incursion into their territory?* Of course, he left the questions unasked, though he was clearly pleased that young Anatoly had apparently arrived at the very same questions.

"I'm afraid, sir, we must risk stirring up Chiang Kai-shek's Nationalists," said Anatoly. "But I—" He looked at Beria and went silent.

"Finish your thought," Stalin commanded. "You have no enemies here."

"With pleasure," Anatoly lied, then continued: "I can explain it best by telling you what I believe this ancient Roman found, and what is going to happen in Tibet—very soon."

Initially, Pliny had realized with a jolt that the decision of the Cerae not to mark him with their stink doomed him to the Scythian fate. He came to this realization during the instant in which he saw the Ceran called Teacher pouring a pot of drill-tipped worms over Severus's head, arms, and chest. Up to that very moment, he believed the creature had turned against her pet and actually thought of Severus's fate as "some justice." And yet, moved by a stubborn ember of compassion for the centurion, he turned away, bracing himself for screams that never came.

When he looked again, the worms were falling away from Severus's body. The swarm of ticks had remained near the rim of the pit for a long time, then scattered and disappeared. Proculus's moments of dread came and went in the very same way.

Finally, when Pliny's turn came, he glared at Severus. Clenching and unclenching his bound hands into fists, the naturalist watched stoically as the Ceran ladled worms from Severus's pit into Proculus's pit, and finally into his own. Pliny set his jaw—determined to accept his fate like a Roman.

But the bites for which I had braced myself were never delivered, Pliny recorded in his codex.

It seemed, to me, that no sooner had they touched, tasted, or smelled my skin, my hair, and my sweat, they were repulsed by me, and fled my body.

I understood then, beyond doubting, that we had indeed been used for a process of training the weapon. The same worms and ticks that did not attack me were collected from my pit and poured upon a Scythian captive who had been brought forth and lowered into the ground. His flesh did not repel them—could not repel them.

And it seemed to me that the unfortunate man was dead in the amount of time I would take to draw a deep breath, hold it reflectively, and exhale.

CHAPTER 17

Dilemma

*The real problem of humanity is the following: We have Paleo-
lithic emotions . . . and god-like technology. And it is terrifically
dangerous, and it is now approaching a point of crisis overall.*
—E. O. WILSON

*Metropolitan Museum of Natural History
Fifth Floor*

S o, do you think Pliny knew the implications
of this?" Dr. Nora Nesbitt asked.
"Of course he knew," Patricia said, ges-
turing toward the codex. "He's telling us right there the step-by-
step procedure for imprinting a biological weapon to attack an
ethno-specific group."

Charles Knight held the newly assembled fragments of codex in one hand, a magnifying lens in the other. "A race-specific
weapon," he said, noticing that his hands were shaking. "Two
thousand years ago."

"How can this be?" Patricia asked. "It would be the biological
equivalent of uranium-235."

"He must have been mad to write this down," Nesbitt said, as
much to herself as the others.

"Ah, but he never *published* it," Patricia emphasized.

"Thankfully," Knight replied. He placed the codex fragment and magnifier down on a lab bench, then buried his trembling hands in his pockets—hoping to shift the conversation away from what had quickly become an uncomfortable topic.

Nesbitt, however, was not about to let the subject rest, even for a minute. "Where, exactly, did they find Pliny's book?"

"Someone concealed it under a wine cellar," Knight said, allowing a degree of impatience to creep into his voice.

"In one of Pompeii's sister cities," Patricia chipped in. "Not quite sure which one."

"And *that's* how it was preserved?"

Knight peered at Nesbitt over his glasses. "You know, I'm beginning to feel a bit like one of those contestants on *Twenty Questions.*"

"Come on, Charles," Patricia said, in her best singsong voice. "You know you want to tell us."

Knight shot his friend an exasperated look, sighed, then continued. "According to Major Dropsy, the fact that the codex was sealed in an airtight, screw-top cylinder of noncorrosive metal probably had something to do with its preservation."

Patricia gave a wry smile. "See, now that wasn't so hard."

Nesbitt ignored the banter. "So Pliny's codex got buried by Mount Vesuvius, on the very same day that he died?"

"Pliny, Pompeii, and thirty thousand people," Knight said.

Nesbitt shot the artist a skeptical look. "And how come nobody recovered it until recently?"

"Well, apparently they came close," Knight replied, resigned now and back in educator mode. "Soon after the blast, Emperor Titus had begun a recovery and aid operation in the region—which included the sinking of mine shafts into sites where the wealthiest Pompeians had lived."

"Ah, the recovery of gold, you mean?"

Knight smiled. "Of course, Dr. Nesbitt. But Pliny's nephew, Pliny the Younger, was instrumental in bringing mining under the volcano to a halt."

"And why's that?" Nesbitt asked.

"Until now, historians figured it was simply a matter of too many earthquakes and too many mine collapses," said Knight. "But after reading the codex you really do have to wonder."

"Maybe Pliny the Nephew didn't want anybody poking around and finding Pliny the Uncle's little secret."

"I'd call this more of a big secret," Patricia added.

"Agreed," Knight replied. "And the only reason to hide the codex from the rest of the empire is if you know the danger is real."

"Maybe even more dangerous now," said Nesbitt. "If something like this got into the wrong hands, it could make what General Ishii Shirō and his pals did with bioweapons in Manchuria look like a church picnic."

"That's a big 'if,'" Knight replied, "but if this is true, then . . ." His voice trailed off, his mind considering thoughts that had suddenly leaped past "uncomfortable" into something darkly nightmarish.

Nesbitt carried her own thought to its next logical step. "Just imagine the Russians or the Chinese getting their hands on something like this."

Patricia shook her head. "I'm not sure I follow."

"What if they took an already fast-evolving pathogen—plague say—and then began imprinting it against Western Europeans."

"*Or* the other way around," said Patricia.

"If both sides had it, you could end up with people sending race-specific plagues back and forth against each other, until the only safe thing to be is—"

"—anything but human," said Patricia.

Nesbitt let out a long whistling sigh, and the room fell silent. "How much does your Major Hendry know about this?" she said, at last.

Once again, Knight lifted the freshly reconstructed page. "He knows quite a lot. And as a point of information, Dr. Nesbitt, he certainly isn't *my* Major Hendry."

Patricia stepped in, giving her friend a moment to cool off. "I'm sure the major's also figured there'd be more revelations, once we got going on this translation."

"Although he hasn't seen these particular fragments," Knight continued, calmer now. "Doesn't know how the pieces fit together, or the story they tell."

"But I'm sure he's got backup copies of all the fragments, right?" Nesbitt asked.

"He provided us with photos initially, so yes, it makes sense that they've got the negatives floating around somewhere."

"If only we could make them disappear," Nesbitt wondered out loud.

Patricia gave a mirthless laugh. "Good luck getting access."

"Actually," Knight said, "this *might* just work out without resorting to cloak-and-dagger foolery."

The two women turned to the artist, who continued. "What's on this page simply expands on things Pliny had written earlier in the codex. And anyone who's read this thing—even parts of it—knows that he had a tendency to repeat himself."

"That's being kind, Charles," Patricia interjected, then turned to Nesbitt. "I often get the feeling that his critics must have originated the term 'beating a dead horse.'"

The biologist nodded. "So, he rambled a lot."

"Yes," said Knight, "but as it turns out, we may be able to use this tendency to our advantage. The point is, that saying we *think* what we found on any given page is simply more of the same—is believable. And if anyone happens to take a close look at the photos of the codex in a year or two, then we're simply eccentrically incompetent—"

"—and not traitors," Patricia said, completing Knight's thought with a dose of skepticism.

"Right," Knight said, crossing his arms. "So what do you think?"

Patricia made an unsuccessful attempt to hide her true feelings about the suggestion. "Well, I wouldn't call it ironclad, Charles, but—"

"In the meantime, maybe we can get our hands on those negatives," Nesbitt suggested. "Destroy them for good."

"You're beginning to remind me of Pliny," Knight said, looking offended that his own potential solution had been summarily dismissed.

Nesbitt, however, ignored the dig. "Let's just hope you're right about having a year or two."

"Indeed," Knight replied, latching on to the hope that they had gotten themselves unnecessarily worked up about something whose very existence was far from a given.

Nesbitt, though, wasn't quite finished. "If what Pliny describes here *is* still active, do you suppose your friend MacCready has found it?"

Patricia Wynters and Charles Knight exchanged glances, then nodded in unison.

Nesbitt pressed on. "And if he brings it back, is there anyone we can trust with it?"

This time there were synchronized head shakes. "Not exactly," Knight replied.

"Meaning, no one?"

"Exactly."

Unlike Knight and Wynters, Nesbitt did not know Mac, Yanni, and Jerry. So, it became easier for her to wish that their disappearance simply meant they were dead. She suspected that what gave Pliny's Cerae a godlike power over life was a hot-spring microbe that could, with practice, be prodded into hijacking and editing the mysterious code of life itself—essentially instantly. If the now-hidden parts of Pliny's codex weren't just a fairy tale, then there existed a lost microbe that enabled one to direct, at will, evolutionary change.

And to whom should America entrust such power?

The military?

The legislature?

The church?

None of the above?

One fact, Nesbit did know: many microbes would not find it difficult to survive whatever environmental changes nearly two thousand years had wrought, even if the valley's hot pools were now smashed and frozen.

What . . . thing might MacCready free from the ice? Nesbitt wondered. *And what will happen to the world if he brings it back?*

Perhaps, she thought, *MacCready would understand the true nature of the discovery and would refrain from bringing it back alive. But what's the likelihood of that? The man is a zoologist and finding an organism that would allow humans to conduct the symphony of life would be the find of the century.*

And so it became possible for Dr. Nora Nesbitt to wonder if there was anyone who knew a way to make sure that Captain MacCready and his friends never came back at all.

CHAPTER 18

Nursery

The idea that science will one day be able to read and understand DNA the way we can now read and even rewrite music is moonshine.
    —LUIS ALVAREZ (1982)

One could write a history of science in reverse by assembling the solid pronouncements on highest authority about what could not be done and could never happen.
    —ROBERT A. HEINLEIN

We have become frighteningly effective at altering nature.
    —SYLVIA EARLE

Outside the Prison Igloo
July 18, 1946

What do you think they did with Li Ming?" Yanni asked, as she and Mac were once again marched out of their igloo prison and this time, to their relief, by Alpha and a rather unassuming duo of Morlock "dog walkers."

Mac bit down on his lower lip, then shrugged, having decided not to tell Yanni what he'd seen the day before—what he'd been forced to see.

For the moment, however, they were relieved to be out of their glorified icebox, setting off on what, except for the previous day's nightmarish detour, was now becoming more or less routine. This time, however, after trekking away from the igloo for approximately twenty minutes, they met up with a fourth creature, who seemed to have been waiting for them. There followed a brief exchange between the Morlocks, after which they moved apart, roughly delineating a small patch of ground where the humans were free to wander about.

"Is it just me, or are Alpha's friends looking even more agitated than usual?" Mac asked, wishing that his ability to decipher Morlock facial expressions were not so frustratingly small.

"You mean *nervousness*?"

"Yeah."

"Something like that," Yanni replied, squinting into the distance. Within their limited radius of view, no pallid corpse plants or plant-mimicking animals were present, and few Morlocks. "I just wish we could see more," she added, waving a hand at the ever-present mist. "I'd love to take a gander at this place without all of this."

Mac nodded, his mind shifting easily into what his late friend Bob Thorne had called "zoology mode." He began by extending a hand into the strange, snow-laden fog. Mostly, the soupy air was just a suspension of microscopic ice crystals, but like Yanni, he knew that this particular mist was home to something far more interesting than perpetually floating snow—something that was, in fact, quite unique.

As if summoned, one of the tiny snowflake mimics twirled

past his face. He waited. Another appeared, then another. "Well, at least they're not avoiding me any longer," he said.

"Maybe that has something to do with not getting your face smashed down into them this time," Yanni suggested.

Even so, it was impossible to get anything like a good look at the flittering creatures. Mac gently cupped one between his hands as it flew by. He could feel a faint buzzing from within, and not wanting to injure the little whatever-it-was, he brought his hands close to his face before opening them, palms up.

There, sitting in the center of his left palm, was a new puzzle to be solved. *If only—*

He forced himself to concentrate on the creature. *The size is right,* he thought, *but it certainly isn't an insect.* Moreover, it was, to his amazement, impossible to place this particular critter into any known phylum.

Mac noted that what the ersatz snowflake *most* resembled was *a ball of dandelion fluff with something that sort of looked like a miniature bat inside.* There appeared to be jointed limbs and a distinct head region equipped with large eyes—each of which the zoologist estimated to be roughly the size of a pinhead. A magnifying glass would have answered the question of whether or not the eyes were compound—like those of an insect. Mac would have bet on the more camera-type vertebrate eye.

R. J. MacCready held his breath, not wanting to disturb the delicate enigma. After a long moment, the little animal seemed to drift off, as if being carried away by a breeze. Mac could see, though, that its departure was not wind driven at all. Instead, its flight mechanics became yet another layer of mystery involving the fauna and flora of this hidden ecosystem. As Mac watched, and all within those same few seconds, the gentle flyer darted into a Lilliputian headwind and disappeared into the snowy mist, obviously intent on rejoining its pals.

Mac turned and saw that Yanni had been watching him.

"Pretty incredible, huh?" she said, moving in to stand at his side.

"I'll say," Mac replied.

These thoughts were entirely forgotten once Alpha decided that exercise time was over, and—with the usual accompaniment of somewhat less-than-gentle prods—Mac, and to a lesser extent, Yanni were herded back toward their prison of ice. The two prisoners gave no thought to the fact that the fourth Morlock remained behind.

Waiting until after the humans and their guards had disappeared into the mist, the lone Morlock headed off in the opposite direction, retracing his earlier steps until he came upon two figures on the ground—their outlines vague, like ancient statues smoothed by erosion.

Li Ming and his copilot had been reunited, though they were currently unaware of each other's paralyzed existence. Staked to the cold earth on their backs, their eyes stared straight ahead, at nothing.

To a friend or even a close relative, the two men might have been completely unrecognizable, covered as they were in suppurating nodules. Extremities that had been deemed unimportant by their own bodies were denied blood flow and were now blackening from oxygen starvation—the warm blood having been directed instead to the core. Had a pathologist been present, especially one with knowledge of pandemics, the doctor might have taken a special interest in the golf-ball-sized "buboes" that rose bubble-like from the necks, armpits, and groins of the staked-out men. But there were no pathologists present, at least none being of the *Homo sapiens* variety. Even so, the Morlock's eyes widened and his head tilted sideways in birdlike fascination, as a particularly large and purplish bubo continued to bud from the right side of the pilot's mouth. Straining the epidermal tissue beyond its shearing point, the balloon-like sore burst with an audible pop and a spray of red matter, laced with little white clots.

The stench of putrefaction would have been nauseating to most humans, but the Morlock expressed a typical hominid smile and reached down, projecting a finger at something emerging from the crater of flesh. Two newly born snow mimics catapulted themselves from the crater's edge and one of them came to rest briefly on a giant finger, before taking to the air. More of the tiny flyers emerged—more and more of them—rising like summoned spirits. They flitted around their giant midwife for a moment, as if celebrating their new lives. Then, in a swirl from a breeze that existed only in mechanized nonsentience, they were gone.

The caregiver took one last look down at the Chinese captives. Pale white, though still giving off faint mists of breath, these were creatures who had only recently believed themselves to be masters of the air. Now, however, they had taken on a far more important role—as the living nursery for a new arsenal of airborne weaponry.

The past seventy-two hours were a blur to Wang Tse-lin. Deprived of sleep, events tended to become mixed up in time, and only occasionally was he able to keep proper track of them.

When Captain Mung's soldiers broke camp after the first night, Wang had looked on with a combination of disgust and fascination while several men were ordered to butcher the body of the slain Yeren.

In less than an hour, two men with knives had skillfully freed large limb muscles and pectorals from their bony attachments. After some initial reluctance, Wang moved in closer and took notes, as if attending a more formal dissection of a particularly rare specimen. *Indeed I am,* he told himself, noting that "the muscles were dark red and thus obviously rich in oxygen-carrying myoglobin—a requirement for efficient movement at high altitude." Wang also observed that the lungs of the Yeren appeared to be proportionally much larger than those of a normal human and furthermore that they possessed two additional lobes ("another way to compensate for the thin air").

However, the dissection comparison broke down when a third man arrived and began salting the flesh while a fourth packed the Yeren in paper.

"The packages looked no different than what one might purchase from a local butcher," Wang eventually wrote in his field notebook.

When Captain Mung's men neared the end of their grisly tasks, the officer pointed to the considerable carnage that had accumulated. "I want no trace of this creature left on the surface. Clean your tools well and bury everything—bury it deep."

"Yes, sir," his men replied in unison.

"No blood and not a strand of hair can be left showing," he said. "Do you understand?"

The four men nodded as one.

Wang had warned his captain that burying what they left behind could not remove all of the Yeren scent from the campsite, or from anyone who had butchered or even touched the beast. It was plain to him that Captain Mung appreciated this fact. Any fool could cross points of no return without foreseeing them, and most did. The scientist understood that only one objective mattered to his captain, the same one with which he had begun—saving his family. Only an hour after leaving the camp, the captain had mapped out a new pass leading to higher ground. What seemed a very long time after that, the expedition was making progress again, and Mung moved backward along his line of men until he found Wang. Without anyone else noticing, the officer passed him one of the small, tightly wrapped packages.

"Take it," he said, "and do so without making a fuss."

Wang tucked the item into his coat.

"Though I did not think so at first," Mung said, "you appear to be a survivor type."

Before Wang could answer, the captain raised his hand in a gesture that meant a response would be neither necessary nor tolerated.

"If I am killed, I am asking you to take this package to my family. They will know what to do with it."

"Should I tell them anything else, sir?"

Captain Mung pondered the question for a moment before speaking quietly. "You're a scientist. Tell them everything—everything you have seen here."

Then, without another word, the officer turned and headed toward the front of the line. Watching Captain Mung, Wang Tse-lin wondered if it was only his imagination that the small package suddenly seemed to weigh considerably more than it had only seconds earlier. Now, beyond the prospect of having to carry dried flesh from the beings inhabiting this region, Wang had been appointed as the family historian of Captain Mung's mission. Few men besides the officer could have anticipated what had already happened—but fewer would have guessed that, while exceptional intuition defined Captain Mung, a failure of imagination could doom them all.

CHAPTER 19

Captain America

There was a man who was interested in the color of music—the connection between light and music—and that was Einstein.
—LEON THEREMIN

The sciences throw an inexpressible grace over our compositions, even where they are not immediately concerned; as their effects are discernible where we least expect to find them.
—PLINY THE ELDER

Metropolitan Museum of Natural History
Fifth Floor
July 18, 1946

D r. Nesbitt, the pleasure is all mine," the smiling naval officer said, holding on to her right hand for what she considered a beat too long. Nesbitt noted that the accent was unmistakably Bostonian, while the attitude that accompanied it spoke of something else—money.

Of course, Nora Nesbitt had recognized the famous last name. She also had to admit that "Just Call Me Jack" was as handsome as advertised. *Although on the seriously scrawny side.* But this too was to be expected. Nesbitt knew as well as anyone that when the curtain finally dropped on the Pacific Theater, thousands of Allied servicemen returned home with an array of unwelcome souvenirs that spanned many of the invertebrate groups she had come to love.

Nesbitt flashed a warm smile of her own and nodded. *Intestinal parasites,* she thought, before recalling the slight tremor in the man's hand. *Maybe even scrub typhus.*

"All right, break it up, you two," Major Patrick Hendry said, initiating a pair of scowls for completely different reasons.

The major seemed to savor the moment, before continuing. "I presume you both know why I've called this little meeting."

It was clear that they did but it was Nesbitt who responded. "Can I assume that there's nothing new on the status of Captain MacCready, Lieutenant Delarosa, and Yanni Thorne?"

"That would be a correct assumption, Dr. Nesbitt."

"But Mac being Mac, that's no real surprise, is it, sir?"

"No, it's not, Lieutenant," Hendry continued. "You of all people should know that Mac has weathered some serious shit storms in the past."

It had quickly become clear to the invertebrate zoologist that neither the man with the Boston twang nor the redheaded major was at all convinced about MacCready's demise.

"Sir," the young officer said, "I am wondering why Dr. Nesbitt is here?"

Nesbitt decided to respond herself. "Well, Lieutenant, because of the scientific nature of this mission, it's been decided that I'm going with you to Tibet."

The young officer shot Major Hendry a piercing look, as if to see if this was all some sort of joke. But the major's expression told him it wasn't.

The lieutenant instantly changed gears, flashing another thousand-dollar smile. "Dr. Nesbitt, have you ever jumped out of a plane before?"

"No, I haven't," she replied. "Have you ever jumped out of a plane more than twenty-five thousand feet above sea level?"

"No, ma'am, can't say I have."

"Well then, I imagine it'll be a new experience for both of us," Nesbitt said, confidently. "And *please*, Lieutenant, just call me Nora."

Major Hendry cleared his throat. "I'm sorry to interrupt the fascinating banter you two are shoveling but I need you to look at these." He broke the wax seal on a large envelope and removed a pair of photographs. "A recon plane took these at thirty-six thousand feet over an especially mountainous section of southern Tibet. We think this is where Mac went in."

"What are those pairs of spokes?" Nesbitt asked.

"Helicopters," Jack replied. "Two of them, right, Major?"

"That's right. Sitting on a shelf of rock."

Jack squinted at his photo. "But those choppers don't look like ours."

Hendry smiled. "That's two for two, lieutenant. They're Russian. Although it's a safe bet they were flown in there by the Chinese army."

Nesbitt handed the photo back to the major. "So what's this mean?"

"It means that Mac and the others definitely have some company up there."

Now it was Jack who handed his photo back. "You mean in addition to the myths and old wives tales, sir?"

Nesbitt broke in. "Lieutenant, we think these creatures are *real*. And the quicker you start thinking that way, the better."

The naval officer gave a nod that was either respectful or condescending. He also apparently decided not to pursue the issue further. "But there's still no sign of Mac, Jerry, or—" He paused.

"Yanni," Hendry reminded him. "Yanni Thorne. And you're correct, there's no sign of them. No signal patterns in the snow, no broadcast attempts—just a blurry mark near these spokes that might or might not be part of *their* chopper. So this is as good a place as any to start looking."

"How many of us are you sending in?" Jack asked.

"Including you and Dr. Nesbitt, eight. Five specialists in high-altitude combat—mostly skiers and mountain corps types."

"Who else?" Jack asked.

"Another old friend of Mac's," Hendry replied. "Seems as if you weren't the only person who got some strings pulled to get on this mission. Guy's name is Juliano—Sergeant Frank Juliano, weapons and munitions expert."

"This Captain MacCready sounds like a *very* popular fellow," Nesbitt said.

"He is!" the two officers replied simultaneously.

She offered a tight smile, hoping that she'd feel the same way when and if they finally met.

> Fort Ethan Allen, Vermont
> July 19, 1946
> Twenty hours later

A HALO insertion, huh? That sounds painful, sir." The comment came from a short man with a hangdog expression.

The five members of the First Special Service Force who were sitting apart from the others in the briefing room exchanged exasperated looks—several of them doing a rather poor job of stifling chuckles. To Major Patrick Hendry and a trio that included Dr. Nesbitt and the Navy officer Mac had once jokingly referred to as Lieutenant Moneybanks, these guys were an odd assemblage, looking more like north woodsmen, hunters, and lumberjacks than soldiers. The major also knew that this was primarily because that's *exactly* what they'd been before the war.

Hendry shot the members of the "Devil's Brigade" a look that immediately put an end to the little joke they were having at the expense of Mac's pal, Sergeant Juliano. The major knew the members of the elite American-Canadian commando unit had gotten their name from the German soldiers they'd terrorized, leaving behind calling cards on their bodies that read *Das dicke Ende kommt noch!* ("The worst is yet to come!").

Hendry turned toward a short, heavyset man who had an uncanny resemblance to the comedian Lou Costello. "HALO, Sergeant Juliano, that's High Altitude Low Opening."

"Gotcha sir, thanks," Juliano said, looking somewhat relieved.

Now Hendry could see it was Dr. Nesbitt and the Navy lieutenant who were exchanging bemused looks. He cleared his throat before continuing with the briefing.

"We're going with a HALO insertion because it'll give you the best chance of getting in there undetected. The problem of course is that you'll be free-falling for approximately ninety seconds and aiming for a narrow mountain pass we've identified as a safe DZ—that's the drop zone, Dr. Nesbitt."

The biologist responded with a self-conscious nod.

One of the Special Forces members raised a hand. "How are we getting in there, sir?"

Major Hendry went on. "You'll be leaving for Ireland within a week, then on to Turkey—which is where you'll board a C-47 specially equipped for the drop—respirators, special protective clothing, and the like. From Ankara you'll be heading straight to the mountains."

Hendry then turned his attention to Juliano, Nesbitt, and the lieutenant. "You three will be training with these fine men for the next few days. Eventually, you'll be jumping in tandem with a trio of them. Before that, though, you'll take a cram course to get you ready for the conditions you'll be facing *and* the jump itself. The last thing you or this mission needs is a broken leg or a snapped back."

Sergeant Juliano raised a hand, and the major nodded in his direction. Somewhat surprisingly, he stood and turned toward the surly-looking Devil's Brigaders. "Hey, you guys carry the Johnson LMG, don't you?"

Five heads rotated toward the man who appeared to stand roughly a foot shorter than any of them. "Indeed we do, Sergeant," said a thickly muscled, blond-haired man with a heavy French Canadian accent. "Are you familiar with it?"

"Familiar with it?" Juliano replied. "I'll say!" Then he gestured to the naval officer sitting next to Dr. Nesbitt. "Lieutenant, did you know the M-1941 was designed by a Boston lawyer?"

"Can't say I did, Sergeant," Jack replied. He glanced over at the Special Forces guys, a bit put out that their attention was inexplicably focused on Lou Costello's twin.

"Well, it's a beaut, Jack . . . I mean sir. Short recoil, rotating bolt, and up to nine hundred rounds per minute! It's a *real* beaut!"

"I guess we're done here," Major Hendry announced, and almost instantaneously, several of the commandos approached Sergeant Juliano, who immediately became the recipient of some serious glad-handing and backslapping.

"So, is it as awkward to carry a loaded Johnny gun as they say it is?" Juliano asked, eagerly.

One of the men pointed to a friend. "As awkward as my last date with his mom."

Major Hendry ambled over to where Nesbitt and Jack sat silently, watching the proceedings.

"It's nice to see that *someone* is fitting right in, isn't it?" Hendry said, making an effort not to smile until he had turned and walked toward the sound of raucous laughter.

August, A.D. 67

N ow that the initial shock had worn off, Pliny and Proculus could fully appreciate the military significance of the very special hell they had somehow survived in the death pits.

More than three hours after the ordeal, as shadows lengthened across the gardens of the Cerae, the two Romans stood on the balcony of their prison cell. The historian was still rubbing uncomfortably at his arms. *There are no ticks,* he told himself—yet again.

"How are you holding up?" Proculus said softly.

"A little shaken."

A sudden movement drew their attention to the adjoining balcony. Severus was pacing back and forth, and though anger and distress were clearly evident, neither man acknowledged his occasional glances in their direction.

"What do you think is bothering the traitor?" Proculus asked.

"Perhaps he hasn't forgiven his so-called Teacher for the treatment he received at the pits."

"Personally I thought he looked quite natural covered in worms," the cavalryman said, grimacing as the female Ceran made her appearance beside the centurion. Severus, though, stalked off, quickly putting as much distance between them as was possible.

"This is getting interesting," Proculus said, watching Severus begin to cross a dangerously narrow ledge that led to yet another section of the balcony.

The Ceran responded by emitting a sound Pliny never expected to hear from her kind—a strangled grunt, reminiscent of a sob. Then, with the speed of a leopard, she was behind Severus on the precarious ledge—gripping his body and contorting herself against him. There was no consideration given by either figure to the great height at which this drama was playing out. Even at a distance, the air was suddenly filled with her stink.

"Disgusting," Proculus said, turning away, though Pliny found himself unable to do so.

He gestured toward the strange pair. "You do your commander a disservice."

"How so?"

"I believe she is simply marking her possession," Pliny said sharply, watching as Severus's initial struggles quickly abated. "I have been observing him more closely since the pits. It is far more of an addiction than a romance."

"Does it matter?"

"It matters to her—which is quite certainly the only reason we are still alive."

The cavalryman shook his head in disbelief. "And all of this is somehow related to the Cerae training an army of ticks and worms *not* to attack us?"

Pliny nodded, watching as the Ceran moved into the chamber, disappearing from their view. Severus began to follow and then hesitated. He turned stiffly toward his friends, attempting, it seemed, to lock eyes with them. His face was void of all emotion but then, for an instant, there was an undeniable spark of recognition.

"Maybe not *fully* addicted," Proculus said, hopefully, raising his hand.

The moment passed.

The cavalryman's hand dropped to his side.

Pliny continued to watch as the end of this particular scene played out—feeling both fascinated and repelled by what he had seen and what he was still seeing. *Has any relationship during the entire history of the world ever begun and turned so complicated in so strange a place?*

Most frustrating for the historian was that he did not possess the proper words to describe it—little beyond the realization that Severus was inexplicably bound to his Teacher. *To her scent*, he thought. *To something he cannot control.*

As if to prove that very point, the centurion turned from his fellow Romans and entered the chamber.

"Do not fight it, my old friend," Pliny said to himself. "To save us all, you must go back to her."

CHAPTER 20

What We Do in the Shadows

*Three things cannot be long hidden: the sun, the moon, and
the truth.*
—BUDDHA

*The Prison Igloo
Seven days after the Fort Ethan Allen briefing
Two hours after the rescue team departed Ireland
July 27, 1946*

Mac drummed his fingers impatiently on
the ice wall. "Well, I guess those little exercise runs are a thing of the past
now, huh?"

"If they *were* exercise runs," Yanni replied. She gestured to a
pair of Morlocks who were headed away from their igloo. As with
similar visits over the past few days, they had dropped off a supply
of food and water inside the doorway, without actually entering.
"Something's *definitely* got them riled up."

"And no more visits to the elephant house, either."

"It's a corral," Yanni said, correcting him. "But do you see the
connection?"

Mac shrugged. "Not much beyond the fact that they've got us locked down."

"We're not gettin' 'musked' anymore."

"You're right," Mac said, with a nod.

Yanni threw a thumb over her shoulder and in the direction of the grass mimics. "We're startin' to smell like humans again. And that ain't good."

"I *thought* those biters were creepin' in a bit closer."

"Yeah," Yanni followed, "too close if you ask me."

That night, Alpha arrived, but like the other recent visitors, he refrained from entering the igloo. Instead he slid open the ice door and gestured for Yanni to step outside. There were no elephants with him and although Mac attempted to follow her out, the Morlock's impossible-to-misinterpret body language quickly put an end to that venture.

Only a few steps from their prison, Alpha knelt down at a spot that had been covered by grass mimics only minutes before. As Yanni struggled to see in the difficult light, Alpha used an index finger to draw a shape in the dirt, then stepped away from her. She followed up by smoothing over his work and scratching in her own set of figures. Looking even more grim than usual, he motioned for Yanni to step away from the drawing.

"Yeah, I get it," she told him.

Alpha reciprocated by adding more figures, then erased their work. Standing, he glanced at the igloo and made something akin to a pointing gesture. Yanni took the hint.

After sealing the door behind Yanni, Alpha gave a few furtive glances before quickly receding again into the shadows.

"What was that all about?" Mac asked, noting that she appeared unusually shaken by what had just transpired.

Yanni flashed a funeral smile. "Well, the bad news is that the Morlocks seem to think we're part of a full-scale invasion."

"Kinda tough to do much invadin' when you're locked in a fucking icebox," Mac said.

Yanni held up her hand, effectively preventing Mac from entering rant mode. "Yeah, well, first, we showed up in a helicopter. Then Li-Ming. Now it appears as if there are more helicopters out there—maybe on the shelf."

"*What?*" Mac exclaimed. "Lemme guess—they're not ours."

"Nope," Yanni replied. "Evidently they belong to the Chinese."

"So we've opened up Pandora's box," Mac said, as much to himself as to Yanni.

She was unfamiliar with the term but definitely caught the drift. "If that's really bad, then yeah—I'd say our long-term prospects for survival just went from 'unknown' to 'completely down the shitter.'"

"So what's the good news?" Mac asked, hopefully.

Yanni shook her head. "You're kiddin', right?"

July 30, 1946

After they had passed three days huddling in tents and simply trying not to get blown off the side of a mountain, the weather finally cleared. Captain Mung continued to lead his men on a meandering, apparently random trek. As often as not, promising mountain passes led up to impossible, suffocating heights—essentially dead-ending and forcing them to turn back. There were no further signs of the Yeren—or of any life for that matter.

On a morning that broke clear and cloudless, Mung's party navigated around the base of another stone and ice wall—this one shaped like the prow of a mighty ship. Rounding the point, they came to a sudden halt, now able to carefully study, for the first time, what appeared to be a misty sea set against white snow. Using a pair of binoculars, Mung searched for a path ahead, finding a labyrinthine series of switchbacks that eventually disappeared into the basin of icy mist.

How much farther to the valley floor? Mung wondered as he felt someone move in beside him. It was Wang.

"The valley described by the helicopter pilot?" the zoologist asked.

"I wouldn't call what we heard a description," the officer responded. "But I believe it is where they went down."

Wang gestured toward the mist. "And you intend to lead us into that?"

"Where else would we go?"

"You gamble with our lives."

"Being born is a gamble," Mung said, turning away to address the line of men.

M ac squinted at the undulating carpet of mini-predators, now massing around the perimeter of the igloo walls. He gave a halfhearted try at some misplaced optimism. "I guess as long as we keep the door closed, we'll be okay."

"Come on, Mac," Yanni responded, with disappointment, before glancing up at the circular opening in the center of the roof. "These things *can* climb."

MacCready abandoned the ruse. "Yeah, they're startin' to already."

Yanni squatted down at the base of the ice wall. "They kinda remind me of army ants."

Mac's back stiffened at the image. Ants. Hive minds and superorganisms. *Tamara.*

Yanni continued, unaware of the memory she had evoked. "You've seen 'em, right? If they run into a chasm of some kind, or an impassable obstacle—"

"—then the action of each ant coalesces into a group unit," Mac recited, in monotone. "The group unit adapts to changes in the environment."

"Yeah, sure," Yanni said, realizing that she had struck some sort of raw nerve. "So they use their bodies to build a bridge."

Mac glanced up at the ceiling opening again. "Or in this case, a ladder straight into our execution chamber."

"Something like that," Yanni said quietly.

Captain Mung Chen and his men had followed the downward-leading switchback for several hours, invigorated that the drop in elevation had made breathing easier but growing ever more cautious as they drew nearer to the surface of the snow-laden mist. The path down presented sheer drops at regular intervals; but it ended at what looked deceptively like the gentle shore of a pearl-white sea.

The temperature has dropped, Wang thought as he donned his heavy gloves again. Glancing upward, he saw that the sky, thankfully still clear, was now bracketed on all sides by sheer walls of stone and ice. A pair of soldiers, sent to scout the trail ahead, was back. Their animated behavior, as they spoke to Captain Mung, left little doubt that they had encountered something worthy of considerable arm waving. A minute later, they saluted and returned to their fellows while Mung headed straight for Wang.

"They say there's flat ground some fifty or sixty meters below the cloud tops—a lot of it."

"The valley floor?"

"Perhaps an hour's march at best," the officer said. "They also reported that they could make out foliage through the mist—*white* foliage."

"Interesting," Wang responded. "Any sign of the helicopter? Or the missing men?"

The officer shook his head. "No, apparently visibility is quite limited."

"So, Captain, what do you intend to do?"

Mung paused, his gaze falling on a cluster of soldiers, buzzing now (albeit quietly) at the news they'd just heard from their comrades. "Well, what I *don't* intend to do is march my men out there and run headlong into whatever attacked Po Han's crew."

"A fine idea, sir," Wang responded quickly. "And we'll be losing the sunlight in another hour anyway."

Mung pointed to a spot back up the trail. "There is a defensible piece of ground several hundred meters back. We'll camp there tonight. I'll go in with a small recon group in the morning. You will accompany us, of course."

"Of course," Wang said.

They turned whence they had come and began backtracking with slow, labored strides toward the proposed campsite. Wang Tse-lin and Captain Mung took a position at the front of the column. The scientist looked back often, drawn by the multiple enigmas of a frost-laden fog bank so flat that it gave the stubborn illusion of being a sea, and by descriptions of ghostly white plants beneath the surface. And somewhere in that white forest, he knew, angry Yeren stirred.

More than once, Wang thought he saw snowy waves lapping against the shore and washing briefly uphill, but they were wispy and seemed to withdraw and settle quickly.

Too many worries, the scientist told himself. *Just a little snow blindness combined with a trick of the late afternoon light.* Wang was therefore able to forget about the waves until he and Captain Mung were alerted to a commotion down along the trail.

Moments later, an anxious-looking soldier arrived and gave an uneasy salute. "Sir, the back of the line seems to have run into a snow squall," he said breathlessly.

Captain Mung nodded. "I see, Corporal. And is there anything further?"

"It's . . . it's the snow, sir," the man stammered. "It doesn't really—"

Someone screamed. Almost immediately there came another cry and another—until the sounds merged into a nightmare chorus.

Captain Mung scrambled past the corporal and a pair of frightened soldiers, followed closely by Wang. Stopping for a moment, they shielded their eyes against the setting sun and were able to discern details within the commotion—just in time to witness a body falling off the side of the trail into open air. Then another, limbs flailing wildly as it bounced off a rock wall.

Wang recognized the man as one of the snipers who had brought down the Yeren. But even worse than the unreality of what he was witnessing was another thought—*These men haven't fallen and they're not being thrown. They're killing themselves.*

"What's happening?" Wang asked, but Captain Mung could

not answer. They both stood mesmerized, eyes widening at the sight of a third man tumbling off the side of the trail—a man who appeared to be tearing at his own face.

What brought Wang back to reality and the need to respond quickly was his own sympathetic nervous system. The swirling cloud of white was now moving with seemingly methodical intent. Following the rough-hewn path, the cloud advanced up the side of the overlook, engulfing more and more of Mung's increasingly frantic expeditionary force as it approached.

But now there would be no explanations, no orders given and none followed. As the officer and the scientist turned away from the madness unfolding below, there existed, for each of them, only a shared biological imperative—one that had originated and evolved over a half billion years. And so Captain Mung and Wang Tse-lin did the only thing that they *could* do—they ran for their lives.

July 31, 1946

Four days after Yanni informed Mac that they were being blamed for the arrival of more unwelcome visitors, the wall of grass mimics outside the igloo had risen to the level of Mac's shoulders.

The Morlocks occasionally gathered outside, seeming to watch the rising tide as humans might watch an animal in a zoo. Their captors continued to refrain from entering the prison. And yet they came and went by the dozens, in a fairly steady stream. It appeared to Yanni that they were more interested in the progress of the bladelike predators mounting the igloo walls than in the humans imprisoned within. A particularly large group of Morlocks arrived just in time to see the highest section of the living wall collapse and slide back to the ground. One of them directed a menacing grimace at the pair of humans, who were now more clearly visible through the ice. The grimace was accompanied by the surprisingly human pointing of a long index finger.

"Well, they've got gawking down cold," Yanni said.

"I feel like we're sittin' in a window at Macy's," Mac said, flashing the finger pointer one of his own digits. Then he finished dividing up what was left of their last food ration, now nearly three days old.

"Everybody loves a public execution," Yanni said, giving a brief nod to an audience that was presently departing—and looking rather disappointed. She took a water-filled earthen jug from Mac. "I wonder if this is how your Christians in the Colosseum felt, waiting for the arrival of the lions?"

"That story is bullshit," Mac replied quickly. "There's no evidence that any of the so-called *damnati* were killed that way."

Yanni threw him a skeptical look. "But people *were* torn up by wild animals—bears and tigers and shit, right?"

Mac shrugged his shoulders. "Yeah, well, that part is true."

"Just not shredded by a psychotic lawn?"

"No, I think they missed out on that one."

"Well, thanks, Mac," Yanni said, turning away from the scrabbling wall of the carnivorous grass and a new group of Morlocks who had come to watch the humans die. "I feel a lot better now."

The snow mimics on the highland trail were not cognizant of success or failure. They worried nothing about life or death or time. They were, in fact, quite incapable of worry at all. Creatures of mechanized instinct, they swarmed and subdued their prey. Hundreds of the tiny flyers had been killed—swatted and crushed by towering mountains of flesh that lumbered and bellowed and fell. Only when the prey had been immobilized— paralyzed now, and so no longer presenting any danger—did the females approach. The males, who were larger in body size and far more aggressive in their nature, were waiting for them. Equipped with a set of mantis-like raptorial legs, they had already pried open eyelids and lips, inviting the females to enter, and to feed, and to lay their eggs.

By the time the sun dipped behind mountain peaks and gales of snow mimics had retreated like a tide into the mist-shrouded valley, there were only the captain, the scientist, and a bewildered private still alive on the trail.

Far uphill of his preyed-upon crew, Captain Mung was moving forward, but he did so in silence and with a strange gait that seemed more mechanical than human. Wang feared that the officer was in deep shock. *And why not,* the scientist thought, *watching his entire force die—many seemingly driven to suicide by a living storm.*

A sudden gust gave him an involuntary start, and reflexively his head snapped back toward the sound. But the rocky trail behind them was empty now—the snow guided now by only gravity and wind. *Mindless.*

Three hours later, navigating under a faint crescent of moonlight, Wang knew that his questions about what had happened— questions that would have held at least a degree of morbid curiosity for him at any other time—currently mattered for nothing. The *real* question, the only question had become, *How can we escape this?*

"We must get back to the helicopters," Wang had informed the blank-faced Captain Mung earlier. But the officer said nothing, pausing for a moment as if deep in thought, before trudging ahead silently.

The third survivor, a thoroughly and perhaps permanently rattled private who had been listening to the one-way conversation, seemed at first only too happy to support Wang's plan. "We *must* get back to the helicopters," he repeated. But instead of offering reassurance, the phrase morphed into a mantra that the younger man mumbled incessantly under his breath.

At some point Wang took the lead, trekking even farther uphill and toward the imagined safety beyond those self-propelled swirls of white death. As the moon passed behind a cliff and darkness overtook them, he led the others into what he hoped was a suitably deep and protective depression in among the rocks. Wang could not shake the suspicion that danger was tracking after them, so he resolved to remain alert through sunrise. By 2 A.M., exertion and thin air had done their work. His head began to slip downward and for a moment, just for a moment, he closed his eyes.

A sound jolted Wang awake. Morning twilight was strengthening toward daybreak and he immediately felt a rush of shame at his weakness. Stepping out of the crevice, the scientist began flexing his limbs, each joint resisting painfully. Captain Mung had evidently arisen earlier. Still silent, he was carefully surveying the lower section of the rugged trail they'd ascended. Wang glanced back into the crevice, then quickly up and down the trail, unable to see the private. Wang and the captain were alone.

"Where is—?" the scientist said, then hesitated, realizing that he did not know the private's name.

"He was over there," Captain Mung said, motioning toward the crevice. "He's gone now." The officer's voice was flat, and lacking emotion.

"Gone?"

"Just as I said."

Wang paused, briefly wondering why he felt no relief that the captain was speaking again.

"Do you think they . . . the Yeren . . . took him?"

The officer, whose stare remained fixed, shook his head. "If so, then why didn't they take us, too?"

"But . . . his pack is still there," Wang said, allowing his voice to trail off as alternative scenarios crept to the surface of his thoughts like dark spirits.

The captain stepped down from his rocky perch, passed Wang, and snatched up his own backpack. "We need to keep moving," Mung said, his face blank. Then, without another word, he headed off in the presumed direction of the helicopters.

Wang scrambled into the crevice, grabbed the remaining packs, and followed.

In the Igloo Prison
August 1, 1946

By nightfall, the grass mimics had climbed to within a few feet of being able to merely inchworm across the dome top, thus allowing them to drop through the circular opening in the ceiling.

Mac and Yanni had spent much of the past hour folding their coats into a makeshift manhole cover they hoped would block the entrance of grass mimics through the hole in the roof. Mac hoisted Yanni up to make the final fitting, bracing, and plugging as best she could.

"You all right up there?" Mac asked her.

"Swell," came the reply. "You know, I never noticed it before, but these things make a lot of noise."

"What kind of noise?" Mac asked, trying to hold Yanni's legs steady as she struggled to completely fill the opening.

"Kind of 'clicky,' you know, like *click click click*."

"They sound kind of crunchy from down here," Mac added.

Yanni was about to say something else when she saw, through spaces in the grass, movement outside the igloo. Someone or something was approaching the jail door.

"Get me down," she whispered.

Mac all but dropped her to the floor, then the pair made a somewhat less than effortless transition into *we-were-just-sitting-around-when-the-hole-in-the-ceiling-plugged-itself* mode.

The igloo door, which had been thoroughly coated in grass mimics a moment before, received a blast of something wet. Immediately the view through the portal of ice resolved itself. The tiny predators had been washed away and were making no effort to climb back. The source of the stream was a matching set of hoselike appendages, which were themselves attached to the stubby-tusked mammoth that Yanni had met in the corral. Accompanying the creature was Alpha, who slid the door open and ducked inside.

Without hesitating, Yanni stood and ran past her stunned friend, apparently intending to throw her arms around the giant. Alpha reacted by stepping back quickly and spreading his arms in an unmistakable threat display. His canines—bared directly at Yanni—were even more of a shock.

"Okay," she said. "I get it."

As Mac watched the strange reunion unfold, he never noticed that a double trunk had snaked in through the open door—at least, not until it sprayed the two humans with an elephant-scented shower of mucus and anyone's-guess-what-else.

MacCready shook himself off like a wet dog.

A moment later, something dropped on him from the ceiling, glancing off Mac's shoulder. He was relieved to see that it was only their coats—the desperately rigged ceiling plug had failed.

If not for that shower, we'd be dead, Mac realized. The little mammoth was suddenly at his side, using the tips of both trunks to simultaneously unfold and give their parkas a protective smearing.

Mac shook his head and turned toward Yanni, who, though apparently still perplexed at Alpha's *don't-touch-me* response, was finishing up a brief figure-drawing session with the big guy.

"Pull up your socks, Mac," Yanni announced. "Alpha says we're leaving."

As Wang Tse-lin and Captain Mung continued their trek toward the imagined safety of the helicopters, the scientist's unease about the other man soon gave way to something far more disturbing.

"Can you feel them?" the officer asked.

"Feel who, Captain?" Wang said.

"Can you feel the presence of the Yeren?"

"No," the scientist replied, trying to discern shadows in the faint glare of moonlight against fresh-fallen snow—trying to dredge up everything he knew about the symptoms of shell shock. It wasn't much. "I haven't felt any presence, sir. But I do know we're close now. Close to the helicopters. Close to leaving this place."

"The Yeren can smell us," Mung said, his voice haunted. Then he pointed to the backpack Wang was carrying. "They can smell that, too."

"I haven't seen or heard a thing, sir," Wang said, holding down his fear as a crescent moon sank behind a cliff, leaving little for him to see *except* shadows. He tried to be as quietly reassuring as possible. "Tell me about your family again. I wonder if I might meet them when we get home."

The captain shook his head. "Give me that bag," he said, quietly but firmly.

"That's all right sir, I'll carry—"

"*Give it to me now!*" Mung shouted, wide-eyed.

Wang did as he was told.

"The Yeren have been tracking this," the officer said, exchanging his own backpack for the one Wang had been carrying. "They *know* what I have done."

"Captain, if you like, we could just throw it over the side," Wang said quietly. "Then we can both go home."

"*No!*" the officer replied, clutching the backpack. "This was for my children! To cure them."

"But—"

Mung drew his sidearm, aimed it at the scientist's face, and took several steps backward. "If you try to follow, if you disobey me, you *will* die."

Wang Tse-lin stood silently and then likewise took several steps backward. Mung turned away from him and began walking downhill. "Can you feel them?" he asked again. "They can smell me."

Then, turning a corner, Captain Mung was gone.

After that, Wang lost track of the hours. Emerging onto the stony shelf on which the helicopters stood waiting, he squinted against the sunrise.

The wind was stronger here and it whipped between the two aircraft, scouring the ground and spinning up mini-tornados of snow. For a moment, Wang's mind flashed back to the swirling clouds that had engulfed the men on the lower portion of the trail. These swirls, however, did not chase him down or drive him to madness. They simply pulled apart and disappeared.

Where are the pilots? he thought.

Wang almost called out, but something stopped him. Instead he trudged a path through fresh snow directly toward the nearer of the two Russian helicopters, noting with unease that one of the engine cowlings had been removed.

Maybe the others are inside, he thought.

As the scientist approached the cargo door, he was startled at the sound of a voice. Wang felt a sudden surge of relief that the voice belonged to a human. There was no relief, however, at the realization that the human was speaking English.

"That's far enough, buddy," said the voice. But before Wang could respond, eight figures seemed to materialize before his eyes—some from behind the helicopters, others rising up from behind a low wall. All of them were wearing white camouflage uniforms and all of them were armed.

Americans, Wang thought.

One of the men approached, the revolver he carried pointing at Wang's midsection. The scientist slowly raised both of his hands, then screwed on a smile. "Chicago Cubs!" he said. "I was student at Northwestern."

"Well, that's your cross to bear," the man replied, nasally. "I'm a Haa-vid man, myself. So what team would I be rooting for?"

"Boston Red Sock!" Wang blurted out, breaking into a real smile.

Now the thin man with the pistol began to smile, too. "Well, he's okay," he announced, looking quite satisfied with himself.

The others moved in closer now, encircling Wang. He noticed that one of them was a woman, and gave them all a respectful nod. "Boston Red Sock," he continued for his captors. "They trade Babe Ruth to Yankees!"

There was a momentary pause and Wang watched with dismay as the first man's smile vanished. His colleagues, though, appeared to think it was all quite funny.

"That's right, Chicago," one of them said, patting Wang on the back. "You tell 'em."

CHAPTER 21

Night Zero

*You can't say civilization [does not] advance. In every war they
kill you in a new way.*
—WILL ROGERS

In the Valley of the Cerae
August, A.D. 67

When Julius Caesar crossed the Rubicon, there was much about which he
should have worried. He could easily
have paralyzed himself with any one of those concerns, but he
prevailed over them, as if they did not exist.

That was more than a hundred and fifteen years earlier, and
half a world away from the realm of the Cerae. At times such as
this, Pliny reminded himself how easily the temptation to obsess
on any single, deadly obstacle could prevent him from doing what
was necessary to survive, and succeed. Caesar's ability to cast his
own psychological traps aside and to focus all of his genius on
solving the challenges ahead, one by one, had always led him to
the right decisions—until, that is, a particularly cold day in mid-
March.

Pliny and Proculus stared silently across the Ceran gardens.

Tonight, darkness was no longer being pushed back by phosphorescence—by living lamps that the Cerae had somehow managed
to control. All the bioluminescence of the gardens, the terraces,
and the pillars had been steadily dimming. The city and the entire valley, it seemed, were going black.

"They're going to war," Proculus said, looking out across the
darkening terrain. "And we're about to be caught in the middle
of it."

Pliny did not wish to dwell on the thought, but he knew the
man was right and that any escape now (even if it was successful)
would likely mean running into an invading force traveling in
the opposite direction. But there was a far greater picture to be
painted here and it had little to do with their escape.

"I know what you're thinking," Pliny said at last.

"Yes. But—"

"Proculus, you must abandon any thoughts of escape. To even
attempt it would be to neglect a far greater duty."

"I don't understand," the cavalryman said.

"We *must* not leave Severus behind."

"And why is that, sir?"

"The Cerae cannot be given a reason *and* a means, Proculus,
for aiming that weapon against Roman blood. All other consider-
ations are secondary. Do you understand me?"

"Yes," said Proculus quietly.

Pliny could see that, like him, the man had no difficulty pic-
turing the Cerae killing them both long before they could ever
flee the valley.

"They'll use Severus or perhaps even our own bodies to train
their living weapons," Pliny said. "Then imagine this nightmare
spreading along Roman roads, westward and into the heart of the
empire."

The cavalryman gave a visible shudder, and after a pause, it was he who continued. "If you're right, then there is one more consideration—far greater than the rest."

"Go on."

"Not even knowledge about that kind of power can escape this valley. I mean no impertinence, but do *you* understand *me*?"

"I do," Pliny replied. "Quite clearly."

The historian waited for a response but there was only silence. "I wonder," he whispered against the night, "what this impossible valley will produce tomorrow."

The Scythian forces had spread across the mountains like a diffuse infection—their widely separated positions making a full assault by the Cerans impossible.

At one encampment, workers were slicing and packaging meat from a bull elephant and two horses—victims of the thin, cold air. The most skilled of the butchers were carefully cutting the flesh of two Ceran scouts into long strips.

Five riders soon departed on horseback to distribute the elephant and horsemeat to other encampments—but the flesh of the enemy was not part of the distribution. The power of Ceran muscle and marrow, having for generations been the substance of local mythology, was now, perhaps, proving to be more than mere myth. Whether the effects were real or imagined, the blood-bright meat of the creatures quickly restored strength and rendered the people of this individual brigade more resilient against heat-sapping winds and snow. Under such cover, the second enemy scout had crept in among them during the previous night's march. Unseen until it struck, the intruder took five arrows before it fell, and the fresh supply of meat and pelts came at the cost of six men.

Here, and at other outposts, the flesh of Ceran scouts was being secretly hoarded and consumed. Not only did it provide the Easterners with restored strength, it invigorated those who believed the stories told by elderly plains people—stories about a race of monsters whose flesh was not simply a curative but whose lair held the secrets of everlasting life.

Captive monks had confessed the existence of a lost city in which towers built from "crystalline gold" blazed under the sun—a promise whose value had become secondary, the Scythian chieftains agreed, should the magical elixirs turn out to be real.

The commander of this particular encampment could not sleep, noticing as well that the rest of the group also remained too energetic for their daytime rest period. She flexed her fingers, admiring the craftsmanship of her new gauntlet glove. Fashioned from a Ceran's forearm and hand, the fingers were still slightly too tight but she knew the leather would soften and stretch before the upcoming fight. The commander acknowledged a pair of armorers, who were even now putting the finishing touches on her new battle gear. They were stretching a Ceran pelt over the frame of a shield she herself had fashioned from its owner's rib cage.

The handiwork of the Scythians was not yet completed.

CHAPTER 22

Breaking Away

I have seen the science I worshiped and the aircraft I loved, destroying the civilization I expected them to serve.
—CHARLES LINDBERGH

The end of civilization will be that it will eventually die of civilization.
—RALPH WALDO EMERSON

There is precious little in civilization to appeal to a Yeti.
—SIR EDMUND HILLARY

The Kremlin
August 2, 1946

Istory had taught Nikita Khrushchev that, from the time of the Mongol invasions through Napoleon and Hitler, Russia had earned its paranoia the hard way.

To him, battles were not exciting victorious endeavors. He hated and feared war but knew that survival meant a constant state of heightened alertness.

Even in the enclosure of the Kremlin (and especially here, this night), Khrushchev understood that paranoia was often the only choice. *Be smart, but never show it,* he decided. *And maybe after Stalin, Beria, and their friends are finished killing one another— maybe, just maybe I'll still be taking in air and in my right mind.*

Unlike his associates, the fifty-two-year-old Politburu member foresaw that Mao Zedong's strategy and logistics must eventually emerge victorious in the current internal conflict with Chiang Kai-shek and the Nationalists. But Khrushchev, of course, kept this idea, like the rest of his thoughts, to himself.

After a very long night of exquisitely manufactured vodka and even richer food, Stalin finally asked, "So, tell me, Beria. Is there any news out of Tibet?"

"Hard to tell, Comrade," the man replied. "Although thanks to a new gift from Comrade Theremin to the museum, information has begun to seep out again, from New York."

"And?"

"And it seems that Anatoly did not overestimate the likelihood of some very dangerous biology."

"I see," Stalin said, "And what has happened with our Mac-Cready problem?"

Beria allowed himself a small chuckle. "I doubt there *is* a Mac-Cready problem anymore."

Stalin grunted approval, then accepted a slice of chocolate pecan pie from the ever-silent Khrushchev. He chewed reflectively and wondered aloud: "Now, what about the Chinese?"

"They sent in three helicopter crews," Beria said. "And are apparently set to send in more."

"Communists or Nationalists?" Stalin inquired, his mouth full.

"Does it matter?" Beria responded, taking what would have been for any man other than the marshall of the Soviet Union a risk with his own life. Even so, the man was relieved when Stalin chuckled. "Whoever they are, they cannot know what we already know about this Pliny and his codex."

"Why not?" Khrushchev asked, timidly.

"No theremin," Beria snapped at him, and after a pause, wondered aloud, "So, what *do* the Chinese know that we don't know?"

Stalin cleared his throat. "More importantly, Beria: how soon can our own team be in there?"

"Logistically, another three days."

Stalin shook his head. "Unacceptable," he said, and threw a glass, causing Khruschev to dodge it in a comically exaggerated manner.

Stalin and Beria exchanged snide looks before continuing to do what they would do until their dying days—they ignored the man.

Beyond the Valley of the Morlocks
August 2, 1946

Under the cover of darkness, accompanied by Alpha and one of the miniature mammoths, Mac and Yanni were led away from their igloo prison and along a rocky trail they had never seen before. Once above the layer of mist and floating snow, they were grateful that their path was made visible (if only barely) by the faint glow of starlight.

Despite the danger, Mac found himself fascinated by the furry elephant—which, as the journey progressed, had become more clearly illuminated by the rise of the crescent moon above the knife edge of a rock formation. This was his first opportunity to walk beside one of the creatures, and to view it up close for an extended period. Unlike the thick, pillar-shaped limbs of the two modern species, this one's legs were significantly thinner—

built for rapid, agile movement. Even more fantastical were the mammoth's feet. Gone were the broadly flattened weight-bearing structures that characterized all proboscideans, past and present.

And instead of a flat pad and some toenails, it's got six stubby digits.

Many hours beyond the valley—and beyond daybreak—Alpha had scouted out ahead, while Yanni knelt down to prepare another round of what Jerry once referred to as "drawing stick figures in the dirt."

"You know that pandas have an extra digit, right?" Mac whispered to his friend.

Yanni shot him an incredulous look. "Ummm . . . that's great, Mac. But what's that got to do with the price of tea in Cuiabá?"

"Helps 'em strip off bamboo leaves."

"Yeah, and?" she said, trying in vain to concentrate on her hieroglyphic figures.

"Well, these mammoths have six toes as well."

"Yeah, I noticed."

"I'm betting the extras are modified ankle and wrist bones—tweaked to take on a new purpose."

"Like climbing around in the rocks and stuff?"

"Right," Mac said. "Evolution doesn't invent. It tinkers with what's there already."

"That's great, Mac," Yanni said, "and speaking of evolution, I'm going to go get Alpha back here." She pointed to her handiwork. "I need to show him this."

Mac replied with a nod as she walked away. "Careful," he called after her.

Glancing down, Mac noted that her symbols had themselves evolved into something far more complex than the simple stick figures she and Alpha had begun with.

Mac caught incongruous movement out of the corner of one

eye. Reflexively, he dropped and rolled to his right. A loud metallic clank accompanied by a spray of sparks exploded so near to his face that the embers actually struck him. He sprang to his feet, instantaneously assessing the threat while already leaning into his next dodge.

During an adrenalized flash of recognition, he saw everything he already suspected. It was the visage of the creature who had murdered Jerry—*back to complete his trophy case.*

In only two seconds, Mac managed three perfectly executed avoidance maneuvers, changing direction each time and increasing the distance from his attacker—but to no advantage at all. The Morlock's reflexes were quicker.

Mac glimpsed the raised pike and barely had time enough to register what was about to happen. And yet, within that same small part of a second, and in a blur of motion that Mac could not quite track, the little mammoth was suddenly between them. With its right trunk, the elephant had whipped something around the back of the giant's head, deftly caught it with its left trunk, and began to pull Scarface onto his tusks.

Mac watched the Morlock's expression change from one of snarling triumph to wide-eyed surprise as the mammoth's tusks drove through his body wall and diaphragm, expertly targeting the heart and lungs.

Scarface dropped, staring at nothing.

The mammoth, looking rather calm, given the circumstances, ignored the body and began wiping its tusks clean in the snow.

"Gotta tell ya, kid," Mac said, "just when I thought I'd seen everything . . ."

The mammoth shot him the briefest of glances before turning his attention uphill. Yanni was running down toward them, Alpha trailing behind.

Having finished cleaning itself, the little mammoth, continuing its nonchalant routine, picked up the woven cord it had used to save Mac's life. *It's the choke collar,* Mac realized.

He looked on with a combination of surprise and awe as the creature reaffixed the restraint around its own neck.

"So *that's* why you guys wear those things."

Although Mac had been involved in the killing of a Morlock, he was relieved when Yanni informed him that Alpha regarded it as nothing more than "pest control." The short conference that followed ended with mutual nods and a bout of hieroglyph-obliterating overkill by the lead Morlock.

"Okay," Yanni announced, "we're headed back to the shelf and the Chinese helicopters. You think you can fly one of them?"

"As long as it's in one piece," Mac replied. His mind flashed back to Li Ming's colleague in the "Trophy Room." *It's a bet those Chinese pilots won't be flying us out of here,* he thought, but left unsaid.

The Navy lieutenant from Massachusetts was growing impatient with delays, brought about by the "sole survivor" from a Chinese expedition. He gestured toward the Asian zoologist. "And we're supposed to believe everything this Red shovels our way?"

In a remarkably calm voice, Wang had managed to inform the Devil's Brigade–led team as thoroughly as he could how easy it was to make wrong turns, and about some of the unique dangers they were now facing.

Of greater concern to Dr. Nora Nesbitt was the fact that, after an uneventful trek to the helicopter site, it was immediately apparent that the two Russian "bananas" would *not* be flying anywhere. Large sections of the engines had been forcibly torn out and were now missing.

"Look, our mission is to get MacCready and his two friends out of here," the lieutenant said. "As for the rest, I think this guy's whole story reeks of misinformation."

The invertebrate zoologist had already determined that, hero or not, the Bostonian was as cocky as he was enamored with the sound of his own voice.

While "Just Call Me Jack" shared his idea about a Chinese hoax conspiracy with Nesbitt, the rest of the team worked with Wang to plot a course that they hoped would lead them to MacCready.

"So, Chicago," said Captain Don Pederson, a thick-necked former lumberjack, "you've seen nine-foot-tall ape-men and killer snowflakes?"

Wang nodded. "As I told you."

"And you're *not* a fisherman now, are you?" the Devil's Brigade leader asked, his men responding with an assortment of snickers and moans. The sole female member of the group looked on with a frown, while Wang looked confused.

"He means you're not prone to exaggeration," Nesbitt explained for Wang, shooting the captain a discouraging look.

"No . . . no, fisherman," Wang responded. "No exaggeration."

"I told you these creatures are real," she informed the group, allowing some annoyance to creep into her voice. "What he's telling us is simply more evidence."

"Any birds?" someone asked, and eight heads, including that of the Chinese scientist, turned to him. It was Sergeant Juliano, the incongruous-looking weapons expert and old friend of the missing Captain MacCready. Juliano scanned the quizzical faces, then shrugged. "I hate birds."

"No birds," Wang replied, as they began the trek downhill. "Birds not the problem."

Long after moonrise on the third of August, the strangest team of travelers since *The Wizard of Oz* was on the move.

Mac, Yanni, and the other two species had neither heard nor smelled any pursuing Morlocks. Nonetheless, the pair of humans snapped into hyperalertness as Alpha, up ahead, halted suddenly.

"Morlocks?" Mac whispered.

"Don't think so," Yanni replied, scanning the shadows and stony crevices, and listening intently.

While Mac and Yanni hung back, the little mammoth moved forward, brushed past them, and stood just behind the giant. Mac watched in fascination as the odd bifurcated trunk split at its base into a pair of arm-length appendages—each with a set of finger-like tips, and each testing the air in multiple directions.

"Something's got 'em worked up," he said quietly.

If either of those things sees us, take the shot," Captain Pederson whispered to the man with the nightscope-mounted carbine. "Aim for the big guy."

As if on cue, both of the strange creatures turned their attention directly at the sniper's nest.

Pederson's eyes widened in surprise. *They* can't *have heard me,* he told himself. *We're a hundred yards away and downwind.*

The beasts—one of the Chinese scientist's "ape-men" and what appeared to be a miniature elephant sporting a shaggy carpet—continued to stare straight at him. *Son of a bitch!*

"Captain?" the sniper lying next to him said, under his breath.

Pederson shook his head slightly, before whispering a response. "Take the s—"

Yanni rushed forward, ahead of Alpha. Keeping one eye on the ice and bolder-strewn incline, she motioned for him to crouch down and for the little mammoth to remain still. All of their attention was focused on a rocky outcropping a hundred yards farther uphill. Then, just as Yanni was about to begin shouting, something unexpected broke the cold silence.

Don't shoot!" came a cry from behind the sniper. "*That's Yanni!*"

Captain Pederson and his sniper turned to see the little weapons expert Juliano frantically waving his arms and running past them and into the line of fire. "What the hell is this?" the thick-necked officer muttered.

The two Devil's Brigaders exchanged exasperated looks, then the sniper turned back to reacquire his target. The giant was gone, as was a creature that reminded him of an elephant in need of a serious haircut.

"Hold your fire," Pederson said, just as Lou Costello's twin reached Yanni and at least one of the others they had been sent to rescue.

The sniper reset the safety.

Those Ruskie helicopters are trashed," Sergeant Juliano told his friends. "Not even *you* could fly them out of here, Mac."

R. J. MacCready shot his buddy an appreciative nod.

Captain Pederson peered over the table of rock and into a thousand-foot drop. "So, you know another way down from here, Captain? Besides the quick way?"

"We don't," Mac replied, "but Yanni's friends might."

"If they aren't halfway back to that valley already," Jack chimed in. He was referring to the fact that, by the time Sergeant Juliano threw his arms around Mac and Yanni, both Alpha and the little white mammoth had vanished.

"They wouldn't do that, Jack," Mac said, shaking his head, though his tone of voice expressed something less than one hundred percent certainty.

"They risked their lives to help us escape," Yanni added, sharply. "I doubt they even *have* a home to go back to, anymore."

"So . . . then why'd they run off?" the Devil's Brigade leader asked.

Mac watched Yanni's transition from defense to offense. "Probably because they were about to get ventilated," she said.

Mac noticed that Pederson also sensed the icy reaction and, knowing she was right, he dialed back on his tone. "Well, Mrs. Thorne, saving you two was quite admirable of your friends, but can you get them back here?"

"I don't know," Yanni replied, still on edge. "*Your* men gonna shoot 'em?"

"Captain Pederson," Mac said, "if anyone can coax them back, Yanni can."

"It's the guns, Mac," Yanni asserted. "You know how they are when it comes to guns."

Mac nodded; but he, Yanni, and everyone else present knew

there was no chance that any of them would be giving up their weapons.

"Nobody's going to shoot them," Mac reassured her, while making eye contact with as many of the team as he could without being too obvious.

"It won't matter," Yanni continued. "If you're holding a weapon, you're goin' over the cliff."

"Excuse me," Pederson said, "am I missing something here. Why do we even *want* those creatures back? We've rescued two of the people we came here to rescue, right?"

There were nods all around from the Devil's Brigaders—but Mac, Yanni, and Jack exchanged looks.

"Whatever you need, I'm in," Jack told Mac and Yanni. Then, turning to Pederson, he said, "You do understand Jerry and Mac saved my ass."

"We know," Pederson replied.

Jack let out a deep breath, then continued. "So, Mac, have you learned whatever it is you were sent in to learn?"

"That and then some," MacCready replied, "as you might have noticed."

At that, Dr. Nora Nesbitt became even more "on mission" than she had at the sight of little "Dumbo," *to say nothing of a living example of Pliny's hairy bipeds.*

"Well then," Pederson said. "We're mostly mission accomplished. Let's find the quickest way out of these mountains—I'd start with downhill, no?"

Yanni gave a derisive laugh. "Look, Pally, Alpha knows the ins and outs of this region far better than we do," she asserted. "Without him, I'm certain we'll run into a slew of Morlocks."

"Morlocks?" Nesbitt asked "Is that what you're calling them?"

"Morlocks, Cerans, Yeren," Yanni addressed the group. "Whatever you wanna call 'em, they'll be happy to show you the quickest way down."

"Oh?" Juliano interjected, hopefully.

Yanni gestured toward the ledge. "Sure. Screaming your lungs out and with your rifles shoved up your asses, sideways."

"And don't forget the killing snow cloud," Wang added. "Only this Yeren will know how to avoid."

"That's right," Mac said. "Without Alpha, we're definitely not getting out of here alive."

"And with him?" Nesbitt asked.

"We're only *probably* not getting out of here alive."

"Well there's a convincing argument," Captain Pederson said. Then he shot Yanni a look. "But we're *not* getting rid of our guns."

"I'll see what I can do," Yanni said, throwing a dirty look at the holstered .45-caliber Colt that he was sporting. With no further comment, she headed off down the trail.

Mac's expression of deep concern turned to a mixture of pride and worry. He did not try to stop her.

"Shouldn't someone go with her?" Nesbitt asked.

"*No!*" Yanni called back without turning around.

Yanni Thorne turned the corner of a switchback and came face-to-face with the miniature mammoth. Taking her by surprise, the creature rushed forward, its bifurcated trunk resembling a pair of welcoming arms. It gathered her in against its forehead for what her late husband might have termed a "slightly less than bone crushing" hug, while simultaneously, Alpha seemed to materialize from the face of a sheer rock wall into the predawn twilight.

Easy there, fella, Yanni told herself, trying to find the breath that the little pachyderm had just squeezed out of her.

Alpha's reaction was far less friendly. By way of a greeting he drew back his considerable set of gums to reveal an even more considerable set of teeth. Then he hissed and gave a short whistling cry, which translated to, *Do not even think of coming near me*—a behavior that continued to leave Yanni perplexed.

"Yeah, nice to see you, too," she told him.

Adding to the peculiarities of the reunion, it was the mammoth and not Alpha who stepped forward to give Yanni an all-too-familiar "finger" poke. What made it even weirder was that the prod was in the wrong direction, toward the downhill portion of the rocky incline—away from Mac and the others. To emphasize the point, Alpha took a few steps, gesturing for her to follow.

"O-kay, I get ya. But I'm gonna need a little favor first," Yanni said, then pointed uphill. The response was nearly as predictable as it was negative.

Yanni decided to try another approach. Kneeling in the snow once more, she drew a series of stick figures, pointed to them, then to herself. Finishing up, she gestured that the three of them should proceed back the way they'd just come.

Alpha gave the artwork a quick glance before obliterating it with a violent swipe of his foot—the little elephant following up with a nasal-powered exclamation point.

"I knew you'd see it my way," Yanni said, then she smiled and started drawing again.

R. J. MacCready's internal alarms had started going off before Dr. Nora Nesbitt got to the question she'd apparently been waiting to ask all along.

"The only sped-up evolution I saw was probably related to the extreme isolation these species are under," Mac lied.

"You mean, like on an island?"

"Yeah, some species get smaller when there are less resources."

"Like the mammoths?"

"Exactly," Mac replied, knowing that at least *this* much was true.

"So this mist-covered valley—none of us gets to see—is really just a kind of island?"

"Right! Nothing magical going on. Just a series of small, isolated populations having no exchange of genetic material with the outside." Mac was in serious lecture mode now. "That type of isolation can produce some weird-looking shit."

"Like Morlocks and mini-mammoths with two trunks and legs adapted for climbing?"

"You got it," MacCready said, trying to be nonchalant as he gauged Nesbitt's response to what he was shoveling. And for her part, the invertebrate biologist simply nodded, appearing to take it all in.

Good, Mac thought, flashing her a smile.

"That's interesting, Dr. MacCready," Nesbitt replied, flashing her own smile. "I was just wondering—"

Her tone told Mac that the charade was over even before it actually was.

"—did you happen to run into any guinea worms that had been artificially selected to become biological weapons?"

Shit! "Guinea worms?" Mac asked, trying not to stutter.

"Yes, *Dracunculus.* Something very much resembling that very parasite was clearly depicted in the Pliny codex."

"And?"

"And it looked like ancient Morlocks had been farming them."

Jesus, Mac wondered, but said nothing. *Were the grass mimics Pliny's worms, two thousand years later?*

"I see," Nesbitt said, wearing a very different smile now, and reminding Mac a little too much of a cat who had just cornered a mouse.

There was a sudden commotion among the others and Mac took the opportunity to step away from what had turned into an uncomfortable grilling by Nesbitt. Two Devil's Brigaders stationed fifty yards down the rugged trail were frantically waving their arms, signaling something important.

An out-of-breath Sergeant Juliano was suddenly at Mac's side.

"You're gonna want to see this one, Captain," the man exclaimed, literally pulling MacCready by the jacket. And as usual, he knew that the little sergeant was right.

As they'd been ordered to do in just such an event, Mac saw that the two sentries had put down their rifles and were now stepping back against the rocky wall bordering one side of the trail. Yanni Thorne gave them a brief nod as she passed. Mac noticed that there was little response from the shaggy-looking miniature elephant that followed her. Offering what Mac considered a slightly less than friendly response, the Morlock flashed a toothy snarl before kicking the two rifles off into space.

"Bad Morlock," Mac said to himself, then ran down to greet Yanni.

Captain Don Pederson called a "humans only" meeting on a barren outcrop some thousand feet above their "thrown overboard" rifles. The focus of discussion was how, exactly, they might avoid dying in one of the various ways that had been recently enumerated by Mac and Yanni. On that topic, had anyone been acting as meeting secretary, he would have noted that even the Chinese biologist had gotten into the act, chipping in—

repeatedly—with a rather squirm-inducing method of demise involving some rather badly behaved snow. And had the meeting secretary taken shorthand notes, the exchange between the parties would have read something like this:

"Alpha says there's only one way to get down from here without getting killed."

"And what's that?"

"He says we need to follow him."

"Where?"

"Up to a place where none of the other Morlocks will come after us."

"And where's that?"

"Ummm. . . . Alpha won't say."

"I still can't see why we don't just head downhill. Whether your big pal there likes it or not, we're not completely defenseless."

"Just keep your sidearms hidden."

"Look, there's a valley full of Morlocks waiting for us to head in the wrong direction. And your little handguns won't matter for shit once they've pulled your balls out through your mouth."

"That sounds painful."

"But that's not going to happen, Sergeant."

"That's good, sir."

CHAPTER 23

When Three Worlds Collide

Change is the law of life. And those who look only to the past or present are certain to miss the future.
—JOHN F. KENNEDY

I don't try to describe the future. My business is to prevent the future.
—RAY BRADBURY

In the Valley of the Cerae
Summer, A.D. 67

As the days passed, Pliny came to realize that Severus was falling even more intensely under Teacher's control than he thought imaginable. At present, he could not determine who the man was anymore: Severus the involuntary traitor or Severus the Roman centurion who was now actively assisting in preparations against the Scythian invasion.

"So you think their main force is still spread over a wide area?" Proculus asked.

"I believe so," Pliny said. "Becoming familiar with the terrain and drawing up their plans."

There was no question that the Cerae too understood what was happening—and how their every effort must be directed against this latest race of intruders. In fact, Pliny's captors were so preoccupied that it was deceptively easy to imagine that he and Proculus could simply retrace their steps to the glacial valley, past the ruins of Pandaya, and all the way to Rome without being captured—at least, not by the Cerae.

Pliny noted that on most nights, Teacher and Severus never returned to their chamber. *Doubtless making more catapults,* he concluded. *And more canisters.*

Nearly two weeks after the weapons test on the Scythians, Severus was finally allowed to speak with his two country-men—an exchange that took place across adjoining balconies.

"Are you with us?" Severus asked. The sound of the centuri-on's voice surprised them at first.

"And are you helping our enemy design new weapons?" Pro-culus snarled. "The same enemy who butchered and desecrated your own men."

"I wasn't talking to *you,* Cavalryman," the officer replied.

Pliny suppressed a smile. *A trace of the old Severus,* he thought. "How are they treating you, my friend?" Pliny countered.

There was no response to the pleasantry, so Pliny resolved to answer the man's question. "I suppose if it is a choice between the Cerae and Scythians, we shall live longer among the Cerae."

"No doubt about who *you* will be serving," said Proculus, still agitated from the scolding. He pantomimed an obscene act.

Pliny scarcely noticed the gesture, deciding instead to offer Severus some advice. He turned his gaze outward, as if he could stare a thousand stadia through buildings and across mountain passes. "From what we know of the old Scythian predecessors, they like the dark," Pliny said. "They'll probably make their next move under the cover of a new moon and thick clouds."

Only after he finished his pronouncement did Pliny discover the centurion had gone.

W hen the Scythians did march against the valley, they struck during a cloudless night, with the full moon glowing balefully overhead.

It was plain that Severus had communicated to Teacher and her brethren, whether he believed it or not, that his two fellow travelers were on the side of the Cerae. On the night of the Scythian march, Pliny and Proculus had an extraordinarily clear view from the great pinnacle—which towered over the cloudy sea like a dark sentinel. The Scythian invasion force entered the valley of the Cerae from five different directions.

"Medusa's eyes!" Proculus said. "It's like watching five rivers pour in."

On opposite sides of the valley, the habitations of the Cerae were no longer in phosphorescent blackout.

A diversionary tactic or traps? Pliny wondered.

He watched Scythians approach narrow entrances into the brightly lit structures before rejecting them for what they were— decoys, choke points. In total, Pliny estimated that these tactics had delayed the Scythian advance by no more than a quarter hour.

On the ridges, elephants appeared, some of them with riders, others hauling wood-framed weapons.

"They've brought their own bolt-throwers," Pliny told Proculus.

Even as they spoke, several of the ballistae were being set in place and aimed at the very tower on which they stood.

Proculus held up one of the membranous, pomegranate-sized bags of worms that Severus and the Cerans had entrusted to them. The disgraced centurion himself had instructed that these needed only to be dropped upon the attackers, should they storm the tower.

The cavalryman gestured toward the invading force. "I'd trade all of these creepers for one of their longbows."

"Get down!" Pliny shouted. The first of the ballista-launched projectiles were already arching high over the moonlit fog.

The two men dove onto the floor of the terrace.

Two rounded stones struck above and below their position, bouncing off the ice and fiber mixture. A third shook the wall behind which Pliny and Proculus had ducked, striking only a few arm lengths from Pliny. The material seemed to be holding together surprisingly well but a piece of shrapnel had torn open one of the worm-filled bags. Yet this too was of no consequence. Detecting nothing to attack, the writhing former contents of the weapon simply moved off in every direction, spreading like petals from a nightmare flower.

Proculus pointed in the direction of the Scythian ballistae. "*That* way," he told the creatures.

"Let me know if they start listening to you," Pliny said, risking a peek across the mayhem unfolding below. "This is not going according to plan," he declared, moments later.

Proculus managed a laugh. "For whose side?"

"Either."

The war elephants were the last to descend with the Scythian horde. A hundred or more of the armored giants moved toward the mist-hidden catapults where Severus and a small team of Cerae worked feverishly to load and fire as many canisters as they could before being overrun. Projectiles landed in clusters along the shore of the false sea, among the densest concentrations of Scythians. The riders reined in their elephants, pausing to assess. The foot soldiers also hesitated, and some of them were already beginning to fall.

Simultaneously, no fewer than a thousand Cerae boiled over the tops of the nearer ridges, whence the Scythians had come. They charged down from the hills at a dead run, some wielding Roman swords and lances, others firing bags of Scythian-seeking death from slings. They had appeared with amazing sudden-ness—as if most of their army, well fed and rested, had swarmed up from beneath the mountains themselves.

The Scythians had no choice but to move deeper into the sea of fog.

On the mist-bound valley floor, the white mammoths were first to sense the approach of the new danger. They were taller at the shoulder, more muscular, and less fleet-footed than their descendants. Their fur was longer, their cranial capacity smaller, and each possessed only a single trunk. Three of them had just helped Severus and two Ceran warriors to realign a catapult, its aiming point directed by spotters above the mist. Teacher was about to give one of them an appreciative pat on its trunk when all three turned toward a sound that neither human nor Ceran could hear. Spreading their ears, the mammoths stood very still for just a moment, then ran off into the mist. All along the cata-pult site, the rest of the mammoths did the same.

"We don't have much time!" Severus called out. Driving home a message that his words did not quite convey, he panto-mimed a rapid-fire sequence to the Cerae. At Teacher's signal, they launched what he feared would be their final volley of canisters.

With no mammoths remaining behind to help realign and reload, and realizing with Severus that they could not possibly reload before being overrun, the Cerae broke open the remaining launch canisters and spread their contents over the ground. Then they gathered hastily into the defensive *orbis* position that Severus had taught them.

The first direct encounter with the Scythian invasion force was with its foot soldiers. They stepped onto ground infested with two species of living weaponry that flowed like a liquid, up their legs and under their armor.

Severus looked on with a combination of horror and admiration as the soldiers advanced, displaying no response to pain—at least at first. More than thirty Scythians came striding out of the snow fog. Though his own sword had been returned to him, Severus found that, surprisingly, there seemed no use for it. Only three of the invaders reached the perimeter of outward-projecting Ceran lances. The last of them pushed a stubby reed between his lips and blew a high-pitched whistle before he died.

The whistle changed everything.

It summoned monsters.

Defensive formations no longer mattered.

The first of the war elephants broke through the Ceran position only moments after emerging from the mist. Clad in thick leather and metal armor, the elephant's headpiece was its most fearsome feature—*at least initially*—baring a huge, centrally located eye.

Cyclops! Severus thought, scarcely noticing its rider at all. Though part of his brain recognized that this was the work of an artisan, there was no escaping the sensation that the eye was staring directly at him and through him. For an instant the image held him spellbound, an involuntary response that had worked exactly as intended by the designers of the headpiece.

During that first instant, a Ceran warrior standing beside Severus, and similarly transfixed, was separated from his head by one of the twin blades affixed to the monster's tusks.

The Cerans who weren't crushed or slashed by the creature during those first moments of contact scattered to either side. Severus sidestepped the behemoth but was knocked to the ground by a Ceran. As the centurion glanced up, the armor-clad Scythian rider reined his war elephant into a remarkably tight turn in preparation for a second charge. One of the Cerans used his sling to launch a tick-filled projectile at the giant. Impacting solidly against a sliver of exposed flesh between thick leather plates, the spidery creatures burst forth but soon fell away ineffectively, like beads of water shaken from the back of a dog. In a moment of pandemonium, the defender had forgotten that his weapon was "trained" to follow only the scent of Scythian flesh.

"Aim for the rider!" Severus called out. Then, remembering the language barrier again, he pointed to the Scythian, who was howling and bellowing as if possessed.

Teacher released her own projectile and struck the mounted attacker square on the faceplate. Others followed her lead, but the rider's armor covered the body so well, and was so tight fitting, that it slowed the penetration of the weapon. During the few extra seconds required for the ticks to find seams and eye slits, the elephant gored a Ceran architect and two warriors with its tusk-mounted blades. A physician was stamped to death at Severus's side, with a warrior simultaneously tusk-flung over his head.

During the next instant Severus was airborne—thrown out of the way by Teacher, who immediately scrabbled up the animal's flank with two other physicians, even more quickly than Severus had seen her kind ascend balconies and ice cliffs.

The centurion pried a lance from the hands of a dead Ceran defender then, taking quick but careful aim to avoid Teacher and her companions, he hurled it at the elephant. Severus had contrived to blind the creature in one eye or at least distract it from the trio of Cerans but the projectile pierced the giant's trunk instead.

Teacher and her two companions drove three lances through the rider, flung him over the side, and began tearing openings in the elephant's armor. Lances of Ceran steel pounded down between its ribs and into each of its huge lungs.

At the moment the beast began to topple, it reached behind with its wounded trunk, grabbed one of the Cerae from its back, and pierced her all the way through on a blade-tipped tusk. As the dying monster fell onto its front knees, Teacher and the other Ceran sprang from its back.

For all the death the elephant had wrought, Severus could see that, unlike the indigenous mammoths with their coverings of dense fur, this relatively hairless giant had been leaking heat from the entire surface of its body. *Already dying before it ever entered the valley,* he thought.

The cries of bellowing monsters and mortally wounded Cerae could be heard from every direction, near and far. Drawn to the catapult emplacements by the sounds of battle and perhaps the scent of a sibling's blood, a second giant roared out of the mist—a bull elephant, more massive than the first. But there was something beyond its size that distinguished the new arrival. It only took Severus a beat to realize that the cyclopean eye of its headgear was completely obscured by blood and flesh. One of the brute's tusk blades had been snapped off near the base, the damage serving as a warning that this beast was even more hot-tempered than the one they had just slain.

The creature's Scythian rider was a monstrosity in her own right. She wore strange armor, more tightly fitting and oddly familiar. Apparently, the protective garments had already taken hits from tick- and worm-filled projectiles but this time the weapon was not only being slowed, it was being repelled. Now, with the rider having fully emerged out of the mist, the familiarity of the outfit became all too horribly clear.

"My gods," Severus whispered, realizing that the rider's gauntlet gloves had been sewn together from the carefully refitted hands of a Ceran. The headgear and most every other covering were also fashioned from Ceran skin. The ticks and worms that had been flung at the rider had mistaken her for one of Teacher's brethren, and now they were falling harmlessly from the armor, like dust.

With a sickening snap, Severus saw one tusk-pierced warrior flying end over end into the fog. Another Ceran stood his ground with a lance of native steel, trying to blind the rampaging beast, but he was not fast enough to escape a blow from the huge trunk. Teacher tried to save him but not even she was fast enough—suffering a slash to her thigh—the tusk blade coming perilously close to severing a femoral artery.

Severus moved in to assist, but Teacher violently flung him out of the fray, then spun back to face their attacker.

The beast charged again, the monstrous rider darting forward over its back and mounting the head as if climbing atop the prow of a ship. Her armored breastplates clothed in real Ceran breasts, the Scythian stood like a figurehead from hell.

Though Severus managed to avoid being stamped flat, a swipe from the creature's trunk cracked several of his ribs. When he looked up, Teacher was already clinging to the giant's sides, pulling away armor, slashing and stabbing.

Struggling to regain his footing and his breath, the centurion coughed blood and picked up another lance, his mind stuck on a single question: *How can I help tear a hole in this thing?*

Severus rose to his feet and staggered toward Teacher like a drunk, vowing to die for her with what little strength he had left.

By the time he stood, Teacher had climbed atop the animal's shoulder. The enraged Scythian repeatedly struck the Ceran in the face with its shield, finally dislodging her. But as the physician fell, she reached one elongated arm behind the Scythian's shield. Locking her hand around a wrist, Teacher pulled the she-beast down with her.

Severus was almost upon them and he knew that death was surely no more than a few heartbeats away when Pliny and Proculus arrived, accompanied by half a dozen Ceran warriors with lances of their own. By the time four lances went through Teacher's torn-away segments of elephant armor and into the animal's lungs and arteries, they were down to three warriors. Within those same seconds, the Scythian's instincts alerted her to Teacher's sudden and repeated glances toward the Roman. In response, the warrior drew a blade and made a dash for Severus.

She never reached him. In a blur of blocking and swiping motions, Teacher disarmed the elephant rider. She tore away the weapon-repelling breastplate and mask of Ceran flesh, then drove the Scythian face-forward into the tick- and worm-covered ground.

Observing that the weapon was still refusing to feed, Teacher ripped away what remained of the mask, then rent the woman's face with teeth and nails—shredding skin and exposing unprotected muscle and bone.

Severus was all tunnel vision now, watching as the enemy's writhing body was driven into the weapon-infested ground.

He watched the ground feed.

Those left standing now saw that Teacher could easily have ended the Scythian's misery with a single neck twist, but the physician had something more vengeance driven in mind. And so the ticks and worms ate their fill.

At some point, Severus realized that Pliny was standing beside him. "If you survive this night," Pliny said, over the eerily human death cries of the bull elephant, "I have one piece of advice for you."

"And what's that?" the centurion replied, wearily.

"Don't *ever* get her mad at you!"

South Tibet
Beyond the Valley of the Morlocks
August 3, 1946

On a day when Mac came to believe the lost world had already produced so many extraordinary dangers that nothing could surprise him anymore, he was suitably surprised by the approach of two more Chinese helicopters.

And thus ended what should have been a brief food and rest stop, near the ledge where Mac's and, more recently, Wang's party had landed. Bristling with guns, the new arrivals zeroed in and circled one of the downed craft as if it were a wounded queen bee.

Mac had no time to appreciate that his insect metaphor was about to get stronger. In the distance, a black speck had been hovering over the Morlock valley, but soon it too was making a beeline for the shelf.

"What the hell?" Mac muttered, watching as a third helicopter loomed quickly into view. *And this one's different from the first two*. Instinctively, he glanced over his shoulder to make sure Yanni was okay. As expected, she and her two woolly pals were already scrambling for cover.

Jack, who had hunkered down beside him, gestured toward the third gunship. "You think somebody's crashing their party?"

"They're Russians," Mac replied. "And I definitely get the feeling they didn't come to this dance together."

"Lucky thing our rifles and Johnny guns got thrown over the side, huh?"

This time Mac said nothing, watching as his friend zigzagged away to find a more secure position. Though he had lost sight of the others, Mac did notice that Alpha was still maintaining his distance from the group. Uphill, and in open view, the Morlock simply pressed himself closer to a wall of rock and ice, quickly becoming all but impossible to see.

Mac caught a flash of movement out of the corner of an eye. Seemingly ignoring the multiple threats from above, now it was the Chinese scientist who had run up to join him. "Those first helicopters, Nationalists!" Wang shouted over the din of blades and engines.

"Yeah?" Mac replied, motioning for him to duck down. "What's the difference?"

"Third one *not* Chinese. Third one Russian."

"So?"

"Communists and Nationalists no like each other."

Before he could reply, Mac saw that, incredibly, two of the Devil's Brigaders had stepped out onto open ground.

What the hell are they doing?

Unarmed, the men waved their hands over their heads.

MacCready recognized a whole new potential for catastrophe. America's uneasy alliance with Kai-shek's Nationalists had worsened the tension between President Truman and the Kremlin. No one knew for certain the new lows to which hatred between China's Nationalists and Communists had sunk, but from the look on Wang's face, at least two sides in this curious triangle were on the verge of a new war.

With this in mind, Mac now realized that the brave men who had stepped out into the open were simply taking their best shot at deescalating the situation.

The first flare of gunfire was therefore all the more shocking because it came from one of the Chinese helicopters, from Nationalist "allies."

The two Devil's Brigaders were still holding up their hands when the back of one man's head disappeared. The other soldier moved with such swift and practiced precision that nothing worse than shards of lead-splattered rock reached him before he was safely behind a mound of boulders.

"So much for your side," Mac told Wang, wondering in the back of his mind if the Nationalists had initially come in trying to learn what had happened to the three prior helicopter crews, or if Pliny's secret codex was not quite a secret anymore. There was no time to examine the question. Mac began blazing a new trail uphill, behind the cover of limestone and ice. A quick glance told him the helicopter that had fired on the two men was now closing in on the survivor's rock shelter—clearly trying to secure an optimal angle of attack, in order to finish him off.

Next, they'll seek out the rest of us, Mac told himself. *Remove all witnesses and maybe no one will ever learn how badly you just screwed up your mission.*

Only now did Mac realize that Wang had decided to follow him.

"So what the hell are your people doing up here?" Mac snapped at the scientist.

"My captain was ordered to bring back Yeren bodies," the man replied, his voice strangely calm, given the circumstances.

Mac nodded in the direction of the choppers. "Looks like somebody changed the plan."

Indeed they had, and now, with the arrival of the Russians and the drawing of American blood, the plan continued to change—at a psychopathic rate. The Nationalist helicopter that had been pursuing the surviving Devil's Brigader found its way blocked by the Russian craft. A hyperamplified speaker system blazed to life above the man's position. In a Russian-English hybrid language that Jerry had once referred to as "Rushlish"—and even with most of the words distorted through the sweep of blades—it was easy to piece the message together. The Russians were ordering the Americans to come out and give themselves up. One word came through with particular clarity: "MacCready."

The Chinese tried to sidestep the Russian blockade, shifting to a new line of fire against the trapped Devil's Brigader. The Soviets moved again into a line-blocking position, reminding Mac of Charles Knight's sculpture of a *T. rex* and *Triceratops* squaring off for battle. The difference was that, at least for now, this standoff appeared to be all show, with little desire by either side to charge. The comparison broke down completely as the second Chinese helicopter moved steadily nearer, making it inevitable that they would soon outflank the Russian on either side.

While the aerial chess match began to take shape, Mac considered the two likely outcomes for those on the ground: *killed by the Chinese or captured by the Russians and disappearing after "Uncle Joe" tortures out all the information he wants from us.*

Mac thought again about Charles Knight's sculpture and the two ancient enemies—*neither quite willing to attack the other.*

"Maybe I can change this," he said to himself, noting that

one of the Chinese helicopters was drifting into just the right geometry and was on the verge of eclipsing the Russian helicopter. Confident that the engine noise would drown out the sound of his sidearm, Mac waited for the very second the airborne geometry became perfect, then fired off three shots and quickly ducked.

Simultaneously, four puffs of smoke shot out from behind a rock shelter on the other side of the Russian helicopter. The bullets bypassed that craft and struck the other. After a moment of confusion, Mac realized exactly what had happened—someone else recognized the same fortuitous geometry and contrived the *same* plan, at the *same* moment.

The two sides were so focused on the trapped American, and on one another, that neither saw the actual shooters. The Chinese seemed only to notice penetrating gunfire from the direction of the Russian helicopter, and vice versa.

"MacCready!" Wang cried out beside him. "Stay down!"

Mac paid him no attention and kept just low enough, peering between rocks, to prevent the now confused and distracted intruders from seeing, and guessing, what had just happened. He had hoped to trigger at least a scrimmage, but what erupted now was a runaway spasm of gunfire that increased in ferocity for the better part of a minute.

The Chinese had nothing more substantial, for protection, than a canvas-and-glue hull. And, although the Russian helicopter came equipped with several patches of armor plating, the Soviets found themselves outgunned by the Chinese.

Within that first minute, within that single sweep of a stopwatch, the crew of the nearer Chinese helicopter were dead even before it fell to the ground. The Russians gained only a brief respite—perhaps twenty seconds more of life, for both of their pilots were slumped dead in their seats from Chinese gunfire. Mac thought he could discern at least two figures struggling into the cockpit as the Russian ship rotated away from him, staggered across the sky, then dropped upon the chopper aboard which Wang had arrived. It shattered against the older machine, scattering fire and smoke and throwing the few who survived—however briefly—into a disoriented, flaming rout.

As Mac watched, the second Chinese helicopter, its engine laboring, disappeared over the sheer cliff, beyond the spot where death had by now claimed the last of the Russian crew.

Reasonably sure that there were no guns trained on them, Mac and Wang bounded down from their hiding place. They reached snow and slid to a stop.

"Stay down!" MacCready shouted, but the surviving Devil's Brigaders were already huddled around the body of their dead friend. Jack was covering them with his Colt .45 and he gave Mac a nod. Taking in the scene, Mac let out a deep breath as Yanni, unharmed, and the little mammoth came out into the open.

"Nice shooting, huh?" Jack called out. "But I'm afraid I've only got two rounds left."

"That was *you*?" Mac followed.

"Yeah," Jack replied. "What's that they say about great minds?"

But staring down at the body of the Devil's Brigader, Mac decided to say nothing.

The Bostonian, however, wasn't quite through. "So, can you tell me why the Chinese *and* the Russians are running air raids on Tibet?"

MacCready shook his head, very slowly. "That's a story for another time," he said. "If ever."

An unmistakable noise distracted them. Somewhere far below the strewn-field of wreckage, the other Chinese helicopter had survived and was—despite the rattle and shriek of an engine in distress—returning.

"Get to cover!" Mac yelled at Yanni, as the little mammoth instinctively placed its own body between hers and the onrushing sound.

Mac turned to face the roar of the approaching gunship, taking a bead on the edge of the shelf where he calculated the flying machine would emerge.

Jack followed MacCready's lead. "What the hell are these guys so hot to find?" he pressed again.

But now there was no time to stonewall or deny; there was only time to face the enemy.

God damn you, Pliny, Mac thought. *Why couldn't you have stayed in fucking Rome?*

> *In the Valley of the Cerae*
> *Late Summer,* A.D. *67*
> *Five weeks after the Scythian defeat*

There were no celebrations among the Cerae—nothing resembling a victory party, no outward expression of triumph.

"They are not us," Pliny warned Severus. "I do not believe we can even call them people."

Within hours, after only the briefest recess for a meal and sleep, the Cerae shifted to a widely communicated and apparently universally agreed-to plan. In response to it, they became as active as a nest of paper wasps.

The winds blew fitfully down from the hills. The mists of the Opal Sea rose and fell in waves, and in the center of the sea, the Cerae themselves were doing what Scythian ballistae had failed to do. They were bringing down the central tower.

"But why?" Proculus asked him.

"It's the most visible evidence of their existence in this valley," Pliny explained. "And a potential beacon to future invaders—a beacon they've decided to extinguish."

In only a month, the tower had been completely dismantled. Architects, warriors, and mammoths now put to the yoke hauled it away piece by piece to some hidden lair.

By Pliny's accounting, the Cerae physicians and architects had suffered something worse than a decimation—battle losses that had now led to a shortage of architecturally talented minds. As a result, Pliny and Proculus were escorted deep into a cave system where they were "invited" to assist in the drawing up of new structural designs. This surprising activity focused primarily on sketching in their own opinions on Ceran plans for underground roof supports. The system was being expanded at a furious rate, much of it branching out into and then remodeling a preexisting labyrinth of natural tunnels and caverns.

On the fortieth day after war's end, Pliny stood on the lip of the balcony he and Proculus still shared. It would be their last day here, since the building was also being systematically deconstructed. The gardens below were a hive of activity in which each of the pallid white plants was carefully uprooted for transport to a new subterranean home.

Pliny shrugged. "By the winter solstice, every trace of these buildings will be gone."

"After their encounters with the Pandayans, the Scythians, *and us,*" said Proculus, "they must know that the world outside is growing larger—and closer."

"And so they've decided to hide every trace of themselves, under the fog and under the ground."

Through a space between stone arches, they watched the frozen body of the great bull elephant being carefully prepared for transport to the caves.

Pliny gestured toward the activity. "Including that monstrosity."

Proculus nodded, but said nothing.

"But what of the weapons they used to destroy the Scythians?" Pliny asked. "What if they decided to train such abominations against Rome?"

Proculus uttered a humorless laugh. "You have raised this question before."

"Yes. And on *that* day we had not yet seen the immensity of such power. I cannot bear to think of these living weapons—or something even worse—following trade routes and Roman roads into the very heart of the empire."

Next door, the balcony Severus and Teacher had shared was being carted away in pieces. Even as Pliny and Proculus watched, one of the worms, fleeing the commotion, inched toward the two of them. Then, sensing their presence, it darted away.

Pliny gestured toward the tiny creature. "The buildings are not all that's changing."

"I've noticed," Proculus replied.

Both of them were aware that physically, the worms were becoming smaller, faster, and seemingly more sleek-bodied than the ones they had seen at the death pits and during the battle.

Pliny did not understand the mechanism involved—no one would for nearly eighteen hundred years. And even then, Charles Darwin himself would neither see nor imagine evolution occurring at such a pace.

As Pliny and his friend prepared to descend from their quarters for the last time, both of them shared something remarkably close to a single thought.

No Roman, no man, can ever know that this place exists.

August 3, 1946

The helicopter was still beyond sight, below the cliff edge and rising loudly on damaged engines. The American rescuers and their rescued were hunkering down for a last stand against the Chinese—mere pistols against machine guns—when Alpha finally reappeared. From a distance, he communicated to Yanni with a series of hand signals and whistling sounds.

"What's *that* all about?" Mac called back to her, his pistol still trained on the edge of the cliff.

"Alpha wants everyone out of here," she said. "Out of here *now!*"

She was pointing uphill, unwisely, in Mac's opinion, in a direction that would make them more easily seen and fired upon.

The Devil's Brigade leader started to object, when Mac held up a hand. "Just, listen to her. Take Yanni and the others and run! Jack and I will follow as soon as we can."

The naval officer from Boston shot his friend a confused *Are you sure about this?* expression.

Yanni could see what the two men had in mind, and she rushed over to MacCready. Grabbing his arm, she began tugging. "No, Mac!" she yelled over the approaching roar. "Alpha wants us *all* out of here. Something about a storm coming."

"What?" Mac said, unsuccessfully trying to break free. "What storm?"

Yanni shook her head and tugged harder. "Not sure, Mac. You want me to stick around and figure out the particulars?"

Mac looked toward the edge of the cliff again. Twin rotors came noisily into view.

All three of them turned and ran.

The helicopter crested the cliff edge and navigated around the fringe of the Russian wreck. Coming close to a full stop, the pilot skillfully held his machine in a hover.

Mac, Yanni, and Jack picked up the pace, trying to catch up with Alpha and the mammoth, who were already far upslope of them. They caught a glimpse of Juliano and Wang, who appeared to be helping Nesbitt along. All three were reaching individual degrees of exhaustion in the mountain air.

Mac sensed sudden danger behind and his body moved instinctively—twisting to one side and knocking Yanni down in the same direction, just as a bullet burrowed through the air above their heads with the hollow sound that could only be heard (and felt) during a near miss. The crack of the gunshot came later.

Mac turned, surprised to see that the man who fired upon them was on the ground, limping. It appeared that he had jumped down more than a full story from the helicopter and decided to pursue them on foot. *Why aren't they just flying up after us and shooting?*

The man, a Chinese officer, emptied an entire clip in their direction but this time he was off target by hundreds of feet. He dropped his weapon and began swatting at himself.

Alpha's storm had arrived.

"*This* way!" Yanni said. Mac and the others obeyed without any further questions at all. Glances over his shoulder provided Mac with only bits and pieces of the picture below. Bright, sunlit streamers of snow rose vertically above the cliff face and above the enemy, as if driven by a howling wind. In another split second he saw the helicopter engulfed. During another glimpse, it was whirling away in apparent desperation—back again toward the terrain that dropped off more than a thousand feet. In the end, Mac paused and watched for nearly a full ten seconds. The Chinese on board were leaping from both sides of the machine. Mac was certain that by the time it began to drift and shudder, and fall out of view, not a soul remained aboard.

R. J. MacCready realized that the storm engulfing the Chinese was full of snow mimics. What he had no way of knowing yet was that he had just witnessed the first use of a racially tagged biological weapon in nearly two thousand years.

Autumn, A.D. *67*

The Ceran domes and the enormous central tower were gone forever.

All of the valley's inhabitants were now involved in a strange endeavor by which an entire civilization was trying to dig a hole into the earth and pull the hole in behind itself.

As the Cerae retreated into subterranean depths, the architects and the physicians seemed to have picked up as many as two hundred words of Latin from Severus, along with the words necessary to join them together in some meaningful fashion. As for learning the Ceran language, Pliny continued to believe he might have an easier time trying to communicate with a fish or a bug.

"This much they do understand," Severus explained one day, as they surfaced into sunlight. "'Pliny,' they say. 'He can be trusted.'"

"How would they know that?"

"Whether it is true or not, they *think* it," Severus replied. "And what if I told you that, should you or Proculus choose to leave this valley, none of the Cerae will stop you?"

"I think I would choose to stay around a while longer."

Proculus nodded. "It may be safer here."

"Nero wanted us to find the Cerae and bring one of their heads home for him," said Pliny. "Even if the ghoul is finally dead, who knows what would happen if the empire really does continue seeking the Cerae, perhaps even more vigorously? The Scythians might end up looking lucky by comparison, even if Rome somehow came out the winner."

"It's an amazement that the Cerae haven't destroyed themselves with their own discovery," Proculus added.

"And if *Rome* possessed such power?" Severus asked.

Without hesitation, Pliny replied, "I believe the empire's wings are made of wax, and always shall be. Give emperors the power to shape life itself? No. If your wings are made of wax, never fly too close to the sun."

"You, too, Proculus?" Severus asked.

"We can never tell of this place," said Proculus. "But if we leave, come with us, brother."

Severus looked down at the ground. "I cannot."

"What?" Proculus shouted. "You, a Roman, choosing these monkeys over us? Are you still a slave to the scent of your she-beast?"

Severus shook his head. "You have seen that she is not well. For this reason, a path is being prepared for me to stay beside her."

"What is the meaning of that?"

"I do not comprehend it fully myself. It is difficult for them to explain, in our words."

What Pliny had been able to see and understand was that Teacher did not appear to be healing from her wounds with the same magical rapidity as the rest of the Cerae. Two physicians had been tending to her continually since the Scythian invasion. Such attention seemed proportional with the serious nature of her condition. There were, in fact, few in her caste left. Because her kind had taken an especially severe beating from the war elephants, Pliny wondered if their population might have been pushed to the edge of extinction.

"How bad is it?" Pliny asked. "Is Teacher dying?"

"You do not understand," the centurion replied. "Her wounds from the battle are completely healed. It's something else that saps her strength."

"What then? This strange addiction between you?"

"Cling to that if you must."

Pliny stared at Severus, then shook his head, very slowly. "Her power over you. It is not what I thought it was, is it?"

"Shall I tell you why I must stay with her, always? Shall I tell you why a path is being prepared?"

"She has softened your brain," Proculus insisted.

Severus managed a quiet laugh. "As most *Roman* women cloud men's minds, from time to time."

"Roman women?" Proculus stammered. "These Cerae are not *us*!"

"Maybe they are more like us than they appear," the centurion said, quietly.

Though the Cerae looked humanoid and at the same time quite different, Severus's suggestion could not have failed to hammer a few cracks into Pliny's presumption that they were a breed completely separate from humans.

"What exactly are you going to do?" Pliny asked.

The centurion glanced over toward the path into the earth, then back to his friend. "I must admit," he said, "I have yet to figure that out."

"Stay with her *always*?" Proculus protested. "Nothing is forever."

"Time will have its say," said the centurion. "It always does."

CHAPTER 24

The Man Who Loved Morlocks

Home is where the heart is.
—PLINY THE ELDER

Glory ought to be the consequence, not the motive, of our actions; and although it happen not to attend the worthy deed, yet it is by no means less fair for having missed the applause it deserved.
—PLINY THE YOUNGER

West, *beyond the Valley of the Morlocks*
August 4, 1946

Death snow," Wang had called it. And, though MacCready had personally witnessed its effects, he found it difficult to comprehend how the same fluffy snow mimics that swirled so harmlessly around him during his entire time below the mist became the fury behind the storm that burst upon the Chinese.

He was thankful that the death snow did not follow them. It had in fact withdrawn with the last Chinese helicopter, but its arrival at the landing area communicated that the minds who had conceived a killing wind, and who commanded it, were on the move.

Past sunset and throughout the night march, Mac had not seen any other Morlocks, but from the way Alpha kept pressing the group forward it was clear that the danger was quite real, and likely gaining on them. The little mammoth, too, was looking increasingly nervous—making frequent stops to sniff the air, before heading off at an ever-more-hurried pace.

By the time the first rays of sunlight touched the ground, Alpha led them far from the cliff-side trail and into a narrow corridor through an ancient seabed of slate. Soon after, what some of the others might have perceived as claustrophobia-inducing walls gave way to an open plain. They crossed over what seemed like miles of stone flakes mixed with the shells of oysters and clams, but these mollusks had been off the menu for more than seventy million years. In silence and with great haste, they eventually followed Alpha from the flatland into a maze of mountain passes bordered on either side by vertiginous walls of rock. Here and there, the walls dripped skyscraper-sized streamers of green icicles.

No time for stopping and looking or asking questions, Mac thought, noting that other sights along the way were just as puzzling. Soaring outcrops of colorful mineral veins appeared to be studded with leafy plants, but they were really primitive lichens and mosses—ranging between blood red and purest white.

"The Hardy Boys," his botanist friend Bob Thorne had called these organisms, which had a talent for growing anywhere and under any conditions. "I've studied lichen that can grow on a dead guy's skull," Bob had informed Mac.

At this point, with the sun having passed high noon and with shadows just beginning to lengthen, R. J. MacCready was simply grateful that none of the local flora had behaved badly.

Despite the apparently desperate push for speed exhibited by the fleet-footed mammoth, Mac found time to make several more observations. He *was* disappointed that there were few if any animals among the lichen and white "moss"—though he knew this was generally the case for such environments—including the most species-diverse regions of all. He recalled the initial shock he had felt during his first trip to a rain forest, this particular one located deep within the Malaysian peninsula. As a graduate student, he'd come to study an oversize species of hairless bat by the name of *Cheiromeles*. He had been anticipating something like a Cecil B. DeMille crowd scene—this one starring monkeys, lizards, and every form of tropical wildlife he knew to inhabit the region. What he got was heat, humidity, and land leeches—hundreds of leeches. But these were not the wormlike parasites Mac had encountered while swimming in Adirondack ponds as a child. These bloodsuckers were six-inch-long hunters, as fast as they were active. And as he soon determined firsthand, their bite made the most pain-dealing bee seem like a mosquito by comparison.

Thinking about the tiger leeches brought back far more recent and even more uncomfortable memories of inchworm grass and skin-piercing bites.

Next topic, Mac told himself

Shifting mental gears, he noticed that Sergeant Juliano was acclimating well to the harsh terrain. Mac knew that the relative lack of wildlife suited him just fine and the little guy actually looked quite content to be where he was. Even the appearance of a lone raptor, soaring overhead, went essentially unnoticed. It glided high enough on an updraft, and disappeared fast enough, that the feather-phobic sergeant never had a chance to complain about it.

Also on the plus side of the ledger was the fact that breathing was becoming easier—far easier. Mac estimated that they had descended at least a thousand feet from the zone Jerry had once called "where helicopters go to die" and now the benefits of additional atmospheric oxygen were becoming noticeable.

Another positive was the ambient temperature—which here and there seemed to have risen high enough to melt an igloo (if there'd been one present). As a result, although the tall massifs that surrounded them were topped with ice, the mountain ravines through which they passed were intermittently bare of snow.

Mac noted the change, then forgot about it until they were passing over an outwash of white earth.

Yanni had stopped abruptly and was kneeling with her hand held flat against the stark, chalky-looking dirt. She broke what had been an hours-long silence. "Mac, feel this ground."

MacCready squatted down beside her and placed his hand down next to hers.

"Jeez, this ground must be twenty degrees warmer than the air," he said.

"What is this stuff?" Yanni asked, gesturing toward the stark white soil.

"It's calcium carbonate," Mac said, noting that there were an assortment of fungal puffballs growing on it, each nearly as pale as its surroundings. And given that there were no dark-colored rocks to absorb sunlight and heat, Yanni asked the very question Mac was beginning to compose.

"So where's this heat coming from?"

"Must be from below," Mac replied. "Geothermal wet spots, maybe? I'm pretty sure carbonate needs warm water to form."

"Kind of like Yellowstone?" one of the Devil's Brigaders added.

"Yeah, kinda like that."

A pair of sharp whistling sounds and a loud grunt terminated the discussion. Mac turned and saw the same man whose question he had just answered stagger forward and drop to his knees. An eight-foot pike had torn through a point directly between his shoulder blades and now extended out through his abdomen. Surprisingly, there was no blood. The soldier's expression showed nothing like pain—only shock at the strange object that had seemingly materialized in front of him. He locked eyes with Mac, then fell forward, his body sliding toward the spear point that had just embedded itself in the white earth.

Now there was blood.

A groan caught Mac's attention and he turned toward it. Another spear had pinned Sergeant Juliano to the ground.

As near as he could tell, at least a dozen Morlocks had found them. Mac and Yanni ran straight for Juliano.

"Your two friends aren't stopping!" Captain Pederson called out, pointing toward Alpha and the little mammoth.

"And we can't, either!" Yanni shouted back, noting that neither of their guides had broken stride and, if anything, they were sprinting ahead at an even quicker pace.

Some of their pursuers were trailing along the floor of the ravine. Others were apparently making a camouflaged approach, using the surrounding cliffs as launching points for their assault. They were also exhibiting an astonishing, perhaps even desperate degree of accuracy.

Especially, Yanni thought, *since they're hurling their steel pikes from something like two hundred yards away*—a feat that would have been impossible even for the most talented warrior in her village.

As if to emphasize the point, another sharp whistling sound provided a half-second warning, enabling Pederson to turn a kill shot from a lance into a glancing flesh wound to his shoulder.

"*Fuck this!*" he shouted as he, Mac, and Yanni bunched together in an attempt to drag the wounded Juliano out of firing range. The particular spear that had pierced the sergeant's calf was hastily removed with no time to consider the additional pain or damage they'd just inflicted and not even enough time to wrap the wound.

Seeing that Mac, Yanni, and now Captain Pederson were struggling, Jack quickly doubled back. Drawing his sidearm, he fired off several rounds into the surrounding cliffs while the leader of the Devil's Brigade took careful aim at what he determined to be the Morlock ground position. Without shifting either his aim or his gaze, he passed Jack three more bullets, announcing regrettably, "Those are the last I can spare you."

"They've tested our logistics," Jack said, making his out-of-breath pronouncement while grabbing a handful of Juliano's parka and more quickly dragging him along.

"I know it," Mac replied, still supporting Juliano between himself and Yanni. Ignoring his shoulder wound, Pederson was now bringing up the rear—ever watchful for more projectiles.

"They know that in a pinch, we'll leave our dead behind," Pederson said. "But *not* our wounded."

"Which serves *their* purpose by slowing us down," Mac added, with a grunt.

The rain of metal seemed to have paused.

"They're probably regrouping, no?" Juliano said, exhibiting a degree of calm that belied his deteriorating condition.

"Sounds right," Pederson agreed.

Up ahead, Nora Nesbitt and the surviving Devil's Brigaders had been ordered to maintain at least eye contact with their non-human pacesetters, and the invertebrate biologist was now waving her arms to signal their position.

"I still can't believe you talked me into ditching those rifles," Captain Pederson told Mac, as they slowly gained ground on the rest of the team. But it was Yanni who replied.

"Listen careful-like this time," she said. "Without Alpha, we're not getting outta here. And if everybody's packin' iron, we don't have Alpha."

"So how come we got to keep our pistols?" Pederson asked, performing a rather skillful backward run, while covering their backs. It was now all so sickeningly clear that if the Morlocks maintained their distance at the two-hundred-yard limit of spear range, then the pistol, compared to the accuracy of the rifles and Johnny guns left behind, would be rendered next of kin to completely useless.

"It's called a compromise," Yanni said.

"Too bad you couldn't have negotiated rifles instead," Jack said.

Yanni ignored the remark. "What I'm wondering is why Alpha's former pals didn't just overrun us as soon as the first handgun was drawn."

"Afraid of gettin' plugged, maybe?" the Devil's Brigader replied.

"I don't think so," Yanni said. "At this distance you can't hit any of them with a pistol. There's something else goin' on—"

Their conversation in retreat was interrupted by Mac. "Incoming! Watch it!" he called, just before a metal shaft smashed down not more than two yards away, propelling a spray of gravel at them. One fragment struck Yanni in the forehead, and a moment later she casually wiped away a thin trickle of blood.

"Yanni, you okay?" Mac cried, nearly letting go of Juliano before instantly correcting himself.

"I'm fine. Just keep going, huh?"

"Their throws are gettin' less accurate," Mac observed. "Strange. I think they're falling back."

"That's good," Yanni responded, "because we need to pull up someplace soon and patch Juliano's wound." *His face is looking too pale,* she left unsaid.

"Don't worry about me," Juliano mumbled, barely coherent. "No birds, though, right?"

Jack shot Yanni a puzzled look.

"Everybody hates something," she whispered. Then she turned to Juliano. "No birds, Sergeant."

"Spear-slinging giants, we got," Mac added.

Jack realized that Mac and his Brazilian friend were trying to keep the wounded man awake and talking. "Nine-footers," he chimed in.

"Well that's good," Juliano mumbled. "I hate birds."

We know, Mac thought. *Just hang in there.* He and Yanni exchanged concerned looks and picked up their pace.

Thankfully, there were no more reports of "Incoming!" from Pederson or Mac—the last spear having fallen short by nearly twenty yards.

Up ahead, Alpha and the little mammoth had finally begun to slow the pace, but behind Mac and his friends, there appeared an unnerving sight—a line of Morlocks spread out across the floor of the ravine. The giants who had been stationed in the cliffs were presently descending to join what now resembled nothing less than a pack of alpine wolves—ready to charge.

"Jesus," Jack muttered, checking his ammo, "we're not out of the woods yet. Nowhere near it."

The Devil's Brigaders, having seen the Morlock formation themselves, moved into position for what was beginning to look like a last stand.

Captain Pederson, who was counting his cartridges, nodded toward the line of creatures. "Remember Custer?" he asked no one in particular.

"Fuhgeddaboutit," Yanni responded.

"Well, it was back in—"

"I *know* when it was," Yanni said. "But this ain't that."

"Yeah, how do you figure?" Pederson said, chambering a .45-caliber round.

"Because I don't think they're coming any closer."

The Morlock formation, which had swelled to nearly two dozen individuals, surged back and forth in the distance, strengthening the imagery of so many wolves—now held inexplicably in place. It was as if a line had been drawn upon on the ground, across which they could not advance, toward something even a Morlock warrior feared.

By the time Mac and his friends had begun closing the distance between themselves and Alpha, the Morlock and his furry little companion had come to a complete stop. Yanni approached him, and though he was still wary of any physical contact, they did undertake another bout of their strange, hieroglyphic communication—this time presided over by the mammoth and somewhat constrained by the gritty substrate they were using as a writing tablet.

As the powwow concluded, and while most of the others were keeping an eye on the distant Morlock pack, the mini-mammoth passed something to Yanni, who nodded and immediately ran back to Sergeant Juliano. Mac and Pederson had by now applied a field tourniquet just below his knee.

"Here, Juliano," she said, "you've got to eat this now, okay?"

Dr. Nora Nesbitt, who had been intrigued by Yanni's interaction with their nonhuman guides, was suddenly at Yanni's side.

"What's that?" she asked, as the wounded man began to chew on what appeared to him to be a handful of leftover spaghetti.

"Just a little home remedy Dumbo picked up," Mac replied, without much thought and without looking up from checking the tourniquet.

"This stuff's okay," Juliano whispered. "Sauce sucks, though."

Nesbitt ignored the wounded man and the chuckles his response had elicited from his friends. "What *kind* of remedy, Captain MacCready?"

Now Mac turned to face the invertebrate biologist. "Well, it's not *Dracunculus*—if that's what you were thinking."

"Who's drunk?" Juliano asked them.

"Never mind, Sergeant," Mac said. "Just eat up all your spaghetti and you'll be fine." Then he addressed Nesbitt again. "Look, if we ever get out of here, there'll be time to talk about all of this," he said. "Right now, I think we can all agree that we've gotta keep moving."

Before she could respond, he and Yanni redirected their attention to Juliano, whose breathing was already starting to come easier.

Before departing, Nesbitt also noted the improvement.

Mac double-checked that everyone else was out of earshot, then turned to Yanni. "I certainly wasn't planning on bringing out that cave pasta—or anything else for that matter. At least not until we've had time to *really* think about it."

"And time is what we *don't* have," Yanni asserted.

Mac gestured toward the sergeant. "Although your elephant pal just put a crimp on that idea, huh?" Mac said.

"Seems that way," she conceded, and making sure to keep her voice low, added, "But that might not be so bad, right? Potential cures for polio, maybe even cancer."

"Yeah," Mac shot back, "then there's Wang's killing snow, car-nivorous grass, and probably shit we haven't even seen yet—all of it sharin' that valley with Juliano's spaghetti."

Deep in thought, Yanni said nothing, so Mac continued. "Just imagine this flora and fauna being toyed with in some lab until they change it into who-fucking-knows-what?"

Yanni uttered a short laugh. "Now where have I heard some-thing like that before?"

The answer, of course, was her late husband.

Yanni nodded toward Alpha and the mammoth. "And if any-body finds out what's really in that valley—"

"—it'll definitely spell the end of *their* world," Mac said, com-pleting the thought.

Misenum, west of Pompeii

A.D. 79

Eleven years after Nero's death, nine years after Pliny's return to Rome

At a quarter past eight on the morning of August 24, the first tremors rippled out from Mount Vesuvius. By noon a giant cloud covered most of the eastern sky.

A distress call was relayed to Pliny's seaside home by flag sig-nal from Herculaneum. The city of six thousand people stood midway between Pompeii and the estate.

Proculus, Pliny thought, before instructing his men to signal back. "We are coming to you, as swift as Mercury."

As Pliny, now an admiral, prepared to cast off, his seventeen-year-old nephew undertook an assignment that had just been given him. Its subject: what to do with the elder Pliny's original notes, the same notes from which the secret codex had been compiled. The young man implored the historian not to sail toward the very danger everyone else was fleeing. But Pliny waved him off, leaving the distraught teen with only a quote. "You may steal that one someday," the older man said, trying to make a joke of the situation. Then, in typical Pliny fashion, he repeated the phrase.

More than fifteen hours later, as the eruption reached its peak ferocity, a family friend on a mission of rescue found the boy at his uncle's work desk, surrounded by history books and apparently reading. *Is he in shock?* the older man asked himself, as all around the quaking grew worse and walls had already begun to crack and fail. The teen was *not* in shock. He had in fact spent the entire night seeking out and sorting through every scrap of paper mentioning the Cerae. He burned them all, in honor of his uncle's wish that their valley, their world, should remain lost.

When the boy, who would become known as Pliny the Younger, left the estate for the last time, he carried a single sheet of papyrus. It bore the very phrase his uncle had emphasized earlier.

It read, "Fortune favors the brave."

It was an epitaph.

W ell, *this* certainly ain't in Pliny's codex," R. J. MacCready told Yanni.

"At least not in the parts we saw," said Nesbitt.

They reached the grotto an hour before sunset.

Several miles beyond their last encounter with the Morlocks, the ravine had opened above what appeared to be an oasis but what the "scientist types" present immediately recognized as yet another microenvironment. Standing on the rim of the craterlike depression, Mac was reminded of the Roman Colosseum's arena floor and the surrounding amphitheater. *Maybe a bit steeper-walled,* he thought, *but the dimensions are just about right.*

The grotto's most startling feature, though, was neither its size nor its shape; it was the fact that every surface had become covered in blood-red overgrowth.

Alpha motioned for them to begin their descent and they moved forward cautiously. Oddly, it was the little mammoth who took the lead during the climb down, while the Morlock remained atop the rim, apparently to stand some uncharacteristic guard duty. Toward the rear of the column were Wang and one of the Devil's Brigaders, carrying Sergeant Juliano on a makeshift stretcher. The color had come back to his face and, despite the size of his wound, those caring for him had discovered that a tourniquet was no longer necessary.

Mac had to smile at Dr. Nora Nesbitt's unbridled joy at her new surroundings. The woman had immediately recognized that there were, in every direction, numerous unique life-forms to study, and in all likelihood, undiscovered invertebrates. She bounded down the rocky incline, reminding Mac of an undergraduate on a field study for the very first time.

Yanni motioned toward the other woman. "You'd better send down someone after her," she told Mac.

"Alpha wants us all down there, no?"

"Yeah, but if she breaks her ass or gets eaten by a tree, that's gonna slow us down real fine."

Mac nodded, no less anxious than Nesbitt to examine what Yanni had described as "a sort of forbidden zone for Morlocks." It was a disclosure that also helped explain why Alpha was acting so strangely. Thankfully, others were now assisting the rapidly recovering Sergeant Juliano, and so Mac was able to make his own observations.

He reached the floor of the grotto with little effort and, turning back, he noted that the Morlock was finally making the descent as well—still exhibiting what was clearly a great deal of hesitancy. The big guy's fur had also taken on something of a reddish hue, though MacCready took little notice, especially when he found himself standing in front of what looked like a cactus mimic that stood almost twice his height.

"Tons of iron-loving microbes and fungi," Nesbitt chirped, moving in to stand beside him. She gestured at the "cactus." "Oh, and mold—mostly red mold with, probably, some bacteria."

Mac took a closer look, noticing that what appeared at first glance to be tiny flower heads were actually black and red sporangia—circular structures that both produced and stored the spores, which were the equivalent of seeds.

Can't be too hard on myself for not recognizing them right away, he thought, realizing that these particular sporangia were half an inch in diameter—hundreds of times larger than anything he'd ever seen on a microscope slide.

Mac extended a finger and gently touched one of them.

Nesbitt cringed. "I wouldn't—"

The sporangium made a barely audible pop and suddenly Mac received a face full of red dust.

"*Blah!*" Mac cried, coughing and taking a step back.

"Never mind," Nesbitt said, which Mac translated as, *Stupid zoologist!*

She continued on, excitedly. "The closest thing you've seen to this was probably growing on an old piece of bread."

Just then, Yanni arrived. "Red looks good on you, Mac," she said, without smirking. "But listen, when you're done with your makeup session, Alpha pointed us to a clearing where we can camp for the night." Then she gestured for him to follow—which he did.

"There's also supposed to be a downhill path leading out of here," she said, under her breath.

"And where's that?"

"At the far side of the grotto."

"And?"

"And it'll take us out of this maze without running into any Morlocks. I don't think they'll come within miles of this place. According to Alpha, we just have to keep winding our way south and downhill. Eventually we'll run into civilization—although he didn't really call it that."

"He's turning out to be a lifesaver, that one," Mac said. "Who'd a thunk it?"

"Yeah, well, he *is* acting kinda weird though," Yanni said, unable to hide her concern. "And these red spores are getting all over his fur. You'll see what I mean."

The others were already starting to prepare for nightfall by the time Mac, Yanni, and Nesbitt rejoined them. Because they did not want to attract unwanted guests of any species, thoughts of a fire had been quickly nixed, so they simply arranged themselves in a rough circle and laid out whatever they could to act as bedding. The temperature in the grotto was nearly tropical compared to what they'd been through, and several of the Devil's Brigaders had already taken off their parkas to use as pillows or blankets.

Yanni gestured toward Alpha, who remained as far away from the humans as he could manage. The Morlock was squatting, and looking rather sphinxlike, with eyes closed. Even in the rapidly diminishing light, Mac could see that Yanni had been right—the Morlock's fur seemed to attract the red spores, in much the same way a magnet attracted iron shavings.

"What, you figured he'd be joining us for poker tonight?" Mac asked, trying to lighten the situation. "Guns, remember?"

"That ain't it, Mac," Yanni said, looking even more worried than before. "There's something wrong with him."

Though Mac silently agreed with her, his attention was soon drawn to the little mammoth, whose behavior was the exact opposite of the Alpha's. Currently, Dumbo (Mac's nickname having definitely caught on) was getting his ears stroked by Wang. An additional positive note was the fact that a rather comfortable-looking Sergeant Juliano, currently reclining against a scarlet boulder, was assisting the Chinese zoologist.

Within a few minutes, Mac too had settled in, and soon he was asleep.

The Red Grotto, Cerae/Morlock Forbidden Zone
August 5, 1946

Dr. Nora Nesbitt awoke at dawn as something lightly touched her face then flitted away.

Sitting upright, she rubbed her eyes and peered around the makeshift camp. There were snores and some sleepy shuffling about, but apparently no one else was awake.

Nesbitt turned her attention to what had awakened her—what appeared to be a swirl of red dandelion seeds. These, though, were efficient fliers, moving upward and changing direction with nothing like a breeze to propel them.

Like insects, she thought, *but different.*

Rising slowly, she decided to follow them.

Jack opened his eyes and stared up at the brightening sky. He wondered how on earth he'd come to such an amazing and terrifying place.

The answer, of course, was his friend R. J. MacCready. And so despite an ever-growing, personal laundry list of ailments—ranging from what he hoped was *only* malaria, to a spine that was becoming the new definition of "completely fucked"—the naval reserve officer hadn't given even a second thought to turning down this rescue mission. Always sickly and rail thin, Jack had long ago come to believe that his time on this planet might be relatively brief. Because of this he'd resolved to live whatever time he might be granted in as full a fashion as possible—and to accomplish something important before he died.

He had no way of knowing or even suspecting that something red and foreign to modern human experience was working its way deep into his tissues, in much the same manner as the microbe with which Yanni had infected Juliano the day before. He would never have believed, on this morning, that instead of death, decades of gradual (albeit painful) healing lay before him.

Below, on the grotto floor, Nesbitt trailed the scarlet swirl—which she'd now determined to contain scores of tiny creatures. They moved like a vapor around rocks and foliage, and she followed them, making mental notes on their behavior, until at last they came to a door-sized opening in one of the sloping walls surrounding the grotto. Then, seeming to hesitate for a second or two, the living cloud dispersed, flying off in separate directions and leaving the puzzled biologist staring into the pitch-black crevice. Nesbitt moved a bit closer and squinted into the dark. She could see that the crevice was actually more like a tunnel, leading a short way into the rock wall before ending in an expanse of light perhaps twenty yards farther down.

The sensible part of Nesbitt's brain, which was usually quite considerable, told her to head back and tell the others. But there was something else, something she could not quite define, and it told her to explore the opening herself—and especially what might lay beyond it.

Before entering the miniature cave, Nesbitt grabbed the closest thing to a branch she could find. Invertebrate lover or not, she had a fear of spiders that was as strong as it was well hidden. She frowned at the flimsy-looking excuse for a stick, which would now serve to clear her way through the tunnel.

"Fuckers beware," she announced to the shadows. Then she ducked into the opening.

J ack sat up, just in time to see the furry little elephant disappearing into a thick growth of mold or fungus or whatever the hell the scientist types were calling it. To the former pampered kid from Massachusetts, who had been turned by circumstances beyond his control into a war hero, everything about this place was just plain weird. Still, he rose quietly, as something about the animal's stealthy departure compelled him to follow it into the undergrowth.

N ora Nesbitt emerged from the short and thankfully spider-free tunnel waving an ersatz twig she'd determined to be a new species of club moss. She planned to add a small piece of it to the specimens she'd already accumulated. Although the biologist hadn't told anyone yet, she intended to carry the collection out when they left the grotto. But what Nesbitt saw upon emerging into the light caused her to drop the moss sample without a thought. The little subchamber was even more thickly carpeted in red than the grotto above.

A half-dozen mold-covered, statue-like figures were arrayed

across the ground of what looked like an open-ceilinged chamber. Her first thought was that they resembled the huge primates MacCready and his friends had been calling Morlocks. But these individuals differed from the hulking creatures she'd already seen—*thinner and somehow more graceful,* she thought. *And exactly like the ones described in Pliny's codex.* The biologist approached the closest of the figures—which, like most of the others, seemed to be sitting on its haunches. The head was almost at the level of her chest, and its face was directed toward the tunnel from which she had just exited.

Nesbitt knelt down and brushed an index finger over what appeared to be a thin layer of red mold. She hoped to scrape away a portion of the stuff to reveal the layer beneath. But the mold, which had a fleshlike consistency, would not budge.

"It's fused to whatever's below it," she said to herself. "Shit, these things are *old.*"

A rustle of what sounded like parchment from behind her caused the scientist to jump, but when she turned around there was nothing.

Nesbitt stood, took another glance at the tunnel exit, then crept deeper among the cluster of figures. She noted that four of them, like the one she had just examined, more resembled Pliny's drawings than the alpha Morlock, while the farthest arrangement—a pair of individuals—suggested something very different. Curiosity drew her closer to this particular grouping.

"This can't be!" Nesbitt said, the sound of her words amplified by the proximity of the chamber walls.

One of the figures was neither Plinean Cerae nor MacCready Morlock. The scientist moved in for an even closer look. It was clearly a Roman officer.

Nesbitt uttered a name that had not been spoken here for nearly two thousand years.

"Severus."

R. J. MacCready knew that something was very wrong, the moment he noticed that Jack, Nesbitt, and the little mammoth were all missing.

He woke the others and within thirty seconds the clearing made an abrupt transition from peaceful to chaotic as sidearms were strapped on and hasty plans formulated to divvy up the search for the improbable trio.

It's definitely Severus and Teacher," Nesbitt told herself, only half-believing her own words. "And they're certainly not statues—they're mummies!"

Through the layer of red mold, it was clear that someone or something had arranged the bodies of the unlikely pair, so well documented by Pliny, into an embrace that had lasted two millennia.

Nesbitt moved in to examine the centurion's upturned face, which held an undeniable expression of calm. Then her gaze turned toward the famous Ceran teacher, whose long, graceful arms were wrapped protectively around her pheromone-addicted captive.

"So it was true," she spoke to Teacher. "What the codex said about you was true."

Nesbitt turned back toward the face of the man Pliny had trusted, then hated, then finally come to forgive. She gave a start and took a reflexive step backward. The centurion's head seemed to have moved, ever so slightly. No, not merely *seemed* to have moved; he was definitely turning toward her in ultra-slow motion—at the rate a thin line of mercury will rise in a thermometer if she were to hold the glass bulb between two warm fingers.

"*Oh my God!*" Nesbitt cried, stepping in closer to Pliny's centurion. "*You're alive!*" Now she looked at the Ceran, lifting her head slowly toward her. "*Both of you!*"

The biologist suddenly understood more clearly than those who were pulling Hendry's strings the implications of what Pliny had found. And, since the Roman had never documented this particular phenomenon, she was the only one who knew. Nesbitt understood, better than even MacCready, what the real fuss would inevitably be, *if word of this ever gets out.*

Nesbitt looked Severus in the eyes, then reached out and touched one of Teacher's hands. It appeared to her that their cells and tissues—human and Morlock alike—had been replaced by or perhaps infused with and redesigned by the strange red mold. *The ultimate in symbiotic relationships,* she thought. *This one between* three *species.*

"You're immortal, aren't you?" Nesbitt asked the pair. Now stroking the physician's hand, she addressed the creature, whose face continued to turn, almost imperceptibly, in her direction. "And you and your kind figured this all out nearly two thousand years ago. Amazing."

Nora Nesbitt smiled and secured her grip on the Ceran's elongated index finger. Then, with some effort, she twisted it off.

J ack had watched the furry elephant with the strange legs and even stranger bifurcated trunk as it sniffed the air around a breach in the rocky wall. It did the same thing to the shadow-filled opening itself. Then, without hesitating, the little mammoth uttered an unnervingly human cry and ran into the dark.

From the other side, someone screamed. Jack ducked into the tunnel and scrambled toward the light. Emerging, he saw something wildly incongruous, the little mammoth—enraged and circling Nora, having already knocked its prey off her feet. The creature seemed ready to charge again and Nora let out another yell, whether in fear, in an effort to scare off the animal, or both, Jack could not tell. But instead of goring or trampling the scientist, it approached slowly, pausing several feet from where she had been standing, next to what looked to Jack vaguely like a statue. The animal's eyes were wide with anger and it bellowed loudly, holding out both of its trunks toward the terrified biologist.

Jack had drawn his Colt but determined that Nora was in the line of fire. Positioning himself for a safe angle, he began a careful crab walk along the red-slicked boulders, slipped, tried to regain his footing, and discovered immediately that he could not. Instead, he redirected all of his forward momentum to a shoulder slam into the pony-sized mammoth's side. The elephant emitted an audible *oofff* and, within the very same instant of that utterance, pivoted toward his attacker. Wrapping both of his trunks around Jack's abdomen, the mini-pachyderm flung him aside with ease. Then the mammoth turned its attention back again toward Nesbitt, who had used the momentary diversion to make a dash for the tunnel. The enraged elephant tore after her, kicking up clouds of red mold and soil as it charged.

R. J. MacCready appeared at the tunnel opening just in time to see Dr. Nora Nesbitt fall to the ground five feet from where he stood, the little mammoth seemingly hell-bent on trampling her to death. Mac drew a bead on a spot to the rear and just below the animal's front shoulder, then fired off three shots—the roar of the Colt .45 magnified by the confined quarters.

The little elephant spun sideways and crashed into the grotto floor headfirst, two feet from the cowering Nesbitt. The animal's breath was a raspy gurgle. Its legs kicked ineffectively, scraping furrows in the ground, now wet from a heart-driven pulsation of arterial blood.

On the other side of the enclosure, Jack was struggling to stand. Observing that the Bostonian was still in one piece, Mac knelt down beside the traumatized biologist. He could hear Yanni's voice now, coming down through the tunnel and calling his name.

Nora Nesbitt glanced back at the fallen mammoth before looking into the face of her rescuer. "Thank you, Captain," she said.

But R. J. MacCready was not in the mood for gratitude, having just been forced to kill a sentient creature that had saved his life on multiple occasions.

"Would you mind telling me what the fuck just happened?" he snarled.

H e hasn't moved an inch, Mac," Yanni said, as they stood beside the giant Morlock they had come to call Alpha.

His pose reminded them both of what were apparently five of Alpha's ancient relatives, housed in a chamber that also held a Roman centurion.

"I don't know what got into him," a sorrowful MacCready had told Yanni earlier. "Nesbitt says she wandered in there chasing what were probably cousins of those snowflake mimics, found what she *thought* were weird statues, and got attacked."

They'd both had some time to think about what happened and now, as the others prepared to move out, Yanni's anger about the shooting of the little mammoth continued to seethe, just below the surface and barely contained. She did not know if she would ever be able to fully forgive Mac. For the moment, though, the two friends came together and stood beside Alpha.

Yanni broke the uneasy silence and spoke softly. "So, this Nesbitt, you believe her?"

"Jack pretty much backed up her whole story."

"Do you think *he* knows what's really in there? That those aren't statues?"

"No," Mac replied. "Although to tell you the truth I have no clue about what's going on with those figures. Do you?"

"Pliny's secret to life itself, I'd say."

Mac shook his head. "Hell, if it is, I say we leave this part out."

Yanni turned her attention to Alpha and nodded slowly. The Morlock had not only gone silent; its entire body was now covered in a layer of red mold that seethed and undulated, appearing (if that were possible) to take complete possession of the giant.

Mac glanced around to make sure there was nobody within earshot. "Look, Yanni, even if Alpha *could* leave—"

"—and judging by those living statues, I'd say that's a long shot."

Mac nodded. "Granted, but I don't think he would anyway. He'd never risk spreading this shit to his kind. It's why he brought us here. He knew the other Morlocks would never risk contaminating themselves."

"And it's also the reason he wouldn't touch us," Yanni added, crestfallen. "He knew we'd eventually be coming here and didn't want his scent on us—or we'd end up like him."

Captain Pederson's arrival curtailed any further conversation. "You two ready to move out?"

R. J. MacCready reached a hand out to Yanni but she looked down at his holstered sidearm and shook her head. Mac gave a last glance back toward the place where the little mammoth lay and said, "Let's get the hell out of here."

Something Wicked This Way Comes

There are known knowns; these are things we know that we know. We also know that there are known unknowns; that is to say, there are things that we know we don't know. But there are also unknown unknowns—the ones we don't know we don't know.
—DONALD RUMSFELD (PARAPHRASING THE
1955 "JOHARI WINDOW")

There's another possibility: the unknown knowns—which [are] the things we know, and then we choose not to know them or not let other people know we know.
—STEPHEN COLBERT (TO RUMSFELD, 2016)

I find the lure of the unknown irresistible.
—SYLVIA EARLE

Metropolitan Museum of Natural History
New York
September 22, 1946

Major Patrick Hendry entered Charles Knight's office and found it rather crowded. It was clear to him that the old artist, R. J. MacCready, Yanni, and Patricia Wynters had been deep in conversation before he walked in. The trio was admiring Knight's latest work—a portrait.

"What do you think?" Mac said, holding the painting out toward the major.

Hendry nodded at the familiar face of his friend—now deceased.

"Mac's gonna put it right next to Bob's."

"That's a great place for it, Yanni," Hendry replied. Finding himself on the verge of an uncomfortable emotion, he turned toward the artist. "You got a real future in this painting business there, Chuck," Hendry said. "If you keep working at it."

Charles Knight replied with a grunt he typically reserved for conversations with the major.

Hendry was just about to place a box down on a small empty table when a panicked look from the artist stopped him. "Don't put it there!" Knight cried.

Hendry looked down. "Hey, nice theremin," he said.

"And don't touch this one!" Knight shot back.

"Okay, okay, I gotcha," Hendry said, deciding to hold on to the box. Then he changed gears. "Well, I'm glad you're all here."

"Why's that?" Mac asked.

"First things first," the major continued. "Each of you take some of these."

Four quizzical faces stared back at him.

"They're from Jack," Hendry said, tilting the open box toward them. "He says he wants you to spread 'em around."

"What the hell is this?" Mac replied, picking up one of the red, white, and blue bumper stickers and a matching pin.

"Your boy's running for Congress!" Hendry announced.

"Yeah, but not in this state," Yanni said, examining one of the buttons.

"How is Jack, anyway?" Mac asked.

"Thanks to your little adventure," Hendry said, "his back was completely screwed. Now, though, he says it's been gettin' a lot better."

Knight chimed in. "Yeah, I hear he's screwing three"—he glanced at Yanni and Patricia—"beautiful Tiffany lamps together."

Patricia laughed. "I've seen pictures of him with some of those lamps."

"Bad back, huh?" MacCready replied. "Anything I can do to help?"

Yanni shot him a dirty look as she attached a campaign button to her blouse.

"Guy's got an interesting future ahead of him," Hendry said, before turning to Knight and Wynters. "Okay, enough about our boy. By my calendar you guys are still on the payroll. So what else have you come up with?"

"Well," Patricia replied, "we finished with the last bits of Pliny's Omega codex."

"And by bits, she *means* bits," Knight said, pouring an envelope full of dust and fragments onto a metal specimen tray. "Most of this stuff was disintegrating before it ever got here," he lied.

Hendry continued. "I suppose all that business about how the Cerans molded life like clay got destroyed, too?"

"Funny," Patricia said, "it turned out to be the most fragile part of the codex."

Hendry gave Knight a knowing nod. "That's . . . um . . . terribly unfortunate," he said, trying his best to sound official.

Never suspecting that Hendry might really have been on their side all along, Knight and Patricia each raised an eyebrow—to Hendry's amusement.

"Did your boys from D.C. photograph those last codex sections?" Wynters asked.

"Hmmm . . . I'd have to check," Hendry replied, a response that Mac would doubtless translate into *Hendry never has to check anything. He's hidden or destroyed some of those negatives.*

The major turned to Mac and Yanni. "All right, final time I'm gonna ask this."

"Go on," came the simultaneous reply.

"Was Pliny's 'molding life' stuff still there and is there any way that it came out with any of you?"

"No, the red grotto was only death, and the stuff you're talking? It was back in that valley—if it existed at all."

"And?"

"And Yanni and I were the only ones who ever got in and out of there alive."

"So what's your assessment?"

"Never saw them doing anything like Pliny describes," said Yanni.

Clearly unable to completely trust Hendry, Wynters said, convincingly, "We know environments in isolation often produce some strange evolutionary quirks."

Hendry shot her a skeptical look. "Like carnivorous grass, angry snowflakes, angrier Morlocks?"

"Look around this planet hard enough, Major," Knight added, "and you'll probably find even stranger examples."

Normally, Major Hendry would have challenged the pair, but he knew that this was anything but a normal conversation. It was more like a dance.

Mac nodded. "So, officially, we're assessing the key feature of Pliny's Omega codex as a naturally occurring evolutionary phenomenon, expanded into a fairy tale."

"And I'm guessin'," Yanni said, "with the Russians and Chinese suddenly having other things to worry about—"

"—like each other." Hendry completed the thought.

Mac grimaced and continued. "Because of that, I think we can keep a lid on this for a while longer."

"A couple of years if we're lucky," Yanni added. "Then somebody's gonna go back in there."

For several seconds there was silence, as they each pondered that particular problem.

"Well, at least that gives us some time to think this through," Mac said, resting Jerry's portrait on the theremin.

"Okay, now that that's settled," the major continued.

"For now," Yanni countered, stopping herself from saying anything more. She and Mac both knew—*we've stopped it for now, but this is far from over.*

"One way or another," Mac had told her earlier, "it's going to come back. Pliny's microbes—wildly adaptable and with numbers on their side."

Yanni also realized that, once again, wherever the road had divided into right decisions and wrong decisions, they had made the best available choice. Yet, once again, every path they had taken seemed, on some level, to have made matters worse.

"For now," Yanni emphasized again, with as much confidence as she could muster, "it *is* settled."

"All right, *for now*," Hendry acquiesced. "What *else* did you figure out?"

It was Wynters who replied. "Apparently, our Roman friends stuck around in Tibet for quite a while—a coupla years in fact."

"Though you'd never know it from reading Pliny's *Natural History*," Knight added. "He covered up those missing years pretty well."

"Anything else?" Hendry asked them.

"Yeah," Knight continued. "Eventually Pliny and his Nubian friend made their way home. And we *know* what happened there."

"What about the other guy, the centurion?"

"We think Severus stayed behind," Wynters said.

Mac and Yanni exchanged brief but knowing glances, simultaneously sharing a thought. *He definitely stayed behind.*

Knight cleared his throat. "Now, Major, I've got a few questions for you."

"Go ahead," Hendry said, crossing his arms.

"So where exactly did they find this codex?"

"Herculaneum, if you want to be precise," Hendry snapped, then checked his watch. "And before you ask your last question, we found it in a cylinder made of some metal—it's probably some new alloy. God only knows why he wrote the damned thing up in the first place."

"He had to," Knight guessed aloud. "In his own way, the guy was an artist."

"Well, artist or not," Hendry said, "someone buried his codex months or maybe even years before the eruption. Buried it deep."

"And then deeper still, I imagine, *after* the eruption," Mac added.

"About sixty feet deeper than Pliny had planned," Hendry said, before turning back to Knight and Wynters. "You two finished with Twenty Questions?"

"Two questions," Knight replied, oblivious to the game show reference. "But for now . . . yeah."

Mac, however, wasn't quite done. "What happened to Tse-lin? He still in custody overseas?"

"For the moment," Hendry replied. "With all he knows, we couldn't let him go back to China now, could we?"

"Right," Mac agreed, "and then there's all that contact he had with us Americans. If he *did* go back home, he could be arrested or worse for less than that."

"Especially now," Hendry replied, "with the little war you guys almost started."

Mac shrugged.

"Yeah, yeah, I know," Hendry continued. "It's not like you sicced that Russian chopper and those two Chinese choppers on each other, right?"

R. J. MacCready summoned his best *who me?* expression.

On the other side of the room, Yanni bit her lip, understanding that this was another of the details Mac had decided to keep from Hendry—to protect them all from an incident that was already widening the rift between China and the Soviets.

Yanni decided to change the subject. "So about Wang Tse-lin?"

Hendry held up his hand, then spoke slowly. "Everything's been arranged." The major shot a wry smile at four faces wearing the same expression of anticipation. He waited a beat, apparently to savor the moment, and then went on. "You can use a new vertebrate zoologist here, right? Especially one who's familiar with a part of Asia we might have trouble visiting ourselves?"

"Sure we can!" Yanni answered, not bothering to check with the three people who actually worked at the museum.

MacCready was momentarily relieved with the news about the Chinese scientist, but his look quickly returned to one of concern. "So, Pat, what about those Devil's Brigade guys? They saw the

Morlocks, or the Yeti or whatever you want to call them. What if *they* say something?"

"I've got that covered, too, Mac," Hendry said. "Anyone who mentions your hairy pals—either species—will get the same treatment that those Night Fighter flyboys from the 415th got when they started chirping about their so-called 'fucking foo-fighters.'"

Now the nonmilitary types in the room shot the two Army guys a trio of quizzical looks.

"Unidentified flying objects they're calling 'em," Mac explained. "In this case, glowing round objects that some of our pilots have claimed to see following their planes around."

Hendry continued. "The bottom line is that everyone considers these guys to be laughingstocks now, and that's exactly what the Devil's Brigaders will face if they start flappin' their lips about fuzzy giants."

"Well, that's sort of a relief," Yanni said. "I guess."

Major Hendry, though, was clearly not finished with the topic and Yanni's halfhearted response served as a reminder. "What about our other problem?" he asked. "Your Dr. Nesbitt?"

The three museum workers exchanged uneasy looks, before Patricia Wynters spoke up, presumably because it had been *her* idea to bring the invertebrate biologist into the project.

"Ummm . . . well . . . as you know, Nora left the museum a few weeks ago," she said. "Rather abruptly."

"She get fired?" Hendry asked.

"No." Wynters hesitated. "She took another job—at a lab."

Hendry was suddenly paying a lot more attention to the conversation, and there was no way he could have missed MacCready wincing. "Where?"

Mac stepped in. "A small lab that nobody seems to know anything about."

"Something about a fruit," Knight added. "Peach Island I think it was."

"Well, that's not very reassuring," Hendry replied. "I'll see what I can do."

Mac nodded a thanks.

"One last question," Hendry said, and this one he directed at Yanni. "Your little elephants, did you get to chat them up like you did with that pair in Central Park?"

"As a matter of fact, I did," she responded. "One in particular."

"And how'd that work out?"

"Badly," she said. "But I'm not ready to talk about it yet." Yanni shot a quick glance at Mac, who was looking downcast. "But there was nothing anyone could have done," she added.

"So how smart do you really think they were?" Hendry asked.

Yanni paused for a moment. "As I've said, maybe smarter than humans," she replied, "and definitely more kind."

Hendry chuckled, then started to head for the door. "Well, personally, I'm glad I missed 'em then."

"Why's that?" Yanni asked.

"If they *are* smarter than us," Hendry said, "maybe they'll be running the show someday. And I'd hate to wake up one morning and find humans depending on the humanity of elephants."

"Could be worse," Mac said, almost to himself.

"Could be a lot worse," Yanni said. Then she quietly took Mac's hand.

On that same afternoon, beneath the snows of Tibet, and in a way that neither the Morlocks nor the humans had ever anticipated, the little white mammoths launched a sudden revolt. It was as ruthlessly brutal as it was competent and when it was over the mammoths had displayed more human behaviors than even Yanni could have imagined.

> Herculaneum Harbor
> Just after midnight
> August 25, A.D. 79

F*inally*, the architect thought, *the last of the boats have been launched.*

Pliny's Nubian friend had spent the better part of the night at the docks, comforting concerned parents and their children, and assisting them into an array of small craft he and a few friends had hauled out from beneath the stone arches of the city's marina. When the eruption began, many had refused to enter the boats. The giant mushroom cloud of black smoke was so distant that most people believed it safer to remain ashore than to set sail onto increasingly turbulent waters. Proculus ordered his artisans and slaves into the first boat—"As an example for others to follow, *and only as a precaution,*" he lied. "You'll probably be home for dinner."

Many of those who had either chosen to stay behind or failed to find room in a boat were now huddled beneath the marina's arches. Each vaulted chamber was a storage room that served primarily as a drydock for an assortment of fishing boats. The arches and chamber ceilings formed the foundations of the city's waterfront buildings—a neighborhood that normally offered stunning views across the Bay of Neapolis.

Now though, the sights and sounds were of a far more frightening nature. The mountain, Vesuvio, had been rumbling for fourteen hours. And though the skies above Herculaneum were still crystal clear and full of stars, Pompeii to the east was now invisible, as were the entire eastern horizon and the stars above it. They were blotted out by an inky black cloud that had risen from the mountain—a cloud rent by forked and quivering bursts of flame, like flashes of lightning magnified a hundredfold. The constant rumbling roar was frequently joined by muffled cracking sounds, and each of these was followed by a growing chorus of moans and cries from those assembled along the shoreline or hiding below the arches.

The Roman stood on the beach in front of the marina, glancing out across the bay. His flag signals requesting more ships to aid in the evacuation had been answered almost immediately—the first from his old friend Pliny. But that had been more than thirteen hours ago and as of yet the architect had spotted no sails—*at least none headed in this direction,* he thought.

What Proculus would never know was that the admiral had set out with a small fleet many hours earlier. To their horror, the sailors found their way blocked by a massive island of floating pumice. But while others turned back or took off in new directions, Pliny continued to steer east, trying to find some way to reach his friend and evacuate anyone with him who needed rescuing. Finally, after a dense rain of walnut-sized rocks began to pelt his vessel, the heartbroken Pliny was forced to turn his ship toward the Isle of Capri.

Proculus now had one eye on the horizon and the other on two carpenters who were attempting to patch the bottom of an old wreck they'd dragged out in desperation.

He tried to stay cheerful, attempting to joke with the children of parents whose only concern seemed to be whether there would be a place for them on the small craft—if it were ever made seaworthy. Rendering everyone's task more difficult was the near-constant shifting of the ground beneath their feet.

Remarkably, those who had settled in under the stone arches, filled only hours earlier by boats, were calm now. Parents were sitting in a circle, with their children sleeping in the middle. Some of them Proculus knew; others were refugees from the direction of Pompeii, stopping here because they were exhausted, or being slowed in their progress by small children. Several women were obviously pregnant and had taken shelter here when they could walk no farther. Their footprints would still be present in the sand two thousand years later.

On the beach, a Roman soldier joined the crowd on horseback. Proculus threw the man a salute and beckoned him to come nearer. He would be a useful pair of hands for either the boat repair efforts or perhaps crowd control, once the last boat was ready to be launched.

"Give us a hand, soldier!" Proculus called to the man. "There's water for your horse and I could certainly use your assistance."

The soldier, though, did not respond. Instead he turned to look toward the volcano, then spurred his horse onward, moving with the flow of refugees.

"*Cowardly dog!*" Proculus yelled, and thought about running after the man.

But now a new sound reached him, like the crash of one mountain upon another—loud enough to hurt his ears despite being muffled and distorted by the dust cloud. Turning in the direction of the commotion, Proculus beheld a fiery red sun—wider than Vesuvio itself, shining out through the columns of black dust and falling to earth at incomparable speed.

The sight of it was absolutely horrifying, making his next thought as perplexing as it was incongruous—given the realization that whole towns beneath the new sun were dying. *Jove, forgive me. It is the most beautiful thing I have ever seen.*

The mixture of gas and lava mist burned hotter than iron

emerging white from a furnace. From the moment it crashed down upon the volcano's sides, it flowed like liquid down the mountain's southern flanks and over the contours of the land— taller than any tidal wave ever recorded by history, and five times as fast. It brightened as it approached, blazing like uncountable millions of stars coming to life, and Proculus could feel their collective radiance against his face.

The disobedient soldier clearly felt it, too, and reining his horse into a tight turn he ran it at full gallop toward one of the arched shelters, giving apparently no thought at all to the people he was about to trample inside.

"*Stop, coward! Stop!*" Proculus yelled.

His command counted for nothing.

The cedar forest north of Herculaneum was being plowed up by a mighty precursor wave of compressed air, clearing a path for the fiery tidal wave. The tallest trees in the empire were snapped above the roots and flung many times their height. They turned slowly and gracefully, end over end as they flew toward the city. The radiance from the wave was so great that each cartwheeling tree was bursting into flames before it.

Proculus would never know that when death came, its touch would last no more than one two-hundredth of a second. Nor would he have cared. During the last moments of his life, he turned once more to face the sea—now illuminated out to the horizon and growing brighter.

With every instant that remained, he searched the great bay— praying *not* to see the sails of Pliny's boats approaching. His prayer answered, Proculus felt relief.

Then he disappeared into history.

Fin

Author's Note

Reality Check

Although the time frames in our novel shift between 1946 and the first century A.D., the tale serves as a fable for tomorrow—in particular, the danger of racially tagged biological weapons. Since 1945, the question has been whether our electronic civilization will survive its nuclear adolescence. As we learn how to read and edit the code of life itself, the genetic frontier looms ahead as another yin and yang, with great promise and great peril. As we write, curing cancer (the Black Plague of the past century) is almost within reach. Racial tagging (and even a person-specific weapon) also represents a looming reality.

What else in this tale is real, or blurs the lines between reality and fable?

To begin, some of the people:

Charles R. Knight (1874–1953) appears throughout as himself. He was arguably the greatest artist of prehistoric life who ever lived. Long before special effects mavens Willis O'Brian (*King Kong, Mighty Joe Young*) and Ray Harryhausen (*Seventh Voyage of Sinbad, Mysterious Island*, and so on), put flesh on an array of creatures no human had ever seen, Knight was already bringing multiple lost worlds alive through his paintings. No one was more influential in stimulating the public's still-growing fascination with dinosaurs than Knight, who (as depicted in our novel) was born in Brooklyn and whose paintings and murals hang prominently in natural history museums across the country. For an amazing look at Knight's life and art, readers should turn to *The Artist Who Saw Through Time,* by Richard Milner.

Knight's granddaughter, Rhoda Knight Kalt, who makes a brief appearance while Wynters and Nesbitt are discussing guinea worms, is a real person. As a child, Rhoda frequently toured the American Museum of Natural History with her beloved grandfather, whom she called "Toppy." As an adult, no one has done more than Rhoda to perpetuate the legacy of Charles R. Knight.

Bernard Herrmann (1911–1975) was one of history's great composers. Born Max Herman in New York City, he wrote the musical scores for some of the classic films of the twentieth century, directed by the likes of Alfred Hitchcock, François Truffaut, Orson Wells, Robert Wise, and Fred Zinnemann. Herrmann, who studied at the Juilliard School of Music and New York University, began his career as a conductor. He won his only Oscar in 1941 for *The Devil and Daniel Webster,* a fact that is a little perplexing when one considers that his groundbreaking musical scores for films like *North by Northwest, Vertigo, Psycho,* and *The Day the Earth Stood Still* were never even nominated. Bernard Herrmann also worked extensively on television, where he composed some of the medium's most highly recognizable music, the themes for *The Twilight Zone* and *The Alfred Hitchcock Hour.* Herrmann died unexpectedly, not long after finishing the score for Martin Scorsese's *Taxi Driver* (for which he picked up a posthumous Oscar nomination).

Alfred Hitchcock (1899–1980) was one of the greatest movie directors of all time. As depicted in chapter 7, composer Miklós

Róza used a theremin in Hitchcock's hallucinatory classic, *Spellbound* (1945). Hitchcock famously paired with composer Bernard Herrmann, whose first meeting we have fictionalized. Their collaborations produced some of their most famous works. Herrmann also wrote the scores for Hitchcock's *The Trouble with Harry* (1955), *The Man Who Knew Too Much* (1956), *The Wrong Man* (1956), and *Marnie* (1964). Hitchcock did not use a musical soundtrack for his classic *The Birds* (1963) but Bernard Herrmann acted as consultant on the creation of the electronically produced bird sounds, heard throughout the film. Their relationship came to an abrupt end during Herrmann's scoring of *Torn Curtain* (1966). Reportedly, studio producers wanted a more pop- and jazz-influenced score, which Herrmann refused to deliver. Nor would he provide a suitable title tune for Paul Newman's costar, Julie Andrews, to sing. As a result, Herrmann's score was bumped from the film and John Addison was approached to write a new one. Despite the stellar cast, *Torn Curtain* became one of Hitchcock's worst-reviewed films (reportedly Newman's Method actor style led to clashes with the director). The director and composer never spoke again. In what was perhaps an even more inexplicable snub than that inflicted upon Bernard Herrmann, Alfred Hitchcock never won the Academy Award for Best Director, although he was nominated five times.

The theremin is an early electronic musical instrument, designed about 1920 by Russian inventor Léon Theremin (born Lev Termen). Originally known as an etherophone, his device is the only musical instrument played without touching it. Its unique sound (once described as a cello lost in the fog and crying for help) results from two metal antennae attached to the wooden body of the instrument—which resembles an old radio receiver. One antenna is a straight vertical rod, usually situated on the right side (for right-handed players), and the other is a horizontal loop that extends out from the left side of the console. The antennae generate an electromagnetic field that extends about four feet around the device and the thereminist (necessitating that the instrument be separated from the rest of his orchestra). As the thereminist places his or her right hand closer to the pitch antenna, the pitch rises, while moving the left hand closer to the volume antenna causes the volume to decrease. These electrical signals, which vary as the thereminist moves his or her hands and fingers within the electric field, are amplified and sent to a loudspeaker. Generally typecast as a means to produce eerie or spooky sounds, the theremin played a major role in the soundtracks of *Spellbound, The Thing (From Another World)*—and Tim Burton's comedic tragedy *Ed Wood* (with Lydia Kavina as thereminist).

Léon Theremin happened to be working on a proximity detector for the Soviets when he developed the idea for electronic music. He also invented a miniature eavesdropping device for the NKVD (which preceded the KGB). One such listening device (aka "the Thing") was embedded in a carved wooden version of the Great Seal of the United States and presented to the U.S. ambassador to the Soviet Union in 1945. It hung in his Moscow residence for seven years until it was discovered by accident (an accident of the Major Hendry kind). We have taken a little creative license in putting Theremin's two most famous inventions together. Léon Theremin as master spy, however, is not fiction.

Pliny the Elder really did exist, really did travel the world as an explorer and writer, and was known for his extraordinary appetite for work. Many of his writings have survived because his nephew, Pliny the Younger, pleaded mercy for the early Christians during a time of political and social upheaval that ultimately eroded, from within, a civilization that was able to control water and steam, and was actually building multiple gearshift devices, at the time it began to fall. During the Dark Ages, Christian monks looked kindly upon the Plinys, copying and preserving many of their writings.

When depicted in fiction, Pliny the Elder has typically (and wrongly) been written as a buffoonish, decadent character. We have taken it as an honor, in this novel, to depict him in a manner more consistent with his writings, and what his nephew and others of his contemporaries wrote about him. We hope we have come closer to the real man, and how he would have reacted if thrust into the lost world of the Cerae.

From the writings that survive (notably his thirty-seven-volume *Naturalis Historia*), history has learned the legends of other lands, as told to Pliny the Elder during his travels. He was, for example, the explorer who gave the world its only detailed account of the strange celibate Essene cult, as related to him by another traveler, about the people who hid the library known as the Dead Sea Scrolls. Historians and naturalists still argue about the extraordinary animals he described from many lands—"what was merely the mythology of some distant tribe, what was real?"

Even his death was extraordinary. The last words attributed to him in this novel were actually spoken by him, as recorded by his nephew in letters to his friend Tacitus—the full content of which can be read in Haraldur Sigurdsson's excellent book about the eruption that buried Pompeii, *Melting the Earth* (Oxford University Press, 1999).

As we depicted, early during the second day of the increasingly violent eruption of Mount Vesuvius, Pliny the Younger was reportedly discovered by a friend to be behaving in a strange manner at his uncle's estate. In his letters to Tacitus, Pliny the Younger mentions that this friend found his insistence on reading history and finishing an assignment from his uncle as quite odd. He never explained this obsession with his uncle's papers, while two whole cities died within his view. In chapter 24, we provided a dramatized explanation for the famous Roman's true and inexplicable behavior.

The Roman cavalryman whose skeleton was found at the marina of Pompeii's sister city Herculaneum has, like Pliny the Elder, been maligned by modern, speculative history. Some fanciful "reconstructions" depict him as a hardened thief who at the last minute had a softer heart than indicated by his rugged features.

We have named him Proculus and, though he is the product of abstract fantasy, the skeleton of a man much like him actually was found, with the healed wounds we have described. He died under the physical conditions we have described, at the time and place we have described, with a gold inlaid silver scabbard for his sword.

In 2015, the Smithsonian Channel's *Mummies Alive* series focused on gold and silver coins in Specimen E26's side "pocket," and on his fine tools, asking, though he appeared to have died in the act of rescue, "Was he a hero or a villain?"

The "thief/villain" speculation is based on a self-perpetuating dogma that Roman soldiers were poor and unskilled and, because this man was apparently wealthy, he must therefore have been looting as the fires of Vesuvius approached. In reality, his finely crafted sword spoke of success within the ranks, and within his extramilitary career. In accordance with historical writings reaching back to the time of Emperor Augustus (including Pliny the Elder, *Naturalis Historia*, 2.93–94), there was much skill, education, and even wealth among the ranks, including Pliny the Elder himself—who, in reality as in this tale, was an admiral at the time of his death, and really did sail off toward the eruption that buried Pompeii and Herculaneum, on an ill-fated mission of rescue.

P liny the Elder did indeed record legends about strange wildlife in lost worlds, sometimes so fantastical that they must generally be regarded as the mythology of distant lands, or misunderstood descriptions of animals (like orangutans) known to biologists today.

The civilization we have called the Cerae are a fictional people, but Pliny did record in his earlier volume, *Natural History* (chapter 24: "Taprobane"), the fragmentary legends of a people with whom we have set out to make our own cautionary mythology resonate. Sometimes called "the Seres," they were encountered during the reign of Emperor Claudius (Nero's adoptive father). There are several spellings for these strange-eyed beings (blue-eyed, it was sometimes rumored), who communicated by "an uncouth sort of noise" and had flaxen hair. The Emodian Mountains (either the Himalayas or mountains nearby) "looked toward" these legendary people, believed by an earlier Roman visitor to have no true or comprehensible language by which to communicate thoughts (and hence the communication dilemmas faced by Severus, which later prove challenging even to Yanni's exceptional skills). Their means of trade was also strange, and we have remained consistent with the ancient legend, according to which, goods were brought down from a distant spot behind the glacial barriers and left at the side of a river, to be removed by local inhabitants. They were said to be a shy and secretive people. Pliny the Elder wrote that those who went exploring ahead of him, during prior decades, were mystified by the idea that this race, with its habit of leaving valuable goods behind, might in doing so be communicating some demand—perhaps to take these goods and stay away. The drop-offs were made to the river civilizations north of Taprobane (Sri Lanka).

Fictional our Cerae are, but we have made sure to maintain a certain amount of convergence with the Greek historian Strabo, who wrote in the fifth century B.C. (in *Geographia*, book 15, chapter 1) about a race in the same region able to control nature to such extent that they converted an ancient wasteland in and around the inhospitable mountains (south Tibet) into very fertile ground, and were able to extend their lives beyond two hundred years.

Pliny also wrote (as in *Natural History* 20, "The Seres") that the race, whose homeland remained hidden, produced varieties of iron unequaled in quality. As legend told it, their forests were white with valuable fleece—which was combed from the trees and sent out to the world in secret and under cover of night. He emphasized (repeatedly) that they shunned direct trade "with the rest of mankind." They were described to him as being "of inoffensive manners," but also monstrous and capable of being provoked to great savagery.

Some ancient historians called them the Sieriz (pronounceable as "Ceres"); others named them the Sinae—later believed to be the Chinese (though there would thus have been some very misunderstood and exaggerated descriptions of the Chinese, with the white fleece combed from trees being, perhaps, a misunderstood account of silk harvested from the cocoons of tree-dwelling silkworms). For the sake of our story, Sieriz—*Ceres*—worked, in terms of describing a cold, hidden world where everything was white, yet fertile. Ceres was a Roman goddess of agriculture and fertility—formerly a Greek goddess, Demeter (a name you may recognize from an ill-fated submarine in *Hell's Gate*).

O ur Prince of Pandaya, and his kingdom's mistake, is fictional. But a place much like it was recorded by ancient historians to have existed near East India. There, according to legend, a royal harbor city was lost during a great flood—approximately where we have let Pliny's expedition find it (or rather, its ruins). Pliny the Elder made mention of the capital city (which he sometimes called Korki Pattinam) while trying to compile reports about the hidden realm of the "Chera" kingdom (our Cerae). A generation earlier, Augustus Caesar received an emissary from the still-intact city in 13 B.C. The historical Pandion (Pandyan)/Tamil capital was shifted after the destruction. This surviving remnant, whose people were said to have been descendants of Hercules, moved south to the island of Sri Lanka (Taprobane) and were known much later as the "Tamil Tigers."

In the time of Emperor Augustus, the people of the doomed city were known as a source of luxuriant textiles, fleece, and spices. Pliny the Elder mentioned a wealthy "Pandu" port that belonged to the "Chera," of whom he wrote that he was unable to learn anything. (Bear in mind that a reason for multiple spellings of the same place, or people, is inevitable in texts that were bound to pick up variations when preserved mainly by recopying, mostly by hand and by monks, throughout several centuries and across different languages.) A contemporary of Pliny, Periplus, referred to an independent district of the Tamil ancestors (Pandu), which, as a civilization, fell under the mysterious "Chera/Chola/ Cerothra" (whom we simply call Cerae). In A.D. 640, the Chinese explorer Yuan Chwang described this same mysterious (Chola) region, home to a once-powerful trading city wiped from the world, unpopulated except for a few lingering savages who lived a sorrowful, troglodyte existence.

There really was, in China, a belief that legendary apelike creatures in the mountains possessed flesh and bones that, if consumed, held curative powers. This, of course, became the basis for the ill-fated expedition into which our character, Wang, was drafted. Additionally, certain fossil remains from apelike denizens of the East actually have led to speculation about lost or undiscovered species as the origin of the still ongoing Yeren and Yeti "sightings." The abduction of poor Dr. Wang by something akin to a cannibal army in 1946 is thus not entirely beyond reason.

In 1935, Dutch paleontologist Gustav von Koenigswald came across a yellowish molar among the "dragon bones" for sale in a Hong Kong pharmacy. Traditional Chinese medicine had long maintained that certain fossilized remains possessed curative properties when ground into powder and ingested. Over the next several decades, researchers recovered several hundred similar teeth and even a few of the lower jawbones that held them. Eventually, and although no cranial or postcranial bones were recovered, anthropologists named the new primate *Gigantopithicus* because of its immense size. Initially thought to be a human relative, scientists determined the creature to be an ape, most closely related to modern orangutans. Certainly the most striking feature of *Gigantopithicus blackii* was its size, with males reaching perhaps ten feet in height and weighing in at nearly 1,200 pounds, actually outsizing MacCready's "Morlocks." Females were significantly smaller, with a body mass that might have been half that of males—a textbook example of a phenomenon known as sexual dimorphism.

Although *Gigantopithicus* was quite possibly the largest primate that ever lived, it also exemplifies how great body size can become a detriment to a species over time. For at least a million years, as many as three species of *Gigantopithicus* lived in the forests of southern China, India, Vietnam, and Indonesia. Evidence from their teeth and jaws indicates that their diets consisted of an assortment of plants, including fruit, leaves, roots, and possibly bamboo. To support their massive bodies, *Gigantopithicus* would have needed to consume large amounts of plant matter, but when glaciers began advancing down from the north around 100,000 years ago, the tropical forests where Asia's apes thrived gradually gave way to cooler, drier savannas. It has been hypothesized that these altered environments could not provide enough food for the giant forest dwellers and they eventually died out (aided, perhaps, by *Homo erectus,* the apparent ancestors of modern humans).

Similar examples of the disadvantages resulting from large body size can be found elsewhere and throughout history. For example, in South America, changing environmental conditions around ten thousand years ago are thought to have been a contributing factor in the extinction of the giant sloth, *Megatherium*. Additionally, since they fed exclusively on blood, *Desmodus draculae,* the large vampire bat inhabiting our novel *Hell's Gate,* likely went extinct after the Pleistocene megafauna upon which they preyed (possibly including ground sloths) disappeared.

For the purpose of this story, we hypothesized what might have occurred if Tibetan branches of some unknown lineage of a once very diversified primate family tree (an ancestor or side branch of *Homo erectus* or some yet unknown group, perhaps) had come into contact with a substance that allowed them to more quickly adapt to harsh local conditions. This boost to the process of natural selection resulted in the fictional Ceran/Morlock classes (with their thick, insulating fur and masterful climbing ability) encountered by Pliny the Elder and R. J. MacCready. What our fictionalized version of the Roman historian and naturalist characterized as "the key to life itself" was also responsible for the other strange species—like predaceous "snowflakes" and lethal grass mimics.

The Yeti or abominable snowman (Pliny's Cerae or Mac's Morlock species) is a giant, apelike biped, said to inhabit the Himalayan region of Tibet, Nepal, and Bhutan. Although the scientific community considers it to be entirely a legend, the Yeti is arguably the most famous creature in all of cryptozoology. The term *abominable snowman* originated in 1921 with Calcutta newspaper reporter Hendry Newman. Evidently, Newman mistranslated a Tibetan colloquialism *metch kangmi* ("filthy snowman")—which was used to describe something rumored to have been seen during a reconnaissance mission to Mount Everest earlier that year. The resulting moniker has had universal appeal, though probably not for primatologists and other scientists attempting to determine if such creatures actually exist. Although there have been hundreds of reported Yeti sightings, photographs of strange footprints in the snow, and "physical evidence" like hair (determined to be from known species, including mountain goats) and even a famed skullcap (also a mountain goat), there is currently no tangible evidence that these creatures have any footing in reality.

The Yeren, recovered by our Dr. Wang Tse-lin, is one of the legendary "Wildman of Shennongjia," reputed to live a peaceful existence in the mountainous forests of Hubei, in eastern central China. Reportedly covered by either red or white hair, the Yeren is said to stand between six and eight feet tall. Cryptozoologists have speculated that it may be a relative of *Gigantopithicus* or a large species of ground-dwelling orangutan.

The real-life Wang Tselin, also a Chicago-schooled Chinese biologist, wrote a detailed report about an examination he claimed to have performed on a Yeren that had been shot and killed in China's Gansu region in 1940. He said the specimen was a nursing female, approximately six and a half feet tall, and covered in dense, grayish-red hair. According to the scientist, the specimen's "face was narrow with deep-set eyes" and it reminded him most of models he had seen of the famous "Peking Man" (a Chinese example of the modern human ancestor *Homo erectus,* thought to have lived between 1.9 million and 230,000 years ago [see Smithsonian Institution: http://humanorigins.si.edu/evidence/human-fossils/species/homo-erectus]). Locals reportedly told Tselin that a pair of Yeren had been observed in the area for more than a month. Unfortunately, there was no follow-up to this story (no photographs, no physical evidence), and it has been difficult to track down additional information on the scientist himself. As the Chinese civil war heated up, he seems simply to have disappeared into history (probably as a casualty). We have taken the liberty of fictionalizing Wang Tselin and his Himalayan adventure, and also given him a more hopeful future.

As with the Yeti and its North American counterpart, "Bigfoot," there is currently no physical evidence that the Yeren (as described by Wang) actually exists. Most skeptics believe that Yeren sightings are the result of misidentification. There is strong agreement among scientists from a variety of fields that any suggestion of a Yeti/Bigfoot/*Gigantopithicus* connection is untenable unless tangible, repeatable laboratory evidence becomes available—such as hair roots with distinctive DNA that does not turn out to come from goats and known species of monkeys (which, so far, has universally been the case).

Our suggestion (in the Epilogue) of a Morlock diaspora was invented to fit certain anecdotal events, actually recorded as far away as Russia. That the Kremlin would be willing (as in this novel) to send military helicopter crews out to investigate rumors of strange creatures is not far-fetched. In the May 29, 2014, issue of the *Huffington Post,* David Moye reported on a 1959 event involving the Russian military: "Mysterious Deaths of College Students Blamed on Russian Yeti." If nothing else, the article and the documentary on which Moye was reporting make for interesting reading and viewing.

While Mac and Yanni have become accidental cryptozoologists, with the exception of very large squids, cryptozoology (certainly in the case of Yeren and their kin) has the curious distinction of being the only field of exploration that has yet to prove that its subject matter actually exists.

Nonetheless, there are a wide assortment of increasingly fascinating—and surprisingly recently coexisting—side branches of our tree of human lineages to choose from as ancestors to the inhabitants of our story's mist valley. The origins of humans, Neanderthals, and other human cousins is not a single, classical poster image of descent leading from an apelike fossil called

"Lucy" to something resembling "Peking Man," to Neanderthals, and finally to fully erect "Cro-Magnon Man." It makes for a visually interesting T-shirt depicting apes walking from left to right along a "ladder of evolution" to become ape-men and erect-walking humans (leading to erect-walking robots). It's a simple and tidy and popular depiction, but it is also entirely wrong.

The ascent of man is not a ladder with a few missing links inserted among the rungs. We, and the few apes that remain on the planet today, are merely the surviving branches of a once (and not very long ago) very luxuriant bush. The lost valley in the maze of the eastern Himalayas is, in this story, populated by one of those missing branches, isolated in a place where the actual process of evolutionary change could be altered.

The complexity of the human family bush is much greater, and more interesting, than previous generations have supposed. The emerging possibility of a human cousin closely related to Peking Man, surviving into recent times in the isolation of an Indonesian island, enhanced the sort of speculative journey we have taken into the isolation of a lost east Himalayan world, as isolated as any island.

In real life, as in the journey we have all just taken together, the genetic distances between our human branch and branches that used to be called "animals" or "ape-men" are being diminished and even blurred. The lessons from studies of ancient DNA indicate a surprising amount of interbreeding, for example, between Charles Knight's Neanderthal "cave men" and "archaic humans" from Africa, also between Neanderthals and a species or race traditionally graded as distinctly *non*human (*Homo erectus,* "Peking Man").

Relevant to the relationship between Severus and a fictional race that looked so physically different as to seem nonhuman, the list of ancient hybrid events is growing: South Africa's *Homo naledi,* the "mystery human," appears to have an ancestry dating back more than two million years (close to the origin of *Homo erectus*). To judge from their fossils, they looked simultaneously very human yet carried a mixture of less human features even more ancient than *H. erectus*. Another branch—*Homo floresiensis,* popularly dubbed "the Hobbit people"—resembled a miniature and more primitive version of "Peking Man," surviving in parts of Indonesia into very recent times (probably post–Ice Age and even into our Bronze Age). Scarcely had the 2003 "Hobbit" discovery begun to be tested and resolved when yet another branch was un-earthed: Denisovan Man, located primarily in Siberia. Though it is Neanderthal-like in appearance, approximately 8 percent of Denisovan DNA seems to have been derived from interbreed-ing with still another new (presently unidentified) human species from Asia—a branch genetically distinct from both Neanderthals and modern humans. Researchers believe that in the Middle East Neanderthal interbreeding with our modern, more thinly boned ancestors took place along the Jordan Valley.

In the November 2016 special edition of *Scientific American: The Story of Us,* Kate Wong and Michael Hammer commented at length on these truly fascinating discoveries. Wong noted that the "mystery human" of South Africa "exhibits a mishmash of traits associated with various hominin species," including some skull similarities to the more apelike *Australopithecus,* commonly known as "Lucy." And yet there is evidence of burial practices and the use of fire, possibly dating back as many as three million years, almost as far back in time as "Lucy." If so, these people could even oust australopithecines from the lineage leading to us (and, in our fiction, to the Cerae). "It may be," Wong continued, "[that] *H. naledi* originated millions of years ago and managed to persist across the ages unchanged, like a coelacanth, overlapping with other *Homo* 'species,' including *H. sapiens.* . . . Possibly, *H. naledi* interbred with our ancestors and contributed DNA to the modern gene pool, like Neanderthals and Denisovians did."

"The roots of modern humans," added Hammer, "trace back to not just a single ancestral population in Africa but to populations throughout the world. Although archaic humans have often been seen as rivals of modern humans, scientists now must seriously consider the possibility that they were the secret of *H. sapiens'* success."

And thus the picture is more complex than you might have supposed. Though it is extremely doubtful that a lost world of Yeti-like Cerae or Morlocks is living and awaiting discovery, we will not be the two people in the room who drop dead from shock if a twig on the human bush looking even stranger than Indonesia's "Hobbits" or South Africa's "Mystery Man" is found to have survived in some remote place, into the Bronze Age or even into Pliny's time.

E lephants, mammoths, and their cousins have a similarly complex ancestry, now winnowed down to only two recognized species: the Indian and African elephants.

Mutations of the kind we have described are not entirely unknown. Nearly four thousand years ago, a pygmy elephant smaller than a Shetland pony inhabited the island of Crete in the Mediterranean, contributing to the idea of the Cerae's mini-mammoths. In Alaska and along some of its offshore islands, the northwest mammoths were still alive when Egypt's pyramids were being built. Among the last of them was a "pygmy" species.

There is also real-life precedent for the "twinning" effect on mammoth appendages, in Mac's time. At the Explorers Club in New York City, visitors to the main lecture hall can examine the fully adult, fully functional-over-a-lifetime quadruple tusks of an extinct woolly mammoth (whether this was a single mutation or a previously unknown type of mammoth continues to be debated). On public display in the same city, at the Ripley's museum on Forty-Second Street, are the preserved remains of an elephant that grew to adulthood in Botswana, and lived until 2005 with a mutation that produced two fully functional trunks (both confirmed, by DNA tests, as belonging to the same individual). The mutation was clearly imperfect, and no one knows for sure whether the two-trunked elephant would have lived to adulthood if not maintained in a "preserve." In the opinion of most veterinarians, the mutation was an impediment. We have bypassed this problem in the novel by presenting as if true the mythology of fantastical Himalayan cure-alls—which, in the world of the Cerae and the Morlocks, influenced the tempo and mode of evolution, rendering imperfect mutations perfect. Thus "little Dumbo's" two trunks become the evolutionary equivalent of giving our human ancestors two hands with opposable thumbs.

As depicted in the Yanni encounters, elephants really are known to have a language at least as complex as the communications between cetaceans (whales and dolphins). Most of the communication has been recorded at low frequencies, beyond human hearing. In Africa, actual "tribal dialects" have been identified among these amazing giants. Once again, a group of animals requires us to ask new questions about the identification of intelligent species, and whether we humans really are the only potentially intelligent creatures now being evolved on this planet.

Sadly (as noted in a September 29, 2016, census summary in the British science journal *Nature*), elephant populations are being decimated. *Worse than decimated.* Between 2006 and 2015, ivory poaching alone had dropped the population of African elephants by 111,000, to only 415,000 individuals. And hence, our fitful moments of wishful thinking, on behalf of elephants: In our fable, living with a microbe that modifies life while reducing the frequent evolutionary mistakes in the raw material of natural selection (random variation), the Morlock misfortune became their failure to notice that brain growth was being enhanced for the enslaved and environmentally stressed mammoths.

When imagining the architecture of a post–Stone Age culture in the eastern Himalayas—where mountains and valleys are being pushed up by the collision of India with Asia—we had to invent architecture with earthquake resistance in mind. As with human architecture, much of the inspiration for long-lived structures comes from nature. One of the most amazing borrowed-from-nature structures on earth is Gaudí's nature- and forest-based design for the La Sagrada Família Basílica in Barcelona. Strong by definition, Cerae and Morlock structures needed more flexibility than stone and mortar, and had to be rendered conceivable based on local building materials, including plant matter and ice.

Ice composite architecture is rooted in reality. For our own civilization, it might actually begin to play an important role in the not-too-distant future. Composites with the strength of concrete and flexibility of steel can be made from materials as simple as pulped garbage or "cotton" spun from recycled plastic.

The ice composite boats mentioned by Jerry as he examined Morlock structures really did reach the experimental stage near the end of World War II. Composite hulls and bunker walls tested well. Cotton balls in ice have proved to be a surprisingly good strengthening material, distributing the force evenly and preventing shattering of the ice even against artillery. An ice composite boat more than thirty feet long, after successful testing under Churchill, was left abandoned at war's end, on a drydock near London—where it took almost a year to melt. (A smaller version, using old newspapers in ice, was famously tested on the American documentary series *MythBusters*.)

The world's first, actual large-scale ice-composite is an underground dam, built in the aftermath of Japan's "3/11 triple disaster" (earthquake, tsunami, nuclear meltdown). Currently one mile in circumference, the dam of ice-and-dirt prevents new groundwater from entering the Fukushima meltdown site and carrying even more radioactive debris into the ocean. The Fukushima ice composite dam is impermeable, non-brittle—and it can be kept in place for centuries to come (if civilization endures). Even in the aftermath of new earthquakes, the dam is easily repaired—in a manner analogous to a living organism healing an injured bone—just as we have indicated for the Cerae and Morlock structures.

There was, in reality, a lost Roman Ninth Legion. The timing of the disappearance varies but it is most commonly believed to have happened about A.D. 120 (and possibly as late as A.D. 160), either in Britain or after a long march eastward through Persia (present-day Iran). The Jordan Valley and India are occasionally mentioned in missing Ninth sightings. Whether they actually wandered into some unknown slaughter, or were simply disbanded and not recorded, remains unknown. We do know, from trade goods found in the cities of Vesuvius and through

DNA tracing the descent of remote Chinese villagers back to Rome, that the Romans did reach as far as China and the eastern Himalayas, in Pliny's time. (See, for example, Nick Squires on Chinese DNA, in the *Telegraph*, November 23, 2010, and National Geographic Society on the study of Chinese mummies with European features and red hair.)

A twentieth-century Chinese army like the one MacCready, Yanni, and Jerry found in "the Trophy Room" really is (like the Roman Ghost Legion) widely reported to have vanished into legend. In the realm of great mysteries, the disappearance of nearly three thousand Chinese soldiers outside of Nanking during the morning of December 10, 1939, remains unsolved. At 4 A.M., Colonel Li Fu Sein (after an inspection of men and equipment) slept for three hours in a truck and awoke to find concealed cooking fires still burning, and camouflaged artillery still loaded and aimed. With the exception of about a half-dozen men at a remote overlook, Sein's entire battalion, including its field officers, had vanished without any signs of combat. During the decades that followed, not even an impostor came forward (as in the manner of Little Bighorn "survivors") claiming to have been a survivor or deserter from China's own "missing Ninth." Farmers westward, upriver, attested that no soldiers at all, and certainly not three thousand of them, ever came through the area, as it could not have gone unnoticed during a mass desertion. To the east of their position, the Japanese never recorded a battle against Chinese defenders or (as was their tradition) the execution of men who surrendered. The most probable explanation: farmers west of the location simply kept quiet about a mass desertion upriver into the mountains, and the lookouts who remained at their post, and who never heard anything about desertion plans, were at their posts for precisely that reason.

Whatever really did happen, the Japanese occupiers of Nanking would have publicized a desertion of this magnitude for its propaganda value. They did not. They were evidently as mystified by the event as everyone else. For the sake of storytelling, we have tapped this mystery on the shoulder and blamed the Morlocks.

This was not the last mass disappearance in China. Almost exactly nine years later, on December 12, 1948, the *New York Times* reported that General Sun Yuan-lians's Fifteenth Army had vanished southwest of Suchow. While they were thought to have surrendered to the communists, or deserted, areal reconnaissance revealed that they appeared simply to have vanished.

Only rumors survive.

On underground realms of the Far East: Even without expansion by Morlocks and their ancestors, Asia already boasts cave systems so large that St. Patrick's Cathedral could easily be accommodated in a small corner. China's Miao cavern, which can be reached only by navigating an underground river, is the largest "supercave" currently known. It contains a stalagmite large enough to engulf the Statue of Liberty from toe to torch tip, and the main cavern is long enough to contain a jumbo jet's entire runway. In Tibet, enormous Buddhist temples have been built inside natural caverns. The cave systems of the eastern Himalayas remain mostly unexplored. The bioluminescent life in the lost world of the Cerae/Morlocks is based on organisms that actually exist—some encountered in caves, others being extrapolations of prey-and-predator relationships studied by colleagues who have visited the ocean's "deep scattering layer" of life and the hydrothermal oases still being explored at the continental spreading centers. Among the strangest observations: organisms that give off a literally blinding, bioluminescent flash to stun predators, or prey, or both.

O n unknown microscopic life and strange microbial symbiotic linkages: Recent assessments using new collecting and culturing methods have revealed that 99 percent of all microbial species (not counting viruses) are yet to be discovered. A good place to begin venturing into and learning about this realm is Laura Beil's introduction to microbial "Dark Matter" in the September 7, 2016, issue of *Science News:* "Out of the Dark: Scientists Discover Bacteria that Defy Rules of Biochemistry." Beil's article is one of the clearest expositions on a field exploding with amazing new discoveries, and we cannot wait until she writes a book.

The fictional Nora Nesbitt's speculation about pheromones and microbes, and what she believed might have taken control of Severus, as reported by Pliny, is based on a strange but true microbial relationship. The cat-rat paradox occurs precisely as Nesbitt described it, in her conversation with Patricia Wynters. Kathleen McAuliffe's profile of parasitologist Jaroslav Flegr—"How Your Cat Is Making You Crazy"—in the March 2012 issue of the *Atlantic* (as well as publications by Flegr himself) would be an excellent place to begin exploring this subject.

The guinea worm parasite (minus the enhancements brought about by a microbe under control of the Cerae) follows its usual life cycle exactly as described by Nesbitt. As an example of how we do not know the measure of some national leaders until after they are out of office, former American president Jimmy Carter, along with his many truly charitable efforts, has brought the world closer than ever to eradicating the dreaded disease dracunculiasis.

The lost worlds of the Himalayas, much as we have described them, really do exist in legends older than Imperial Rome. One lost tropical valley, located east of our fictional mist valley and believed in the West to have existed in legend only, actually was discovered early in the twenty-first century.

We owe much to these long-standing oral and written traditions about mystical hidden valleys in the eastern Himalayas and Tibet, and in particular the Shambala legend. The mythical kingdom is mentioned in ancient Buddhist and Hindu texts with origins going back to at least 200 B.C. Predating Pliny's Rome, the legends spoke of magical substances and secret healing practices.

The tales first emerged into popular Western culture in the form of a novel about a man who crash-landed in an airplane, on the fringe of the hidden realm. This was Talbot Mundy's *Om: The Secret of the Ahbor Valley,* published in 1925. Eight years later, in his retread of Mundy's story (*The Lost Horizon*), James Hilton renamed the hidden world Shangri-la. This place-name never existed, until Hilton. Shambala (sometimes spelled Shambhala) is the proper name, of legend.

As further examples of how we have tried to keep our story consistent with Eastern traditions about the lost world: In China and as far north as Russia, legends actually do describe jewel-like cities hidden in the mountains—cities in which the people vary from enlightened to very warlike and even enlightened in the bodies of large monkeys. Their central hidden realm is shrouded in white mists and there are cave systems that, as tradition describes them, have spread out widely under the world. Apocalyptic prophecies are linked to the innermost realm—according to which, during a universal outburst of evil when humanity is governed by the furies of greed and war and as the leaders of all the doomed nations peer into the abyss, something spreads out of Shambala to save humanity from itself.

Shambala is the hidden realm that Westerners have been seeking since at least the time of Vatican expeditions sent during the tenth century, based on the belief that it was a surviving remnant of Eden. Evidently there were no expedition survivors. About 1534, Jesuits returned to Rome with further tales of Shambala. The Vatican library preserves hand-drawn maps of hidden worlds, encircled by mountains and strange waters, and showing encounter points with Buddhist monks, living in temples at altitudes of seventeen thousand feet. The monks had described mythical women, "extraordinarily angelic yet as wild as snow leopards," according to the twenty-first-century explorer Ian Baker.

It is Baker whose expedition discovered the strange, tropical oasis of "Pemaku," nestled deep within an east Himalayan labyrinth of valleys, with snowcapped mountains and glaciers towering overhead. Following the path of the nineteenth-century explorer John Whitehead, Baker did find a cave, river, and waterfall system consistent with one of the valleys described by Jesuits centuries earlier. The world Baker found descended below five thousand feet and was carpeted with strange, isolated plant life (members of his expedition are, at this writing, still identifying specimens with medicinal potential). More than a century earlier, his predecessor Whitehead had given up, writing that the search for the magical waters and plants of a lost Himalayan paradise "can be characterized as one of the great romances of geography and one of the most obsessive wild goose chases of modern times." Whitehead noted that not even guides could get him past the unknown (cryptic and feral) guardians: "They kill Tibetans on principle."

In 1924, the Russians sent an expedition into Tibet and the

eastern Himalayas, searching for Shambala. They failed. Later, the Nazis sent expeditions (expecting to find a cave leading deep into the Earth, where dwelled the perfect, white-haired Aryan race). The German expeditions were launched in 1930, 1934, and 1938. Most of the Germans were believed to have frozen to death. (For the purposes of our fable, look in the Morlock trophy room.)

Ian Baker noted in 2016, while lecturing at the Explorers Club in Manhattan, that there are legends of other hidden realms west of his "Pemaku" site. Ancient texts speak of "the secret gate . . . The people who know the key have hidden it from outsiders and especially from the Chinese. . . . [T]he way in is guarded by a long-haired, extraordinary animal." Texts also describe tall and terraced waterfalls, and tunnels behind life-giving waters, going deep into a mountain.

According to Baker, mentions in sacred books of hidden gorges carpeted with strange plants that impart longevity and memories of past lives are part of an amazingly symbolic language—next of kin to Western civilization's oldest fables. "The big mistake is to take the texts too literally."

And thus, bold traveler, you will read bamboo annals describing something in a remote valley "harder than a tiger, to tame. And at the heart, at the final stage of deification [and realization], the colors in the guarded place are orange and red, like a fiery tiger." *Logic and reason fail you*, the annals warn. "And an ancient figure in red fire riding with a pregnant tigress. And an image of redness beyond anything you have been ready for."

Although we have a red grotto consistent with the texts, Baker believed, as not actually existing in physical form, a world beyond the tropical, unpopulated Himalayan oasis he discovered. "The Shambala story may even be based on *this* oasis," he said. The innermost secret realm in a more distant fog valley may, he suggested, "in the symbolic language of the region, really refer to a hidden realm that is inside of you, rather than being literally a physical place."

Paraphrasing Mircea Eliade on this subject (from *Myths, Dreams and Mysteries: The Encounter Between Contemporary Faiths and Archaic Realities,* Harper, 1975), Baker concluded, "At the commencement and at the end of the religious history of humanity, we find again the same nostalgia for Paradise. The myths by which this ideology is constituted are among the most beautiful and profound in existence. They are the myths of Paradise and the fall of immortality of primordial man . . . and the discovery of the spirit."

Or, as we have depicted it, the gates to Paradise can also swing open into Hell.

There really do exist many written warnings against seeking out and then entering the center of the most secret of the lost worlds. According to one ancient text, "Without proper vision, if unready, you bring unpredictable disaster. Disaster for all."

On racially tagged bioweapons: Fortunately, at our present point in history, the development of such weapons is restricted by the fact that viruses (the most likely tools) tend to mutate too rapidly to be practical for this kind of weaponization. However, talk of such weapons (mostly in a "defensive" context) had been in the air by the time our first novel, *Hell's Gate,* originally planned as a stand-alone cautionary tale, was purchased with a request for a sequel. Though we have described this danger in terms of a modern-day fable, as with most fables, it carries a real warning. In this case, the warning points toward a reality hiding somewhere not very far ahead, like a monster under the bridge we are approaching. If there is time enough to start thinking about what might be hiding under humanity's bridge to the genetic frontier, and to take action before we actually get close enough to be in danger, then it is logical to do so. Many aspects of our scientific fable are, in fact, science eventuality. It's time to start the conversation.

Acknowledgments

The authors would like to thank Gillian MacKenzie for continuing to be the best literary agent that anyone could ever hope for. Thanks also to Kirsten Wolff and Allison Devereux at the Gillian MacKenzie Agency for their hard work.

A very special thanks to our talented editor Lyssa Keusch and to her colleagues at William Morrow.

We are grateful to Patricia J. Wynne for the amazing figures of Tibetan wildlife that grace our novel.

Much gratitude to James Cameron and James Rollins for their support.

A special shout-out to Robert Ruotolo for generously giving his time and bringing us up to speed on all things helicopter-related. We thank our friends in the USN and USMC, and we carry with us always, alive in our memories, those who did not make it back to shore.

From Bill Schutt

I am deeply indebted to my friends and colleagues in the research community and at the American Museum of Natural History for their advice, support, and friendship. They include Ricky Adams, Frank Bonaccorso, Catherine Doyle-Capitman, Kristi Collom, Betsy Dumont, Neil Duncan, John Hermanson, Mary Knight, Gary Kwiecinski, Ross MacPhee, Shahroukh Mistry, Scott Pedersen, Nancy Simmons (it's good to know the

Queen), Ian Tattersall, Elizabeth Taylor, Rob Voss, Sean Werle, and Eileen Westwig.

A very special thanks goes out to my wonderful friend and co-conspirator Leslie Nesbitt Sittlow. Leslie and my "brother" Darrin Lunde spent many hours reading through early versions of *Codex* and they were always there to provide friendship, laughs, and sound editorial advice.

At LIU Post, thanks and gratitude to Ted Brummel, Gina Famulare, Kathy Mendola, Katherine Hill-Miller, Jeff Kane, Jen Snekser, and Steve Tettlebach. Thanks also to my teaching assistants, LIU graduate students Elsie Jasmin, Chelsea Miller, and Kayla Mladinich, for making my life so much easier.

Sincere thanks goes out to Bob Adamo (RIP), Frank Bacolas, John Bodnar, Alice Cooper, Aza Derman, John Glusman, Art Goldberg, Chris Grant (Yoga Farm, Lansing), Kathy Kennedy, Lisa Kombrink, Suzanne Finnamore Luckenbach, Aja Marcato, Elaine Markson, Carrie and Dan McKenna, Maceo Mitchell, Farouk Muradali; Gerard, Oda, and Dominique Ramsawak, Jerry Ruotolo, Laura Schlecker, Edwin J. Spicka, Lynn Swisher, and Katherine Turman.

Special thanks also go out to Dorothy Wachter and Carol Trezza—for being wonderful "second moms" to me back in the day, and for encouraging my dreams of becoming a writer.

Finally, my eternal thanks and love go out to my family for their patience, love, encouragement, and unwavering support, especially Janet Schutt, Billy Schutt, Eileen Schutt, Chuck Schutt, Bob and Dee Schutt, Rob, Shannon, and Kelly Schutt, Dawn Montalto, Donna Carpenter, Don and Sue Pedersen, Jason, Geoff, and Chris Langos, my grandparents (Angelo and Millie DiDonato), Erin Nicosia (American Cheese), and of course, my late parents, Bill and Marie Schutt.

Selected Bibliography

Baker, Ian. _The Heart of the World_ (Penguin, 2006) and "The Secret River: Plants, Alchemy, and Immortality in Tibet's Hidden Land of Pemaku," _National Geographic Adventure_, 2010. (See also, regarding Russian and Chinese legends of Shambala: http://studybuddhism .com/web/en/archives/advanced/kalachakra/shambhala/russian _japanese_shambhala.html.)

Bisel, Sara. _Secrets of Vesuvius._ New York: Scholastic, 1991.

McAuliffe, Kathleen. "How Your Cat Is Making You Crazy." _Atlantic_, March 2012.

Milner, Richard. _Charles R. Knight: The Artist Who Saw Through Time._ New York: Harry Abrams, 2012.

Nielsen, R., et al. "Tracing the Peopling of the World Through Genomics," _Nature_, January 19, 2017, pp. 302–310. (NOTE: The rapidly developing discovery of unknown human-like relatives is beginning to look like only the tip of a rather large iceberg, including one species that, in a manner similar to our fictional Nesbitt specimen, is known only by a broken off finger fragment.)

Suetonius, Gaius (translated by R. Graves, M. Grant edition). Nero [in] _The Twelve Caesars._ New York: Penguin, 1979.

For a compilation of what little history survives the legend, see W. H. Schoff, "Tamil Political Divisions in the First Two Centuries AD," _Journal of the American Oriental Society_ 33 (1913): 209–13, and K.A.N. Sastri, _The Pandyan Kingdom: from the Earliest Times to the Sixteenth Century_ (Madras: Swathi Publications, 1972).

For an introduction to the Scythians, see Jeannine Davis-Kimball, *Warrior Women: An Archaeologist's Search for History's Lost Heroines* (New York: Warner, 2003) and A. Karasulas and A. McBride, *Mounted Archers of the Steppe 600 BC–AD 1300* (U.K.: Osprey Publishers, 2004).

On elephant vocalization, see Caitlin O'Connell, *The Elephant Secret Sense: The Hidden Life of the Secret Herds of Africa* (MA: University of Chicago Press, 2008) and Carl Safina, *Beyond Words: What Animals Think and Feel* (New York: Holt, 2015). To actually listen: http://www.cbsnews.com/news/the-secret-language-of-elephants2/ and http://news.nationalgeographic.com/animals/what-elephant-calls-mean/.

About the Authors

BILL SCHUTT is a vertebrate zoologist, explorer, educator, and author. He is a research associate in residence at the American Museum of Natural History and a professor of biology at LIU Post. Bill's first book, *Dark Banquet: Blood and the Curious Lives of Blood-Feeding Creatures,* was praised by E. O. Wilson, the *New York Times,* and Alice Cooper. His latest nonfiction book, *Cannibalism: A Perfectly Natural History,* is a widely acclaimed exploration of cannibalism in nature and among humans. Bill lives with his wife and son on the East End of Long Island.

J. R. FINCH is the pen name of a painter, history buff, and cave explorer. He lives in New York with three cats.